BLOOD LOSS

Book Two of The Young Blood Trilogy

T. Marshall Bunn

Belief Creating Reality Publications

ROCKVILLE, MARYLAND

Belief Creating Reality Publications
Rockville, Maryland
www.youngbloodtrilogy.com

Publisher's Note: This is a work of fiction. Names, characters, places, and incidents are a product of the author's imagination. Locales and public names are sometimes used for atmospheric purposes. Any resemblance to actual people, living or dead, or to businesses, companies, events, institutions, or locales is completely coincidental.

Excerpt from *Dracula* by Bram Stoker, 1897, in the public domain

Cover photo by Nicci Trent

Book Layout © 2014 BookDesignTemplates.com

Blood Loss: Book Two of The Young Blood Trilogy/ T. Marshall Bunn. -- 1st ed.
ISBN 979-8-9861016-2-0

Library of Congress Control Number: 2022910506

Acknowledgments

As far as the trilogy goes, this book was simultaneously the most difficult and the most fun to write. Apart from the self-discipline it took for me to occasionally write outside of my comfort zone, there was quite a bit of research involved, and I need to thank the following people for their help: John Bankhead of the Georgia Bureau of Investigation and Cpl. David Milford of the Richmond County Sheriff's Office for their advice on the law enforcement aspects of the story; Col. Neal Trent, U.S. Army (Retired) as well as Dan Brown of the U.S. Army Signal Corps Museum at Fort Gordon for their guidance and education on the military; and Susanna Rosen for her help with the one and only illustration of the series.

Thanks also to Rachel Brune, Gypsye Legge, and Stephanie Stewart for their help with proofreading and their thoughts on my early drafts.

The young do not tell themselves to the young, but to the old, like me, who have known so many sorrows and the causes of them.

— Abraham Van Helsing, 1890

Now no matter, child, the name:

Sorrow's springs are the same.

— Gerard Manley Hopkins, 1880

CONTENTS

CHAPTER ONE

CEMETERY

On a chilly November night, a young, dark-haired boy screamed. Surrounded by tombstones, he lay on his back, arms pinned helplessly at the wrists by the beautiful, blonde girl who straddled him, her wide smile punctuated by two sharp fangs. The boy knew that he was about to die, and as the girl leaned forward and lowered her head toward his neck, he understood with remarkable clarity that what was happening was all his fault.

CHAPTER TWO

BEGINNING

Excerpts from the journal of Raymond Adrian Young

July 12, 1982

Hello! My name is Ray (Raymond). I am begining this journal today. Back in school, Mrs. Brinson read us a book about a boy who kept one (journal). So I thought Id do one too! (Carolyn or Susanna if you read this I will tell on you to Dad and you will get in trouble.) I live in Augusta, Georgia in a house on Aumond Rd. We have a dog, King, who is a St Bernard. We got him to replace Susanna's mean cat who scractched me in the face and left a scar on my cheek. Im glad hes gone!

More later.

July 13, 1982

I hate Susanna! She is so mean and unfair. Carolyn is just as bad! She tried to put up a bucket of water on my door and soak me. It got all over everything and Susanna yelled and made us both clean it up. (At least we got it done before Mom and Dad get back.)

CHAPTER THREE

MIDDLE

Excerpt from the diary of Carolyn Leigh Young

July 13, 1982

Sometimes I wish I didn't have a brother and sister. Okay, maybe that's too harsh. But I swear to God, they get on my nerves like nothing else.

I tried this thing on Ray as a joke like they do on TV when they rig a bucket over the door and it dumps down on the person when they open it. Instead of a bucket, I used a trash can (one of those plastic ones). I tricked him by saying he should go outside and play with King, set the whole thing up, and waited for him to come back.

So what does he do? Instead of opening the door quickly like your supposed to, he messes it all up and the whole thing comes down not on him but the rest of the floor, and there's water everywhere and he's all like "what? duhhh" And I realize that I really should've thought about this better. Susanna comes down and is all "WHAT DID YOU DO OH MY GOD BLAH BLAH BLAH I'M SO IMPORTANT AND IN CHARGE

God I hate her. We got it all cleaned up and everything is fine. But I get soooo sick of her being such a stuckup b— and Ray being, well, he's not as bad as her, but it just stinks being the middle kid, ya know? Susanna gets all the flowers and pretty stuff and cheerleading and whatever, I get stuck with nothing but handmedowns and crap.

And Ray's "the baby," and a boy, so he gets all that kind of attention too. I might as well not exist.

CHAPTER FOUR

END

Pages from a notebook belonging to Susanna Michelle Young,
March 1983
(later torn out and burned)

Just some thoughts on the potion that Robert and I developed together. (Those notes are in my Chemistry folder.) The experiment is at an end, and I should probably just throw all of those pages away, but it doesn't feel right to just get rid of two months' worth of work. And maybe there are other reasons, too. But for the purpose of these notes, I felt like I should document as much as I can remember.

It's hard for me to talk about this without getting into the emotional side of things. No, Susanna, you should focus. Deep breath. It's over with him now, and it's for the best. But goddamnit I miss him already. He was just so... intriguing? Is that the right word? Let's face it, he could be kind of a dick, all full of himself, but maybe there was something to admire about that? Better a bad boy than a mama's boy, our beloved cheerleading captain always said. But really, I sometimes didn't know if I was coming or going when it came to him.

Alright, alright, alright. Stop being so dramatic. About the potion. It was something he was working on before we started dating, something to do with behavior modification in the mice. That much I remember. Also something to do with the effects of different chemicals and substances on them, like that one he mentioned (already can't remember the name) that's the same one that causes alcoholism in people. Tetra-something... Q? Hopefully I can look that up later.

Anyway, he first showed me the effects when he'd gotten it to the stage where a mouse treated with it would become aggressive and bite another one. I shouldn't have found that as fascinating as I did, but there was just something so weird about seeing a plain old ordinary mouse go from calm to vicious after a single injection. I've always had a thing about needles, though, and that's the reason he later changed it to something that could be given orally. Or at least, that's what he told me.

Little by little, he and I tinkered with the formula and found ways to alter just how the mice transformed, mentally and physically. Some of the ingredients were... questionable, I guess you could say, but I went along with it. That was part of the thrill, I suppose. If I asked him where he'd gotten some of the more racy (illegal?) bits, he'd just give me that smile and almost wink as he said, "I have my ways." That always got me. Stupid, stupid. Sorry, I should stay on topic.

Before we knew it, what we found ourselves making were vampire mice. It was weird seeing that the first time, the way the transformed one latched onto the untreated one's neck (or what passes for a mouse's neck), the "victim" struggling and screeching until it was drained of blood. It just kinda took off from there. All these other vampire-like traits, we found, could be built in, just by tweaking the potion correctly. (I won't even get into what happened to the times when we got it wrong. That got really gross sometimes.)

Building on this idea also meant giving the mice the same vulnerabilities as real vampires: garlic, sunlight, running water, etc. I wasn't even sure how he knew how to link whatever ingredient to whatever trait, but like I said, I went along with it. Sometimes he would work on it when I wasn't there, then be all eager to impress me with some new development. I have to admit, it worked. The moment when he was all "Hey, watch this," and was able to make one of them turn into a tiny little bat, well, it blew my mind.

I can't say for certain whether or not he tried the potion on himself without telling me. The way it went with him in the lab that afternoon, he talked like he hadn't, but looking back on it, I'm not sure I believe him. This was the point when we'd already found that, while the antidote (which we developed because it eventually made more sense to reuse the mice instead of euthanizing them) did work, it was really slow, but exposing the changed mice to enough of the "anti substances" (garlic etc.) turned them back to normal much faster. Plus there was the time when one of the mice managed to bite him, and I worried that maybe that would affect him somehow, but we didn't build in the, you know, contagiousness part of it, even though we probably could have. Traditionally, that was how it worked for real vampires (if there even is such a thing), but it wasn't part of our experiment.

Anyway, he got it in his head that we could try the potion on a person, and I think he actually had some idea of using some unsuspecting person as a guinea pig, which I wasn't okay with. "Or you," he suggested, and I was like 'hell no.' He said he was joking, but again, I'm not so sure now.

So it was decided that he would take it, which meant that we had to use some black garbage bags to block out the windows in the lab and keep the sunlight out. It was supposed to just be a quick test, and then he'd change himself back immediately. But that wasn't how it went. I got scared when he first began to change; it wasn't as straightforward and simple as it was with the mice. He was breathing heavy and closing his eyes and sweating and all... It really scared me. I was afraid he might die for some reason. But that was nothing compared to how he got once the change was complete.

When I saw that look he got in his eyes, that malicious hunger... I knew immediately that this was a mistake. The bloodlust we'd instilled in those simple mice was now in him, and there I was, a tasty little meal. He didn't even have to say anything, just smile. Oh my God, those fangs... I still shudder when I think about it.

I ran, which was stupid because the stuff I needed to ward him off was right there on the table. But I panicked, you know? It's a really weird feeling to suddenly feel like your life is in danger, and I hope I never feel it again. He chased me around the lab two or three times, and I even got the sense that he was enjoying it, toying with me. He might very well have killed me.

We ended up by one of the blocked off windows, and he caught me, grabbing me hard. There was nothing sexy about it this time (as opposed to other stuff we've done, I mean); I was just terrified. Fortunately for me, he'd grabbed me by the upper arms (I still have the bruises), not my wrists, so I was able to pull at the garbage bag and rip it off the window. Oh, and just before that, he leaned in and said something like, "Come on, just a little taste…" (I have goosebumps while I write this.) That scared me more than I've ever been in my life.

But the sunlight worked, and he was back to normal in an instant. I fell down, too scared to even cry, or maybe too angry. He didn't even remember what happened at first until I told him. And then he apologized like a billion times, but I insisted that he stay away from me. Eventually, he got pretty freaked out too, then swore up and down that he'd never want to hurt me, and he later tore out the pages from his notebook that had the formula on them and shoved them into my hands, saying I should take them and burn them.

We tried to make things work for a very very short time, but I told him today that I don't ever want to see him again if I can help it. It's a good thing that there isn't much left of school, and I've already changed seats so I can sit on the other side of the room from him in class. I know it was the potion and all, but damn it, it's really hard to forgive some guy after he's tried to kill you. I don't even know what we were doing, trying to make this whole vampire thing happen. Sometimes I wish I'd never laid eyes on him.

I have to admit, though, that maybe there might be something to this that's worth keeping. Maybe under the right conditions, this potion could actually do some good. I'm not talking about the vampire aspect, or at least, not the killing part of it. But we built in some pretty neat and, I don't know, useful parts as well? Like the resistance to aging and death. That was nifty. And the way the mice were able to change form and fly? Sure, that's pretty damn cool, too. I don't even know just how all that worked, but it did. Maybe if I feel up to it later, I can do my own experiments and see what I can do with it all.

But for now, I'm just going to have to step back from this. It freaked me right the hell out, and Robert too, I know, so I think I'm just going to file everything away for now and not think about it for a while. I've got other stuff to think about anyway, like graduation, then college. I bet Charleston is going to be a blast.

CHAPTER FIVE

FATHERS AND SONS

Jim Broyles prided himself on being a fair man. In his younger, more athletic days, he'd had it drilled into him by his father and his coaches the importance of things like sportsmanship, honesty, and fairness. Unlike some people he could name, he was a firm believer in the old cliché: "It's not whether you win or lose; it's how you play the game." As long as one did their best and played by the rules, that was what counted. The success one gained from playing sports wasn't measured in how many points were scored or how many games were won. What mattered most was improving one's self, physically and mentally, learning from mistakes and doing better with each try.

He'd worked hard to instill these values in his two boys as well. They may not have been as physically adept as he was back in the day, but he hoped to make athletes out of them soon enough. Brandon, the older one, had some interest in both football and soccer, but he'd failed to master either so far. That would come with time, though, Jim was certain. The boy just needed more practice and self-discipline.

It was Shawn that he worried about more. It had taken him a while to settle on any kind of interest in sports, and his gangly frame, pale skin, and high-pitched laugh had made him the target of a group of bullies at his school when he was in first grade. Or maybe it wasn't that exactly; kids could be mean, sometimes for no real reason. Jim knew that, and he'd been the same way at times. But whatever the cause, these particular mean kids had started picking on his son and had even taken to making fun of the family name, calling him "Shawn

Balls" instead. Things escalated to the point where Shawn got beaten up by them at recess one day, and the teachers seemed unconcerned or unwilling to do anything about it.

Jim wasn't about to let his son grow up to be a wimp. One day, this boy would be a man, and running away wouldn't solve anything, not now, not ever. So he tried to teach Shawn how to defend himself, but the boy had no idea how to throw a punch. According to the way he'd described and demonstrated it, when attacked, he'd tried to hit back by swinging his arm laterally like a baseball bat, which the bully simply ducked under and then sprang up from below, nailing Shawn right in the gut and knocking the wind out of him. This left him groaning on the ground in pain, and the boys left him there to suffer, writhing in the dirt.

Despite the protests of their mother, who wanted to find a more diplomatic solution, Jim had taken Shawn into the den that evening and sat forward in his recliner, palms held up. "Now, go on," he said. "Hit them as hard as you can." The pale, little red-haired boy pounded away as best as he could, but honestly, there was little to no strength behind his blows.

What ended up making the bullies leave Shawn alone, Jim later learned, was a combination of two things. Once the situation had played itself out, he and his friends simply avoided those mean boys at recess as best as they could, sticking closer to the teachers on the playground. But prior to that, it was Brandon who had intervened, he and a couple of his classmates intimidating the other boys and threatening them if they bothered Shawn again. It may not have been the perfect solution, but it worked. It was good of Brandon to stick up for his little brother.

That had been a year ago, and since then, Brandon had continued to look out for Shawn. As a result, the younger son seemed to gain more confidence, looking up to his big brother and wanting to be more like him. Jim provided his own guidance, including encouraging both of them to pursue athletics. The latest effort involved the Run for Life race at the YMCA, a charity event whose ticket sales would benefit the local chapter of the Red Cross.

"I want you boys to run the best race you can," he said to them the Saturday morning of the qualifying race. "I fully expect to see you both running across that finish line ahead of everyone else." He wasn't entirely serious when he said this; what mattered most to him was that they tried their best. He hoped that the wry smile he gave them conveyed his deeper sentiment.

"But what if the other kids beat us?" Shawn asked, sounding more whiny than Jim liked. The boy then let out a little grunt as his brother shoved him slightly.

"Don't listen to him, Dad," Brandon said with a smile very much like his father's. He looked like a miniature version of him, while Shawn was a bit of an anomaly in terms of family traits. Jim's friends liked to joke that, because neither he nor his wife Jane had the boy's fiery red hair, he might be "the son of the milkman." That wasn't true, Jim knew; the genes were in the family. Jane's brother had the same look to him, also sporting a long, deeply orange beard. Truth be told, he was a tree-hugging, guitar-playing hippie, and the resemblance had always bothered Jim more than he liked to admit. Physical similarities or differences aside, he always planned for his two boys to follow in his footsteps. After all, what father wouldn't?

As far as the race was concerned, he'd been put in charge of it by a friend of his who worked at the YMCA, which he was grateful for. Being a coach at a local school, he could get a little stir crazy just sitting around during Augusta's summer months. Getting involved in something like this, particularly one that was for such a worthy cause, gave him a good feeling.

The idea of including the boys sprang from a conversation he remembered having a couple of years back with another local coach when they met, a man who apparently had a son about Shawn's age. "Track is a good sport for smaller, less 'manly' boys, if you want to put it that way," this Coach Hendricks said to him. "Because they're more lightweight, there's less weight to carry, see? So they can move faster. It's not like in football, where the bigger you are, the better."

Because of his insistence on fairness and — though he wouldn't outright admit it — a strange sense of fear over being accused otherwise, he advised Brandon and Shawn not to go around telling all the other kids that he was their father. "I mean, if they ask, sure, don't lie or anything. You know I don't want you to do that. But just... Don't offer it, all right? If some of the kids know your dad's in charge of things, they might think there's some favoritism going on."

"Sure, okay," Brandon said, and Shawn followed with an obedient nod.

"And there *won't* be, by the way," Jim added meaningfully. "You get out there and you give it your all."

"We will," Brandon said.

"Yeah," Shawn added, smiling along with his big brother. They were good kids.

So when the qualifying race was over and one of the other children suddenly jumped onto Brandon and started beating on him, Jim felt a mixture of confusion, protectiveness, and anger. At first, he hadn't even realized what was going on. When the dark-haired boy — who looked a little like Brandon himself, Jim realized — ran over and tackled him, Jim first thought that he was just being playful, his mind briefly flashing back to visions of high school and college football. Sometimes, the guys would get rough in their congratulating each other, but it was all in fun. It became clear in just under a few seconds, though, that this boy had very different intentions.

After grabbing the boy off of Brandon and restraining him, Jim wanted to know just what this little brat's problem was. Some other children — the boy's friends, he assumed — had run up from somewhere and were showing concern as well. Was the kid just pissed off because he hadn't won the race? Both Brandon and Shawn had, in fact, along with some other girl, but his pride in his sons was quickly spoiled by this other boy's complete lack of self-control.

Things took an unexpected turn once the aggressive boy calmed down and stopped spouting obscenities long enough to accuse Brandon of cheating. Worse still, he claimed that he'd thrown a rock at him during the race. Jim couldn't imagine his own son doing something so despicable and underhanded. "Is that true?" he asked him.

"No, it's not true. He's lying." Shawn backed his older brother up, saying that the accuser was just being a sore loser, and Jim was inclined to agree. He'd noticed that this whiny little brat had been lagging behind the other runners for most of the race anyway, so it was most likely that he was just making things up to compensate for his own shortcomings. His opinion was reinforced when the boy's story changed halfway through, claiming that both Brandon and Shawn had thrown rocks, and by that point, he'd had enough. He knew in his heart that his boys would never do something like that. He'd raised them better. Whatever this undisciplined little shit's problem was, he was out on his ear. And where were his parents, anyway?

Jim ceased caring once the offending party was on its way; he needed to salvage the situation and get things back to being fun and fair for the rest of the children. No point in letting some sore loser ruin it for everyone. Once things settled and were back to normal, he was able to be proud of his sons again. Thank God they weren't as bad as whoever that other child was.

The incident wasn't even mentioned to Jane that night or the following evening when the official race was held. It just didn't seem worth bringing up. She wasn't there when it happened even though she was supposed to be; she also worked at the YMCA in the promotions department and had been involved in the planning of the whole event. She'd been amazing at getting everything organized, but on Saturday, she'd had to go visit a friend in the hospital who had been in a terrible car accident, though luckily, he'd wound up being okay.

Jane, bless her heart, had still managed to come through with everything, right down to the last-minute arrangements of getting a photographer from the local newspaper to cover the Sunday night race. It would be good publicity for everyone involved, and the man, whom Jim only met briefly that night, said that he'd try to get something put into the article encouraging readers to donate more money even if they hadn't been able to make it to the event.

Jim felt immense pride in seeing both of his boys lined up along with everyone else at the starting line, eager to start the race. He gave them each a subtle wink and a thumbs-up just before he started the countdown, and they returned the gesture with their smiles. It would have made his night if they managed to nab at least second and third place each, but even if they didn't, he'd be proud of them and know that, through everything, they'd learn the importance of good, honest competition. Even if they lost, they'd still grow up to be winners.

He blew his whistle, and the runners were off. He kept a close eye on both of his boys, eager to know how the race would turn out. It was only about ten seconds in that he realized that there was a problem.

Brandon, who had been running along normally, started looking around like something had distracted him. Shawn did something similar, and whatever it was also made him stumble and raise a hand to his head. Other children started doing the same, and then Jim saw more clearly what was happening: Several things that looked like small, black birds were flying right at them, circling around their heads.

Jim reached for the whistle on the cord around his neck, wondering if he should stop the race. If these things — birds, or bats, or maybe some really big aggressive insects, like cicadas? — were interfering, it would be only fair to start the race over. But then Shawn toppled over onto the ground as one of the dark flying shapes seemed to latch onto the side of his neck, and Jim began to panic. He found himself saying over and over in his head, *Get up! Get up!* But his youngest son didn't move.

Some of the other children had kept on running, seemingly unaware that anything out of the ordinary was happening. Jim felt extremely angry about this, his panicked mind spewing hatred at these ignorant and unconcerned children. Part of him knew that this was unreasonable. But more than anything else, he knew that he had to put a stop to all of this. He started blowing his whistle repeatedly, running fast to catch up to Shawn, to help him.

He was distracted by another unbelievable, unacceptable sight: Brandon had also gone down, attacked by one of these flying menaces. This couldn't be happening. He stopped for a moment, stunned. He didn't know which way to go, whether he should run to one boy or the other. They both needed his help. He had to do something.

A flapping noise filled his left ear, and less than a second later, Jim felt a sharp pain on the side of his neck. He could feel the tiny beast on him, its wings wrapping around his throat as it held on, and he tried to reach up to pull it away. But something strange was happening. As he tried to move, his limbs felt sluggish, like he was underwater. His legs gave out beneath him, and there he was on the ground, paralyzed.

The revelations hit him in quick succession. This animal — whatever it was — was killing him. He had no way to fight back. He could only stare helplessly at the growing chaos around him, the dirt that had gotten into his eyes stinging, maybe even more than the wound on his neck where the tiny, deadly creature was still attached. Everyone was running around and screaming, some of them being caught by the flying menaces and going down. Where he'd fallen, he couldn't see the section of the stands where the crowd was, but he was pretty sure they were in just as much danger. He wondered where Jane was, if she'd managed to get away.

Then he realized that she was probably on her way over to him or their boys, wanting to help. He wanted to get up, to warn her off and tell her to run; it was too late for them. But he couldn't move, and he felt so weak and helpless, then angry at himself for that. For a moment, he thought he could feel himself standing up just as he'd pictured doing, but the sensation repeated, then repeated once more, and again…

He realized that it was dizziness he was feeling. The ground was still in the same place, but his increasingly numb body felt like it was tumbling forward in quickening circles. A memory surfaced, something his doctor had once said.

The doctor had told him that one of his pet peeves was the way that dying people were almost always portrayed in movies, whether they were fatally wounded in a shoot-out or expiring on a hospital bed after a long illness. Inevitably, the person would be speaking in a rough voice, looking pained as he said something like, "Tell… my wife… I love her… *ughhh…*" or something similar just before they went. But it wasn't like that in real life. Most of the time, people died while unconscious or in a stupor, so they were in no shape to give profound speeches.

Jim knew that it was his turn now, and, like the person in his doctor's story, he wouldn't get the chance to tell Jane — or his sons — how much he loved them.

CHAPTER SIX

BOYFRIENDS AND GIRLFRIENDS

It wasn't that Leslie was promiscuous — far from it, in fact. For one thing, she was still a virgin, despite having managed to rack up a whopping total of thirteen different boyfriends by the age of seventeen. But that was only because she was particular about what she wanted. She'd had plenty of relationships that just hadn't worked out, and she'd learned over the years not to waste her time.

There had been plenty of heartbreaks along the way, especially during the early years. Her first boyfriend back in seventh grade had dumped her, and she'd cried for days. All of those things in the songs she grew up liking came true, and she listened to the most upsetting ones on tape over and over as she wallowed in her misery. That was what the best country music had always been about: heartache.

She had grown up some since then. It wasn't that she'd grown cold, not exactly. But while some of her girlfriends would spend months trying to make something work with a boy when it clearly just wasn't going to, Leslie had learned how to spot the signs of a failing relationship early on, cut her losses, and run.

Not all of those boys had been complete wastes of time. Things always started out fun, and even for the ones with whom things had ended badly, there were little bits here and there she could look back on with a smile. Her best friend, Kim, had sometimes joked that she "went through boyfriends like toilet paper," which made her laugh up to a point. But she didn't like the implication that the joke also meant that she treated them like shit, which she tried not to do. Though sometimes, that became necessary.

She could tell that she was on her way down that road with her latest boyfriend, Stephen, someone she really never should have started dating in the first place. Or, at least, she should have gotten to know him better first. If she had, she wouldn't have gotten into a relationship with him. He was a nice guy and all, but too nice. That was the problem. Well, that, and the fact that he hadn't ever had a girlfriend before her, or maybe he'd had one or two. He'd been kind of vague on that.

Breaking up with Boyfriend Number Twelve, Wayne, had been easier. She'd had a job back then, the one at the school supplies store, and that had given her an excuse. Sure, it was only part time, but between that and school, her exams, and dealing with all the crap at home with her mom, things were just way too stressful to add a boyfriend on top of that. She'd just barely gotten the credits she needed by the end of eleventh grade, and she worried about how that might affect things once she started applying for college the following year. If she even stood a chance of getting any scholarships, it was time to buckle down and stop playing.

"I've had three or four years of playing," she said firmly to Wayne during their break-up conversation. "I've gotta do what's right for me."

A *"Sorry you feel that way"* or *"You do what you have to do"* might have been better than the "Whatever, bitch" she got back from him, but it was good enough. Things were over between them, and having a reason to hate him made it easier, plus it justified the "Fuck you" that she gave in response.

Stephen was a different story. It had taken her too long to figure it out, but the fact of the matter was that he was so grateful to finally have a girlfriend that he would put up with just about anything. She'd tried being mean to him, to be irritating to the point where plenty of her past boyfriends would decide that she was "just too much" or throw easy grenades at her like "What's your problem?" But Stephen just stuck with it, which in a way was admirable, but not exactly. He wasn't a total wet noodle — a term Kim liked to use — and he could even snipe back at her when they got into a playful fight.

But they barely had anything in common. She liked country; he was into more popular music. And he even seemed to look down on her for being into country, like it made her some kind of dumb redneck or something. It had been something they'd joked about early on, back during the flirting stage. Then it became something they just didn't talk about. The same had been true for his interest in stupid things like *Star Trek* and all that. What kind of guy got all into a TV show from something like fifteen years ago?

By the time the relationship had hit its third week, the only time they didn't snipe at each other was when they were making out. That was the one thing they were really good at together, and damn, he sure could kiss. She'd miss that, she knew. But there were other boys out there, and honestly, she should have stuck to what she'd decided after Wayne and just been on her own. It was time for a change.

Sometimes, it had been easy. Just a simple "I want to break up" and that was it. Other times, that would be met with resistance, so she'd have to do things to make the guy want to leave her, to make it seem like it was his idea. But with Stephen, she knew it was going to be more difficult. Letting him down easy might not even be an option. He'd already failed the first test, one that had worked a couple of times before: cutting her hair really short and getting her mom to give her a home perm. Boys liked long hair, plain and simple. And they'd get pissed when she cut it short.

But no, Stephen, even though he'd expressed the dismay she'd expected him to, insisted that they would be okay, that he loved her no matter what. Worse still, he'd started saying things about how much he'd hate to lose her, how miserable he would be. This was going to be hard.

Leslie also wasn't the kind of person who chickened out of things, but for whatever reason, she did on the Sunday night that she'd planned to go over to Stephen's house and break up with him. She knew that she needed to be firm, and she had rehearsed the scenario in her head over and over. With as much practice as she had, it should have been easy.

The problem was that, honestly, she had in fact started to fall in love with him, maybe just a little bit. There definitely was an attachment there. And it scared her. He really was a great guy. But with all of the things they didn't have in common, she believed deep down that if they stayed together, things still wouldn't work out. And it would hurt even more once it finally did end. Best to do it now, to rip off the Band-Aid, so to speak.

She could see it in her head: knocking on the front door of his house, waiting for him to open it up, then holding up his class ring, indicating that she was ready to give it back to him. Early versions of this fantasy had her calmly and profoundly explaining to him every reason why things had to be this way, which he would grudgingly accept, then stand there at the doorway while she walked back to her car. Maybe it would be raining, too. She had some lines rehearsed, like how Stephen needed to learn not to be dependent on someone else for his happiness. There might also be some appropriate song lyrics she could throw in, too, but she wasn't going to sing them, just say them and pretend that they were her own words.

This plan had been forming in her head almost as soon as Stephen had left her house the night before, and she'd avoided talking to Kim about it. For some reason, Kim had been really for this relationship, some bullshit about Stephen being able to straighten her out, whatever that meant. She had in fact talked Leslie into dating him in the first place. When she had tried to talk to her about her doubts, Kim had been dismissive, telling her she was just throwing away another good guy. But that was just it. Sure, maybe he was a good guy, but that didn't mean he was good *for her.*

She had spent all day Sunday — including not paying attention during church — painfully anticipating the confrontation, and the closer it got to the planned time that evening, the more nervous she got. When Nicola, her little sister, reminded her of the race she was running in at "the Y" (as her parents called it) that night, she felt a huge sense of relief. She'd forgotten all about it, despite her promise to be there.

Nicola was such a little attention-seeker, and yet, it's not like she had to fight for it. She was the young, cute one, plus she was good at everything she tried. School, sports, music, you name it: She was at the top of her class. Even so, there was always all this pressure on Leslie to be a good example for her, to be the big sister. Honestly, she really did admire the little rat, which was her playfully mean nickname for her because of some weird obsession she'd always had with cheese. That little girl was going places and, once she was old enough, would probably break a lot of hearts, even more than Leslie herself had managed to rack up over the years.

So, despite the occasional resentment she'd felt toward Nicola, coupled with the guilt she'd had heaped on her for blowing off attending the rehearsal race (or whatever it was called) the day before, Leslie was relieved to have an excuse not to go to Stephen's. She felt better, including physically; her stomach had been hurting more and more as the day had gone on.

Later, at the YMCA, she began to feel distracted once more, even angry at herself. All she was doing was putting off the inevitable. She should have just gone ahead and gotten it out of the way. Finally, she shook her head to try to clear her thoughts, her dark brown curls bouncing wildly as she did so.

"Are you all right?" her mother asked her, sounding more irritated than concerned.

"Yeah," Leslie said, feeling a little embarrassed. "Just, um… Headache." She wasn't sure why she'd lied about that. More honestly, she added, "Feeling kinda out of it. Didn't get a lot of sleep last night."

"Well, I've been up since six o'clock this morning," her mom said bitterly, "and you don't hear me complaining."

You just did, Leslie thought, but she kept it to herself. Her mother was always doing that, having to top everything that was said to her. If you had it bad, she had to have it worse. She and Nicola were a lot alike in some ways, and sometimes Leslie wondered if that's why their dad had left, outnumbered by three moody, unpredictable girls in the house. There were probably other reasons, though.

As the race began, she promised herself that she would put Stephen out of her mind and pay attention to her sister, and for a few moments, she actually was into the whole thing. Nicola, not surprisingly, stayed near the front of the pack of running kids, and she couldn't help but be impressed. She barely even noticed when one of the slower runners seemed to trip and falter, figuring that was just part of the sport, some of them screwing up more than others.

But it soon became clear that something was wrong. Another of the racers, a boy, fell down and skidded along the dirt; it looked painful. The man in charge of everything, some fat guy with a whistle, ran out towards him. Some of the competitors started slowing down to see what was going on, but others, including Nicola, hadn't seemed to have noticed anything. Then another boy went down, and shortly after that, the fat man did.

Leslie had been meaning to get her eyes checked; seeing things in detail from far away had gotten more difficult the past few months. But she also hated the idea of getting glasses, and she wasn't sure if she could just go straight to contacts or what. Regardless, she now regretted that she couldn't see just what was happening to these people, what was making them fall over. Worse still, none of them were getting up. Finally, she saw what the cause was as more and more screams erupted around her.

These tiny, almost invisible black bats were flying around and biting everyone, and she had no idea what to do. She wanted to run, but she wasn't sure where to go. She felt her mother gripping her wrist, so tightly it felt like she was going to break it. "Come on!" she shouted, but Leslie pulled away.

"Wait! Where's Nicola?" She looked around the track frantically, trying to spot her. She wasn't where she'd last seen her.

"She's over there!" her mother yelled, but Leslie couldn't tell where she was talking about. The crowd was becoming increasingly panicked, and she felt herself shoved from behind by someone. This caused her to slide down to the next row of bleachers, pain exploding in one of her shins as she landed.

Recovering, she looked around again, still hoping to see Nicola among the fleeing people. More than that, she began to fear that one of the motionless bodies on the ground might be her sister after all. And then she saw that, bizarrely, there was some red-haired guy with a big camera just standing in one place, whipping his body around as he snapped away, getting pictures of the chaos all around him.

Wow, now that's dedication, she thought to herself, almost finding it funny. But then she came to her senses, knowing that she needed to do something. She couldn't find her mother anymore, and as more people around her pushed and tried to clamber to safety, she found herself, like the photographer, just standing there. She simply didn't know what she should do.

Too late, she realized that she shouldn't have hesitated. If she'd kept moving, she might have been able to avoid the bat that suddenly zoomed toward her, right at her face and then around to the side of her neck. For a split second, she'd clearly seen its eyes, these shiny, black orbs that looked like little, polished pebbles. She'd also seen its open mouth with its tiny, sharp teeth, which she could now picture clearly as they bore into her flesh. Somehow, that made it hurt more, like the time she remembered getting her first shot from a hypodermic needle:

Seeing it pierce the skin of her arm had been a terrifying and painful experience.

As she collapsed, she could feel herself growing weaker; she didn't even have the strength to try to pull the creature off her neck as it drank the blood from her body. All she could see was the silvery metal of the bench on which her face was pressed, and she was vaguely aware of her arms dangling in the open air beneath it. There were these horizontal grooves on the bench that would probably leave an impression on her cheek, and for a moment, she felt embarrassed, wondering what that would look like later. Then she realized that it didn't matter.

Unlike that tetanus shot all those years ago, she wouldn't be feeling the pain and the soreness for days, angry at her mother for not warning her ahead of time what that mean doctor was about to do to her. They'd just sat her down, not even telling her what was going on, and stuck that horrible needle into her as she cried out. She'd been bitter about that whenever the memory resurfaced. But this time, she didn't know who to be mad at.

As the dizziness and disorientation increased, she wondered if her sister and her mother had managed to get away. She wondered how Stephen would feel about all of this, how much the loss of her would upset him.

And then, she didn't wonder anything at all.

CHAPTER SEVEN

COUPLE

"Don't think I didn't see that," Kathleen said sharply, her arms folded.

"See what?" Matt said exasperatedly, though he was pretty sure he knew what his girlfriend was getting at.

"You were totally looking at her!" she said, stomping her right foot into the dirt.

"What? Which one?"

"Well, I do hope it wasn't the younger one," Kathleen said. "She couldn't have been more than like thirteen. But the brunette. You were all like, 'I'm sure Cliff can give you a jump!'" She said this in a goofy voice, gyrating her hips as she spoke.

"I don't talk like that," Matt said impatiently, "and I didn't do some stupid moving around like this." He mocked the gesture she'd made.

"Yeah, but you thought it."

"I was talking about their car," he insisted. "They said they needed a jump-start. It was a joke. And everyone laughed but you." In the flickering light from the campfire, Kathleen's expression was hard to read. He wasn't sure if she was really mad or just picking a fight for the fun of it. Hoping to change the subject, he walked over to the styrofoam cooler and pulled off the lid. The water and ice cubes inside made a slushing sound as he pulled out another beer.

"Don't you think you've had enough of those?" Kathleen asked.

"Oh, God, don't start," Matt said, becoming more annoyed. "This is only my third one. And we came out here to have fun, you know?"

"I just worry sometimes," she said, her voice becoming more quiet.

"About what?" he countered, becoming more defiant. He reached into the cooler again, then pulled out another bottle and handed it to her. "Loosen up, already. Remember what you said earlier. It's summer, so every night is Friday night."

"It's Sunday," Kathleen said sharply, taking the bottle but not making a move to open it. Then she let out a laugh. "Fine." The beer let out a familiar hiss as she twisted off the cap.

Matt eyed her as she took a swig from the bottle, then took one of his own. It was always hard to tell with her whether she was genuinely mad or just playing around. Sometimes, his misunderstanding of that led to some genuinely nasty fights. The girl was like a minefield.

"Say," Matt said after a swallow, "now that the others have gone, you wanna…?"

"Wanna what?"

Matt gave a nod to his left, toward the direction of the lake. There had been some talk of them going skinny-dipping, and now that the rest of the guys had gone off to help those two girls, Matt hoped that Kathleen would follow through.

"No," she said.

"Why not?"

"I just don't."

"You said earlier you'd…"

"I know what I said!" she almost shouted, then seemed to catch herself. "I just… changed my mind, is all."

Matt wasn't sure what to say. If he wasn't careful, this could erupt into another real argument. Their friend Cliff had once commented on how they, as he put it, "knew how to fight," that they were able to work through their problems rather than bottling things up and letting them get worse. He started to question her further, but something strange distracted him, a flapping sound that passed right over the two of them.

"What…?" he began, but the thing — whatever it was — had come and gone too quickly. He looked behind him in the direction it seemed to have gone. Had it been an owl?

"I've been meaning to tell you," Kathleen began, apparently oblivious to what had just happened, "I don't want to have sex again until after we get married."

Here we go again, Matt thought. They'd had this conversation probably four or five times over the two years they'd been going out, but they'd always gone back to having sex again. Kathleen's family was Catholic, and she often got caught up in all of the requisite guilt that went along with that. But he also knew that this particular argument was sometimes a ploy she used to try to get him to propose. She had an almost freakish obsession with getting married before she reached the age of twenty, and while he did genuinely want to marry her someday and could often picture that future, he just wasn't ready. He felt that they were still way too young, that they should finish college first and get their careers going.

"Kathleen, look," he said, stepping forward. "You know I love you. I always have, and I always…" He broke off because he heard something.

It sounded like Cliff's voice, or rather, him yelling. He had always been a party animal, so Matt was used to him showing off and letting out big cheers, especially when he got drunk. The sound came from the direction he and the others had walked, but there was something disconcerting about it: It sounded more like he was hurt. Matt looked around, but Kathleen called his attention back to her.

"I'm serious this time," she insisted.

"Did you hear…?"

"Yes," she said with a severe frown. "I heard Cliff being his typical drunk self…" She stopped suddenly, her eyes going wide as two more screams erupted from the darkness, ones that sounded like they'd come from Eric and Lance, their other two friends.

"Matt, what the hell is that?" she hissed, dropping her beer and rushing forward to grab onto him. She then remembered the two girls that the guys had gone off with, half expecting to hear their screams come next.

"Something wrong?" a voice that sounded like a girl's said from behind her. Kathleen spun around, surprised to see two boys walking towards them just a little more quickly than she was comfortable with. She had no idea who they were or what they were doing here, and it occurred to her that they looked way too young to be out here at the lake this late on a Sunday night.

"Who…?" she and Matt said together, then broke off when they realized they'd been speaking simultaneously. Under any other circumstances, they would have laughed about that; it was something they frequently found themselves doing. The two of them really were a lot alike, often thinking the same thing. It was one of the benefits of having been a couple for so long.

"You kids shouldn't be out here," Matt said, and the nervousness in his voice only added to Kathleen's own. "It's not… It isn't safe."

"Oh, we know," the shorter of the two said, the one wearing glasses. The taller, more lanky one, whom Kathleen noticed was almost as tall as she was, let out a high-pitched laugh, pretty much a giggle. They stopped their approach, the taller boy holding an arm out in front of his friend as they got nearer to the campfire.

"Remember what she told us," he whispered to the shorter boy, who nodded. They took a couple of cautious steps away from the fire, then eyed Matt and Kathleen again.

"Are you hungry?" she found herself asking. She had suddenly gotten it into her head that these might be two lost runaways, the skinniness of the taller boy vaguely reinforcing this idea. This notion was more comforting than the other one forming in the back of her mind; there was something almost predatory looking about these boys. "We've got some crackers over here, and some marshmallows and…

We were going to make s'mores…" The words died in her throat as the taller boy spoke, his wide smile punctuated by two long fangs.

"Oh, we're hungry, all right," he said, the evil look in his eyes made all the more menacing by the way they glinted in the firelight.

With that, he rushed forward and pounced onto Matt. Despite his bigger size, he seemed helpless against the assault, collapsing onto the dirt and screaming as he went down. Kathleen cried out as well, horrified at what she saw happening to her boyfriend, but it was less than a second before she too was attacked by the other boy.

"No!" she tried to scream, but the word dissolved into a groan as the vampire's fangs sunk into her neck. She collapsed to the ground, completely unable to fight against him despite the fact that he was only a little more than half her size. The pain made her want to flail about, but her body just wouldn't respond. All she could do was lie there, staring up at the dark sky and the barely illuminated trees, the sound of her own blood being gulped down the throat of the monster that was going to take her life. She probably only had seconds left.

Kathleen had always believed in the supernatural, but she'd never given any serious thought to the existence of vampires. And yet, here she was, being killed by one. But she did believe in psychic powers, and she'd occasionally liked to imagine that the bond between her and Matt could go so far as to be telepathic. He'd never been all that into the idea, but he did sometimes humor her when she'd brought it up.

So here, in her final moments, she did her best to send him a message: *I love you.*

Love you, too, she thought she heard back.

CHAPTER EIGHT

THE NEWS

Dana McKinley's work was important to her, though she bristled at being called a "career woman." There was just something about the term that rubbed her the wrong way, almost like it was a backhanded compliment. Sure, this was the '80s, and she was all about progress and women being able to have careers every bit as much as men did. But more often than she liked, any conversation or discussion that included that particular term seemed to have a subtext to it that in order for a woman to be successful, that meant that she had to sacrifice other, more traditional things, like having a family.

But that wasn't the case for Dana. She had a family, and as seriously as she took her work, her husband and daughter meant more to her than anything else. They were the true center of her life, and if she'd ever had to choose between them and her job as co-anchor of Channel Four News, her family would have won hands down. Fortunately, she'd never had to make that choice.

She knew plenty of women who had been perfectly content to marry men who were well off and live out the rest of their days as housewives, and she didn't begrudge them that. But she'd always wanted something more. When she was feeling truly honest with herself, she would have to admit that the life she had wasn't the one she had once dreamed of, but that didn't mean that she wasn't happy with it. She was. If her younger self had been able to look forward ten years and see how she'd ended up, she might have been disappointed, but Dana wasn't that naive, starry-eyed teenager anymore.

Broadcast journalism wasn't even something she had been interested in back then. Her dream had always been to become a famous actress, something she eventually learned to stop telling people as she got older. It wasn't just that it was such an unrealistic goal; it was that the motivation behind it was a little embarrassing.

As a teenager, she'd idolized Grant Pullman, one of the hot, hunky soap opera stars of the late '60s and early '70s. He'd played a doctor on *General Hospital* for a while, which was where she'd first seen him and fallen in love. He had these dark, full eyebrows and a smile so arresting it could stop an oncoming train; basically he was the epitome of charm as far as Dana was concerned. Like many soap actors, he'd moved around from show to show as the years went on, later playing a night club owner on *The Guiding Light,* then even being a nasty villain on *The Edge of Night.* She didn't even care which role he played; he was gorgeous, and she wanted nothing more than to one day meet him and be with him for the rest of her life.

She could picture it, and she often did, fantasizing in countless scenarios about how wonderful their life together would be. It was this ongoing fantasy that led her to pursue acting herself, and if things went right, she too would become a part of the soap opera world, hopefully moving to New York or Hollywood or wherever she needed to go, just so long as she ended up in Grant Pullman's arms one day.

Of course, things didn't work out that way, but she did enjoy acting in high school and later on in college. She performed in several plays, and while being on stage and being afraid of messing up or forgetting her lines made her nervous, she found that it was a good nervousness. The payoff was always there at the end: The applause from the audience was like a drug. She wondered if Grant Pullman felt the same way about his acting. One day, they would talk about it, maybe cuddled up together in front of the fireplace in his huge and lavishly furnished house. For some reason, she always pictured a white bearskin rug in this story.

Near the end of high school, she'd applied to various colleges around the country, and while she disappointedly did not get accepted at New York University, she was invited to matriculate at the University of Southern California. Surely, that would get her close enough to the Hollywood scene and on the road to fame, fortune, and more importantly, the actor she'd been infatuated with since she was fourteen. But something got in the way: a wonderful guy named Mark whom she started dating just a few months before the end of high school.

Mark was great, funny, and smart. He certainly wasn't bad looking, either, and she'd even told him during the early flirting stages that he reminded her quite a bit of one of her favorite actors. It didn't take her long to fall in love with him, and by the time the summer was halfway through, she gave up on the idea of USC and decided to just stay in Augusta to be with the new love of her life. Part of her felt disappointed in herself for that, like she'd given up on a dream and just settled for something more mundane. But as time went on, she knew that she'd made the right decision.

Dana stuck with acting, becoming involved with Augusta College's Drama Guild. It was fun for a little while, but she grew increasingly irritated with the other students. Some of them were nice, but there was a lot of cliquishness going on, the older people being jealous and excluding newcomers like herself. Added to that was the way the faculty seemed to be rather full of themselves, acting like they were big-name Hollywood directors when, truth be told, they were nothing more than professors at some little-known college in Augusta, Georgia, a place most people had never even heard of.

But Augusta was her home, and while she may not have loved it, it was where she was. Her initial jealousy over many of her friends going off to colleges out of town was mitigated when a third or so of them wound up failing out during their first semesters due to partying too much, most of them returning to Augusta in shame. At least she'd chosen to stay home, and even if it weren't the most exciting place in the world, she wasn't alone.

The Christmas before they were both due to graduate, she and Mark had exchanged presents as usual. While Mark always appreciated the thoughtful gifts she picked out for him, he took a keen delight in her doing the same, watching her eagerly as she opened each one. He also liked to surprise her, plus he seemed to get an almost perverse pleasure in having her shake her wrapped presents in the days leading up to the holiday and try — almost always incorrectly, by the way — to guess what they were.

One mystery present in particular had her baffled: a large, sturdy box that felt completely empty. Most boxes had some kind of mass in them, some clue as to their contents. But this one literally felt empty. Try as she might, she couldn't guess what was in it, and no matter how much she prodded Mark for clues, he wouldn't give in. It would have been frustrating if he weren't so sweet.

The day finally came when she was able to tear off the paper and see what was inside, though Mark had tortured her further by making her save this one for last. Inside, suspended by a series of rubber bands, was a much smaller box, which explained why nothing had been able to rattle around inside. But it wasn't just any kind of box; she recognized it for what it was immediately.

Her hands were shaking too much to extricate it from the elastic network, so Mark helped it along, sliding off of the couch and getting down on one knee to face her while Dana put her hands to her mouth, gasping as she held back tears.

Their marriage was good and solid, but the romance was marred by one painful fact that became apparent early on. Despite their best efforts, Dana couldn't seem to get pregnant. They'd always wanted children, and they wanted to get started on having them right away, but something just wasn't working. It was heartbreaking, but they were both determined to make it happen.

This was one of the reasons why Dana kept working. Mark was well off, working his way up in the sales department at a local company that built and sold golf carts, one of the town's leading industries. So in theory, at least when they had just been talking about getting married during the years leading up to it, Dana could have become a stay-at-home mother. But the recurring doctor's appointments, which then led to fertility treatments that failed multiple times, necessitated a dual income.

She didn't mind working. If nothing else, it kept her mind occupied and helped stave off the depression she sometimes found herself slipping into. She didn't know — and the doctors seemed to go back and forth on it as well — whether it was her husband's fault or her own why she couldn't manage to conceive. Regardless, she felt betrayed, sometimes by her body, other times by God.

An internship during college at one of the local news stations had led to a part-time job and then a full-time one, initially doing production behind the scenes instead of in front of the camera. By that point in her life, Dana had accepted that she was more likely to get work that way; her childhood dreams of fame and stardom would have to wait, maybe forever.

Her first on-air stint had come about purely by accident when the regular co-anchor had unexpectedly been taken ill, which was later revealed to be due to her own pregnancy. She kept it to herself, but this made Dana burn with jealousy, angry over the fact that this other woman could have a baby when she was having her own fertility issues, which had just recently come to light. And while she nervously stumbled and stammered her way through the opening minutes of that first night on the air, her Drama background paid off. The acting instinct kicked in, and she was a hit with the higher-ups at the station, finding herself occasionally filling in for the woman whose job she would eventually take over once she became a mother.

Without meaning to, Dana grew up and became a professional. Her shoulder-length blonde locks gave way to a sensible, feathered coiffure, just as the groovy, flared pants of her youth were replaced with skirts and heels. She reported the news along with seasoned on-air veteran Britt Hinson, putting on a smile when talking about pleasant things, or sporting a practiced, concerned look when it was necessary to convey the more grim stories.

And finally, in the spring of '78, the doctor told her what she had been waiting to hear for what had felt like an eternity: She was going to have a baby. For the first few months, she lived in terror that something would go wrong, that she might wind up having a miscarriage and be even more devastated. But that didn't happen, and Melissa Annabelle McKinley came into the world without a hitch. She was the best Christmas present a mother could ever hope for.

There was a part of her — selfish, Dana knew — that worried that while she was on maternity leave, her fill-in anchor might take over her job permanently. But even if that had happened, she wouldn't have been heartbroken over it. Sure, her family could still use both her and Mark's incomes to make up for all of that lost money. The two of them joked that Melissa, or Missy, as they took to calling her when she was old enough to talk, was "the most expensive baby ever," but she'd been worth every penny. And even if they had been forced to just rely on Mark's salary, they still would have been okay. But as much as Dana enjoyed her newfound, hard-earned motherhood, she still enjoyed her work, which she was able to return to soon enough.

She genuinely felt that her job was an important one, putting a familiar and comforting face on the news that sometimes wasn't all that enjoyable to report. Her local fame wasn't the kind she'd pictured as a child, all of those glamorous parties and photo shoots like the ones depicted in the magazines. But she was still something of a celebrity, if a small-time one. People recognized her when she went to the grocery store. Her alma mater even got her to give a talk to one of their Journalism classes, which was a strange feeling. She took some pleasure in this, but deep down, it wasn't what really mattered to her.

Mark and Missy, the home they had, the life they lived: That was the center of her existence. Even if something happened to her job — if some new, up-and-coming or better looking upstart wound up taking it from her — she wouldn't have shed many tears. If anything happened to her husband or daughter, though, that would be what would make her world fall apart.

While her job was to report the local news, she or Britt Hinson — they took turns — also had to cut away halfway through each broadcast to briefly focus on national and world events, a tie-in to the network broadcast that followed their own show. More often than not, this was the part of the show that Dana disliked the most. The news around Augusta could range from the unpleasant to the light-hearted, but when it came to worldwide stories, these were almost always negative. There were hostage situations, plane crashes, assassination attempts, and, most frightening of all, the ever-increasing tension between the United States and the Soviet Union.

Dana tried to ignore the things her more cynical friends and colleagues said, their fears that one day, something would snap, and World War Three would break out. The nightmare scenario of a nuclear holocaust wiping out all or most life on the planet in a storm of fire and ash was just too terrifying to contemplate. People would say things like, "What kind of a world is this to bring a child into?" That made her angry more than afraid. She'd worked so damn hard to bring her daughter into existence. What right did a bunch of trigger-happy politicians and overgrown bullies have threatening the lives of the people she loved?

So she remained defiant, at least internally. Her family would be okay; they had to be. She had to believe that in order to get through day to day. There was no point in living in fear. The news was something that happened to other people; she just talked about it on the air.

"Who did your braids?" Dana asked her daughter with a knowing smile.

"Umm…" Missy said, rocking her body back and forth with her hands behind her back, avoiding eye contact. Then she looked her mother straight in the eye and said with a wide grin that still had all of its baby teeth, "Maybe it was Daddy?"

Mark, who had been looking on with amusement, suddenly got a shocked look on his face, almost like he thought he was going to be in trouble. He looked at Dana with near desperation, shaking his head quickly but saying nothing.

Dana laughed loudly, kicking her head back. She tried to regain control, attempting a stern expression. "Missy, you know what we've told you about telling lies."

"I *know,*" she almost sang, hanging her head. "It was *me.*" She sounded disappointed at being found out.

Naturally, Dana knew what had happened even before she'd asked her question. Missy had tried unsuccessfully to french-braid her hair once already, and the results were laughable, but it was cute all the same. She was envious of one of the other girls in the neighborhood whose mother had done her hair up this way just a couple of days ago, and Dana had promised to do the same for her. She just hadn't had time given how much work had been keeping her busy. Apparently, before coming to visit her at the TV station this evening, Missy had tried once again to do it herself; she was a stubborn little girl.

Dana leaned forward in her chair towards her daughter, and all of a sudden, Missy turned away, covering up her eyes. "Missy, it's okay," Dana said quickly, gently grabbing her tiny arm and pulling it from her face. "I'm not mad." The girl turned back to her, sniffling a little. "Go and find Aunt Patty," Dana said, pointing. "She's in the bathroom down the hall. Remember? The one on the right."

"Okay," she said, quietly but more calm.

"Tell her Mommy said for her to redo your braids," she said, giving her most comforting smile. Missy beamed back at her, then scampered out of the room.

"She just wants to look as pretty as her mom," Mark offered with a smile. "She asked me earlier tonight about the people who do your hair and make-up before your shows."

"She did?" Dana was aware that the family usually watched the 6:00 broadcast from home, Mark being under strict instructions to change the channel or at least turn the sound down if a story came up that was too graphic for Missy to handle.

"Well, she didn't put it like that, not really. It was more like, 'Daddy, who does Mommy's *booooty?*'"

Dana looked confused for a moment, then let out another huge laugh. About a week ago, she'd let Missy go along with Carla — the same girl whose braids she envied — and her mother while she got her hair done at the salon, which the mother referred to as "the beauty shop." Missy had mispronounced the phrase as "the booty shop" once she'd gotten back home, and despite their efforts to teach her the correct pronunciation, their little girl kept getting it hilariously wrong.

Recovering, Dana said, "Well, maybe I'll let her come by one night and get her own *booty* done by one of the girls while I'm getting ready. If Britt can spare them, anyway. I swear that guy spends more time in make-up than I do."

"Mr. Helmet Hair…" Mark said playfully, repeating an old joke of theirs. He sat down in the only other chair in the small office, glancing at the papers on the desk behind his wife. "Started working on the eleven o'clock show, I see."

Dana sighed and swiveled her chair around, then began sorting through the sheets. "Yes. In fact, I need to get going soon. Mr. Hel… *Britt* and I have to go through tonight's copy."

Mark suppressed another laugh. "I still want to try it out, you know."

"Try what out?"

"My tennis ball theory." Part of their long-running joke about Britt's hair was that it was so heavily sprayed up, if one were to throw a tennis ball at it, it would bounce off.

Dana giggled, turning back around to face him. "Don't you dare." Then she changed the subject. "Anyway, I'm glad you all stopped by. Wish I had time to go with you, but, well, you know."

"I know." He paused, then added with a slightly evil grin, "That's what I get for marrying a career woman."

"Don't start," Dana shot back through clenched teeth, but she wasn't really mad.

A few minutes later, Patty, Mark's sister, came in through the door. The two of them both had dark brown hair, as did Missy, and she'd told Dana that most of the time when she was out with her daughter, people assumed that Patty was her mother. It was an understandable mistake, but she'd grown tired of correcting people, sometimes not even bothering to.

The woman was a godsend. Dana's and Mark's busy work schedules could have made raising a daughter impossible, but Patty had been more than willing to help. There had been some discussion of making her into a live-in nanny, but Patty — who wasn't married and had no children of her own — insisted on keeping her house on Central Avenue, the one she and her brother had inherited from their parents several years ago. She still spent the night plenty of times at Mark and Dana's when necessary, but there was something in her, maybe pride, that demanded some sense of self-identity. Dana understood that, and she was beyond grateful for the help her sister-in-law provided.

Missy sidled in behind Patty, a huge grin on her face. Her braids had been done properly, and she bounded over to her mother. "See?" she asked excitedly.

"See what?" Dana joked. "Did you… Let's see. Did you change your shoes?"

"My *hairrr, Mommyyy,*" Missy almost growled, but she was in on the joke this time.

"Yes. You look *boo-tiful.*" They both laughed, though maybe for different reasons. Dana straightened up, looking around at Patty and Mark. "Well, you all go and have fun at dinner." Her voice retained the somewhat fake, sing-song way that adults spoke in while around children, mostly for their benefit. She faced Missy again, getting up from her chair but kneeling, remaining at floor-level and taking the girl's arms in her hands. "We still have a deal, right?"

"Yes, Mommy," Missy said, sounding a little perturbed.

"You eat all your vegetables at dinner, and then you can get dessert."

"Yes, Mommy," she repeated. Then she got a pensive look on her face. "Do you think they'll have pizza?"

Dana let out a small laugh, knowing the fancy restaurant that they were heading to. "No, sweetie, not at The Plantation House. It's much more upscale than that."

Missy's face fell. "But…" Her nose began to wrinkle and redden, a sure sign that she was about to cry. "But I wanted pizza!"

Patty quickly leaned over and put a hand on Missy's shoulder. "Sweetheart, I promise you. What they have at The Plantation House is much, much better. Really nice food. You'll like it. I swear."

Her impending crying fit seemed to have been averted. She turned to face Patty, then asked her softly, "Do they maybe have pizza for dessert?"

Patty shook her head. "No, darling. But maybe… Maybe they will. Or they might have something better! I've heard they've got this really great thing called turtle cheesecake."

Missy frowned and furrowed her little brow, seeming to mull this over in her head. "Is that anything like the chocolate moose?" she asked.

Patty laughed gently, but Dana cringed, remembering a dining disaster from a little over a month ago. Missy had been promised a chocolate mousse for dessert at a similarly upscale restaurant, then had thrown a tantrum when it arrived. Dana and Mark couldn't understand why she'd been so upset and refused to eat it, and the rest of the night hadn't gone well. It wasn't until after Missy was in bed and the three of them were discussing it that Patty figured it out: The girl had misunderstood the description of the dish and had expected something similar to a chocolate bunny like the kind she'd gotten at Easter, only in the shape of a moose.

"No, not at all," Patty said, still being as smiling and reassuring as always. "It's better. Much better. I'll explain later, once we're in the car."

The girl seemed to relent, but there was still something reserved in her manner. "Okay." She then leaned in closer to her aunt, thinking that she was whispering too low for her parents to hear but really just hissing. She hadn't mastered that skill yet and thought she was being stealthy. "But if the turtle cake isn't good, maybe *then* we can go get pizza."

Patty nodded conspiratorially, pretending that she didn't think Dana and Mark had overheard. She straightened up, smiling brightly as Dana mouthed to her the words: *"No pizza."* Patty winked back, acknowledging their understanding. Her house was down the road from a bar that sold pizza and beer, but aside from just serving it to patrons, their food was also available for take-out. A couple of months before the "chocolate moose" incident, Patty had gotten Missy some pizza from there, which she loved so much that she ate to the point where she got a stomachache that kept her up all night. That hadn't been a pleasant thing for Dana to come home to after work.

Her husband, sister-in-law, and daughter departed, and Dana eyed their backs suspiciously, wondering if Patty would in fact honor their agreement. There was no reason to think that she was being dishonest, but there had been at least a couple of times when Missy's persuasiveness had won out. This thought was derailed by a suspicion of a different kind, and Dana quickly moved over to the chair where Mark had been sitting.

He had this bad habit of not tucking his wallet all the way into his back pocket, and it sometimes fell out, particularly when he wore dress pants. She'd gotten used to checking behind him. Relieved, she saw that it wasn't in the chair, but that didn't mean that it might not fall out and get wedged between the car seat and the door, which had happened more than once. She shook her head and told herself she was worrying over nothing. If Patty wound up having to foot the bill at the restaurant tonight, Dana would pay her back. That, too, had happened more than once. She sighed, thinking to herself that she loved Mark dearly, but the man would lose his own head if it weren't attached.

In the minutes leading up to airtime, Dana and Britt sat behind the news desk, alternating between talking about the stories they were getting ready to report and making small talk. Dana hated having to start off a show with bad news, though Britt was in favor of it; he thought that it grabbed viewers' attention right away. Tonight in particular, they were going to have to lead with a story that fell into this category.

Over the past two nights, a series of vicious attacks by some unknown flying animals had resulted in the injuries and deaths of more than two dozen people around town. Because of the severe blood loss the victims experienced, there was some speculation about the animals actually being vampires, but that was just stupid, Dana felt. There was no such thing. Britt agreed, and they'd decided earlier that evening to avoid using that word in tonight's broadcast. At the very least, it was bad journalism to report speculation, and sensationalism was even worse.

The broadcast began as usual, the anchors composing themselves as they heard the opening theme music and the announcer's voice playing quietly over a speaker elsewhere in the studio. The rectangular, red light on the front of one of the cameras lit up, and the cameraman pointed, giving the hosts their cue.

"Good evening," Britt began in the same cadence he used every night, "and welcome to Channel Four News. I'm Britt Hinson."

"And I'm Dana McKinley." The light on the second camera went on as Dana turned slightly in her chair to face it, then began reading the teleprompter. "More tragedy has occurred in the Summerville area of Augusta tonight in what appears to be the latest in a series of unexplained killings."

After the show was over, Dana made her way back to her office, exhausted. Some nights were better than others, but this was one of those where she was looking forward to getting home as soon as possible. She cringed as she heard a voice call out from behind her: "Miss McKinley!"

She turned around to see Anthony, one of the guys from the production room, hurrying up to her. He was a nice young man, if a little ineffectual, and she had a soft spot for him due to the fact that he currently held one of the VTR editing positions she'd once done as an intern. She sighed.

"Anthony, I've told you. You can call me Dana. It's okay."

"Sorry," he said, holding out a hand in front as if to shield himself. He caught his breath as he stopped in front of her, then delivered his message: "There's a couple of policemen here to see you."

"What, now?" she asked, surprised and a little angry. She had an idea what this might be about: There was an upcoming charity event that the local police department was organizing, and they'd already been pestering her to host it. It wasn't that she didn't believe in the cause; of course it was good to make people aware of the dangers of drunk driving. She'd told them on the phone that she would consider the offer, but what made her the most reluctant to accept it was that it would mean even less spare time to spend with her family. She hadn't explicitly stated that, though, but she was beginning to think that she was going to have to. Good cause or not, it was rather tacky of them to show up at her work this late at night.

Dana looked up at the ceiling, fighting back another exasperated sigh. She knew better than to lash out at one of the lower-ranking staff; she'd been on the receiving end of that plenty of times in her younger days. She'd always vowed never to become a prima donna.

Regaining her control, she asked Anthony where the police were. "Front lobby," he said with a hint of a smile. "I made them wait there. Something about a missing wallet... I'm not sure. The guy wouldn't tell me much of anything, even when I kept asking. Kind of an asshole, really."

Dana relaxed, letting out a little laugh. "Well, now I'm really not surprised. On a few levels, in fact." Aside from tonight's annoyance, she'd occasionally had other troubles when dealing with the police, who could sometimes be stingy with information when they chose to. "I think I know what's going on. Thanks, Anthony; I'll take care of it."

He nodded at her and grinned as she walked past him, down the hall and in the opposite direction from her office.

She was surprised to find that only one of the policemen was in uniform, a squat, grey-haired man with a moustache. The other man didn't even look like a cop; if he were one, he was wearing what they called plain clothes. As she approached them, she put on her best professional smile.

"Mrs. McKinley?" the taller man asked, the one not wearing a uniform. Neither he nor the other man looked particularly friendly.

"Yes," she said brightly, extending her hand to shake his.

The man returned the gesture, but there was something odd in his expression. "I'm sorry we weren't able to get in touch with you sooner."

"I take it this is about my husband's wallet?"

"That's..." the man began, but then he stopped short. Dana was prepared to joke around about her husband's chronic irresponsibility, but this man's tone was a little too serious for her liking. "I'm afraid..." He stopped again, clearing his throat. "I apologize, ma'am. It was because of the misplaced wallet that it took as long as it did to find out who to notify. This is Officer Harbin..." he gestured to the man beside him, and Dana suddenly realized that she recognized him from the footage used at the beginning of tonight's broadcast. "And I'm Randall Milton, County Coroner. Your husband is a Mr. Mark McKinley; is that correct?"

"What's this about?" Dana heard herself asking. "I mean, yes." She was almost whispering now, her heart beginning to race as the man continued to speak.

"I'm afraid I have some terrible news, Mrs. McKinley. It's about your husband, your daughter, and a Miss Patricia McKinley…"

Dana's world fell apart.

CHAPTER NINE

ENOUGH

Excerpts from the diary of Carolyn Leigh Young

June 28, 1983

I'm not sure what to do. We're still doing the vampire thing. I'd be lying if I said that it wasn't pretty cool at first, but I kinda hate saying that. I only went along with it because I thought the whole "vampire potion" thing was a load of bullcrap, just something Susanna made up to make Carl feel better. Ray's other friend Tim was pretty convincing, too. I wonder about that kid sometimes. He's almost too smart. Scares me a little. Or he would if he wasn't so damn annoying with how smart he is. Nerd.

But here's my point: they all said we could undo the potion after we took it. Like there's another one we can take that undoes it so we're normal people again. We were only supposed to be vampires for a little bit anyway, but it's been... how long? Three days now. Or nights. It's weird getting used to all that. But I just think we've done it long enough. I want to get back to normal. And I feel bad about all the killing. Like that little girl outside the pizza bar/place tonight

. . . . .

Ray was just in here wanting me to come watch TV with them. No. Where was I?

I just feel all complicated about it. This is pretty darn amazing, that we're able to do all this. The whole bats and flying thing, that's cool. But it's got to be wrong, killing. And Susanna's being her usual self, all in charge and telling everyone what to do. I wonder if I can talk her into putting a stop to this soon. I don't want it to get out of hand, or maybe it already has. I'll let you know how it goes.

June 30, 1983

I don't know what's wrong with me, why I'm feeling so weird. I can't stop, and I don't want to. I'm craving it like you wouldn't believe. I just can't get enough of their

. .

Forget it. I thought I was going to write more in here, but I've got better things to do. There are people out there waiting.

CHAPTER TEN

JASON'S STORY

Jason and the girl sat together in the front of his parked car, but the two of them didn't know each other. They'd been talking for several minutes now, and by the time Jason realized that he'd never even asked the girl her name, that made him feel awkward. He couldn't seem to find a way to just throw in, "Hey, what's your name?" without it sounding like he was trying to pick up on her, which was the farthest thing from his mind. He was in way too much pain to even think of doing something like that.

But the girl was nice enough, and she'd been a good listener, letting him ramble off all of his thoughts about what he'd been through the past few days, which had been hell. The town seemed to have been overrun by vampires, which was supposed to be impossible, but he'd seen it firsthand. In fact, he'd barely escaped with his life. And that was the problem.

Jason had been coming back to this parking lot — this exact parking space, in fact — the past few nights. He wasn't even sure why he kept doing it, but it seemed to bring him some sort of comfort. At the very least, he felt like he owed it to his girlfriend. She was dead now, and he kept replaying in his head the night she'd been killed, wishing he'd done things differently. Every night up until this one, he'd been on his own, sometimes bawling his eyes out as he beat himself up inside, feeling guilty for having survived. He knew that it didn't make sense, but he didn't care.

"But why?" the girl asked. "Do you think it would've done you any good to die along with her?"

A flash of anger ran through Jason at this question; it seemed rather cruel. But then he realized that the girl was right, and he said so with a sigh. "You look a little young to be a shrink," he joked, surprising himself at being able to find any humor in all of this. But it was a nice outlet; in a way, he wasn't poking fun at this girl as much as he was at the dull, pinch-faced older woman he'd been forced to talk to the past couple of days. "Maybe you should do that when you grow up."

"If I grow up," the girl said sadly, looking away from him and out the windshield.

"What do you mean by that?"

"Now who's the shrink?" the girl asked with a pointed look. Jason found himself feeling nervous. The girl wasn't unattractive, but she was definitely too young for him, and he began to wonder if he'd made a mistake by offering her shelter in his car. But when he'd spotted her wandering across the parking lot earlier, he'd decided that it wasn't safe for her to be out on her own, particularly this late at night and with everything that had been going on around town.

"I... Look, maybe I should take you home. Do you live far from here?" He began to reach for the keys in his pocket.

"No," the girl said sharply, reaching for his hand. It was warm on his, and he again felt uncomfortable. He wasn't sure how old she was, but she was definitely in jailbait territory. The girl drew back, then settled back down in the passenger seat. "I mean... I don't want to go home. Not yet. There's... things going on."

Jason began to feel sorry for her, wondering what she could be referring to but thinking he might have some idea. "So you're a runaway," he said.

The girl seemed to think for a moment. "Yes. I suppose I am."

He wasn't sure what to make of that. "Bad things at home, huh?" The girl nodded. "I can understand that."

"You can?"

"Well, kind of. I'm not supposed to be out here tonight, either. In fact, it's probably stupid for me to keep coming out here night after night, you know, after what happened."

"Your family doesn't know you're out tonight, do they?" the girl asked, a slight smile creeping into her expression. "You snuck out."

"Yeah," Jason smiled. "But it's therapeutic. I guess. Not even sure what the point is."

"Maybe you're hoping she'll come back."

His smile disappeared. "What?"

"That's how it's supposed to work," the girl said simply. "A vampire kills someone, and then they come back to life as a vampire themselves. Is that what you're thinking's gonna happen?"

"What? No! I can't even…" He paused. "At least, I really hope not…" He shuddered.

"Don't worry," the girl said, looking away. "From what I've heard, that hasn't been happening. The people getting killed, they just… Well, they just die." She looked back at Jason, seeing the pained look on his face. "Sorry. That was probably a mean thing to say."

He sat there in silence, putting his hands onto the steering wheel, then leaning his forehead onto them. He breathed in deeply, and the girl could tell that he was trying to keep from crying.

"Sorry," she said again, reaching up and touching his right arm gently. "You wanna tell me more about her? Just who was she? What did she look like?"

"Well, that's the thing," he began.

His girlfriend wasn't the prettiest girl in the world, but that hadn't mattered, not really. While most guys went for the tall, blonde, voluptuous kind, Jason had fallen for this tiny girl in his English 102 class, loving everything about her, right down to her beak-like nose and cropped, frizzy brown hair. She wasn't ugly, though, not in the least. She was just kind of "off," attractive mostly because she was different and smart. She had a wide smile that spread across her face, coupled with a devilish glint in her narrow little eyes, always looking like she was up to something.

She lived in Grovetown, a country town way out to the west of Augusta, but Jason didn't mind driving out there almost every single day to see her. It was worth it. Putting up with her trailer trash family was more difficult, but again, she was worth the trouble. To him, she seemed so unlike the rest of her family, a diamond in the rough.

"I'd hoped to take her away from all that," Jason said, "once we had enough money saved up for an apartment. Just never got the chance." He paused, thinking that the girl might say something sympathetic, but she just sat there. "I've gotta say, I miss her so damn much, but I'm not going to miss dealing with her alcoholic stepfather. God, he was an asshole. All full of himself, refusing to speak to me most of the time whenever I came over. Like I wasn't good enough or something."

"Hmm," the girl said, but that was it.

Jason went on to talk more about their relationship, including how he'd hoped to marry his girlfriend someday. But all of that was cut short on Monday night when they'd been walking back from the record store to his car, and she'd screamed when she'd spotted the dead bodies in the parking lot.

"At first, I was mad, thinking she'd just seen a spider. That was one thing about her that always got on my nerves, the way she'd shriek her damn head off if she saw one of those things. There was this time when we were driving, and a spider started crawling across the windshield, and again, there she went, jumping up and down in the seat, all *'EEEEEE! EEEEEE! EEEEEE!'* To the point where I just had to yell, 'Shut up!' I mean, it was on the damn *outside* of the windshield. It wasn't going to come in through it and get her." He let out a small laugh.

The girl shrugged her shoulders. "I'm that way about roaches. I know they can't really *do* anything to you, but they just creep me right the crap out."

"Yeah. I mean, I guess I can understand it, but damn, calm down." He said this last bit as if it were addressed to his now dead girlfriend, and he began to feel sad again.

"So, she saw the bodies…?"

"Yeah," he said, picking up with his story. "We pretty much walked right up on them. And then I saw what she was pointing at: not just the people, but the vampire bats floating in the air right above them. We'd seen the news, what had happened last night. And there it was, happening right in front of us. I froze for a second, then grabbed her and told her, 'Get to the car!'"

"And she didn't make it?"

"Almost. She almost did. That's the thing I keep running over and over in my head. I got my side unlocked…" He turned and looked at the driver's side door, taking a breath and then looking past the girl to the other door, seeming to forget that she was there. "I got in. I was safe. Just barely. But before I could unlock her door… She was beating on it with her hands." He mimed doing this, one hand flat, the other a fist. "She looked so scared. And then… Then one of the bats got her on the neck, and she fell onto the window… Her face…"

Jason's voice was becoming more emotional. He was reliving the moment, just as he had done countless times since that night. "And I just panicked. I could see the other vampires flapping around out there, trying to get in, and if I opened the door to try and help, they would have… they…" He breathed deeply, then continued more firmly, trying to fight the way his voice was quavering. "I panicked. Plain and simple. I turned the key and started up the car, and before I knew what I was doing, I backed out and sped off. I felt so damn guilty about that. But I just had to get out of there. There was nothing I could do." He stopped, rubbing his hands up over his face, his fingers pushing up the lid of his baseball cap.

He took a few moments to compose himself, then continued, this time more quietly. "And you want to know the really messed up thing?"

"What's that?"

"She actually *liked* vampires. Like, the stories and all. She even wrote some of her own, thinking maybe she could get them published."

"Were they any good?" the girl asked, tucking a lock of her short, blonde hair behind one ear.

Jason let out a small laugh, shrugging. "I suppose. Kinda. Not really my thing. They weren't just vampire books; she called them 'erotic vampire fiction.' Lots of sex and kinkiness in them. She was more into that kind of stuff than I was. We're talking, *lots* of sex. There was some other writer she was trying to be like; can't remember their name." He let out another slight chuckle, staring straight ahead. "Sometimes I wonder if she actually got off when they bit her."

"What?" the girl asked, sounding somewhat angry. "Are you serious?"

Jason seemed to remember himself and his surroundings, then felt embarrassed. "Sorry. I'm sorry. I shouldn't be talking like that around someone so young and innocent."

"I'm fourteen," the girl said firmly. "And I'm anything but innocent."

This caught Jason off guard, and he began to feel uncomfortable again. The girl didn't sound like she was trying to come on to him, but then he wondered just how long she'd been on the streets. He'd heard of women having to sell their bodies just to survive, but if this poor girl had been doing the same… And what if that's what she was expecting from him? He was now seriously regretting letting her into his car.

"Look, I don't know if…" He wasn't sure how to continue.

"What was her name?"

"What?"

"Your girlfriend. You've been talking about her all this time, and you haven't once said her name."

Jason felt a strange combination of relief and trepidation. He'd feared for a moment there that the next thing out of her mouth would turn out to be a solicitation, but she'd asked a valid question instead. "I know, I know," he said, facing the steering wheel as he gripped the top of it again. "It hurts to say it. When I do, I…" Again, he didn't want to finish his sentence. The sound of her name made him want to cry, particularly when he spoke it. It had been the last thing he'd called out to her before she'd died.

And he didn't want to break down and cry in front of this stranger. He didn't like crying in front of people at all. His father had always discouraged tears, viewing them as a sign of weakness. As he thought this through, Jason realized that this was probably one of the main reasons he'd been coming out here on his own the past few nights.

"Tell me," the girl insisted.

"Carol," Jason forced himself to say, surprised at how he didn't lose control. "Her name was Carol. And I loved…" His heartfelt confession was interrupted by something totally unexpected: The girl in the passenger seat burst out laughing.

Jason turned on her, seeing that she'd cut her laugh short by covering up her mouth. She quickly recovered, shaking her head. "I'm sorry. That was rude. It's just, well, I couldn't help but laugh at the coincidence."

"What are you talking about?" he asked, surprised by how angry he felt. He'd been pouring his heart out, but this wasn't the reaction he'd needed.

"That's the same name as me!" the girl announced, her hand still covering her upper lip as she spoke. She then cleared her throat and tried to look more serious, putting her hands back down by her sides. "Well, almost, anyway. My name's Carolyn."

Though slightly bewildered, Jason tried to salvage the situation. "Really. Well. Yeah, I guess that's an interesting… My name's Jason, by the way."

The girl turned in her seat, turning her body to face his for the first time as she pulled her knees up closer to her chest. "Jason," she said with a nod. She seemed to be thinking, her eyes darting to one side as she gathered her thoughts. Then she looked back at him, a slight smile on her face. "You're an asshole."

He felt his mouth fall open, too stunned to speak. "And a coward," Carolyn added, which made his face grow hot with anger.

"How the hell dare you come in here and…" he began, but his words left him as the girl interrupted him, her smile broadening and her fangs showing.

"I'm so glad I happened to find you tonight," she said. "Now *that's* a coincidence. We were really pissed off when you got away the other night."

Jason turned as fast as he could to reach for the driver's side door, fumbling for the lock. There was a rush of movement from behind him, and then it was too late.

CHAPTER ELEVEN

BAD BEHAVIOR

It had been a dumb idea. It would be a while before Travis would admit that, but part of him knew that it was true. It had taken him weeks to work out the plan, then a few more to drum up the courage to follow through with it, but he'd been determined to see it through. Unfortunately, that hadn't been enough, and here he was in the back of his parents' station wagon, full of shame and regret.

Travis had loved Angela more than anything, and it broke his heart when her family moved away to New York. And while the two of them stayed in touch and tried to keep up a long-distance relationship, he could tell that things were slipping. The letters had become less frequent, and long-distance phone calls were expensive, to say nothing of forbidden. He'd made the mistake of running up a huge phone bill last September, which had gotten him in trouble. He was no longer allowed to call Angela, plus his father kept encouraging him to just give it up and move on. He hated him for that.

He didn't care if there were tons of other girls out there; all he wanted was to be with Angela again. She was perfect, pretty, funny, and everything he'd ever dreamed of. Most of the other girls at school barely paid him any attention, but he was fine with that. They weren't her.

Once he'd been forbidden to call her, he'd started riding his bike to places he knew had pay phones; he'd gotten good at spotting them whenever he was out of the house. He would save up quarters, sometimes for weeks at a time, then bike out to a shopping center or similar place to call his beloved. She always seemed glad to hear from him, and the very fact that he had to sneak around, that their continued romance had to be a secret, made it feel even more special.

The desire to run away from home and be with her had built up slowly, but it came to a head one horrible afternoon at school during P.E. class. Travis had never been that great at sports, and this particular day, he and the other boys had been instructed by the teacher how to do layups, a particular shot in basketball that he just couldn't seem to master.

Coach Kearns had the students practice the shots, but no matter how hard he tried, Travis just couldn't get a single one to go in. It was frustrating, to say nothing of embarrassing; everyone else in the class had eventually managed to do it and were allowed to sit down. And the coach wouldn't let him off the hook, even when he tried to give up. He was near to tears when, after more than two dozen tries, he kicked the ball down the length of the court, ready to storm off. But Kearns intercepted the ball and rolled it back up to him, shouting back, "You're not getting out from under that net until you do a layup!"

Whether it was luck or the fact that he'd been praying to God over and over to just make one of the stupid shots finally connect with the backboard and bounce down properly through the rim, it happened eventually, and Travis stormed off to the locker room in tears, humiliated by the experience. He didn't even care if he got in trouble for blowing off the rest of the class, and he secretly dared anyone to give him any crap over what had happened or how he'd acted. He'd never been more angry in his entire life.

So that was the beginning of it, his decision to leave everyone in his shitty life behind and go start a new one with Angela in New York City. When she'd first moved there, he hated any mention of the place. But from this point on, he began to feel excitement over the idea of living there, being with his girl, and getting away from stupid, boring Augusta.

The two of them had talked about the possibility of him moving there somehow, but they both knew that it was unlikely that he would be able to convince his family to do so. While her father had moved there for work, his own parents both had steady jobs in the Richmond County school system. They'd completely dismissed his initial plea for them to move when Angela's family had first left. Such a suggestion wasn't even worth considering as far as they were concerned.

Travis, meanwhile, vehemently rejected any thoughts of Angela moving on in a romantic sense, of her finding somebody new. What few friends he told about their situation warned him that this might happen, but this just made him angry. In time, he learned to stop talking about her to most people. They didn't understand. No one did.

The day of the P.E. class incident, he'd gone home and fantasized about leaving home with nothing but his bike and a backpack, wondering how long it would take to go all the way to New York. He'd get there, find Angela's house (or "brownstone," whatever that was), and the two of them would collapse into each other's arms in happiness. Maybe her parents would take him in and let him live with the family, or if not, he and Angela could run off to somewhere else entirely, living happily ever after.

Realism set in after a while as Travis worked to perfect his plan, which included confiding in a couple of friends at school. While some people knew about Angela, Amber and Jake were the only two he let in on (most of) the details of the big secret. Amber was a girl in the grade above him who had once had a long-distance relationship herself, but that had fallen apart after a while. Like Travis's father, she had initially tried to convince him to give up on Angela, but at the same time, she seemed to understand his longing to somehow make it work.

Jake was an okay enough guy, and he'd been the one to talk Travis out of trying to ride his bike all the way up north, doing the math and pointing out that trying to make it that many miles just wouldn't work.

What's more, Travis's idea of taking his bike onto the interstate to get there was impossible. "The cops will pull you over for that in the first five minutes," Jake said to him with more than a little condescension.

Amber helped him work out a more practical scheme, getting a cab to pick him up from his house (or somewhere near there) in the middle of the night, then having that take him to the bus station. In one of the notes the two of them passed back and forth in Geometry class, she included the phone number for Greyhound, along with this advice:

After 24 hours, the police will have an APB out on you. So you have to make sure to pick a trip that will take less than that. Don't choose any that stop off in other cities out of the way. That will take up time. Once you're there, you should be home free.

You sure know a lot about this, Travis wrote back. *How come?*

Missed opportunity, was all she wrote in response. He didn't pry, even though he wanted to.

Jake, meanwhile, he intentionally misled, along with anyone else who happened to ask about his mysterious, faraway girlfriend. Though some surmised that Travis was just making this girl up in order to appear like less of a loser, Jake still believed the story, which was the important thing. But then Travis started lying about where Angela lived, claiming that she and her family had moved to Los Angeles and were no longer in New York. "They move around a lot," he'd say.

This was a red herring, an attempt to throw his family and anyone else off the trail in case they tried to come after him. By telling them that Angela had moved to California, that meant that if anyone figured out that he'd gone to be with her, they'd be looking on the wrong side of the country. And while Jake was a friend of his — even if a somewhat tenuous one at times — Travis felt almost no qualms about using him as part of his deception. He even delayed his planned date of departure for two months just so this lie would sink in, not just with Jake, but with everyone else.

"Where you going?" the cab driver asked in a dull tone.

"Southeastern Stages," Travis said, having rehearsed this countless times in his head. "Time to go home."

"You mean the Greyhound station?"

"Yeah." He'd expected to have to give a lengthy explanation, a story he'd concocted about how he was in fact from New York and was going back there after having run away. But this man wasn't like the chatty, interested cab drivers he'd seen on TV. He didn't even speak again until the end of the trip, and only then to announce how much Travis owed him for the fare.

He had originally planned to leave the house that morning before sunrise, but he'd overslept, screwing up his plans. His first thought upon waking up late was to just abandon the plan and save it for another morning, but he was already packed, and he didn't want to put it off any longer. That meant waiting around for his parents to leave the house along with his baby sister, which he knew they'd been planning on doing that day. It took forever, but they finally left, and he called the cab as soon as he saw the station wagon exiting the driveway.

He got his ticket with little trouble, and not long before lunchtime, he boarded the bus along with his backpack. The bags of chips to eat and the paperback books he'd brought with him were meant to last the length of the trip, though he'd been too nervous and excited to bother with them for the first hour. It was finally happening. He was going to make it.

"Do you know it's against the law to tell a policeman even the smallest lie?" the officer sternly asked Travis at the Greyhound station in Fayetteville, North Carolina.

He was in tears by this point, scared shitless over having been caught not even halfway up the coast. Earlier, this policeman and a bus station employee had found him in his seat and asked him, "Are you Travis Eldridge?"

"No," he lied, having practiced for this too in case it came up. "My name's Grant. Grant Pullman." It was a name he'd plucked from the credits of one of his mother's soap operas, and it seemed like as good of an alias as any. It was only as he spoke that he realized how phony it sounded. Within minutes, he was standing outside the bus, the employee unloading his suitcase from the compartment underneath while the officer continued to bombard him with questions.

He was taken to the police station, then questioned by the officer, who went from being hostile to more sympathetic as time went on. Travis explained about wanting to see his long lost girlfriend, and he was even offered a chance to call her to tell her he wasn't going to make it. He refused, not wanting to embarrass himself even further. He had in fact not told Angela he was coming; he'd been planning to show up at her door and surprise her. She would have been so happy. They both would have. But somehow, he'd gotten caught.

"Might be just as well we found you when we did," the officer said, leaning back in his desk chair. "I once did something like that for a girl I'd been with. Kinda the opposite of what you're sayin'; I was the one who had to move away. But I went back and saw her, turned up right outta the blue where she worked; hadn't seen her for months. But because she wasn't expectin' me, she was more shocked, even mad. Then I had to find out the hard way that she'd gone and gotten herself a new guy."

"She wouldn't do that," Travis hissed under his breath, meaning Angela.

"I'm just sayin', son, that maybe you shouldn't've tried to do this all underhanded. Maybe if you'd done it more by the book…"

Travis shot him an angry look, but he quickly lost his resolve. Being defiant to this man wouldn't do him any good. He was already scared enough about the idea of being put in jail once this conversation was over.

"Look," the man said, "I can tell you're not a bad kid. Believe me, I've seen plenty. You just made some bad decisions. So I'm gonna do you a favor. I'm not gonna arrest you, not formally. Otherwise you'll have a record."

"Thank you," Travis managed to say, fighting back tears again. He was sick of crying in front of people.

"All right then," the officer said. "Now let's get your parents on the phone."

The next few hours crawled by. The brief exchange with his father on the phone had mostly consisted of him apologizing, then his dad saying, "We're coming to get you, son." Travis wasn't used to hearing his dad's voice so broken and tearful. In fact, he couldn't remember ever hearing him sound that way. That just made him feel worse.

Because he wasn't being formally charged, Travis wasn't placed in a holding cell or anything nearly as dramatic as he'd pictured. He was exhausted, and so he was allowed to lie down on two cushioned chairs pushed together into a small, makeshift bed, waiting for his parents to arrive.

During that time, he was kept awake by the occasional conversations, both on the phone and with co-workers, that Sergeant Jellyroll had. That wasn't his real name, but it was the moniker that Travis mentally assigned to him when he thought back on the incident, already forgetting whatever he was actually called. He was a walking stereotype with his moustache, fat gut hanging over his belt, and twang-talking machismo. Even though Travis was grateful for the leniency the man had shown him, he couldn't help but feel contempt for him all the same.

He drifted in and out of consciousness as Sergeant Jellyroll rattled on and on to people about this and that, often angrily talking about the various characters he was having to deal with and describing them with more variations on the word "ass" than Travis had previously thought existed. "This jack-ass wants to tell me…" "Dumb-ass said that he…" "That stupid shit-ass said…" He even tried to make a game out of it at one point, trying to count how many times an "ass" variant was spoken. But he gave up when the term "suck-ass" was introduced, laughing to himself but still angry at the overall situation.

His mother and father eventually arrived. Travis sleepily got up from the chairs when he heard his mother down the hall inquiring about "Travis Eldridge, the runaway?" He broke down in her arms as she hugged him, apologizing and feeling terrible about the hell he knew he must have put her and his father through.

It was well after dark by the time they left the station, and so began the long, mostly silent drive back to Augusta. His parents were a lot less mean about things than he'd expected, their initial reprimands to him being tinged with relief that they hadn't lost him after all. They didn't even ask him why he'd run away in the first place, which both relieved and bewildered him. "We'll talk about it later," his mother assured him as he collapsed into the back seat. He wasn't looking forward to that conversation.

As the car rolled along in the dark, Travis found himself unable to sleep, and he alternated between being mad at the people who had foiled his plan and being mad at himself for even attempting it. How had it been that they'd been able to find him so quickly? According to Amber, the police weren't supposed to have been looking for him until twenty-four hours had passed. There should have been plenty of time for him to have made it to New York.

When the family stopped off at a gas station in South Carolina, Travis was alone in the car with his mom for a few minutes. There was a question he wanted to ask, but first, he tested the waters, trying to make small talk. "So where's Sarah?"

"We left her at home with a sitter," his mother said matter-of-factly. Then she turned around in her seat to face him. "We didn't want to upset her with all of this. She wouldn't have understood."

"I know. I'm sorry." Then he put forth the real question he'd been wanting to ask: "How did you manage to find me, by the way?"

His mother sighed. "It wasn't easy. After we found the note you'd left, we called all over the place, and I tell you, I was really panicking."

"Sorry," Travis repeated, turning his head to avoid the look on her face.

"But then we called Amber's house, and she told us what we needed to know."

Travis clammed up. His mother said something else about how dangerous what he'd done was, but he wasn't listening anymore. By then, his father had paid for the gas and was back in the car, and the rest of the ride home was in silence.

Lying down in the back seat once more, Travis thought things through. Why the hell had Amber ratted him out? She was supposed to be the one person he could trust about this whole thing, the only person who'd actually known where he was headed. She'd helped him. But then he remembered something else: She had occasionally acted like she was attracted to him.

Amber wasn't hideous, but she certainly wasn't all that pretty. Their friendship had been kind of back and forth over the years, but there had been a time in middle school when she'd seemed interested in him. He just didn't feel the same way towards her, and he thought that they'd had an understanding once that was clear and they were just friends. Now he was beginning to wonder if she'd had an ulterior motive all along, that maybe if she sabotaged his chances with his long distance girlfriend, he might somehow default back to her.

Travis pictured Amber in his mind. She had this weird look to her where her facial features seemed to be just a little bit too small, sort of bunched together. Her tiny eyes, button nose, and narrow mouth all sat beneath her high forehead, leading him to give her the unflattering nickname "Tennis Ball Face." By contrast, Travis himself was tall and lanky, and something about the shape of his neck, sloping chin, and cropped, pale blonde haircut had earned him from her the equally distasteful label "Q-Tip Head."

That had been how they and the other kids in school had insulted each other in their early teens. But in time, they'd gotten to where they were on more friendly terms, and the animosity subsided. Again, there had been a short time there when Amber seemed to have wanted something more than friendship, but he thought he'd quashed that. Now he was beginning to wonder if she'd intentionally screwed up his plan to be with Angela.

Travis's anger mounted the more he pondered this. He pictured himself punching Amber right in her tennis ball-sized face, that stupid, selfish bitch. How dare she connive to keep him away from the love of his life? Did she really think that it would do any good? He was going to give her an earful once he got home, really telling her off once and for all.

The car continued to roll along, the constant motion of it on the highway almost managing to sing him to sleep. But there was another question that kept him awake: Should he tell Angela about all of this?

Maybe he should. She'd probably appreciate the effort he'd made, hopefully thinking it was romantic. His thoughts began to drift towards attempting another escape sometime later, but taking a cue from Sergeant Jellyroll's advice. While he'd liked the idea of showing up unexpectedly and surprising Angela, it might work better to coordinate their efforts. The two of them could run away to somewhere else altogether, maybe even California, this time doing it by plane rather than by bus. It was a complicated idea, but given time, he'd work it out.

Shannon Pierson wasn't a bad girl, or least, not *that* bad. She certainly didn't have a reputation as a dishonest person, but then, that was kind of the point. The loud-mouthed, troublemaking girls, the ones screaming for attention by acting out and driving their parents crazy, well, those were easy to spot.

Her particular brand of badness was more subtle, and she was good at being sneaky enough to keep it hidden. As far as most people were concerned, she was a goody two-shoes, and she was fine with them thinking that. It made hiding her deeper self that much easier. It was one of the reasons why she'd stayed active in the Girl Scouts for as long as she had, well past the age when it was considered by her peers to be the cool thing to do. She'd say it was for noble reasons like being active in the community and giving the younger girls someone to look up to, and maybe that was true, but it wasn't the whole truth. A lot of it really was for appearances.

She was fifteen, not old enough to get a real job yet, but she'd managed to establish herself around the neighborhood as a responsible and reliable babysitter. Because of this, she didn't come cheap: She offered her services at no less than two bucks an hour. She'd reminded Mr. Eldridge of this when he'd called and made last-minute arrangements with her earlier in the night, and he'd insisted that it was no problem and that he really needed her to help them out.

The details were vague, but she got the sense — both on the phone and after her arrival at their house — that there was some kind of crisis going on. Mr. and Mrs. Eldridge had to go out of town unexpectedly, and for whatever reason, they weren't able to take their four-year-old, Sarah, along with them. Shannon wondered why their son, Travis, wasn't around to look after her, but then she figured out that maybe that was the crisis. Mrs. Eldridge confirmed this when the two of them spoke privately, but she asked her to keep it quiet. As far as everyone was concerned, they'd just had to go out of town on a little trip, and they'd be back sometime very late tonight. It was even expected that Shannon would spend the night, which she'd charge extra for, but no one seemed to mind. She certainly didn't.

Shannon didn't know Travis well; he was in the grade below her. But she did wonder just what was up. The guy was kind of a nerd, but maybe, like her, he had some darker secrets. Had he skipped town for some reason? Maybe after he got back, she could ask him about it.

Looking after Sarah wasn't hard. After dinner, there was a little bit of TV watching, then some playing around with her Barbie dolls. Shannon figured that once Sarah was older, she'd look quite a bit like a Barbie herself, with her light blonde hair and wide, blue eyes. She was cute, almost stereotypically so, and she was used to getting her way. But she was a good kid.

Finally, Sarah's night wound down with an improvised bedtime story. This was one of the things Shannon prided herself in being good at, particularly when it came to dealing with younger kids. Rather than just reading them some picture book, she would make the story a collaborative effort, starting it off with a few lines of narrative and then asking, "So what do you think happened next?"

The child would come up with something, and Shannon would continue along that riff. The two would bounce back and forth, trading places as narrator. More often than not, she'd found that the girls she babysat were better at this than the boys. There was one boy who seemed to get bored with the concept and tried to outsmart her: When it was his turn for the third time, he simply said, "And then everyone died. The end." But most kids weren't like that; they liked playing along.

When it came time to turn out the light, Shannon would tell the child to continue the story in their head, promising that the next time they spoke, she would be eager to find out what had happened. Truthfully, in most cases when she put a child to bed, it would be days or even weeks before she actually saw them again. It was just something to say to the kids, a way to comfort them by showing interest, to give them something pleasant to think about while they drifted off. It wasn't like she really cared about the further adventures of Flopsy the Bunny or whoever, but she faked it like a pro.

Once the lights were off and the child was safely tucked away, that was when the real fun began.

Again, Shannon didn't actually think of herself as a bad person, but she did like being sneaky. There wasn't any malice behind it, not really, but she did like getting away with things. It had started when she was a little girl, creeping around the house and going through her parents' bedroom while her father was away at work and her mother was elsewhere, like out in the garden or watching TV. She knew she shouldn't be rifling through their dresser or looking under their bed or in their closet, but she could, and that's why she liked doing it.

Sometimes, she would try on her mother's clothes, which were of course way too big for her, but it was fun playing dress-up. This had in fact started with her getting into her mother's make-up, but she'd gotten caught and in trouble for that. So she learned not to get caught. And really, while the thrill was in doing something she wasn't supposed to do, she was also just naturally curious. She enjoyed finding new things, particularly hidden ones.

This mildly sociopathic hobby expanded once she was older and started babysitting, and once she knew that she could get away with it, it was hard to resist the temptation. Each new house presented new opportunities for discovery. She didn't steal anything; she knew better than to leave a trail or to give people any reason to suspect what was going on. She became an expert at memorizing the exact layout of a drawer's contents before going through them, later placing everything back precisely as it had been.

Once theft did enter into the picture, it was always done very carefully, and only after she'd been to a particular house several times. The family had to trust her, to not even suspect that if something went missing, she was the one responsible. And it was never anything big: a ring here, a pair of gloves there. That part of it didn't excite her, anyway, not really. She just liked exploring the hidden places.

She'd even sneak into a family's liquor cabinet if it struck her fancy. Some families were more careful about theirs than others. But as it turned out, Shannon found that she didn't actually like to drink. The fumes that would waft out of a bottle as she opened it would burn her eyes and make her want to gag. Even so, there was a small delight in taking a sip. No one would ever know.

She wondered from time to time if she might apply these skills in a more noble fashion once she grew up, perhaps working for the FBI or somewhere like that as a spy. But that would require admitting that she was as good at this kind of thing as she was, which would kind of defeat the purpose of being sneaky.

No one knew about her boyfriend, either. Joel went to Copeland, a different school from hers, and they'd met at the mall where he worked. Her parents didn't want her going out with anyone who was old enough to have his own car, so like many other aspects of her life, she kept him a secret. Over the past month or so, she'd occasionally gotten him to come over when she was babysitting, but only in cases like tonight when she knew that it would be safe. There had to be enough time to spare in order to make it worth it, and as far as she knew, the Eldridges wouldn't be back until well after midnight.

They made out on the couch as quietly as possible, each of them enjoying in their own way the forbidden nature of what they were doing. Shannon hadn't yet given up her virginity to this boy, but she was pretty sure she was going to. Not tonight, though, and certainly not with a child sleeping upstairs.

She'd debated whether or not to invite Joel over this particular night. Sarah's parents had warned her that the girl sometimes got out of bed in the middle of the night. They'd said it was sleepwalking, but Shannon suspected that it might be something more simple than that. Maybe, like her, the little sneak just liked getting up and wandering around at night because it was something she wasn't supposed to do.

She remembered an incident from her own childhood, when she was even younger than Sarah. Ever curious and observant, she'd noticed that when a grown-up came to retrieve her from her crib, they would push down on a thin metal handle on the side, causing the bars to slide downward and make her easier to get to. One afternoon, not long after they put her down for a nap, Shannon reached her tiny arm through the white bars and pushed down the handle. Within moments, she'd made her escape. No more baby jail for her. Shortly after that, she crawled along the floor, up the hall, and to the kitchen where her mother and grandmother were. Her mother gasped with surprise and fear when she saw her, her hand shaking as she put it to her mouth. To Shannon's two-year-old mind, it was the funniest thing that could have ever happened.

As far as this night was concerned, she found that she couldn't pass up the opportunity to invite Joel over. There was just too much time that she couldn't waste, time she could spend with him. And he too was taking a risk, sneaking out of his house to come see her. It was fun.

It was sometime after midnight when Shannon began to get nervous, thinking that she heard noises. This would cause her to stop making out with Joel, much to his annoyance. "Will you calm down?" he whispered after the second time. "I didn't hear anything."

"You sure?" she hissed back.

"Yes, I'm sure," he said deeply, his fingers pressing into the small of her back meaningfully. "Come back down here."

Shannon complied, leaning down to kiss him some more. She knew that it was getting late and that she'd have to make him leave soon, but there was just something about the firm way he held her that made her wish this could go on forever.

All of that stopped when she heard a piercing shriek. It came from somewhere outside, and she knew instinctively that it was Sarah. She leapt up from the couch, vaguely aware of how she may have kneed Joel in the process, but she didn't even care. It was every babysitter's worst nightmare come to life, something happening to the child you're supposed to protect.

Shannon staggered towards the front door, her heart racing as she saw that it was slightly ajar. She tried to remember if she'd locked it earlier when she'd let Joel in, but that didn't really matter, not anymore. She ran to it and flung it open, and what she saw confused her.

It looked like some girl was holding Sarah in her arms protectively, bending down and nuzzling her affectionately. For a split second, she was grateful. Whoever this stranger was, she appeared to have rescued the little girl from whatever had made her cry out. But all of that changed when Shannon got a few steps closer, and the situation became clear.

It wasn't a girl, at least, not an ordinary one. The blood that dripped from her mouth as she looked up made Shannon freeze in her tracks, terrified. She'd heard on the news the past few nights about there being vampires, but she hadn't really believed it, not until now. The vampire girl smiled at her predatorily, then tossed Sarah's limp form onto the grass like a rag doll. Sarah let out a whimper as she landed, which gave Shannon a smidgen of hope. At least she was still alive.

Joel stumbled out from behind. "What the hell's…" he began, but he stopped short when he saw the vampire girl, her short blonde hair wafting in the light breeze as she stepped forward.

Shannon turned to face Joel, disappointed to see that he looked just as scared as she was. "Do something!" she pleaded.

"Yes, do," the vampire said with some delight, and Shannon turned back around to see that she was spreading her arms invitingly. "Or else I might make a meal out of your little girlfriend here."

Shannon heard Joel's racing footsteps as he whizzed past her, then past the vampire, who pursued him. That gave her a chance to run over to Sarah, who still lay prone in the grass. Before she could get to her, she was distracted by a stifled scream from Joel, whom she saw had collapsed about halfway across the lawn. The monstrous girl, however, was nowhere to be seen. Like Sarah, Joel still seemed to be moving, slowly writhing on the ground but not getting up. She felt the urge to run over to him, but she still needed to check on Sarah first.

There was a strange flapping sound that rushed toward her out of nowhere, and then she felt a sharp pain on the side of her neck that made her scream. Something instinctual made her cover her mouth as she did so, remembering that she wasn't supposed to be out here this late at night and that she didn't want anyone to hear her. Almost immediately, she realized how stupid that thought was. She needed to get back inside, to get to the phone and call 911.

She started to stagger back to the front door, but her legs gave way beneath her. She struggled to get back up, but she could barely move. The vampire's bite had done something to her, almost paralyzed her somehow. From where she lay, she looked up and saw the other girl again, who seemed to have materialized out of thin air.

"Decisions, decisions!" she said quietly and with a broad, fanged smile. "I can't decide which one of you to save for last." She looked around, presumably at Joel and Sarah, but Shannon could no longer see them from where she was. "Or who to finish off first, for that matter," she added evilly.

Shannon struggled to speak. She wanted to beg the girl to stop, to just go away and leave them alone. *"Pp... pp..."* she sputtered, and her body shivered involuntarily.

"Yes?" the girl asked with mocking, sadistic politeness, leaning forward with her hands on her knees.

"Please..." Shannon managed to croak out.

"Oh, all right then," the vampire said cheerfully, practically leaping forward onto her hands and knees, her face now inches from Shannon's. "If you insist."

Shannon had always thought that vampires were supposed to be older, aristocratic gentlemen with pale skin and stupid accents. This girl looked, aside from her menacing fangs and callous manner, like someone she could have gone to school with. In fact, she'd begun to wonder if this stranger might in fact look vaguely familiar. By then, though, the girl had bent down past her field of vision and sunk her fangs into Shannon's neck. Pain blazed through her, but she couldn't even scream this time.

It was an odd feeling, her body growing colder as the life was drained away. It was also strange psychologically, knowing that she was about to die. She wanted to cry, but she wasn't even able to do that. Somewhere nearby, barely audible over the hideous sound of the vampire's gulps in her ear, she could hear poor little Sarah, whimpering in a sort of steady whine.

Travis was grateful that the long journey from North Carolina was over as the station wagon bounced slightly upward, entering the driveway. It was already after 1:30 in the morning, and he was beyond tired. He hoped that his parents would just let him skulk off to his room with his suitcase and backpack without bursting into some lecture about how horrible of a son he was for worrying them and trying to run away. Hopefully, if things went the way they had for the past few hours, everything would remain unspoken, at least until tomorrow.

What he didn't expect, either for himself or his parents, was for the three of them to find the lifeless body of his little sister on the front lawn along with two other corpses. His mother fell apart, his father called the police, and Travis wondered if he'd ever be able to sleep again.

CHAPTER TWELVE

THE PLAN

Note left for Carolyn Leigh Young by Susanna Michelle Young
the night of June 30, 1983
(later torn up and discarded)

Carolyn,

This is my third try, so hopefully you'll be reading this. I keep starting the note and then crumpling it up and throwing it away. What you need to know is this:

- Don't freak out when you read this.

- The boys talked me into slipping the antidote for the potion to you, and they're planning on killing you once it changes you back to human. It's taken a long time to work, which is why you've been feeling and acting so weird and vicious lately, I'm pretty sure. Sorry I couldn't tell you earlier; I've been going along with it but trying to figure a way out.

- You'll probably change back sometime during the day while the rest of us are asleep.

- I don't know why I'm making this a list. Whatever.

- Let everyone sleep and wake up at the usual time after sunset, and pretend you're still a vampire.

- Before that, you need to prepare some things so you can change the rest of us back.

Oh, I should explain. Aside from using the antidote, there's a faster way to cancel out the potion. The things that normally kill vampires (the sun, garlic, crosses, running water, etc.) will do it too, and immediately. The others don't know this yet. You're going to need to set things up so it's easier to do that to the rest of us. It's going to be tricky to get it right so that no one winds up getting killed. Okay, back to the list:

- Before we get up, turn the water to the house back on.

- Get the garlic powder from the spice rack in the kitchen and keep it in your pocket. You might need it to defend yourself, and we can use it later.

- There's some black paint in the storage shed if I remember right. Use that to paint a big cross on my bedroom door. (I'll explain later.) Keep quiet and don't wake anyone up. You know how we wake up hungry.

- Once everyone is up and ready to go out and feed, play it cool and act like nothing's wrong. Get it so we're all in the kitchen, then use the sprayer by the sink on me. That will change me back. You won't be able to get all four of us at once, so just aim for me.

- While they're disoriented and surprised, we'll run up to my room and lock ourselves in, and the cross on the door will keep them out. I've got some other supplies up here already that we can use to defend ourselves and change them back.

P.S. Good luck!

CHAPTER THIRTEEN

JOURNAL

Excerpts from the journal of Raymond Adrian Young
(later censored with marker in 1985)

June 23, 1983

Mom and Dad are going to thier conference tomorrow and Susanna will be taking care of me and Carolyn again. They said Tim and Carl can come over and stay too! They'll be in sleeping bags in my room. Carl has a big race to run and wants to practice in our yard.

June 24, 1983 – July 1, 1983

NO "REPORT"

July 2, 1983

Sorry I didn't write the last few days. Carl and Tim were here, and I didn't want them to know about this. They might've thought me writing in a journal was like keeping a diary like a girl and made fun of me.

We had a lot of fun being ███████*. It was dangerous but we got away okay. Mom and Dad come back tomorrow, so we have to make sure the house is cleaned up. Carolyn and I painted over the stuff on the doors so they won't be able to see.*

I wonder if we'll be able to ██████████ *again next year!*

January 18, 1984

Watched a documentary on PBS tonight about psyhcic powers. I wish I had ESP! It would be neat if I could be like the Tomorrow People.

CHAPTER FOURTEEN

ROBERT'S STORY, PART ONE

"Nuh-*uhh!*" Pat said. "You're not an alien!"

"I am too!" Rob insisted, looking around as he made a shushing gesture to his friend. "Don't talk so loud! It's a secret."

"Then how come you aren't green or have antennas or something?"

"Because I'm only *half*-alien," he explained. "I was beamed into my mother's stomach, born to look like a regular baby. Really, I come from the planet Saturn." As he spoke, he eyed Pat gravely, gauging his reactions.

"My dad said there's no life on Saturn," Pat said, folding his arms.

"Not on the planet, there isn't," Rob said with a clever smile, "but there is on the rings."

That seemed to get through. Pat's expression changed from cynical dismissal to wonderment, though still cautious. "Really?"

"Really. And Miss Holloway, she's an alien, too. A bad one. That's why she's always so mean."

Pat, who had gotten yelled at by Miss Holloway that morning for what he felt was no good reason, nodded. "I can believe that!"

Rob nodded as well. "It's not just her, either; it's her and some of the other teachers. But they're in disguise."

"All of them?"

"No, but some. I'm still trying to figure out who. I can… sorta sense it. And there may be some other good ones, ones who are on our side."

"But what do they want?"

"What else? To take over the Earth."

"We've got to do something!"

When Robert Trueblood was older, he'd looked back on his friendship with Pat, wondering what had ever happened to him. He'd changed schools after second grade, and while they had talked on the phone a couple of times after that, they quickly lost touch. But there had been something fun about those days, convincing his friend that he was a supernatural being and that the two of them were all that stood between malevolent aliens and world conquest. Of course, there had never been any real proof of this, and it's not like they really could have done anything had the story been true.

Sometimes, Robert even wondered if there had been some truth to the whole thing after all. The older he got, the more the world tried to convince him that things like aliens and magic weren't real, but he still believed that they were on some level. In fact, he'd seen what he believed to be evidence of that, at least within himself. For one thing, he was psychic.

It took him a while to even realize it; for the longest time, he'd thought that he was just like anybody else. But he would have dreams about certain things, only to have those events play out the next day or soon after that. Often, he would think something, and then somebody he was talking to would say the exact same words only seconds later.

One morning during fifth grade, his friend Richie was freaking out because he had lost a check that his mother had written, one that he was supposed to give to their teacher for the monthly book club order. He knew that he'd get in trouble for this, but Robert somehow knew where to look. "Check under the top book in the stack under your desk," he said, his eyes not meeting Richie's but instead staring off into space and slightly downward. His tone was even and matter-of-fact.

Richie bent down and rifled through his books, still panicked, and then he froze. Moments later, he slowly stood up from where he'd been squatting, holding the check in his shaking hand. Wide-eyed, he practically whispered to Robert, "How did you know?"

Robert shrugged. "I just did."

He confided his secret to Richie, who turned out to be something of a blabbermouth. Robert found himself having to backpedal when other kids in the class questioned him about his supposed powers, a few of them genuinely intrigued, but most of them just ridiculing him for believing in such a thing. He told them he was just pulling a prank on Richie, and their friendship ended soon after. He learned then that some people just weren't trustworthy.

From then on and throughout high school, he'd learned to play his cards close to his chest, and this gave him an air of mystery that he found he enjoyed. People might think he was weird, but he was okay with that. Puberty had been somewhat unkind to him in the beginning, turning him into a tall, lanky guy, but things evened out, his dark hair and eyes combining with his devilish grin to make him quite the charmer. Teachers liked him because of his obvious intelligence and mostly good behavior, and his peers, male and female alike, saw him as a good guy.

Even so, he was still careful about whom he let get close to him. He wasn't terribly popular, but again, that was okay with him. He had his secrets and wasn't keen on revealing them to anyone he didn't deem worthy. Sometimes, he would even make stories up about his past just to see how people would react, like the time he convinced several people in his World History class that his father worked for a secret department of the government that was training people to use ESP to spy on the Russians. He also had a story about a former girlfriend of his who had been kidnapped by the mafia, her family having been forced to pay a huge ransom but then keep quiet about it, lest they come after her again. That was why it hadn't been in the news, he said. There were even times that he got so entrenched in these fantasies that he'd start to believe in them himself.

His psychic powers were real, though, but only rarely did he reveal them to anyone. There were two opposite ends of the spectrum: those who would laugh in his face and those who would freak out if they believed him. Sometimes, he doubted himself, wondering if maybe the skeptics were right and it was all in his head. A quick test with Zener cards, the kind with the different symbols on them that were used to test psychics, would dispel these doubts. He could put a spread of them face down on a table in front of him, touch the top of each one, feeling a weird tingle in his finger as he tried to guess which symbol it contained. Most of the time, he was right.

This was all well and good, but he wasn't sure how useful it was. What he really wanted was the power to control people's minds, to be able to project his thoughts outward into theirs. In a sense, he could do that with the way he manipulated people with his stories, but it would have been a lot cooler if he could literally make people do whatever he wanted.

Aside from the one he'd made up, Robert did indeed have a handful of girlfriends over the years. Most of the relationships were short-lived, though. Either he would grow tired of them and move on, or other times, they would realize just how full of shit he was and call him on it. His first one in sixth grade failed to fall for his attempt at resurrecting the alien invasion story, this time claiming that their P.E. teacher was kidnapping their fellow students, turning them into slaves, and replacing them with identical clones. He'd meant for the story to be a test for the girl, seeing if he could trust her with some real secrets of his, but she just told him he was crazy and dumped him.

Another ruse with a later girlfriend had the opposite effect. When he was sixteen, he claimed that he had previously dated an actress who was currently on the TV show *Eight Is Enough*. There was a grain of truth to this particular lie: The same girl who had dumped him in sixth grade was named Connie Beecham, and her name was similar to one of the actresses on the show. What was funny was that "his" Connie and the one on TV actually did look quite a bit alike, so it was easy for him to carry the fantasy along in his head that they were the same girl. The reason for the discrepancy in their last names, Robert claimed, was that she'd changed hers for acting purposes once she'd supposedly moved to Hollywood all those years ago. In reality, he had no idea where the real Connie had ended up.

This vicarious claim to fame, whatever purpose he thought it might serve, only wound up making his current (and real) girlfriend Celia jealous. True, that had been part of his intention, but only to the extent that it made his past seem mysterious and intriguing, just like most of his stories did. He didn't want this secret trumpeted around the school, nor did he expect for Celia's insecurity to blow things way out of proportion. She constantly barraged him with accusations of him still being in love with this previous girlfriend, dramatically lamenting the fact that she wasn't good enough or pretty enough in comparison.

"And what if she moved back here?" Celia demanded, fuming.

"What?"

"Would you leave me for her? I bet you would."

"How can you think that?" he asked, trying not to picture the pretty actress in his head. He'd also wondered sometimes what might happen if he were to ever run into the actual Connie he had known again. "Celia, you know I love *you.* " As he said this, he held her more tightly.

"Yeah, I'll bet."

"I do!"

The sad thing was that, even though they broke up not long after this conversation, he really did.

Robert had kicked himself for ages after that. If only he'd told Celia the truth, things might have been different. But the problem with being such an expert liar was that he never could admit that he was lying. He hated being found out. His stories were his way of controlling reality, shaping not only the way that others saw him but also the way he saw the world. Really, he just wanted life to be interesting.

He was used to getting his own way, at least, most of the time. This was something that his peers occasionally attributed to him being an only child, this stereotype that children like him were spoiled. But he didn't buy that. He'd worked hard to accomplish the things he'd done, and as far as school was concerned, he'd earned every A he'd ever gotten. He was brilliant, and while he tried not to be a braggart about that, he knew deep down that it was true.

He'd never lost his ability to be charming, and he could lie and manipulate better than anyone he knew. But what he really wanted was to find someone who would appreciate him for who he was at his core, somebody that he could reveal all of his secrets to. The falsehoods he spun around himself were like land mines, traps meant to catch anyone who dared to get close but wasn't good enough to get to know the real him inside.

The fantasies weren't just to make him seem more interesting or because he got a kick out of fooling people. It was because that without them, the world was too boring. The funny thing about what got him together with Susanna was that for once, he didn't have to make something up in order for it to be extraordinary.

"Hey, do you like mice?" Robert called out to the pretty brunette, leaning against the doorway of the lab. The two of them had talked a few times before over the course of the school year in their AP Biology class, but not often.

Susanna skidded to a halt, her shoes slipping. It wasn't her most graceful moment, but she recovered, fixing Robert with a perplexed look and smiling. "That's got to be one of the weirdest pick-up lines anyone's ever heard."

"It's not a…!" Robert began, then stopped short. He felt his face flash with hotness, but he fought his nervousness down. "Look, just come here. I want to show you something."

She looked from one side to another, then cautiously followed the weird boy into the lab. While his back was to her, she checked her black sweater for stray pieces of white lint; she'd been finding them at random places all over it the entire day and been picking them off. "If you think you're going to fling some little rodent on me and make me scream, you've got another thing coming, buddy."

Robert laughed. "No, nothing like that." He knew that Susanna wasn't some delicate little flower.

They'd never been great friends, but their paths had crossed from time to time over the years. In eleventh grade, there had begun a running joke between them involving her and her fellow cheerleaders selling spirit ribbons to support Westlake's football team. The first time, she'd approached him in the hall and asked him if he'd like to buy one, just as she'd been doing to everyone else that day in a bright, friendly manner.

"And what if I don't?" he asked, more playful than rude.

Not missing a beat or changing her tone, she replied, "Then I'll kick you in the balls?"

Robert couldn't help but laugh, and he forked out the cash, graciously accepting the ribbon and its accompanying football-shaped sticker, which he attached to his shirt and wore the rest of the day. He didn't go to the game, but then, he almost never did.

Throughout that year's football season and again the following year, the joke was revisited, Susanna approaching him with her usual "Would you like to buy a spirit ribbon," his pretense at refusal, and her threatening something violent. "I'll stab you with a fork?" "I'll hunt you down and kill you?" "I'll burn down your house?" It was cute the way she combined menace with charm.

This afternoon in the lab, he did intend to freak her out, just wanting to get one up on her for once. He hadn't planned it or anything; she just happened to be walking by the door when he'd started to step out for a pee break, and once he saw her, he couldn't resist the opportunity.

"Here," he said, stopping at a table in the lab and gesturing at the cage. There were two white mice in it, crawling around and acting normally.

"Yes, they're cute," Susanna said, unimpressed. "My little sister had some a few years ago. Our dad got her one for Christmas, thinking he'd just gotten her a nice little pet. The day after Christmas, it turned out that 'Mr. Mousey' was in fact 'Mama Mousey,' and all of a sudden, there was a whole bunch of them. Didn't turn out well."

Robert laughed. "I can imagine."

Susanna peered over the cage, her eyebrows raised. "What, no wheel or anything? They're going to get bored."

"No, they won't," he said with a grin. "Watch this." He picked up a hypodermic needle from the table, and Susanna drew back.

"What are you going to do with…?" she hissed through her teeth. Then she tried to compose herself, folding her arms. "I really don't like needles."

Enjoying her discomfort, Robert said in a deep voice, "Don't worry." With that, he opened the lid of the cage, then grabbed one of the mice with one hand. With the other, he injected something into the helpless rodent. He then released it, closing the lid as he drew back, gently placing the needle back onto the table. He noticed that Susanna had averted her eyes when the injection had been given, but she'd since looked back to see what this was all about.

"So what's that supposed to…" she started to say, but then there was some movement from the cage.

The mouse that Robert had given the experimental potion to suddenly went crazy, leaping onto the untreated mouse and biting at it with intense fury. Its victim squealed and struggled, trying to get away. Robert expected Susanna to flip out at this point, but to his surprise, she just leaned in closer and watched, her mouth gaping open.

After several seconds, Robert intervened. He'd seen this happen before, so he rescued the victim mouse by reaching back into the cage, firmly pulling the newly violent one away and tossing it to one side. With his other hand, he quickly placed a large piece of plexiglass from the table into a groove in the cage, separating the two subjects. The seemingly rabid one continued to throw itself against the transparent barrier, eager to get to its wounded companion.

Robert leaned back, eyeing Susanna. She straightened up as well, letting out a tense sigh. "That was…" she began, her eyes still wide. "What the hell did you give him?"

From that point on, Robert learned not to underestimate this girl. She hadn't gotten all scared and run away, and while he initially felt disappointed by that, he soon found himself intrigued. Apparently, she felt the same way, though it took a while for him to figure out whether it was him or the potion that she was more interested in. Regardless, she asked him more and more about it, and before long, she was helping him perfect it.

The development of the potion had started out a few months earlier as a collaboration between Robert and a teacher's assistant, a college guy named Jonathan. He was interested in the effects of different chemicals on the brain, and because he knew that Robert had aspirations of becoming a scientist like his uncle William, he picked him to be his own assistant. Originally, the research was focused on alcoholism, something that Robert had a vested interest in because of his father.

The man may or may not have been an alcoholic; Robert was never clear on whether his father actually depended on drinking or just really liked doing it. A wealthy real estate agent, he was successful and well regarded in the community. But when he got to drinking each night after dinner, he'd suddenly get inspired to work on these big projects around the house, often dragging Robert into them against his will. Whether it was working on one of the family cars, maintaining his 100-gallon fish tank, or something else, it was not uncommon for Robert and his dad to find themselves working well into the wee hours of the night, the elder not wanting to stop, particularly the more bourbon-fueled he became.

As a boy, Robert hadn't minded this so much; it was kind of fun. But the older he got and the more he realized that it was the bourbon that seemed to make these projects drag on late into the night, the more he began to resent his father. As a teenager, he wanted to differentiate himself from his parents and forge his own identity, but that was hard to do when he kept being roped into these things he didn't care about. And while his dad never got violent as a result of his drinking, he did sometimes become annoying, rambling on and on about things he thought were deep and profound. As a result, even though some of his high school friends got into drinking, Robert himself refused to do the same.

Jonathan had encouraged Robert in this choice, warning him that there was a chemical in the brain, probably hereditary, that caused alcoholism. That was why it tended to run in families. If Robert had the same gene as his father that made him susceptible, he might very well fall into that trap if he so much as took his first drink. The experiments with the mice were meant to be an extension of this same line of research, which other scientists had conducted before.

There were other aspects to it as well, including behavior modification. With the addition of various combinations of chemicals, it was found that the mice could be manipulated into doing various things. Some of this involved mazes and rewards and such, and under the influence of different variations of the potion, the mice were more motivated to do certain things at some times, and less so in others. Robert found the whole thing fascinating.

Things fell apart when Jonathan ended up in trouble with the law. Robert never got the full story, but it had something to do with him being involved with an underage girl. To make matters worse, he'd tried to lie to the girl's father over the phone by pretending to be a policeman, something about a fake investigation into his behavior. That had landed him in jail. Robert was disappointed by this to say the least, both by his friend turning out to be a criminal and by how this put a halt to their research.

He soon recovered, though, continuing to work on the experiment on his own thanks to the support of his teacher. But without Jonathan's guidance or adequate supervision from that teacher, things took a darker turn, and Robert strayed from the idea of trying to find a cure for alcoholism. Instead, he found himself trying to see just what is was possible to get these mice to do.

By the time Susanna came into the picture, Robert had gone down the path of becoming the ultimate control freak, drunk not from alcohol but from the power of being able to turn these mice into tiny little monsters, attacking each other according to his whim. It excited him. If he ever stopped to think about just what this said about him as a person, if there were anything wrong with him that drove him forward, that voice in his head would quickly be silenced by some weird, unspoken ambition to just keep moving forward.

The idea of turning the mice into some kind of vampires sprang from a few places in the dark corners of his mind, though looking back on it, he wasn't entirely sure of the order in which things happened. He'd always liked the vampire myth, his earliest memory of it being the cartoony depictions of Dracula that usually cropped up around Halloween. They were silly, all *"Bluh, bluh! I vant to drink your blood!"* He never took them seriously.

Some time after that, he'd happened to catch part of a Dracula movie on TV one night when he wasn't supposed to still be up, but his parents were elsewhere in the house and didn't know that he was still watching TV in the den with lights off and the volume way down low. He knew he wasn't supposed to be watching it, but something made him want to just the same. In the movie, this Dracula was downright menacing and terrifying, blood all over his face as he hissed and attacked people. It made it very difficult for Robert to fall asleep that night.

There was a girl he knew in second grade, Nancy Bloodworth, who had this thing where she liked to gross out the boys on the playground by kissing them against their will, not on the lips but just wherever she could manage to. At that age, boys thought that girls were icky, and she liked to play with that idea. It was similar to the idea of "cooties," but she called it "the kissies." He'd been the victim of her assaults plenty of times.

Once they'd called a truce and things were okay between them, Nancy also told him about how she liked to give herself bruises, sucking on her skin until the blood seeped through it. She also liked to, whenever she got injured and had a scab, pick at it to make it bleed and drink some of the blood out of it.

"Are you a vampire?" he asked her once, but he didn't really mean it.

"Maybe," Nancy said with a wicked smile. "Are you scared?" He wasn't sure. "I have the right last name for it, though!"

Robert was confused. "What?"

"*Blood*worth! Good name for a vampire. Hey, you do, too! True*blood.* We should get married!"

"No!" Robert practically screamed. The thought of that was appalling.

Yet another time, Robert had gotten a nosebleed, something that happened to him every now and then as a little kid. He had no idea why they happened, but because of his experiences with Nancy, he thought that it might be cool to intentionally drink the blood rather than focus on trying to stop the flow.

"Don't do that," his babysitter told him, helping him clean up with tissues. "It's gross."

"No, it's neat!" Rob insisted.

"Do you actually like the taste?" she asked with a frown.

"Yeah!"

"Rob, no," she said, dabbing at his nose with the tissue. "You don't want to drink blood. If you do, you'll become a vampire like Dracula, who killed his mother. You don't want to kill your mother, do you?"

Young Rob pondered this for a moment. "No." It wasn't until he was much older, once he'd actually read *Dracula,* that he realized that his babysitter had completely made that up. There was nothing in the book about that happening.

So with all of these old stories in his head, it occurred to Robert that it might be interesting to not only make the experimental mice aggressive, but downright deadly. To his surprise, Susanna went along with this. In time, he told her more about his past, revealing deeper secrets. For the first time in his life, he felt truly comfortable doing that with someone.

Not unexpectedly, she'd been skeptical when he told her about his psychic powers, but she quickly came around when he demonstrated them to her with his set of Zener cards. Once again, she didn't get freaked out; she just leaned in closer to him.

"So," she said, "these psychic powers of yours. What are they telling you about me?"

Robert smiled. "What do you mean?"

Fixing him with a stern gaze, she said, "Read my mind."

"Susanna, it doesn't really work like that."

She pouted, looking down at the table. "That's too bad." Aware of her leg brushing up against his, he asked her why. "Well, if you really could see into my mind, you'd know how much I want to make out with you right now."

The romance was a fun one, better than anything Robert had experienced before. Part of him knew how lucky he was to have landed a catch like Susanna, but the more arrogant side of him felt like he deserved it. He was brilliant, and so was she, and the two of them made a great team. He lied to her about the fact that he was a virgin, knowing that she'd slept with at least two boyfriends before him. If she could tell during their first night together, she didn't let on.

Sometimes, he felt like he was in over his head, both with her and in terms of the speed at which the potion was coming along. But he quickly shoved thoughts like that aside. What was happening in his life right now was amazing.

Things went south when the development of the potion reached its logical conclusion: It needed to be tested on a human being. He'd considered trying it out on himself, but he didn't want to admit that he was a little too scared for that. He didn't want to try it on his beloved Susanna, either, in case something went wrong. There was some talk of slipping it to some unsuspecting victim, but the two of them decided against that; the results could wind up being disastrous. If it were going to be done at all, it had to be in a laboratory setting.

So he did use it on himself, and he wound up almost killing Susanna in the process. They were both very lucky that she was able to change him back to human before he could manage to do that. He barely even remembered what he'd done under the influence of the potion; it almost felt like a bad dream, but the fallout from it was definitely real. He genuinely regretted what he'd done — or tried to do — and more than that, he was so shaken up that he decided not only to end the experiment but to get rid of all evidence of it.

Things fell apart between him and Susanna shortly afterwards despite his best efforts to save the relationship. It broke his heart the way she suddenly became so cold to him, but he couldn't really blame her. He'd tried to kill her, even if he hadn't really been himself at the time. He wished he'd never started the whole thing, and part of him blamed Jonathan and hoped that he'd rot to death in jail.

That should have been the end of it, but it wasn't. Robert had given Susanna all of his notes and the formula for the potion, telling her to burn them. That had been a gesture of goodwill, hoping that it would prove that he still loved her and would never do anything to harm her again. He thought it might win her back, but that didn't happen. She just cut him out of her life, not even bothering to say goodbye to him when they graduated high school a couple of months later.

When the news reports of vampire attacks around the city began to crop up near the end of June, it didn't take Robert long to figure out what had happened: Susanna had used the potion herself. Not only that, but she must have recruited some other people to take it as well, given that the reports cited multiple attackers. The police and other officials wanted to insist that this was just the result of some rabid bats or birds or some other bullshit like that, but Robert knew better.

His emotions were all over the place. Once he got over the initial shock, the idea that his former girlfriend was out there killing people made his stomach turn. More than that, she had a grudge against him, so he began to fear for his own safety. What if she decided to come after him, maybe to settle the score?

It was a good thing that she didn't know where his new house was, he realized, which made him feel a little better. Just after graduation, his father had set the family up in a nice, new place, a huge house out in Evans. This suburb of Augusta was only beginning to be built up and developed, so homes were few and far between out there. It was quiet, secluded, and — most importantly — safe. At least Robert hoped it was.

The killings went on for nearly a week, then stopped as abruptly as they'd begun. Robert had no idea whether or not Susanna and her group had been killed, or maybe they'd just taken the potion for a limited time, then changed themselves back to normal. By the time he'd worked up the courage to call her house, he was told by her mother that she'd already left for college in Charleston. He didn't dare say anything about the potion or the vampire attacks, which by then most of the city seemed to have already forgotten. But at least he knew that Susanna was still alive.

"Is this Robert?" Mrs. Young asked, her voice suddenly shifting from pleasant to icy.

"Yes, ma'am, it is."

She paused. "Listen, I don't know exactly what happened between the two of you, and frankly, I don't need to. But she made it clear to me that she does *not* want to hear from you anymore. I think you'd better just let it be and accept that she's burned that bridge behind her. Do you understand me?"

He wanted to protest, to insist that he just wanted to know if Susanna was all right. But it sounded like Mrs. Young was capable of being just as stern and adamant as her daughter, so he gave up on trying to further the discussion.

Robert's outlook on life became bleak after that, and it took him a long time to sort through his feelings. His parents couldn't understand why he'd suddenly slumped into depression, abandoning his plans to go away to the University of Georgia, possibly returning to Augusta afterwards to attend its local medical school. And he refused to explain why.

They tried sending him to a therapist, but Robert certainly wasn't going to tell her the truth about everything. It bugged him the way that the woman was able to get some things out of him, like his resentment over his father's behavior when he drank and the way his mother could be something of a drama queen. So he reverted to form, spinning yarns about his childhood that sounded interesting but were completely made up.

At first, she'd believed him, but as the stories became more outlandish, Robert could tell that this was one person he couldn't fool. She called him on his bullshit, trying to get him to tell her what was really going on. That just made him more angry. After only a few sessions, he refused to go back, and he got the feeling that the bitch was glad to see him go.

Nevertheless, some good did come out of his short-lived therapy sessions. He'd picked up on some of the techniques that the woman had used to interrogate him, tactics she tried to use to get him to admit to certain things that he wasn't comfortable facing. Left alone with his thoughts and not being pressured to confess them to some stranger, he began to understand himself more.

For one thing, he'd thought for a long time that his feelings toward Susanna centered around being heartbroken and missing her, but there was a much stronger emotion at play here: jealousy. That vampire potion had been his project. It wasn't Susanna he wanted back nearly as much as it was the potion, the potential it had to give him power.

He'd felt a sort of second-hand guilt about the people who had died while his ex-girlfriend had used the potion, but deep down, he'd wished that he had been the one leading that mysterious group of vampires around town, taking down helpless victims at whim. This revelation scared him, causing him to crouch down on the floor of his bedroom, his arms holding his knees to his chin. But after only a few moments of thinking through it all, he realized that it was the truth. He then started laughing to himself, struggling to keep it from getting too loud lest his parents overhear.

From that point on, Robert had a new goal: to create the vampire potion again. For a little while, he'd still hoped to re-establish contact with Susanna, to confess to her that he wanted in on the action, but he eventually had to admit to himself that this was impossible. He wondered if he might run into her during the Christmas season when she would presumably be back in town visiting her family, but that never happened.

He went by their old haunts, all the places they'd gone together as a couple, hoping that she might show up. He'd rehearsed what he would say to her if they ever did speak again. He even tried reaching out with his mind, hoping to somehow psychically compel her to connect with him, but he wasn't surprised when it didn't work.

She was probably avoiding him, hiding out at home with her stupid family. Maybe she — like he had initially — had been scared by what the potion made her do. If that were the case, he needed to give up on his fantasies of getting her back by his side, the two of them using the potion together. He craved that darkness and power, and if she was too weak-minded to handle it, then that was her problem.

Over the next several months, he did his best to recreate the potion from scratch, but despite his efforts, he just couldn't get it right. Jonathan was nowhere to be found, so that avenue was out. He wound up accidentally killing the mice that he had, the pretense having been that he was keeping them as pets. This disturbed his parents even more, so he had to abandon that approach. There was no way he was going to be able to experiment in a way that didn't spell his own doom; he didn't want to wind up as dead as those mice.

Eventually, it occurred to him that if science couldn't help him achieve his goal, maybe the occult would.

Robert had convinced his parents to purchase a VCR that year for his birthday, claiming that it was something his former therapist had said might help. It wasn't hard to cook up a story about how watching movies at home and getting glimpses into these other people's fictional lives was somehow therapeutic, expensive though it was. Part of this was just Robert being his usual manipulative self, but more than that, he found that this was a useful tool for his new line of research.

There were video rental stores beginning to crop up around town, and Robert would sometimes spend hours perusing them and their printed catalogs for titles that interested him. There was the occasional frustration when a particular movie was only available on VHS instead of Betamax, but he still found plenty of horror movies to rent, including vampire ones.

Some of them were hokey, but for the most part, he found himself envying the villains and monsters on his television screen. Most of the time, the demons were defeated in the end, but Robert always rooted for them just the same. He enjoyed the victories they achieved early on in each film, whether it was brutal murder, demonic possession, or something equally unsavory. He even felt sexually aroused by this, particularly when the victim was an attractive girl. That was a recurring theme, and he was more than fine with that.

The vampire movies didn't do much for him in terms of figuring out how to become one himself. In almost every case, becoming a vampire required being bitten by one, and it wasn't like he could just look one up in the phone book. But there were variations on the myth that hinted that witchcraft and demonology might be the way to go. He was also drawn to the notion of satanic cults, which he understood were in fact real things, not just spooky occurrences in movies.

In both the films he researched and occasionally in the TV news, there were mentions and even depictions of real-life Satanists performing dark rituals. Many of these involved animal sacrifice and human torture, even twisted perversions of the Christian faith. The more racy material he could find, both in print and on film, showed naked virgins tied to altars and people in long cloaks performing their blasphemous ceremonies by candlelight. All of it fascinated him.

Meanwhile, he was attending the local college, mostly to appease his parents; he hadn't even declared a major. He had casual friends and kept most of his secrets, just as he'd always done. Rarely would he let anything private out, and only then if it served his deeper needs. Case in point: a guy in his Pre-Calculus class named Colin.

"Did you see that stuff on the news last night about that satanic cult they found in Utah?" Robert asked Colin. There had in fact not been such a news story, but there had been similar ones in the past.

"No, man, I missed it," Colin said. "That kind of shit freaks me out anyway."

"Oh, you should have seen it. It was some scary shit. There were people performing all of these evil rituals, even kidnapping babies and sacrificing them to the Devil."

"No way." Colin let out a small shudder.

"Yeah, totally. The police rounded them up and everything. And they found something like twenty bodies buried in this cult leader's basement."

"Shit, man, that's fucked up."

"I know! I wish I could find out more about it, though."

Colin drew back, looking frightened. Robert tried to hide his enjoyment of that. "What? Why?"

"No, no, nothing like that," Robert said, flashing one of his charming smiles. "I'm not really into it or anything. It's for my Sociology class. I'm trying to do a paper on it this quarter, but most of what I can find is only in these really old books in the library, nothing current. It'd be cool if I could find someone around here who was actually into that kind of thing."

Colin looked around the student center, checking to see if anyone was paying attention. Then he leaned in closer to Robert, lowering his voice. "Actually, I kinda know this guy."

"What guy?" Robert was playing it cool, but the truth was that he'd already overheard Colin talking about someone he'd met at a bar a couple of weeks ago who claimed to be a Satanist. He'd waited until today to try to get any information out of him, not wanting to let on that he'd been eavesdropping. "You mean a real-life Satanist?"

Still looking somewhat scared, Colin went on to retell his story to Robert, who pretended he was hearing it for the first time. With a little prodding, he spilled more details, including how this man was apparently part of a small group of people in Augusta who practiced this "religion," though Colin scoffed at calling it that.

"You think you can get me in touch with him?" Robert asked, eyebrows raised. In a way, this conversation wasn't all that different from ones he'd had in the past when he was working on the vampire potion. Back then, it had been certain drugs he'd been trying to get his hands on, like the mushrooms that a friend of a friend of his was able to get by sneaking onto cow pastures out in Appling.

"Sure, I guess so. I gotta tell you, though, the guy's kinda spooky."

"I'm sure he is," Robert said with a grin. "But I can handle that." If his saying this made Colin uncomfortable, Robert didn't mind at all.

"Look," the man said to Robert, "I'm afraid you've got the wrong idea."

The conversation hadn't gone well. Per Colin's instructions, Robert had met up with him at Tip-Top, the combination bar and pizza place that he'd been to plenty of times in the past, but he'd stopped going there in recent months because it reminded him of Susanna. Some of his old high school friends also frequented the place, and because of how his life had changed, he felt uneasy around them. But he'd brave the bar at least one last time if it meant finding out what he needed to know from this mysterious Satanist.

Colin had introduced the two of them, then left them at a table to talk, again seeming a bit shaken. Robert, meanwhile, was eager to learn all he could from his new acquaintance, a slightly older man named Adam.

At first, Adam had seemed quite friendly, greeting Robert with a firm handshake and starting off their conversation pleasantly. "So you want to know about Satanism?" He almost seemed to be joking, and his blithe manner wasn't what Robert had been expecting.

"Yes. Very much so."

"And this is for a paper you're writing at college?"

"Actually, no. That was just… Well, it's what I told *him,*" he said, glancing off in the direction he'd seen Colin go.

Adam looked confused. He was a normal enough looking man, which sort of disappointed Robert. He'd expected somebody more sinister looking, maybe with a dark beard. But this guy looked more like some kind of salesman, all affable and ordinary in his button-down oxford shirt. "What do you mean?" he asked.

"I think you know," Robert said, trying to sound intriguing. "What I'm interested in is what's real, the power that you have access to. I have some of it myself. I've been psychic all my life, been in touch with mysterious things." He expected the man to be impressed.

"Really," he said flatly.

"Yes, definitely. I mean, as far as real satanic stuff goes, I know some of the basics, but what I'm interested in is deeper than that. I want to know how to really do things, to take part in the rituals. I've heard you might be able to help me with that."

Adam eyed Robert suspiciously as he spoke, but he'd been expecting this. It wasn't like some master of the black arts was going to open up to him immediately. In fact, his plain appearance was probably all part of the disguise. One documentary in particular that he recalled had emphasized that, the fact that there were witches and demonologists all around, hidden in plain sight. He just wanted in.

"Just what is it that you're after?" the man asked him.

"Everything," Robert said cryptically, then felt disappointed when this didn't elicit the reaction he was expecting. He decided to be more forthcoming. "Look, I just want to expand my natural powers. There are things I need to make happen, spells I want to do, people I want to make pay for the things they've done. I'm totally willing to do whatever it takes, no matter how dark. I'm ready to devote my heart to Satan."

That was when Adam laughed, which was something Robert was not expecting, nor his declaration that Robert had what he called "the wrong idea."

"I mean it!" Robert insisted. "This life hasn't been what I…" He stopped, not wanting to lose control. He needed this guy's help, and for that, he needed to be taken seriously. He breathed in deeply, steadying his hands beside him as he straightened up and leaned forward. "I just really need the help I know you can give me. I'm willing to do anything. I'm not afraid of the darkness, the sacrifices, any of that."

"Kid," Adam said almost pityingly, "you're in way over your head. I can't help you."

Robert wasn't used to being talked down to, and it made him angry. He knew that the man was testing him, but his patience wasn't inexhaustible. "But that's where I *want* to be," he pleaded. "Deeper than I've ever gone."

"You have absolutely no idea what you're talking about," Adam said more firmly, the amusement on his face beginning to fade. "I could try to explain to you about things like greater magic and lesser magic, but I can tell that it wouldn't do any good. You won't be able to listen."

"What's that supposed to mean?"

Adam paused, looking down at the table thoughtfully and spinning his glass slightly with his thumb and forefinger. The ice cubes jiggled and spun more slowly. He looked up again, fixing Robert with a gaze. "What if I told you that there's no such thing as Satan?"

This time it was Robert who laughed. "What? That's stupid. How can you be a Satanist and not believe in him?"

Adam's face went blank for a moment, and then he grinned, almost imperceptibly. "You make your own God. Or Devil."

Robert was beginning to get fed up. "Look, just stop with all the cryptic talk. I need your help, or at least, I need to talk to someone who's not going to waste my time with a bunch of philosophical baloney." He stared, trying to get through. Usually, he won his arguments with charm, but every now and then, he had to do so through intimidation.

"Go fuck yourself," Adam said smoothly, then stood up from the table, holding his drink.

This shocked Robert, and for a moment, he let the man walk away. But he couldn't let this opportunity go. He jumped up quickly, rushing after Adam and grabbing his shoulder to stop him. As he spun around, part of his drink spilled on his hand, which he glanced down at before fixing Robert with a look so white-hot with anger that it made him involuntarily draw back.

"Sorry," he almost whispered. "I... I didn't mean to..."

Adam stepped forward, and Robert, even though he was several inches taller, fought the urge to back even farther away. A few people had taken notice of the confrontation, so Robert was grateful that Adam kept his voice down as he leaned in and spoke. "Whatever it is you think you're after," he said slowly and deliberately, "you need to drop it. Otherwise you'll get what you deserve. You don't want help from a real Satanist; you fucking want Vincent Price."

Robert seethed as the finality of the words sank in. He didn't like how scared he felt, either.

"Happy Halloween," Adam taunted, then turned his back once more and walked casually to the bar, taking a seat.

"It's November," Robert muttered under his breath.

"Welcome to Dairy Queen, can I take your order?"

For most of the people who worked at the fast food restaurant, those words spilled out like a bored mantra. But Robert looked forward to each approaching customer, at least when he had a co-worker for an audience on the nights when he worked the drive-thru.

"Just a minute," a voice crackled over the speaker next to the cash register.

Robert pushed the "talk" button, then said, "Goat head when you're ready," fighting back a snicker before releasing the switch.

Jennifer, the hot little brunette by his side, giggled fiercely as she covered her mouth.

"Shh, shh." Robert laughed, enjoying the routine.

"Okay, we're ready," the voice called out after a few moments.

Robert pushed the button as he got himself back under control. "Goat head." Jennifer couldn't fight back her cackle this time, and Robert wondered if the customer outside had heard it.

Because of the poor quality of the drive-thru speaker, Robert knew that the people on the other end of it thought he was saying "go ahead," and none of them had ever indicated otherwise. But to his co-workers, it was obvious what he was saying, and he enjoyed their simultaneous awe and discomfort at the reasons behind his joke.

Since his encounter with that asshole Adam, Robert had intentionally ignored his advice and continued on with his desire to pursue Satanism. Whatever that boring old fart had tried to do by discouraging him, it hadn't worked. Instead, he continued to develop his own beliefs, even coming up with rituals that he quietly performed in the safety of his locked bedroom after his parents had gone to bed. He slowly accumulated an arsenal of candles and other magical paraphernalia, growing more confident in his abilities as time went on.

Aside from the psychic powers he'd had all his life, he'd begun to develop new ones, though they were subtle and not all that useful. One of them was that, when it was a windy day outside, he found that he could make the wind blow stronger whenever he wanted to, then relax his influence and allow it to decrease. This was one of the things he kept to himself, knowing how much it would freak people out. He found that if he muttered certain incantations to himself, the effect was stronger, and lucky for him, the words didn't have to be real ritual ones from an old book. They were just things that sounded powerful to him, and that was enough. In time, he hoped to make this power strong enough to use the wind — or even just the power of his mind alone — to blow certain objects around, an idea that occurred to him when he saw how the wind gusts he seemed to command could blow patches of sand aside.

He kept this darker side hidden from the right people, like his parents. But as far as his co-workers were concerned, he actually liked telling them that he was a Satanist. It scared them, but he assured them that he wouldn't do anything bad to them as long as they didn't piss him off.

As for why he was working in fast food, that was another rebellion of his, something to get under his father's skin. He was still attending college, but he felt like he was faking his way through that and not caring. His father had insisted that he get a job, suggesting something in sales, like at one of the department stores in the mall. From there, he could work his way up and possibly become a good enough salesman to take over the family real estate business. But Robert had no desire to pursue that or anything else that college might have to offer. He had his own secret plans.

He justified the Dairy Queen job as a different kind of career ladder. As he told his disappointed father, there were people who had worked with the company for a long time and were store managers who did quite well for themselves and made good money, even supporting their own families. This was true, but Robert was still lying when he pretended that he wanted to follow in this path and actually cared about things like customer service and doing the jobs that other people thought were lesser. He even managed to successfully make his parents feel guilty when he called them out for being snobs to suggest that such work was beneath him. But the bottom line was this: He liked fucking with people, and he always had.

That was another thing he liked about working there. Aside from the middle-aged managers who had made this career their own and were good at what they did, the restaurant was mostly crewed by high schoolers and early college-age kids who barely even wanted to be there. Robert mostly didn't either, but he found that he liked being in the company of younger, impressionable youths. If nothing else, they were more likely to believe his stories.

Now just past the age of twenty, he was in something of a middle ground between the older professionals and the younger crew members. The managers could be charmed and manipulated in certain ways, but he didn't bother with his more outlandish stories when it came to them. Those were reserved for the other co-workers, who for the most part believed him.

Sometimes, his lies served a purpose, like when he wanted a particular night off and needed someone to take his shift. But other times, he just enjoyed seeing what he could get past people, like the time he told a rapt crowd on break about when he was a little kid and some guy broke into his house, so he hid out in a closet with a knife and then killed the man when he was discovered. When one of the boys balked at this and wondered why he'd never heard about it in the news, Robert insisted that it was hushed up by the police because he was a minor at the time. That seemed plausible enough for the rest of the wide-eyed listeners.

"That was really brave of you," Jennifer practically whispered.

"No, really, it wasn't," Robert said to her, locking his eyes on hers. "I was pretty messed up by it for a long time."

Jennifer sighed with sincere pity, her bright blue eyes practically melting under his gaze. She really was quite the little hottie, and the fact that she was only sixteen bugged Robert, but only a little. Would it really be so wrong for him to hook up with her? She was so damn gorgeous, and she certainly looked older than she was.

Robert continued to mislead his co-workers, usually covertly but sometimes blatantly, just for fun. There was one time when he told a lengthy story about some woman he knew who tried shoplifting from a store, only to get chased by a security guard who grabbed her leg as she was trying to jump into her car to escape, and the more she struggled, the harder the man pulled.

"Did she get hurt?" asked Oliver, one of the guys at the table.

"A little bit," Robert said, his tone still stern. "He pulled on her leg for a long time."

"Man," Oliver said. "I bet that hurt."

"Yeah, it did. Do you know how long he was pulling her leg?"

"How long?"

"About as long as I've been pulling yours with this story." Robert waited a couple of seconds for the joke to sink in, and then the table erupted in laughter. Jennifer made it a point to laugh more loudly and longer than the others so that Robert would look over at her.

The more the two of them talked, the less Robert fought his desire for Jennifer. It wasn't that she was particularly bright, but he could tell that she liked him, and that was enough to stir up some interest. He even felt flattered that such a pretty young thing would want to be with him, much as he had when things had taken off with Susanna two years earlier.

They had to be careful, though, to keep their relationship officially a secret. The managers looked down on co-workers dating each other, but more importantly, it was technically a crime for Robert to be sleeping with an underage girl. The closer they got, the less he cared, and honestly, being with her felt like one more thing to be getting away with.

Another thing Robert liked about Jennifer was her malleability, how easy it was for him to get her to do things. When she mentioned one day that one of her friends had dyed their hair red and that she was toying with the idea as well, Robert told her that she should, that it would look good. The next day, she greeted him with fiery red tresses. He'd already known about her reputation for being "easy" in other ways, but he was after more than just that.

As his desire for her grew, so did his wish to make his vampire fantasy a reality, and he had every intention of involving her in that. While he pretended to listen and to care about her plans to study cosmetology at the local technical college, what he had planned for her was more important. Once he let her in on the secret, it wasn't hard to convince her of its reality and of how amazing everything would be. He didn't care — and soon neither did she — that he would be taking her away from her family. He'd never even met them anyway; Jennifer had warned him that her strict father wouldn't approve of him.

So things played out as they did, Robert going from being the workplace trickster who shocked his friends with satanic "goat head" jokes and gave them fake palm readings (just an excuse to hold girls' hands, really) to being the guy who never came back to work one day, disappearing under mysterious circumstances. He and Jennifer knew that people would figure out that it was no coincidence that she'd disappeared at the same time, but that just added to the drama and their enjoyment of it.

Keeping Jennifer concealed in the basement that first day so that his parents wouldn't find her wasn't all that difficult, and once his mother and father went out for the night, the two of them set about what Robert hoped would be the final and most important ritual.

Leading up to this, things had been going increasingly well on that front. While his early attempts at rituals had left Robert with little more than a feeling of sneakily doing something forbidden, they had by this point progressed to where he was actually able to hear the voice of the Lord of Darkness himself, at least in his head. The voice — and damn it if it didn't sound quite a bit like Vincent Price after all — instructed him to bring Jennifer into the fold, and the two of them would go on to do great things, including getting revenge on Susanna for daring to defy his will.

"Will we really get to live forever?" Jennifer asked Robert in her high-pitched, delicate voice. It was one of the many things about her that Robert loved, the way she sounded almost musical when she talked. Her wide, ice blue eyes gazed up at him as she cupped his hands in hers, their chests close together. She looked so perfect in her floor-length black velvet robe, its drooped hood supporting her straight, dark red hair. The candlelight flickered throughout the room, making her round face seem to dance in a dark symphony of shadows.

"Yes, my dear," he said to her. "You and me, till the end of time." It didn't matter that it was a corny or clichéd thing to say; it was true. He had no doubt of that.

She smiled even more broadly than usual, and Robert drew back from her meaningfully, still holding her hands. She was the most beautiful thing in the world, and soon, she would be that way forever.

Robert released one of her hands but held onto her with his left, the two of them turning to face the chalk pentagram on the floor. "We call upon you, our lord," Robert said, his voice deep and theatrical. "Come to us and make our desires come true." He felt Jennifer's hand shift, turning so that her fingers were intertwined with his, their wrists pressed tightly together, just as he'd instructed her.

"We call upon the powers of darkness," he continued as they raised their arms upward, "to take us into their fold and make us one with them." He could feel his excitement building, a tingling sensation beginning to grow across his scalp.

"We call upon the unknown names of the great ones of the past, that they may bestow their greatness upon us!" His voice increased in volume as his breathing grew more passionate, and he could feel Jennifer gripping his fingers even more tightly, her breathing also growing stronger.

"Please," she cooed. "Come to us, please."

For a second, Robert felt annoyed. He'd told her before the ritual to leave the talking to him, so he was surprised when she chimed in with her own supplication. He thought of turning to her to give a disapproving look, but then he decided to just go with it. If she was as into this as she appeared to be, then maybe that's what was needed. Instead, he just gave her hand a squeeze, not sure if he meant for it to encourage her or to remind her that he was in charge.

"Come to us, please!" he said more loudly, repeating his girlfriend's words. "Demons of darkness, forces of fate!" The more poetic he sounded, the more powerful he felt. He continued along similar lines as his heart beat faster, his emotions growing more and more intense. Jennifer occasionally whispered her own echoes of what he said, which added more to the experience.

After only a minute or two, Robert became lost in the moment, practically screaming his words, feeling the air vibrate around him. This had happened in previous rituals up to a point, but never this strongly. He'd never been able to go this far. As before, he began chanting the nonsense words and names that came into his head: *"Rixunok! Zedzek! Tekonerak! CAM-TOM-FOR-FEE-LI-YAH-MOR-TOR-TAYYY!!!"* His entire body began to shake with fervor.

Jennifer remained silent, but she continued to grip Robert's fingers with her own, and he could feel the shaking of her body as her arm quivered back and forth. This was really happening. The ritual was going to work. Robert imagined that an earthquake was occurring, and everything felt just as important as if one were.

His eyes had been shut for a while as he'd been speaking in tongues, summoning the unholy power. He then glanced to his right, reaching out to the nearby stool that held the sacrificial knife. Really, it was just one of his father's hunting knives, one that he'd stolen from him for the purposes of this sacred ritual. The plan, which he'd played out in his head countless times leading up to this night, was to use it to slice the skin of his palm and then Jennifer's, the two of them letting the blood drip onto the pentagram on the floor. That was what Satan had instructed him to do. Nervousness and — dare he think it — fear began to well up inside of him; he wasn't looking forward to the pain.

But in the intensity of this moment, a new set of instructions was fed into his mind as soon as he gripped the rubber handle and picked up the blade, feeling its weight. Yes, blood needed to be spilled, but more than that, a sacrifice was necessary.

Jennifer stumbled slightly as Robert pulled her closer to him, his left hand still tightly gripping hers. She looked surprised, but he could tell that she was just as caught up in the ritual as he was. "Trust me," he said to her deeply, and she nodded meekly, which was exactly the reaction he wanted.

With that, he rotated his hand and hers so that their wrists were facing upward, then plunged the serrated knife deep into her forearm, dragging it towards him viciously as he gritted his teeth.

"OWWW!" she shrieked in surprise, then continued to scream as he kept his grip on her, not letting her get away as the blood began gushing out. For a fraction of a second, he felt guilty, but then he did

the only thing he could do: In the same motion he'd used to slash her wrist, he let the blade skip from out of her flesh and then into his own, slamming into his wrist and ripping up his arm, the veins tearing apart and spewing forth the precious lifeblood.

Jennifer fell to her knees and struggled against him, but Robert was barely aware of it. Both of their wrists were pouring the dark redness all over the place, spilling out onto the floor. She continued to scream, unable to get away from his grip at first, but then he found that he couldn't hold onto her.

"Ow! Ow ow ow ow owwww!" she wailed, scrambling around on the floor like a maniac.

"Stop!" Robert called out as he leapt forward. He pounced onto her as the blood continued to pour out of them, their frantic motions smearing the chalk on the floor.

"Be still," he said to her, not entirely sure of himself as he managed to immobilize her. He wasn't certain if he was trying to comfort her or just shut her up.

"It hurts, it hurts, it *hurts...*" she kept whining, trembling in his grip. He couldn't see it, but he was pretty sure she was gripping her wound with her other hand.

"I know," he whispered into her ear, feeling the pain from his own wrist. "Just give it a second. It will all be over soon." He fought back from what his mind was telling him to say, which was more along the lines of *Shut up, bitch.*

Any second now, it would happen. The Devil would make them vampires. They'd both be okay. But then he realized a very uncomfortable truth: First, they both needed to die.

Robert wasn't sure just how long the two of them lay there. Jennifer stopped shaking after a while, and so did he. He thought that it was just because he was the stronger one, the man who had orchestrated all of this. But when he tried to move, he found that he couldn't. He was just lying there, his body holding the unmoving corpse beneath him.

He tried to stand up, hoping to survey the scene, but he literally could not move. It was almost like he were made of stone, a human-shaped statue. He was still aware of his surroundings, the room bathed in candlelight, the floor damp with his and Jennifer's blood. When he tried to blink and then couldn't, panic began to set in.

Even more disturbing was the fact that he was no longer breathing. If he'd been able to, it would have been in quick gasps, but even that was lost to him now. Equally disappointing, but at this point not much of a surprise, he discovered that he no longer had a heartbeat.

This wasn't what he'd expected death to be like. Surely there would be a tunnel with a light at the end, or at least, shouldn't his spirit start floating up out of his body? And if he and Jennifer were supposed to be transformed into vampires, why hadn't it happened yet? Had the ritual failed after all?

A resigned calm began to creep over him as his thoughts drifted to other places, other times. He remembered fooling Pat into thinking he was alien. He remembered drinking his own blood as a child and the girl who had first inspired him to do that. There was his babysitter, lying to him about Dracula. He could see Susanna with him in the Biology lab, the two of them perfecting the potion. And he could see Jennifer, her gorgeous face contorted in a combination of pain and pleasure the first time they'd had sex. He began to wonder what would come next, if anything.

Much to his dismay, he found that he had a long time to think about it.

CHAPTER FIFTEEN

ROBERT'S STORY, PART TWO

There was a gap in Robert's mind, he realized as the blood rushed down his throat. He couldn't remember how he'd gotten here or even who it was that he was drinking from, his massive strength causing some of the woman's bones to pop as he gripped her tightly. She wasn't dead yet, but she was already past the point of being able to put up any kind of a struggle. Robert continued to gulp the precious blood down, feeling himself grow stronger as his victim slowly slipped into lifelessness.

As he stopped drinking, he became aware of the sound of someone else swallowing nearby, a girl sprawled over the prone form of a man on the floor. The back of her head was to him, but then he remembered a name: Jennifer. He also recognized the man that she was finishing up. It was his father, or had been until just recently.

Robert looked back at the limp rag doll of a woman in his arms, her head lolling back at an angle and her neck torn open by two round holes. This had been his mother, but rather than feeling sad about seeing her dead, he felt a smug sense of accomplishment. He let go of what was left of her and let it topple from his arms, the body's head hitting the floor with a loud *thunk*.

The noise startled Jennifer, who stopped her feeding and looked up at Robert sharply, her mouth smeared with blood. For a moment, she looked frightened, but then something seemed to spark in her eyes. She smiled widely, her two large fangs showing prominently. After letting out a short laugh, she stood up quickly, racing forward into Robert's arms.

The memories came flooding back into Robert's mind. The satanic ritual had gone as planned. He could remember chanting along with his beloved, the two of them calling forth the powers of darkness while the pentagram on the floor began to pulsate with light. It had hummed more intensely as the power built up, causing the entire room to shake, but he hadn't been the least bit afraid. Finally, a blinding flash burst forth from the symbol and knocked them to the ground, killing them instantly. It was only when his parents had come downstairs to the basement that the two of them were resurrected as vampires, the smell of fresh blood awakening them. Before the helpless humans knew what hit them, they had become Robert and Jennifer's first victims.

Initially, Robert was glad to be rid of his parents, and he was content to let their bodies stay in the basement until he felt bothered to bury them. This house was his and Jennifer's now. But it soon became clear that he still needed his mother and father for practical reasons, so he used his newfound powers to bring them back to life, but under his control.

Just how he knew how to do this — or even that he could do it — wasn't clear. It was like the knowledge was just there, implanted in him somehow. It must all have been part of the dark gifts he had been given by the Devil, his lord and master to whom he was eternally grateful. With a wicked smile, he realized that "eternally" was more true for him than it was for most other people.

And so he used them, the recreations of his parents, who could still act like regular people when needed but were, for the most part, mindless zombies. They were puppets, a necessity to tie up loose ends and make it so that Robert and Jennifer could continue to live comfortably and without raising suspicion. Of course, if anyone got too close, they'd have to kill them, but he hoped it wouldn't come to that.

Robert's father sold — practically gave away, in fact — his real estate business to one of his colleagues, dodging questions when they got too prying. He insisted that he and his wife were happy with their early retirement. A story was concocted that the family would be going overseas for an extended trip, which included making arrangements with the power, water, and gas companies to pay all of these utilities months in advance.

"Yes, that's right," Robert's father said cheerfully into the phone. "Thank you. I certainly will." After a pause, he added, "You do the same." As he placed the receiver back onto the phone, his expression went from a broad smile to completely vacant, his eyes staring straight ahead.

"Well done, Father," Robert said with a sneer. "Now go back down to the basement until I have need of you again."

The blank-faced man stood up from the table and did as he was instructed, not even seeming to notice Jennifer as he slowly glided past her.

The girl regarded their plaything with amusement, then sidled up to Robert, slipping her arms around his waist and kissing him gently. "When was the last time we fed them, do you think?"

"Hmm? Oh, I don't know." He said it like he barely cared, but then he nodded. "Actually, you're right. It's probably been at least a week." The two of them had found that they didn't have to kill all the time in order to survive, even if they really did enjoy doing so. As for the two mindless revenants in the basement, who usually just spent their days and nights sitting in two easy chairs and staring into nothingness, Robert and Jennifer occasionally brought home leftovers from their killings, just enough to keep them sustained. They probably weren't in any danger of actually dying again, but if they went too long without feeding, their bodies started to age more rapidly.

As long as they were still needed, they were a burden, and Robert was looking forward to the day when he could get rid of them permanently. In time, he would stage things so that it appeared that his parents had died during their fictional overseas trip, and all of their assets would be left to him. But that was several months down the road; he had more immediate concerns.

The next few months were focused, among other things, on spying on the Young family and hoping to find a way to get to Susanna again. At first, Robert just wanted to prey on her, but his ambitions quickly grew into something more complex and sinister. Jennifer was completely on board with this as well, enjoying the excitement of it all.

Sometimes, they would spend hours peering in through the windows of the Young house on Aumond Road, listening in on conversations. As bats, they were virtually invisible in the dark. There were even times when they sneakily made their way inside, hiding in corners of the ceiling or behind pieces of furniture while they conducted their surveillance. If someone in the family started to detect their presence, it was simply a matter of projecting a telepathic command to them to make them forget. Since his resurrection as a vampire, Robert's psychic powers seemed to have increased exponentially, growing stronger all the time.

This mental prompting was also something that could be used to find things out, getting Susanna's family members — especially her two younger siblings — to unconsciously feel compelled to start talking about her and when she might be coming home from college again.

Robert was both surprised and delighted to find out that the wave of attacks that had occurred two years earlier had in fact involved not just Susanna, but these two children as well. They'd all been in on it, using the potion and even bringing in some of the young boy's friends as well. He'd always assumed that Susanna had recruited other people her own age, but the fact that her guinea pigs had turned out to be children made the whole thing deliciously perverse. Even better than that, there were plans for the group to get together this summer and take the potion again. This was when Robert, with Jennifer's help, began developing his own plan.

As far as feeding was concerned, the two of them concentrated on homeless people, whose bodies they then hid. Other times, they would fly to one of the nearby towns outside of Augusta and prey there, again hiding the bodies, usually in some undeveloped woodland area. They wanted to remain under the radar, not cause a panic like Susanna and her careless group had done before, leaving drained corpses all over the place and attracting the attention of the police and the news media. Vampires were supposed to remain hidden in the shadows.

By the time July came and Susanna's group had gotten together again, what Robert had in store for them was epic. He was going to let them have their fun for a little while, but he and Jennifer would always be lurking behind the scenes, waiting for the moment to strike. Susanna, her sister Carolyn, her brother Ray, and even Ray's dumb little friends: They were all going to crumble beneath his power. It was only a matter of time.

CHAPTER SIXTEEN

TOUGH LOVE

If there was one thing that Randy Whitaker believed in, it was the right to protect his family. Until tonight, that had been more of an abstract thing, an imagined scenario that, while he hoped it would never actually happen, he had always been prepared for. A proud, card-carrying member of the National Rifle Association, Randy knew that the right to bear arms wasn't just something guaranteed by the Constitution. It was more than a right: It was a privilege and a responsibility.

That said, he didn't necessarily believe that every single person should have a gun. Criminals and crazy people certainly shouldn't. That was the one part of that damn Gun Control Act from back in the day that he agreed with. He worried, though, that things were about to get worse. With President Reagan getting shot a few years ago, there was a lot of talk about tightening the laws even further, and he knew what that would lead to: just more restraint against law-abiding gun owners like himself. He wasn't a criminal, and he certainly wasn't crazy, even though some of his neighbors thought that he was being too paranoid about this whole vampire mess that had cropped up recently.

That had started two years ago, first with an attack at the YMCA in town in which many innocent people lost their lives. The authorities did little to protect everybody from the killings that went on for days, thankfully miles away from his family's house in Evans. It frustrated him that nobody would actually do anything, and then when the attacks stopped, everyone acted like nothing had even happened. But Randy knew deep in his heart that it could always start up again. And he'd been right.

Just over the past couple of days, there had been reports of vampire sightings, and lots of people were disappearing. For some reason, unlike the last time, bodies weren't being found, but Randy knew that there was a connection. He knew the legends from when he was a kid, even if he hadn't believed in them back then. Vampires killed people, then brought them back to life as more vampires. That had probably happened last time, too, but you couldn't trust the news to report the truth. First Amendment or not, the press could lie. He'd always had more faith in the Second Amendment anyway. Authorities could lie, too.

He'd loved taking his boys, Eddie and Jeff, on hunting trips. The day little Eddie brought down his first deer with a rifle was the proudest day of his life. Jeff, who was two years younger, still had a way to go before he was proficient with a weapon, but he'd get there, Randy knew.

When the two of them came running and screaming through his front door earlier tonight shrieking about vampires being after them, he took them at face value. It was an attack on his family, one of his greatest fears. He'd hoped that being this far out from Augusta, they'd be safe, but apparently that wasn't the case.

"They were right there!" Eddie shouted. "Bats! Talking to us and everything! They wanted to kill us!"

Randy seethed with anger, feeling his face grow hot. He looked down at his younger son, Jeff, and felt even more angry upon seeing the tears in the little boy's eyes. No piece of shit vampires were going to threaten his flesh and blood.

He also felt a sense of vindication. Most of the community hadn't even wanted to believe that what was happening now and what had gone on before was actually vampires. He hadn't believed it either at first, but when he found out that one of his supervisors at the golf cart plant had died as a result of this, that hit really close to home. The fact that the authorities kept wanting to deny the reality of the situation just reinforced what he already knew about the unreliability of government, from the local to the highest level.

Ignoring the protests of his wife, Lynn, he'd flung open the door and confronted the evil bastards, scaring them away with his rifle. Guns weren't supposed to be effective against vampires according to most of the stuff he'd read or seen in movies, but Randy knew better than that. You put a hollow point bullet into anything, and it will surely fuck it up.

It took a while for Randy to calm down once the confrontation was over, and even then, he knew that it might not really be. The vampires, which he now knew without a doubt were real, were still out there, and they might come back.

Since those earliest attacks two years ago, he'd learned all he could about vampires and what was needed to defend against them. He'd built up an arsenal of special weapons to use in case of an attack, which he kept locked in a trunk in the living room. He didn't care that his hunting buddies scoffed at this, joking stupidly on one of their trips that maybe he should be on the lookout for a vampire deer or maybe even a vampire otter in the river. The threat was real, and what was happening tonight proved that to him, even though he'd known it all along.

The boys were scared, and so was Lynn, but he didn't need her getting all hysterical, not now. She was a good woman, but ever since her menopause had started kicking in, she'd have these times where she'd go batshit insane for no reason. Things that she'd normally have blown off seemed to make her angrier than a hornets' nest on fire, but once she calmed down, she was back to the sweet little lady he'd married.

A few months ago, one of these tantrums of hers had ended up with him having to slap her to make her stop screaming at him, which wasn't something he was proud of. It wasn't even over anything that big; she'd just lost her shit one night because the boys wanted to camp out in the yard, and for reasons that were, well, unreasonable, she didn't want them to. He tried to get her to talk things out rationally, but it was like she wanted to fight. When she was younger, sometimes that could be cute, but this wasn't one of those times.

"I'm not playin' with you!" she screamed at the top of her lungs.

"I know you're not, woman!" he bellowed back, thinking he could shout her into submission.

"You know as well as I do that those boys have no business being out in the middle of the yard on a night this cold!"

"No I don't know that! That's what the tent and sleeping bags are for! They'll be all right!" He'd taken them camping before, real camping out in the woods, and on nights even colder than this one. "Just let them have some fun for once!"

Randy was pretty sure he knew what was going on deep down in his wife's mind, at least in the bigger picture. Menopause meant that her eggs were running out, that she soon wouldn't be able to have children anymore. Lynn had made it clear to him that she still wanted to have a little girl; Eddie and Jeff were their only children so far. And Randy wouldn't mind them having a baby girl either, so they'd been trying to get her pregnant just one last time. They hoped that God would bless them with the daughter they both wanted, but if that wasn't his will, then that's just the way things had to be. Randy could accept that, but Lynn couldn't yet, and he suspected that this was what was at the core of her unpredictable flare-ups.

Even so, they kept trying. Boy, did they keep trying. And while that wasn't a bad thing, the woman damn near wore him out sometimes. But what he'd playfully tried to get through her head tonight was that letting the boys camp outside was a perfect opportunity for them to "try" some more.

But instead, she'd turned into a hellcat once again, eventually lunging at him with her arms flailing as she shrieked, "Don't you tell me what to do!"

Finally, he'd had enough, and before he knew what he was doing, he shoved her back from him and slapped her clean across the face. That shocked her into silence, and the entire world seemed to stand still. His arm hovered in the air in the aftermath, and he looked at his hand, then at her as she clutched the side of her head, looking at him in disbelief.

She stomped out of the house, screaming obscenities as she went, and Randy wasn't sure what to do. Part of him felt like she'd deserved it, but a much bigger part hated himself for what he'd done. After speeding off in her car and being gone for at least half an hour, she'd come back, refusing to let him speak to her.

The whole time she'd been gone, the boys had been hiding, apparently having witnessed the confrontation or at least having overheard it. They were scared, and Randy was scared, too, shaken not just by what had happened but by what he had done. He heard the boys' whispers coming from the pantry, and rather than opening it to tell them that everything was okay, he just let them stay in there, not sure what to say to them.

Apparently knowing that the pantry was somewhere the boys liked to hide, Lynn found them almost immediately once she got back. Randy eavesdropped from a couple of rooms over, hearing her console them and saying something that included the phrase "could never leave my babies." He felt like such an asshole.

This wasn't helped by the fact that Lynn walked around the next three or four days sporting a black eye. Apparently, he'd hit her a lot harder than he'd realized. They didn't speak at all, and the boys would barely talk to him either. Needless to say, Randy slept on the couch for a few nights.

He was glad that Lynn was just a housewife and didn't have a job to go to where people might see the damage, though to be honest, he could barely look at her either. The entire family was eerily quiet, and he found himself rushing to get to work rather than endure the uncomfortable silence at the breakfast table each morning where everyone avoided eye contact. Even at work, he mostly kept to himself.

The point when things started to get back to normal surprised him, particularly the way it happened. Still in the doghouse, Randy had spent each night after dinner in the den watching TV. Normally, Lynn sat in there with him, but on this second night after their fight, she was still avoiding him. He felt bad about that, but at the same time, he didn't know what the hell to say to her. He was sorry, but somehow that just didn't seem like enough.

Eddie came into the room, glancing at the TV for a moment and then walking purposefully over to his father's recliner. Randy looked down at him, trying to read his expression. A memory flashed across his mind, one that he now found he had mixed feelings about.

It had been last summer, the two of them sitting in the family's pickup truck, waiting at a red light on Gordon Highway. They were in the left lane, the turn signal clicking away as he waited for the green arrow to come. Eddie was only nine years old at the time, but Randy had already started teaching him how to drive, sitting the boy on his lap in the driver's seat and letting him learn how to steer the truck while he worked the pedals, though under safer conditions than this, like on their property back home.

"Go!" Eddie had insisted once the cars to their right had gone on, their lanes having received the green light. But because of the way this intersection worked, their own lane still had a red light, so they weren't allowed to go yet.

Randy patiently explained this to his son, how they still had to wait and why. When the green arrow lit up, the car in front of them sped into a U-turn, despite the fact that there was a "No U-turn" sign beside the traffic signal. Randy maneuvered the truck into its planned, proper left turn onto Milledgeville Road, noticing the cars waiting to turn right onto Gordon Highway that could very well have collided with the reckless driver had they not been paying attention.

"See, now that's a good way to get hit," Randy said to his son.

After a pause, Eddie asked, "What's a *bad* way to get hit?" The kid was definitely a smart-ass, which could occasionally be funny but was usually just irritating.

Barely taking his eyes off the road, Randy reached up with his right arm and smacked the boy hard on the back of the head. He cried out in pain, clutching his head with his arms. *"That* way, smart aleck," Randy said through clenched teeth.

It wasn't like he went around beating his kids all the time; he only did it when they needed disciplining. He was a firm believer in the "spare the rod, spoil the child" philosophy, and he made sure it was always clear that the boys knew why they were being punished, even if it was for something they'd done hours before he'd gotten home from work. And they did; they weren't stupid. Usually it was a quick cause-and-effect kind of thing, like the time Jeff had started gyrating around like some kind of disco dancer near the end of a church service when the choir started singing the benediction. One quick *pow* to the head was enough to make him stop embarrassing the family.

The incident in the truck had blown over soon enough, and Randy and Eddie were even able to laugh about it later on. Eddie had been trying to be clever, but then, his father's response had also been a bit on the smart-ass side. One time when Jeff was acting up at the dinner table, Randy said to the elder brother in a leading tone, "Think it's time we showed him what's a good way to get hit?" Jeff, who had apparently already been told the story, clammed up immediately. That set the other two off laughing.

Tonight, things were different. There was still the tension in the house over the fight with Lynn, and this was the first time that either of the boys had approached him voluntarily. He thought that Eddie might be in need of some comfort, to be told that things were okay.

Randy may not have been the most mushy guy in the world, but he wasn't afraid to tell his boys that he loved them.

It had already been a couple of years since Eddie had gotten too big to climb up into the recliner with him, though Jeff still did that sometimes. Even so, there was something in Eddie's eyes that seemed to indicate that he missed being able to do it, and Randy thought of making an exception for him in this case, just for old time's sake. But instead of making a move to try to get up into the chair, Eddie just knelt down and rested his hands and chin on the armrest like he'd taken to doing recently.

"Hey, son," Randy said.

"Hey." The boy seemed to be having an internal dialogue, though he never took his eyes off his father's.

Heart-to-heart conversations weren't a big thing in the Whitaker home. Even when there were fights or hurt feelings, it was very rare that anyone apologized afterwards. Instead, the way that people in the family made up with each other was to start talking again, usually with no mention of what had happened before.

"I was thinking about going fishing this weekend," Randy said. Really, he'd just made this up on the spot. "You think you and Jeff might wanna come? We could take the boat up to Modoc, try out a place a buddy of mine told me about."

"I don't know. Maybe." He didn't sound very interested.

Randy wanted to ask him what was on his mind, but he wasn't quite sure how to say it. He wanted to talk to him about what had happened with Lynn, maybe to apologize to him, if not to her directly. Maybe if they could start talking about it, he could instill it in his son that you should never hit a woman, despite his bad example. *Women should be loved and protected. They take care of us in their way, and we should take care of them.* He ran some of these words over in his head, but he wasn't sure if Eddie was quite old enough to hear them.

"You worried about your mama?" he managed to ask.

"No, not really," he said with a shrug, looking away for a moment. Then his eyes shot back to meet his father's, a hint of anger in them. "Look," he said, uncharacteristically firm all of a sudden. He stood up from where he'd been kneeling, his hands still in place on the armrest. He was just barely tall enough to where their eyes were on the same level, given that Randy was sitting in the recliner. "I just want to tell you one thing. If you ever hurt Mama again, I *will* kill you."

Randy was floored. Just for a moment, Eddie looked and even sounded just like his grandfather. But he was still a little boy, and Randy could tell that he was on the verge of faltering, unsure if he should be standing up to his dad like this.

"I…" Randy began, then just nodded, swallowing hard. He didn't actually feel threatened; he knew that he wasn't in any real danger from a ten year old boy. It was the courage he was showing that surprised him. "Okay, son. I understand."

"Good," Eddie said, narrowing his eyes and looking more confident. With that, he turned and walked out of the room.

Randy stared at his son's back as he went, letting him have his moment. A lesser man would have blown up, jumping up from the chair and bellowing, *"WHO DO YOU THINK YOU'RE TALKING TO?"* just before throwing the little brat through a wall. It's what his own father would have done, God rest him.

But Randy learned something in that moment, both about his son and about himself. He didn't have anything to worry about, and his son was well on his way to becoming a real man someday. He'd taught him better than he'd realized.

On this summer night when the vampires had attacked, Randy set about some more father-son bonding, but there was a more urgent reason for it this time. If those pieces of crap came back, the Whitaker men were going to be ready for them. He didn't say so out loud, but he'd been kicking himself for not getting the anti-vampire weapons from the trunk when he'd gone to confront the monsters at his door.

Instead, he'd just gone for his rifle, a knee-jerk reaction based on other scenarios he'd imagined and practiced for, just in case some lowlife tried to break into his house in the middle of the night. But these weren't some black people trying to steal money for drugs; these were real killers, monsters straight out of a horror movie, and the right weapons were needed for the job.

Lynn wasn't too keen on Eddie and Jeff getting involved, but Randy insisted that it was important that they did. For one thing, it helped to defuse the fear of the situation, to know that there was a way to fight back and be prepared. The bigger weapons — the rifles, crossbows, and regular bows and arrows — were his to employ, but he saw nothing wrong in letting the boys handle the wooden stakes. Like any weapons, it was a matter of holding and using them properly, and most importantly, not getting injured in the process. Things like garlic and crosses were safe enough for them as well, but when Jeff tried holding his cross like a handgun and going *"peww peww peww!"* with it, Randy decided to let Eddie be in charge of it.

It was just as possible that the vampires wouldn't even come back, something Randy tried to reassure his wife of when the boys were out of earshot. Fortunately, this was one of the nights when she wasn't having hot flashes or flying off the handle, so she was more willing to listen to reason.

Eddie and Jeff, meanwhile, almost seemed to hope that there would be another confrontation, certain that they and their dad could defeat the vampires. "We're vampire killers!" Eddie exclaimed.

"Yeah! Vampire killers!" Jeff echoed.

This led to the creation of a crude flag, one made with one of Randy's undershirts, black magic marker, and Lynn's reluctant but eventual sewing of the fabric onto a small wooden rod. On it were written in all capital letters the words *VAMPIRE KILLERS*, and the boys looked on proudly as their father rigged it up on the front porch just below the Confederate flag that had flown there for years. By this point, the whole thing was kind of a game, and even Lynn couldn't deny that it was nice to see the family getting together behind a common cause.

Randy hadn't fully expected there to be a second attack, but sure enough, it happened, and it wasn't nearly as cut and dry. This time, the vampires managed to make their way into the house. He was proud of the way his family fought them off, keeping the flying menaces at bay with their weapons. Even Lynn, armed with nothing more than a clove of garlic, managed to stand her ground.

There were five of them, these weird, hovering black bats that could even talk. To Randy's surprise, they didn't sound like he'd expected: some deep-voiced, foreign-accented kind of pansies. Instead, the few times they spoke, they were more like girls, and normal-sounding American ones at that.

There wasn't much time to ponder this, as things escalated to the point where he'd shot at one of them when it zoomed for the window, but he missed. The bat fell to the floor, and in the confusion, the rest of them had flown back out the front door. Randy swore, annoyed briefly that his sons weren't doing much more than standing there, having dropped their weapons in shock.

"Pick them up!" he shouted at them, trying to ignore what he'd seen happen to Jeff's pants. The little guy had pissed himself. Yeah, that would help.

Randy caught a glimpse of red hair, the top of someone's head as they started to stand up from behind the couch. This must have been one of the vampires emerging in its human form, he thought, and as soon as he had a clear shot, he was going to blast that motherfucker into oblivion, right through the heart. Then he remembered that given the number of shots he'd fired already, his rifle was empty. He started to grip at the string of garlic cloves around his neck, ready to hurl them at the intruder.

But then something weird happened: There was a puff of smoke, and then there wasn't a person where he expected to see one, but another bat. It zoomed over the back of the couch and right past him, and a shriek erupted. Randy knew the sound all too well: It was his youngest son. Horrified and expecting the worst, he spun around, but rather than seeing little Jeff being preyed upon by the bat, he was just squatting there terrified, his hands covering his eyes. Eddie, meanwhile, was pointing at the open front door.

Randy stomped over to it, peering out and raising his rifle threateningly, even though it was empty. He stepped out onto the porch. "You'd better not fucking come back!" he screamed.

The following evening, Randy came home to something he really didn't want to hear. "What do you mean you called the police?" he yelled. "You don't think we can handle this ourselves? It's not like they're going to do anything anyway."

"It seemed like the right thing to do," Lynn insisted. Randy glared at her. "They should know where those vampires have been! You said yourself last night that you didn't think they'd been this far out from the city before, so don't you think it's important that people know that?"

Randy had to admit that she had a point, so his anger dissipated, at least toward her. Then it shot back up when she told him the rest of her story: They were sending out a deputy to get a statement from the family. He griped about this some more, going on about how Lynn knew his feelings on the police and about having strangers in his home. This devolved into further ranting about the cops being jackbooted thugs who weren't good for anything other than scaring people and threatening their personal freedoms.

There wasn't anything that could be done; the man was on his way. But then an hour went by, then another, and Randy began to feel more self-righteous. The all-important jerkoff had probably changed his mind and decided that he and his family weren't even worth talking to, that they were somehow beneath him and the rest of those stuck-up city folk.

While waiting, the family had their dinner as usual. Lynn could cook a venison sausage that could knock you on your ass, no doubt about that. Randy knew that he was a lucky man to have a wife who was so good in the kitchen.

He also noticed that Eddie and Jeff seemed to keep giving each other strange, secretive looks throughout dinner, but he opted not to ask them why. Instead, he waited to see what they were up to. After dinner, he kept his distance and didn't let them see as he watched them sneaking into the vampire weapons trunk, pulling out crosses, garlic, and stakes. He'd suspected what they might be planning, but rather than reprimand them for it, he instead found it endearing. There were his two little boys, wanting to be all grown up and defend the family.

While Lynn cleaned up in the kitchen, Randy craned his neck around the corner as he kept an eye on the boys, making sure that they weren't trying to get into any of the more dangerous weapons. He could barely hear them speaking in hushed tones, Eddie taking charge and speaking to his little brother with authority. What few words he could make out let him know that the boy knew what he was talking about, warning Jeff against touching the more dangerous stuff.

He had to duck back behind the door frame to keep from being seen, and when he looked again, he just managed to spot them heading for the front door. He waited patiently as he heard one of them — Eddie, most likely — opening it slowly as they snuck outside. Randy went to the living room window and peered out, his suspicions confirmed. The boys were going to their tent, ready to camp out there another night and ward off the vampires if they attacked, which he was certain they wouldn't. He and the rest of his family had already shown them who was boss.

Even so, it probably wasn't a good idea to let them play out their fantasy all the way. It was still a little while before sunset, so they were definitely safe, but he wanted to let them have their fun. He admired their bravery and enthusiasm. When Lynn asked him where they were and he told her, things took an unpleasant turn.

"What?" she shouted at him. "What the hell are you doing lettin' them go out there? After what happened last night?"

"Calm down," he said. "It's still light outside. We can make them come in before it gets…"

"I am *not* in the mood for this kind of crap right now!" she fumed, stomping past him and towards the front door. He made a move to stop her, then thought better of it. Too much of what was happening reminded him of that horrible night when he'd wound up hitting her, and he didn't want a repeat of that. Better to just let her have her way.

Moments later, he watched as Lynn dragged the boys inside, each one held by their wrists as they squirmed against her. She was raging at them at the top of her lungs: "…the police would think when they come by here and I tell them that I've let my children be outside when there're vampires flyin' around? I'm surprised you're not covered in bites already! Come here, let me look at you…" She released Eddie, then twisted Jeff's head back and forth as she examined his neck. He shuffled off to one side with a scowl as she grabbed Eddie and did the same.

He fought her off, then pleaded to his father. "Daddy! Make her quit!"

"Honey, I really don't think there's harm in them just…"

"Don't you start with me!" she yelled angrily, straightening up as she let Eddie go.

He looked up towards his mother with scorn. "We haven't been bitten or nothing. It's not even dark yet!"

"That's enough out of you!" she shrieked at him, raising her arm and pointing over his head. "Go to your room! Both of you!"

Eddie gave one last pleading look to his father. "Daddy…!"

Randy just said resignedly, "Do what your mother tells you, son."

As the sun went down, Randy and his wife sat mostly in silence in the living room, still waiting for the policeman to arrive. Lynn seemed to have calmed down, but he wasn't about to rattle the hornets' nest to be certain, only to have her go off again. Finally, some headlights shone across the room through the front window, a sign that a car was pulling into the driveway.

Randy got up and headed over to the front door. "Let's get this over with, then."

He heard the car come to a halt on the gravel driveway and waited for the deputy to approach the house. But for some reason, nothing happened for a long time, not even any footsteps. He looked out through the peephole but couldn't see much; the weird, distorted lens wasn't much use unless someone was standing right on the porch. As he continued to wait impatiently, he figured out what was probably going on.

"I swear… goddamn cops," he muttered, then raised his voice so that he'd have an audience in his wife. "They just love sitting in their damn car and making you wait, pretending they're doing something. Makes them feel all important." He knew this from his experiences of getting pulled over for speeding in the past. They liked to make you sit there and sweat, building up the tension.

Randy got tired of standing by the door, so he wandered back into the living room. He debated to himself whether or not he should sit back down; he knew that as soon as he did, the police officer would finally deign to grace them with his presence. Lynn rolled her eyes and gave him a little smirk, her expression seeming to say, *I know. You're right.*

After what must have been a good five minutes, there was a knock at the door. Randy dramatically walked over to it with a sigh, fighting down the urge to say something like *It's about damn time!* as he turned the deadbolt with one hand and the doorknob with the other. But when he swung open the door, the sight that greeted him was not what he'd expected. Instead of some uniformed policeman, there were two young people, a boy and a girl dressed in black, elegant clothes. They looked like two high school seniors on their way to the prom.

"I'm sorry," Randy said in surprise. "Can I… Can I help you? We were expecting someone else."

"We know," the boy said in a strange voice, his eyes narrowing. He was skinny, but the same height as Randy. The red-headed girl was at least half a foot shorter, all tarted up and smiling up at him with her wide, blue eyes. There was something unnerving about both of them.

"You're not with the police, are you?" Randy asked, thinking that it was a dumb question as soon as he'd asked it.

"Oh, no," the girl said, still smiling. "We already took care of them."

Randy felt a stab of pain in his heart, his scalp going numb as he suddenly realized who these people were. Lynn called out to him from the living room: "Is something wrong? Aren't you going to invite them in?"

He started to say something to her to warn her, but he suddenly found that he couldn't speak. He couldn't even turn his head or move any of the rest of his body. He just stood there, completely still, unable to look away from the boy and the girl standing in front of him, smiling at him with their fanged teeth.

He wanted so hard to tell Lynn to stay away as he heard her get up from the couch and walk up behind him, still wondering what was going on. Without being able to look over, he could still hear her stopping in her tracks as she started to say, "What's*sssss…*" The word seemed to sputter out and fade, like tires skidding on the pavement. And then she just stood there too, frozen, as the vampires looked at them with sick, satisfied smiles.

Randy realized what was happening, and his heart raced. He wanted to fight back against the mind control he and his wife were obviously under, but no matter how hard he tried, he just couldn't. These were obviously the vampires who had attacked their house the night before, but now they were here in their human forms, not just bats flapping around and threatening them.

"Actually, you're wrong about that," the dark-haired boy said, looking him in the eye. "That was a different group of vampires, ones that we've been following around and checking up on." If Randy could have flinched, he would have. He hadn't said a word, but apparently, his thoughts had been read. These vampires were some kind of psychics, and they had complete power over him.

"So, really," the pretty girl added, "no, we haven't dined here before. But if you wouldn't mind, we'd like a table for two."

The male vampire laughed, and then his companion did too, and Randy felt appalled as he found both him and his wife absently turning around and leading the two monsters through their house and all the way into the dining room, just walking along like nothing was out of the ordinary. Every fiber of his being was screaming at him to fight back and not let this happen, but he couldn't do a thing.

Randy and Lynn were like puppets, their faces blank as they seemed to politely pull out the dining room chairs for the two vampires to sit in. The whole thing was like some sort of sick stage play, and just when Randy thought things couldn't get any worse, the red-haired girl asked, "Aren't we missing somebody?"

His heart sank as he watched his helpless wife puff up for a moment, her expression still vacant as she called out: "Boys?" She sounded just like her regular self, not the controlled thing she'd become. He hoped that maybe Eddie and Jeff wouldn't hear her, or maybe they'd ignore their mother out of spite, still mad at her over tonight's earlier clash. But inevitably, they came.

"Mama?" Eddie asked as he and his brother walked through the living room toward them. Randy couldn't even look over to see; his back was to them. He kept trying to scream at them in his head, telling them to run, to get to the trunk of weapons, anything. "Who's...?" he began, but then Randy heard his and Jeff's footsteps stop.

"Hush, little one," the tall vampire said, his hand raised and his leering grin never fading. The boys then approached more slowly, eventually making their way into Randy's field of vision. When they stopped walking, all four members of the family were lined up side to side, like soldiers in formation. The vampires sat in adjacent chairs on the opposite side of the dining table from them, looking up eagerly.

"So!" the male vampire exclaimed, clapping his hands dramatically. "Who should we have to eat first?" The girl cleared her throat meaningfully, getting his attention. She gave him a glare that seemed to mean something to him, and he grinned more widely. "I'm sorry. You're right, my love. The lady should be allowed to place her order first."

Randy was disgusted, not just because of what was happening but over the fact that this fiend, wherever he had come from, was downright full of himself. The little shit couldn't have been more than twenty, but here he was in Randy's house acting like he goddamn owned the place, coming across like some pompous, Hollywood actor. Then he remembered that vampires didn't age, so maybe the kid was actually a lot older. Either way, Randy would have sworn he was some kind of queer if it weren't for the beautiful girl by his side, whom he had to admit was quite a looker. Then he felt guilty for thinking that.

"You dirty old man," the girl suddenly said with mock indignation, looking Randy right in the eye. "What would your wife say if she could hear you thinking things like that?" She then leaned forward and looked over at Lynn, putting a hand up to her face like she was whispering a secret to her, but she never actually lowered her voice. "Your husband is thinking about how much he wants to fuck me."

Randy wasn't sure if he turned red, but his face did feel suddenly hot. How dare this little whore say something like that in his own house, and worse still, in front of his children? As the two disgusting creatures laughed over this, all he wanted to do was break free of their control and beat the two of them to death with his bare hands.

"Now then," the boy said, still with the same shit-eating grin. "Waitress, would you care to tell us about tonight's specials?"

To his horror, Randy had to stand there and listen while his wife politely described him and their sons like they were items on a menu. "We have the Randall Gerald Whitaker, a vintage 1945 with a robust, hearty flavor. I have to warn you, though, that there's a high fat content in him that may upset your stomach." She began walking in front of them, gesturing animatedly as she spoke. There was something weird about her face, the way it was stretched in a wide smile, but her eyes still looked straight ahead, devoid of life. Randy knew that none of what was coming out of her mouth was actually her; it was what these vampire trash were making her say for their own amusement.

"If that isn't to your liking," she continued, "we have these two young specimens, the Edward Lee Whitaker, vintage 1975, and the slightly smaller but still succulent Jefferson Davis Whitaker, from 1978. As I'm sure you know, veal like this has a much more tender flavor to it, less smoky and polluted by age." She paused on the other side of their youngest son, and Randy could just barely make out the way she gestured towards herself in his peripheral vision. "And finally, there's me, the 1951 Lynn Atchison Whitaker, if you're interested in something with more of a bouquet."

The vampires looked across the family, contemplating their choices. With a decisive nod, the girl said, "I think I'll have the Lynn." She narrowed her eyes at the woman.

"And you, sir?" Lynn asked pleasantly. There was no hint of fear in her voice, but Randy knew that she must be terrified, just as helpless as the rest of them.

"Oh, the same for me," he said coolly.

"Excellent choice," she said, then sauntered over to the table. She kept that same fake smile, her eyes still vacant. As she moved to stand between the two "guests," they each repositioned their chairs to make room for her. Next, Lynn spread her arms and rotated her hands so that her wrists were pointing upwards, each one near the bloodthirsty creatures' mouths.

They gently took Lynn's wrists in their hands, and the boy lifted Lynn's right one slightly as he smiled at the girl, gesturing like he was toasting her with a wine glass. The girl giggled slightly and did the same. It was a disgusting, sadistic display, but what happened next, even though he knew it was coming, was too painful for Randy to watch. Unfortunately, he had no choice, and he hated the fact that his kids were going to have to see it, too.

The vampires, eyes fixed on each other, leaned forward and bared their fangs before sinking them into Lynn's wrists. Lynn didn't even flinch; it was like she couldn't feel a thing. She just stood there unmoving with that stupid grin on her face, looking almost like a mannequin, and if Randy could see a hint of pain in her eyes, he tried to pretend not to. The sound of fierce swallowing filled the room, and he wished he could somehow shut it out. Little by little, Lynn's arms and the rest of her exposed skin grew paler. He couldn't take it anymore, and all he wanted to do was scream. This was torture, plain and simple.

Randy did find that he could at least turn his eyes far enough to one side that he couldn't clearly see what was going on. He could still hear it, but there was at least some relief in not having it in clear focus. He wanted to tell Eddie and Jeff to do the same, but there was no way to.

Just before looking away, he'd noticed the angle of the red-haired girl's head, the way the top of it was turned toward him. For a moment, he wondered if this was the same person he'd seen the night before getting up from behind the couch, the one that turned into a bat and got away. But then he remembered what the boy had said when they first arrived, something about them being a different group of vampires. Just how many of these damn things were there?

His thoughts were interrupted when he noticed some movement, and he involuntarily turned his eyes back to see what was happening. Lynn had collapsed, her chin catching on the edge of the table as she fell. Her face still held that sickening grin, but her skin had gone almost white. The bloodsuckers were continuing their unholy feast, and as Lynn's drained body slid behind the table and out of sight, Randy tried not to think about all the deer he'd killed, ones he had gutted and drained. He thought of the trophies he had mounted along the walls of their living room, wondering if these disgusting beasts had similar displays of human heads in their own home.

Then he remembered what he knew about vampires and what happened to their victims, and this frightened him even more. What was going to happen to his wife, to the rest of them? Were they going to be turned into vampires as well? He couldn't stand the idea of Lynn, the boys, and especially him becoming like that, maybe even enjoying it because of whatever demonic forces took them over after death. Soon, he might be the one invading someone's home and performing unspeakable acts.

"That was good," the hideous girl said, wiping the blood from her face with a napkin. The grace with which she did it, like she was some polite little debutante, made it all the more disturbing.

"Yes, wasn't she?" The boy turned to face the remaining family members, his look of arrogance making Randy sick to his stomach. "So, dessert?"

"Oh, I don't know!" The girl held a hand to her belly. "Between that one and the policeman, I'm not sure if I have enough room. Should we get a doggie bag?"

The boy let out a small laugh. "We don't have a dog, Jennifer." So that was the little bitch's name. Randy wondered if Eddie and Jeff were thinking about how they'd been trying to talk him into letting them get a dog. He'd been planning to; he just hadn't gotten around to it yet. Now he never would.

"You know what I mean!" she cooed. "Play along."

The boy smiled, but then he stood up from his chair, pushing it behind him. "Actually, no, we can't. No more time for theatrics.

Remember, Susanna and the others are probably on their way." Who the hell was Susanna?

"Oh, right," the girl said. "I almost forgot." For the first time that night, Randy saw a different expression on her face other than self-satisfaction. "Can you sense them? This far away, I mean."

"I'm not sure," the boy said thoughtfully. He looked up into the air, his mind seeming to drift off somewhere else. It was then that Randy felt it happen.

This whole time, there had been a grip on his mind, and it was accompanied by a low, throbbing sound in his ears that had been going on for so long that he'd stopped hearing it. But somehow, it had stopped. Randy could move again, and he realized that the psychic hold on them had been released when their captor had tried to sense these mysterious others, apparently breaking his concentration.

His first instinct was to lunge at the boy and choke the life out of him, but he needed to be more methodical. The vampires hadn't seemed to have noticed yet that he and the boys were free, so if he could maintain the element of surprise, he just might be able to get to his weapons in time.

All of that was spoiled when his youngest son shrieked out, *"Mama!!!"* and began racing around the side of the table.

"Shit!" the girl Jennifer hissed, seeing what had happened. She turned to intercept the boy, but Eddie rushed forward and grabbed him by the arm, pulling him backwards.

"There isn't time!" he shouted. "Get to the tent!" The two young boys began running across the living room toward the front door.

"No!" Randy shouted after them. "The trunk! Get to the...!" His words were cut short when that same mental force took hold of him again, like a fist closing around his mind. Once again, he was paralyzed, and he hated the fact that he'd missed his chance. He was frozen in mid-stride, and just a second or two later, he saw the same thing happen to Eddie and Jeff, though in their case, they actually stumbled to the floor and skidded across the carpet, almost like they'd been shot.

Jennifer stopped her pursuit, then turned back to look in Randy's direction. But really, she was looking past him like he wasn't even there, and she said to the boy with a sick smile, "They skinned their knees. I can smell their blood." She closed her eyes and breathed in deeply, smiling as she sniffed the air. "Oh, I can smell it."

"Yes, I'm sure you can," the arrogant prick said from behind Randy.

You piece of shit, he thought. *If you had any balls, you'd fight like a real man, not hypnotize us like this.* He wasn't sure if his words could be heard, but then, the way Jennifer looked at him and grinned wickedly seemed to indicate that she had.

"Oh, Robert, he's right!" she squealed, pressing her hands together. "Let them loose. It will be more fun that way."

There was another smug chuckle from behind him, and Randy felt the hold on his mind disappear. He relaxed into a regular standing position, his mind racing to figure out his next move. The trunk of weapons was just on the other side of the room, and he could probably make it to it in just under four seconds if he was lucky.

Similarly, Eddie and Jeff began moving again, getting up from the floor. They were only a few feet from the trunk, so they stood a much better chance. Jeff had tears streaming down his face, but Randy hoped that at least his older son could keep things together.

Jennifer began creeping towards them, an evil sneer on her face. "I'll give you a head start," she practically sang.

With that, his face a mix of fear and determination, Eddie once again grabbed his little brother's arm and pulled him up from the floor. But rather than going for the trunk like Randy had hoped, they headed for the front door. He realized what they were thinking: They had weapons outside in their tent.

Before he could protest, Randy heard a huge commotion behind him, and he turned to see that Robert, the other vampire, had somehow slung the entire dining room table into the china cabinet behind it, leaving glass and broken dishes everywhere. Somewhere under that mess was his wife's body. Robert leered at him, obviously proud of his display of strength. His left arm was still extended behind him, and Randy realized that the boy must have hurled the table with a single swoop of his hand.

"So, come on," he taunted. "Fight like a man."

As soon as he made his next move, Randy realized that it was a stupid one. He should have run over to the trunk, but he couldn't resist his primal instinct, the urge to just scream and rush at this intruder, this monster who was destroying his family. He obviously outweighed the little prick, so he was surprised when his lumbering approach was quickly halted, and he was hurled backwards. He sailed across the room like a football, crashing into one of the living room chairs and toppling over along with it. It hurt, but he still had some fight left in him.

His efforts to recover were interrupted by Robert looming over him, then picking him up from the floor as if he weighed nothing. "Come on, Randall," he said. "You can do better than that." Randy felt dizzy as he was hurled back across the room and against the wall, his body crashing into two of the mounted deer heads. They fell to the floor along with him, and he wondered for a second if any of their antlers had managed to pierce his flesh.

Luckily, they hadn't, and Randy got up from the floor, his body racked with pain. He was pretty sure he had some broken ribs, and his vision was going blurry. But he still wasn't about to let this piece of shit get the better of him. He stood firm, holding his fists up in a fighting stance.

Robert laughed slowly and dramatically, again seeming like some corny horror movie villain. He'd had that air to him the entire night, like some dumb, young kid trying to act like a bad-ass without actually being one. Randy knew maturity and experience when he saw it, and this kid just didn't have it. He was a fake, despite all of his apparent power. As he panted heavily and tried to regain his strength, Randy swore to himself that he would teach this little brat a lesson.

Minutes later, Randy breathed his last breath. Leading up to it, he found himself overwhelmed with feelings of sorrow, helplessness, and anger. He barely felt the pain anymore; the blood was draining out of him quickly as the vampire Robert slurped it down. There was something sickening about how intimate it felt, like this faggot was enjoying sucking on another man's neck.

But as his life ebbed away, the biggest emotion Randy felt was guilt. He was faintly aware of the little boys' screaming coming from outside, but he couldn't tell which boy was which. There was a sound of running steps nearby; one of them might have been trying to get back into the house. He tried to hope that at least one of them would manage to survive, maybe even kill the vampires and save the day, but he knew that this was just a fantasy.

He hated the vampires, but he loathed himself even more. Despite all of his toughness, all of the weapons at his disposal, he'd failed to protect his wife and children. He'd failed as a husband, as a father, and as a man.

CHAPTER SEVENTEEN

PARTNERS IN CRIME

"Phillip Cooke speaking," the man said brusquely into the receiver.

It was the way he always answered the phone, as automatically as other people might say "Hello" and just as quick. Sometimes, this threw callers off, and they'd stammer out something like, "I'm trying to reach a Mr. Phillip Cooke…?" That got on his nerves, but it also gave him a sort of righteous anger. Most of the time, he held himself back from saying something sarcastic along the lines of *"Didn't you hear what I just fucking said?"* He had less restraint when it came to telemarketers, though.

More importantly, he needed to keep his cool in order to be professional. The person calling might be a potential customer, so there was no benefit in being a jerk right off the bat. While his day job was working as the maintenance man for an apartment complex, he also did some work on the side in freelance appliance repair. He was pretty much a jack of all trades, able to solve a wide variety of household problems.

But tonight, it was his boss calling, Nate. "Phillip, it's me," he said. "Sorry to call you so late." He barely sounded like he meant it. "Did you manage to get 706 done before you left today? The tenant just called me *again* to ask."

Phillip rolled his eyes. "Well, that's what you get for giving her your home number." He waited for a laugh from Nate, but it didn't come. "Anyway, yeah, you can tell Miss Harper that her precious damn AC is working again."

That finally got a laugh. "I know. Like she even needs it when she's out of town. Probably so her precious little Fifi or whatever the little yap-dog's name is won't get too hot."

"While he's shitting all over the carpet, probably," Phillip added with a sneer, which got another small laugh while he pictured the miniature poodle that had given him so much trouble earlier in the day. Some of the tenants' pets were fine. Cats were much easier to deal with; all they did was hide themselves from view when a supposed stranger like him entered an apartment.

"I had to grab the stupid little mutt and shut him in the bathroom while I worked on it," he continued. "But yeah, it's done. Little Miss Harper can come back from wherever the hell she went and enjoy her frigid apartment at its usual 60-degrees setting."

"Asheville, I think," Nate said. "She really keeps it that cold?"

"Yep. I swear I don't know how she lives like that. Can't imagine what her electric bill must be every month."

"And you still say she's not a good candidate?" Nate asked, his voice suddenly more quiet.

"Nah. Nothing but old lady stuff in there. The TV is way too big, one of those console ones. And the stereo, well, same thing. Big turntable with an 8-track built in. Size of a small couch, and definitely not worth it."

"Nothing else worth taking?"

"There's some jewelry, so maybe. But I can't tell if it's actually valuable or just some tacky old lady costume crap. We could always hit her and take our chances."

Nate paused for a moment. "Better not. If there's not enough worth going for, I'd rather keep her here, not scare her away."

"And lose rent," Phillip added, a hint of acid in his voice.

"You know how it works," his boss replied, and he found himself nodding, despite his dislike for the slimy guy he worked for. But they had a good thing going, and he knew that.

Nate was the manager of Woodland Ridge, an apartment complex not too far from the border of Augusta and its neighboring communities to the south, an area not officially named but still known as South Augusta. It had a reputation for being full of poor people, both black and white. Those who were more well off lived in Augusta proper or its richer suburbs to the west, and whether or not the people there openly said so, they looked down on their southern neighbors, avoiding that part of town whenever they could.

This worked to both Phillip's and Nate's advantage. If you were rich enough to live in the wealthier parts of Augusta, then good for you, but there were plenty who just couldn't swing that. Woodland Ridge offered residents an opportunity for comfortable living at an affordable price, the trade-off being that they were at risk for getting burglarized. No one really liked to talk about that, and the people who ran the place certainly wouldn't admit to it. The property wasn't in the ghetto, but it was near enough to it that whenever break-ins did occur, it was an unfortunate but not entirely unexpected thing.

What the residents didn't know was that not all of the burglaries — which occurred every couple of months or so — were perpetrated by outsiders. The scheme run by Nate, Phillip, and their other partner in it, Doug, went like this: As the manager, Nate knew which apartments had security systems in them and which ones didn't. He encouraged tenants to get them installed, but they weren't mandatory. However, he conveniently had contact information for his friend Doug at L&K Security, which he passed along to renters in the hopes that they would take him up on his offer. If they did, that would mean extra business and commission for Doug. If not, then that meant that their apartments were possible candidates for a staged break-in.

Where Phillip came into it started with his ability to "case" each apartment. As the maintenance man, he was regularly allowed into each place whenever work and repairs needed to be done, so he knew which homes had valuable stuff in them to steal. VCRs, stereos, and jewelry were the top things to look out for, anything that could later be sold at a pawn shop. If someone happened to have enough potential loot and also weren't fortunate enough to have one of L&K's alarms installed, that made them a perfect target.

Phillip could easily move about the apartment complex during the day without arousing suspicion; everyone was used to see him going from one repair job to the next. Once the decision was made among the three partners to "do" an apartment, as they called it, Phillip would let himself in with his key, take whatever valuables he deemed necessary, then hide them in one of the maintenance closets in the hall for later retrieval. Upon leaving the apartment, he would lock the door back and use a crowbar to break it open so that it looked like someone else had broken in.

Inevitably, the tenant would come home, see what happened, then call the police and complain to Nate. The police wouldn't do anything more than fill out a report and go about their merry way. And even if they bothered to investigate the crime and dust for fingerprints — which Phillip knew they never actually did despite such depictions in cop shows — he'd have a legitimate excuse for previously having been in the apartment given his role as repairman.

The victims, understandably upset, would sometimes hem and haw about moving out after the event. If they did, Nate would benefit by charging them extra money for breaking their lease, but if they stayed, they would be further encouraged to buy a security system from Doug. Phillip, sent to repair the door that he had to pretend he hadn't damaged himself, would often wind up in conversation with these people, faking sympathy. He'd sometimes feel guilty about this, but every now and then, if circumstances lined up right, he was able to deflect things.

"I don't want to point any fingers," he would say in a low voice, "but the people in the apartment downstairs from you just moved out. Could've been them, you know. No one woulda looked twice if they saw them carrying off your stuff, you know, mixed in with theirs." What he didn't say was that he and the others occasionally timed their burglaries to coincide with people moving out just so he could use this particular misdirection.

Once everything had calmed down, Phillip took the stolen goods to a pawn shop and got money for them, which was divided more or less evenly (depending how honest he was feeling each time) among the three. Occasionally, but fortunately not often, they'd all go out to a bar together and toast themselves for their evil accomplishments. Despite the thrill over getting away with this ongoing scheme, Phillip felt uneasy around his two accomplices, particularly Doug, whom he suspected had a cocaine habit.

Maybe that was why Doug needed the extra money. Really, all three of them had excuses and justifications for why they did what they did. For Nate, it was that the company that owned the apartment complex didn't pay him enough, and he had a wife and kids to provide for. In fact, all three of them did, and they each felt underappreciated at their jobs in terms of salary. Phillip's first inclination was to blame Nate; surely the cheap bastard could pay him more if he wanted to. But he just passed the buck and said that it was the fault of the parent company, not him. Maybe it was true.

Sometimes, Phillip regretted leaving his job at Fort Gordon, Augusta's local Army base. He'd worked there as a civilian, doing various maintenance jobs for the families that resided on post. It was pretty much the same job he did now, only surrounded by lots of loud-mouthed guys in camouflage with obnoxiously perfect posture. He'd grown increasingly annoyed with all of those big shots who were so full of themselves, but over time, he'd built up a loyal clientele among some of the ones who eventually moved off post and into regular homes elsewhere in the city.

He'd done good jobs for them, plus he got along with people easily. As far as everyone knew, he was a nice guy, and that helped earn him extra work. An officer would move to some nice subdivision in Augusta or Martinez, then call Phillip once they discovered what was wrong with the house and needed fixing. Things got even better when these same guys started recommending him to their neighbors or to other recently transferred soldiers who moved into new homes, and there would be even more money coming in.

Confident that it was a good decision, Phillip quit his job at Fort Gordon and tried to go into business for himself. But he quickly learned that freelance work wasn't as steady and reliable as he'd thought. His wife, Monica, bitched him out for this, and it wasn't long before he was looking for employment again and wound up with a lower paying job at Woodland Ridge. Things stabilized eventually, the work on the side and "the real job," as Monica called it, bringing in enough income to be comfortable, but just barely. They had two little girls to support, she reminded him almost daily.

The three men's joint criminal activities gave them a weird feeling of delight over getting away with what they did coupled with a sense of uneasiness and suspicion. Each man was pretty sure they had enough dirt on the others to keep any one of them from bailing out or, worse still, talking to the police.

Again, Phillip was pretty sure that Doug was into coke. The guy was just a little too hyper and animated, especially whenever he came back from the bathroom, a concentrated but slightly lifeless look in his eyes as he settled down and found his way back into the conversation. Nate, meanwhile, had hinted once or twice about getting extra money from the company that owned Woodland Ridge, plus there was that time that he mentioned something about "losing" rent checks from tenants, complete with the hand gesture that indicated quotation marks. Phillip tried to inquire further, but Nate changed the subject.

They all had their secrets, and while Phillip tried to pretend that he was strictly on the up-and-up with them, he knew that they — or at least Nate — suspected his alcoholism. And sure, if the guy wanted to believe that he secretly struggled with the bottle and went to AA meetings and all that crap, fine. It wasn't true, at least, not in the way his boss might be imagining.

When he'd been younger, Phillip had been an unapologetic drunk. He was the life of the party before failing out of college, and even then, he didn't stop drinking. People close to him pitied him, claiming that he hated his life and drank to escape it, but that wasn't really the case. Even if his life were shitty, he still had a good time with it. Maybe he was just too drunk to notice how bad things were. If that were escaping, he was fine with it. It was better than being miserable.

Little by little, his friends grew up and got married, and it was his turn to feel pity for them. Their wives would put an end to their partying, maybe not all at once, but eventually, making them settle down and become fathers. The wives themselves would get fat, then complain if the husbands said anything about it. Phillip didn't want the same fate for himself, but inevitably, it came.

He tried to play it off as finally deciding to grow up and change, and if anyone noticed that his and Monica's little girl Naomi was born just under eight months after their wedding, they didn't say anything. The woman already had a daughter from a previous marriage, a little brat named Charlotte, whom it took Phillip a long time to tame.

What happened between him and Charlotte was never spoken of. Monica didn't have a clue, and that's the way it would stay. As far as she was concerned, little Charlotte had just had a change of heart and decided to stop fighting against accepting Phillip as her dad. Her silence and withdrawn manner around him was interpreted as obedience, maybe even fear, but a healthy kind.

She wasn't the first girl he'd molested. As young as age fourteen, he had — as he put it when he thought about it all these years later — gotten practice on his little sister, who was ten at the time. He'd liked how it felt, but she hadn't, and when she threatened to tell on him to their parents, he turned it around on her. "It's your fault I did this. You tempted me, like Eve did to Adam with the apple. If you tell anyone, they're going to think you're a trashy little slut. Is that what you want? All your friends to start calling you Bridget the Slut?" He then taunted her, making up a repetitive song out of that nickname. She never told a soul as far as he knew.

He'd regretted it when he got older, feeling genuine shame. When Bridget was thirteen, he found out that she'd been raped by a boy in the grade above her at school, and he beat the boy so badly that he wound up in the hospital. Whether or not this made things better between him and his sister, he wasn't sure, but it definitely made him want to change his ways. He got right with God, joined the youth group at church, and prayed every night until he felt that he'd gotten the forgiveness he deserved.

What he struggled with in subsequent years was the latent desire that he was so ashamed of. He knew that it wasn't right to be attracted to prepubescent girls, but he still was. He didn't really like girls his own age, not in the way he knew he was supposed to. Sure, he could fake it, being all macho around his guy friends as they checked out the cheerleaders or whoever else. Maybe there was some genuine attraction, but it was rarely if ever returned. Phillip had always been a heavyset guy, and girls tended to pass him up for the hunkier types.

That built up resentment in him, but at the same time, on the very rare occasions when it did seem like a girl might like him, he saw it as a chance at true redemption. Maybe he could have a real, normal relationship, at least on a superficial level. But there was just something gross about girls past a certain age, once they got "all stupided up," as he put it, with their stinky-ass hairspray, make-up, perfume, and all that shit.

He sometimes wished that it could be possible for women to be more like little girls, a way to keep them the way they were before they started becoming all complicated and headstrong, shaving their legs and creating all these arbitrary rules and chivalrous bullshit. Little girls were easy to control; they didn't make you jump through hoops.

Phillip knew that these thoughts were supposedly wrong, and he learned very early on to keep them to himself. The one time he tried to brag to a friend of his at school about how he'd lost his virginity at such a young age and how it had happened, it was met with a horrified look coupled with: "Man, that's really screwed up. You did it with your *sister?"*

He backtracked and laughed it off. "Naw, man. I was just kidding. Wanted to see if you'd believe me." His friend just shook his head, mouth slightly ajar. "Ha ha! You did! Loser." It never came up again.

Maybe it was just society that was wrong. He'd heard about girls in Japan (or maybe it was China) getting married to adult men as young as age fourteen. Why couldn't they have that here in America? But he knew he wasn't going to be able to change an entire country's views on his own. If he weren't careful, he could end up in jail.

As an adult, Phillip struggled to settle into the roles assigned to him: husband, father, stepfather, sober person, repairman. There were other identities, the ones he kept secret and tried to tell himself weren't there: pervert, drunk, thief, liar.

With two children in the house, he'd eventually sworn off drinking, especially once he realized that it contributed to some of his darker, supposedly buried tendencies. Every now and then, his job would get too stressful, and he'd lapse back into drinking in order to feel better. That should have been the end of it, just a quick night of nostalgic indulgence to shake off the stress. But what was intended to be just a couple of drinks would turn into half a dozen or more.

Monica would complain, and he'd shout that bitch into submission, letting her stomp off to bed and slam the door. That was fine, he'd think defiantly, then have his way with Charlotte, swearing her to secrecy and shaming her into silence. "No one will believe you if you tell them about thish," he'd slur and whisper to her as she hid her face in her pillow afterwards, trying to keep from crying because he'd already fiercely warned her not to. "They'll think you're making it up to get addenshun… Attention. Lying. You liar. Filzzy… filthy liar. Don' be like tzhhat."

The morning after, waking up on the couch, Phillip would only vaguely remember these things. He'd try to tell himself that they were only dreams or fantasies, that he hadn't actually done them. Charlotte's averting of her dark eyes and acting like a frightened rabbit around him for days or sometimes weeks afterwards told him otherwise. This would cycle him back into promising himself that he'd never drink again and do such terrible things, God willing. It happened several times over the years. At least he'd never done anything to Naomi. She was way too young, only four years old by the time he'd started working at Woodland Ridge.

He wasn't sure what his involvement with the intricate scheme of thievery that he, Nate, and Doug had going on did to him in terms of his other vices. But in a weird sort of way, it seemed to help. He knew that it was wrong, stealing from these people and lying to their faces afterwards. Nate and Doug were evil opportunists, and he wasn't any better. But there was something oddly comforting in it, this idea he developed that maybe, if he continued to be involved in this particular version of badness, it would keep him from doing the other wrong things he sometimes felt tempted to do.

Maybe all men had a certain reservoir of evil within them. It was just there, something inside that could never be denied. So it had to be let out, expressed in whatever terrible ways it needed to be. If that were true, then maybe he could vent his evilness in this way, rather than backsliding into drinking or taking out his sexual frustrations on his twelve-year-old stepdaughter.

God, I hope so, Phillip thought with a sigh. His side projects, doing maintenance in other people's houses, had brought to him yet another thing besides supplemental income. These people had homes, families, and yes, daughters, some of whom were right in the age range that turned him on.

He hated admitting that to himself. The people liked him, parents and children alike, and there were times when he had to force himself not to stare too hard at the little girls who caught his eye. His hair and beard were a mix of premature grey and black, what some people called "salt and pepper," and that, combined with his rather large gut, made him look like a slightly younger version of Santa Claus. A girl in one of the homes he worked on even said so one time, nearly: "You're like Santa Claus's little brother!"

He laughed with her and went along with the joke, as did the parents. Further laughs were elicited when he let out a cheery "Ho ho ho!" But he stopped short of voicing the thought that ran through his head, something about getting the little girl to sit on his lap. That would have been too much of a giveaway. Later on, thinking back to this conversation, he wondered if he might somehow be able to work as a department store Santa during the Christmas season, but that wouldn't be a good idea, he decided. For one thing, that would involve letting little boys sit on his lap as well as little girls. He may have been a pedophile — he hated that word; it sounded so clinical — but he wasn't a queer.

The second week of July hadn't been a good one so far. Nate was stressed out, worried over not hearing from Doug for a few days. He'd tried calling him both at home and at work, but there was no answer at either number and no reply to the messages he'd left. At L&K Security, Nate could understand why no one else had picked up the phone; each of the agents there had their own phone lines. He didn't understand why Doug's wife or even kids hadn't answered until he remembered that they were out of town visiting his mother-in-law. Still, that didn't explain why Doug himself seemed to be missing.

"Calm down," Phillip said to Nate. "Maybe he's just busy."

"He's always busy," Nate practically growled, glancing at the calendar on his office wall. "But he never takes this long to call back."

Phillip knew why Nate was particularly worried this time, but it was on more than one level. The three had agreed long ago that if any one of them got caught by the police committing their various criminal activities, they wouldn't rat the other two out. Even so — and none of them ever said this aloud — they all knew that this promise might not hold up in reality if the situation were to come about. There were things like interrogations, plea bargains, or just simple betrayal. No honor among thieves, and all that.

"You think he got caught doing drugs?" Phillip asked, trying to keep the playfulness out of his voice. Nate glared at him. "Don't think I didn't notice. Guy's a walking time bomb, I think."

Nate's angry look softened as he sighed and put his head in his hands, elbows resting on his desk. "I hope you're wrong." He looked back up again, smearing his hands back across his face and then looking off to the side as he sighed more heavily, clearly exasperated. "But then, given what's been happening, I halfway hope that's what it is."

Phillip knew what he meant, but he didn't really approve of the thought. This vampire crap had started around town again, folks claiming to see vampires and lots of other people going missing. It had been going on for a few days, and Nate was pretty freaked out about it. He didn't want to give any details, but apparently he'd either seen someone get killed when this stuff happened two years ago or just knew someone who'd died back then. Phillip was curious, but he could tell that prying too much would be a bad idea.

Regardless, Nate was clearly concerned that Doug might have become a victim of this latest wave of vampire attacks, if that's what they really were anyway. Maybe this was also shell shock; the guy had been in Vietnam, after all. Phillip sometimes suspected that his claims like "the things I saw back there" or "you'd just laugh if I told you because you'd think I was making it up" were full of shit; he'd heard plenty of malarkey like that from other people during his time working at Fort Gordon, some of which might have been true but could just as easily have been bravado. But the more forgiving side of him wanted to give Nate the benefit of the doubt.

After a couple of days of this, Nate was such a basket case and so thoroughly annoying that Phillip decided that the best thing to do would be to distract him. They'd been planning to rewire the cable TV in his house the following weekend, but he took the initiative and insisted that they go ahead and do it Tuesday night.

Cable TV was great, this paid service that got you twenty channels on your TV instead of the standard three or four broadcast stations. Lots of people had this if they could afford it, but the shitty scheme that the local cable company pulled to get even more money was that if a family wanted this capability on more than one TV in their house, you were supposed to get them to send a technician to come out and do all kinds of work to install extra jacks in the walls for each TV. It was overly complicated, unnecessary, and worst of all, expensive. All one really had to do was run extra coaxial cable from the main jack to all the other necessary rooms in the house using splitters, something Phillip was capable of doing for a lot cheaper. There was some crawling around in basements and drilling holes in the floors to make it work, but it was a much better deal than letting CSRA Cable screw you out of an extra hundred bucks. Phillip would do it for less than half that much for his friends.

After work, the two of them went to Phillip's house to have dinner with his family. While they'd originally talked about just each going home and then Phillip going over to Nate's later, plans changed. He didn't say so outright, but Phillip had an idea that with the way Nate was acting, he might take out his stress on his family. So to spare them that, he brought his boss home, correctly predicting that being forced to be polite in the Cooke household would be yet another useful distraction for him.

Everyone got along well. Monica was the perfect host, all smiles despite the fact that she'd grumbled over the phone when Phillip told her that he'd be bringing someone extra for dinner, which meant that she'd have to be sure to cook enough for five. The girls were well behaved; even Naomi managed to keep from acting up too much. Of course, she demanded attention like any five-year-old would, all proud of herself for having recently been promoted to sitting in a "big people chair" as opposed to the wooden high chair that she'd been using since she was a toddler. She still needed some extra pillows in order to be tall enough to reach her food, though.

Charlotte was her usual melancholy self, but she was still courteous enough. She knew to do that whenever they had company. Phillip could have reprimanded her when he noticed traces of make-up on her that he could tell she hadn't quite managed to wipe off, despite his having forbidden her to wear any at all. "All the other girls my age can wear it," she'd insisted, but he'd been adamant. He didn't like her trying to do herself up and look like a grown-up. If nothing else, it made him uncomfortable. But it wouldn't have done anybody any good to make a scene, so he decided to let it slide for tonight. She was probably putting it on with her other friends at school, then taking it off before coming home. The next time he caught her defying him like that, he'd punish her for it. His house, his rules.

Phillip and Nate left the house later than planned, having gotten caught up in after-dinner conversation with Monica. It made Phillip a little uneasy how much she seemed to want to keep things going, like she was trying to impress his boss. Maybe she was just being the good wife, talking up Phillip's reputation for being a good repairman around town and all that, but he couldn't help but feel insecure that she might be trying to flirt instead.

At any rate, they swung by the Radio Shack store in Augusta Mall to pick up the cables and connectors that they needed. Because they knew that it would take a couple of hours to get all of the work done rewiring the house, it had been decided that Phillip would spend the night in Nate's guest room. Phillip was fine with that, and it gave him a sense of satisfaction that his boss felt that comfortable with him doing so.

Sometimes, he found it funny how people naively trusted him, letting him into their homes. He knew how dark he was on the inside, the desires he felt that he usually kept in check but still thought of acting upon. His feelings on this fluctuated between stealthy triumph and hidden shame. Nate only had a young son — no daughters — so there was no chance of any temptation there. Even so, he knew that he wouldn't be able to turn off his "radar" upon entering Nate's house, eyeballing the place for things worth stealing. He probably wouldn't ever get the chance to actually do anything like that, nor did he actually want to, but he was curious all the same.

Nate froze in his tracks when he heard the first scream. It was pretty far away, but not by much. They were in the mall parking lot on their way back to the truck, and Phillip tried to be dismissive of the sound.

"Come on," he said, "it was probably just some dumb teenage girl making a joke. Let's…"

He was interrupted by another scream, this one obviously from a man and much nearer, followed by more yelling as people began to panic. Nearby, he could see them running around among the rows of cars as they tried to avoid whatever it was that was happening.

"Shit," Nate hissed, ducking his head down. He began to sprint across the pavement, his hands waving over his head as he ran in what Phillip realized was the same direction as before, hoping to reach the truck. Everything sunk in very quickly: Nate was right, and there really were vampires in Augusta. They were in the middle of an attack. This must be what it felt like to be in a war.

Phillip thundered after him, also hoping to reach the truck in time, suddenly feeling stupid for insisting on holding onto the plastic shopping bags that held the equipment they'd purchased. It seemed so trivial in light of the fact that people were being killed all around them, but he held on to them just the same. The weight of the heavy rolls of cable bounced against his legs as he ran.

And then Nate went down, skidding onto the pavement immediately after some small black shape zoomed onto his neck and remained there as the man quivered, then went limp. Phillip could see it, clear as day under the bright glow of the purplish streetlights, a bat feeding on his employer, his friend. Nate's blue eyes stared up into nothing, his face fixed in a mask of terror. The good-looking, dark-haired guy who had been the charming, professional face of Woodland Ridge was now becoming a pale corpse.

Phillip broke away from the horrible sight, realizing that his breathing had turned into some kind of repetitive vacuum cleaner-like sound. Was this hyperventilating? He'd always heard of it, something other people did, like when they were too scared to get onto an airplane or something like that. He was pretty sure he'd seen that happen on TV. But here he was, apparently doing the same thing.

There was nothing he could do for Nate. He was already dead. So he did the only thing he could do, which was to continue to run for the safety of his truck, hoping that none of the vampires would catch him before he got there. To his surprise, he managed to yank the door open and clamber inside, slamming it behind him and shoving the locks on both sides of the vehicle down before collapsing onto the vinyl seats, terrified out of his mind.

Still shaking, he straightened up and looked around, certain that at any second, one of those horrible bats might come beating against his windshield or the windows, demanding to be let in. But he appeared to be safe, and so he fumbled the keys out of his pocket, started up the truck, and sped out of there as fast as he could.

He was barely even aware of it until he was about halfway there, but Phillip realized that he was driving to the liquor store. It was some kind of subconscious thing, he guessed, maybe a defense mechanism. His breathing had more or less returned to normal, but he was still scared out of his mind, traumatized by what he'd seen and what he knew could have happened. He kept running it over and over in his head, then found himself feeling short of breath again when he began to imagine that bat preying on him instead of Nate.

Everything felt like he was sleepwalking. He faked politeness with the cashier as he made his purchase, almost wanting to tell the guy what had happened but also not daring to talk about it. No need to involve anyone else. He just needed to be alone with his thoughts.

He considered drinking from the bottle of vodka right there in the parking lot, but he was afraid that someone might see him, worst of all the police. So instead, he drove over to the church near his house. He'd known since his early twenties that the police never patrolled its parking lot. Maybe they naively thought that no one would be so low as to commit a sin there, like public drinking. It was a good place to hang out at night undisturbed.

And so he did, his nerves slowly numbing under the influence of the alcohol. It didn't do much to keep his mind from racing, though. What was he supposed to do now? Should he even bother to go to work in the morning? His boss was dead. Maybe he should call the parent company and let them know. Should he talk to the police and tell them what he'd seen? No, fuck that. No police.

His mind ran in circles, becoming more fuzzy as time went on. The vodka burned his throat, but he didn't care. After a while, that became numb, too, his vision more blurry. Pretty soon, he'd have to stop drinking or else risk becoming too drunk to make it home. He knew that Monica wasn't expecting him back at the house, but maybe he could sneak in and pass out on the couch. He could explain things to her in the morning.

But there was another feeling building in him. He knew it would probably come, and eventually, he felt that familiar, weird tingle deep down that happened when he knew that he was about to do something he shouldn't. Charlotte would hate him for it, but then, she already did, so what was the difference? He needed the release, plain and simple. And then, feeling even more ashamed, he began wondering if Naomi was old enough to start taking on the burden as well.

CHAPTER EIGHTEEN

FRAGMENTS

Pages from a notebook belonging to Susanna Michelle Young

7/11/85

So Robert's dead. I'm not sure how I feel about that. Relieved? Guilty? I don't know. I thought I would have more to say in here, but now I don't feel like it.

12/23/85

Home for Christmas. Again, I thought I had something to say, but when I try to, the words don't seem to want to come. Maybe if I try doing them in haiku? That could be fun. Let's try it.

Home for Christmas now
Don't really care what I get
Presents are for kids

Halfway through college
Majoring in English sucks
Wasting Dad's money

Never mind. This is stupid and getting depressing. Maybe I'll write in here again, maybe not.

6/29/86

~~Turning 21 in a little under a month~~

Turning 21
in a little under a
month. Like it matters

He was in control
The entire time. Now what?

CHAPTER NINETEEN

AMELIA'S STORY

Amelia missed her father. But as far as she was concerned, she was the only person alive who still did. Oh, sure, her mother had been upset when he died; they all were. But the older Amelia got, the more resentful she became.

Bitterness was nothing new to her. Her life over the past few years had been nothing but one crappy experience after another, and it seemed like that started the night she and her mother got the news of her father's death. It had been less than a month before her ninth birthday, which she spent the majority of crying her eyes out because her daddy wasn't there.

There had been a lot of crying in those days. Her little sister, Megan, had been four at the time, old enough to know that Daddy was gone and to be sad about that, but still too young to understand everything that had happened. Mom — they'd both called her "Mommy" back then — had been pretty hysterical, her repeated cries of "What am I going to do?" echoing in Amelia's mind to this day. But looking back on it, she saw that as rather selfish. It was like she was more concerned with herself than with comforting her two little girls.

And Mom did figure out what to do: She uprooted what was left of their family, moved them all to Savannah where the rest of her relatives were, then got remarried. Amelia had never forgiven her for that.

"I need for you to be okay with his," her mother had insisted on more than one occasion. "Okay?" Then more firmly: *"Okay?"* Something in her tone seemed to forbid anything other than compliance. As time went on, Amelia realized that even if she hadn't been "okay" with these things, it wouldn't have mattered.

The first time she could remember her mom saying that to her, Amelia had in fact been very much in favor of the decision and barely needed persuading. It was shortly after her first day—what turned out to be her only day — at her new school. It had been a horrible experience, and she was glad to leave the place behind.

She'd felt quite the opposite when she'd applied and been accepted a few months earlier. St. Joseph's was a good school; she knew that not everyone could get into it, and you had to be smart enough to pass special tests in order to go there. Her father had been so proud of her and shared her enthusiasm for being accepted to such a prestigious place. It was expensive because it was a private school, but apparently that had something to do with why she would get such a good education there. She didn't fully understand all of the details, but she adopted her parents' opinions easily.

After Daddy's death, money had been something that her mother had complained about increasingly: Words like "income," "insurance," and "tuition" were thrown around quite a bit. There was even talk of not letting her go to St. Joseph's after all, but Amelia insisted, and her mother relented. It was what Daddy would have wanted.

But almost as soon as she got there, Amelia regretted it. She'd heard some people talk about how being the new kid at school was scary, but she'd blown this off.

Before her father's death, she'd been looking forward to this, to making new friends, which she hoped would be exciting. Now things were different, and she was a lot more sad, but maybe things would get better in time. Everyone — the grown-ups in her life, anyway — told her it would.

That first morning, no one would talk to her. Everyone looked at her strangely, some of the girls even whispering to each other behind cupped hands as they looked at her with sideways glances. The teachers were friendly to her, and while that had been enough for her at the start, she felt increasingly out of place.

Not long into the day, everything went to hell. The teacher — whose name Amelia already couldn't remember nowadays — started asking the class what they'd done over the summer. Her blood ran cold; she certainly didn't want to be called on. What was she going to say? *Hi, I'm Amelia, and my dad got killed by vampires?*

Even worse, some of the other kids brought up that very thing. This one idiot, some boy, even seemed to think it was cool. "All these people died!" He said it like it was something exciting, not the horrible tragedy that it was. Her father wasn't the only person who had been killed that week, she knew. But his death was the one that mattered to her the most, maybe the only one that truly did.

Some other girl started bickering with the boy about it, claiming that the whole thing wasn't even real. But it sure as hell was real to Amelia. She hadn't spent the past two months crying over nothing. All of the pain flooded back, the recollection of how he'd been at the racetrack that night taking pictures for his job at the newspaper, something some woman he knew had gotten him to do. Her mother had always resented this arrangement for some reason; Amelia wasn't clear on the specifics.

But it had happened, and her father had died along with the dozens, maybe hundreds of people that night and the following several days as the vampire attacks continued. Some of this she learned later, not this particular summer, including the fact that some people seemed to be in denial that vampires were involved at all. She knew better, but she also really didn't like thinking about it.

And yet, here it was, that very debate popping up in her classroom, everyone talking about the one thing she wanted to avoid. It was too much for her, and she broke down in tears, embarrassment making her wish she could hide under her desk. Before she knew it, she felt a hand on her shoulder, which made her jump. Through blurry tears, she looked up and saw the tall figure of the teacher, who gently asked her, "Amelia, are you okay?"

It sounded like the dumbest question in the world, and a wave of anger rushed through her as she fought back the urge to scream, *No I'm not okay! What do you think?* But that would just make things worse, and she restrained herself.

Actually, no, that wasn't how it happened at the time. That was how she thought about the incident later when she would replay it in her mind. The disbelief over the seemingly oblivious question, her imagined response — all of that came later. In reality, she'd been too upset and scared to be that defiant.

Instead, she just shook her head and then covered her face, wishing she could disappear. It was like the ostrich trying to hide its head in the sand: If she couldn't see all the other kids glaring at her, that made them seem less threatening. Or it should have. Still, to her credit, the teacher persisted not only in trying to comfort her, but doing so as quietly as possible. Sometimes she hated the woman when she remembered this story, but deep down, she knew that she was just trying to help.

"Sweetheart," the woman's voice hummed in her ear, "this is about what happened to your father, isn't it." The question sounded like a statement.

Of course it is, she bitterly thought in her angry recreations of the interaction later. But in fact, she'd just sniffled and whispered, "Yeah. I'm sorry." What was she apologizing for?

She felt the hand on her shoulder disappear, only to reappear on her wrist with a gentle tug. "Come with me," the soft voice said, and with that, she was being led from her desk to the classroom door, all eyes upon her. She did her best to keep her face hidden.

Amelia made less of an effort to fight back her tears as they talked outside the classroom door, further embarrassed by the snot that was beginning to drip from her nose. She wiped at it with her fingers, only to find that there was nothing to wipe those on but her jeans.

"I'm very sorry about what happened in there," the teacher said. "Kids can be… well…" She paused. "And I'm sorry about what happened to your father. It wasn't all that long ago, was it?"

"No," she said, shaking her head quickly and taking a deep breath. At least talking made her have to stop bawling. "'Bout two months, I guess."

The woman's intimidating form towered over her, certainly bigger than her mom, maybe even as tall as her dad had been. Noticing this made her want to break down again. But for some reason, Amelia's latest statement seemed to shock the woman, causing her to put her hands to her mouth with a gasp. She squatted down again, like she had by the desk earlier.

Looking Amelia straight in her eyes, she asked, "Your father… did he…?" She looked away for a moment, then back at her. "Was he one of the ones who passed away because of the…?"

Just say it, you cowardly bitch, Amelia's older self said when recollecting this. "Yes," she whimpered, tears overwhelming her again as her body began to quake. "The vampires did it."

"Oh, bless your heart," the woman said with a sigh, and she leaned forward and hugged her. It was an odd feeling, being hugged by a stranger like this, but it certainly wasn't the first time it had happened. There had been plenty of that during her father's funeral, which was another memory she didn't like reliving.

All of a sudden, something occurred to Amelia, and she pushed back from the embrace. "How did you know my daddy died?"

"Oh," the teacher said with an odd expression, sort of a smile, but also sad. "Mr. Neal told me." This was the school principal, whom Amelia had met before during her application process. She liked him; he was a friendly man with a shiny, partly bald head. Something about him exuded warmth and cheer, and she'd always felt at ease in his presence. "He thought it would be a good thing for me to know in case... well, in case it came up."

Like now, when I broke down and made a fool of myself in front of everyone, Amelia thought later on. But instead of saying that, she just looked down, her eyes focusing on a dark crack between two slabs of grey pavement.

"Look," the teacher said, and Amelia faced her once more. "You're upset, I know. And it's okay. Maybe it would be a good idea for you to go home for the day. You won't miss too much class material, and we can catch you up when you get back."

A wave of relief went through Amelia as she quickly nodded. She certainly didn't want to go back inside and face all of those mean kids.

The drive home was an awkward affair. Her mom seemed mad, but Amelia didn't actually get the sense that she was in trouble. Megan, meanwhile, seemed oblivious to everything, bouncing around in the backseat while she quietly talked to a bright green puppet in the shape of a frog wearing a bow tie.

"I should have known it wouldn't work out," her mother said with a scowl, staring ahead through the windshield.

Amelia had told her everything that had happened, including how she got lost on the way to the principal's office and had an encounter in the hall with the janitor, a big black man who'd scared her at first. He'd turned out to be friendly enough, helping her find her way, but most of the time when he'd spoken to her, she couldn't understand what he was saying.

"That was probably just his dialect," her mother said dismissively. "You shouldn't be so quick to judge."

Amelia didn't even know what that meant. Ignoring her confusion over the unfamiliar words, she continued her story about how the lady in the office had been kind of mean to her, but Mr. Neal had been nice. "Then he told the mean lady to call you and come pick me up."

What she didn't tell her mother was what had gone through her head before she'd gotten lost. While she'd initially been looking forward to seeing the principal again and being comforted by him, it occurred to her that it was weird that he'd told her teacher about her father's death. Mommy had made it clear to Amelia that she shouldn't go around telling people that, something about "keeping it in the family." Whether or not that made sense, she'd gone along with it.

She was okay with Mr. Neal knowing, but why had he blabbed it to the teacher? Did everyone else know, too? And if all of the kids and maybe even the woman in the office knew, why had they all been so mean to her? These thoughts occurred to her again during the ride home, but they were interrupted by her mother, who announced something that would turn out to be life-changing.

"Look, I've been thinking about this, and I really think it's the best thing for all of us." She paused, pursing her lips. "Amelia, I'd like for us to move. Me, you, and Megan."

"Move? Where?"

"To Savannah. I just don't think that this is the right place for us anymore. Not after all that's happened."

Amelia had heard her mother use that phrase plenty of times before as well: "after all that's happened." It had come into play a lot since Daddy had died. And in that moment, it seemed to make more sense than ever. "After all that's happened" meant a lot of bad things: the loss of her father, the constant sadness and crying, the problems Mommy had worried over and complained about like money, and even the experience at school that day.

Her mother went on talking persuasively about how moving back to where she'd grown up would be good for all of them. There was something almost pleading in her voice. "I need you to be okay with this decision," she said. "Okay?"

Amelia thought for a moment. It didn't take long. If moving somewhere else could fix things, if it would make everything stop hurting so much, then she was definitely for it. She'd never moved away before, though she'd heard of other people who had. It even sounded exciting. "Okay," she said decisively, not knowing that she would hate herself for doing so later.

"Meals on Wheels!
Meals on Wheels!
More and more food for
Meals on Wheels!"

The group of five or six girls bobbed up and down as they sang this song over and over, tormenting Amelia Wheeler. It was a stupid nickname, "Meals on Wheels," based on both her real name and the fact that she was heavyset. She wasn't even sure what the real Meals on Wheels thing was about, just that it existed, something to do with giving food to poor people, or old people, or maybe poor old people. She didn't care. All she knew was that this was how these girls in the upper grade pointed out that she was fat and made a huge spectacle of it.

Growing up, Amelia had never been particularly thrilled with her body, but she hadn't been taught to hate it until the fifth grade. Aside from being heavier than other girls, she was also taller; she'd been the tallest person in her class almost her entire life. It hadn't been that big of a deal to her early on, but the older she got, the more people pointed it out. Often, strangers assumed that she was older than she was, equating her larger size with an older age.

Again, she didn't see anything wrong with this from first through third grade, thinking that it was kind of cool to be so far ahead of everyone else in terms of growing up. She'd even started wearing a training bra before any of the other girls in her class in fourth grade. But her pride in this supposed achievement quickly turned to shame when she found out that the other, prettier girls in class began whispering about it behind her back like it was a bad thing, like something was wrong with her.

The fact of the matter was simply this: Amelia was awkward. What few friendships she managed to make felt empty, just like the rest of her life. Things had been so much better when her father was still alive, or even if they hadn't really, things were so crappy these days that she tended to think of her life before the summer of '83 as all sunshine and rainbows in comparison.

Moving from Augusta to Savannah had seemed like a good thing at first. She hadn't minded staying with Grandma and Grandpa, nor had Megan. It had always been a good time when visiting them in the past. Even sharing a room with her little sister wasn't so bad, at least, not in the beginning. After a while, Megan did get on her nerves, and they fought, but then, sometimes sisters did that. Her mom, meanwhile, seemed more gloomy.

"I feel like a failure," she overheard her mother say to Grandma one afternoon.

"You're not," the gentle old woman said. Amelia had always liked her. Nearly every time her name came up, a memory of the smell of pound cake would spring up in her mind. It was one of her favorite things to have. "You've still got two beautiful little girls."

"But I can't do enough for them!" Mom practically shrieked. It was weird seeing her like this, even after all this time. Before her father's death, Amelia had often been afraid of her mother, this strong, disciplinary figure who would yell her head off over the slightest misstep.

But since the tragedy, she'd seemed a lot more fragile. It was one of the reasons why Amelia went along with her "I need you to be okay with this" pleadings early on, like when she'd insisted on sending her to Kellerman Elementary, a public school. This disappointed Amelia a little; she'd been looking forward to attending private school since that's what her father had been setting her up for her all that time. Even though St. Joseph's in Augusta hadn't worked out, she'd assumed that she'd attend fourth grade at a similarly good school once they resettled in Savannah. But Mom insisted that they couldn't afford it.

Kellerman was kind of okay, but not for long. Given what had happened her first and only day at St. Joseph's, she'd been more shy about trying to make friends, but some encouragement from her grandmother prompted her to at least try. Quite a few of the kids came from single-parent households, something she was still trying to get used to herself, but she thought that maybe this could be a starting point for some friendships, a commonality. Most of these kids' family situations were the result of broken marriages, though, not death.

Amelia ignored her mother's earlier advice about keeping what had happened to her father a secret, which turned out to be a mistake. Some of her new friends were sympathetic when she told them that her father had died, but once she started talking about vampires, things changed. People didn't believe her; they thought she was just making things up to get attention, and she was shunned as a result.

Looking back on things once she got to her next school after Kellerman, Amelia wondered if her being perceived of as a liar wasn't the only reason why she'd had so much trouble fitting in. Maybe she really was ugly. She'd never thought of herself as unattractive before, but the rich, snotty kids at Savannah Prep made it quite clear to her that she was.

By this point, her adolescence was in full swing, and she wished she could will her body to stop what it was doing. She would have given anything to remain below five feet tall and under a hundred pounds. Everyone, boys and girls alike, loved to point out how weird she was, and not just the ones in her own class. As cruel as the kids back at Kellerman had been, that turned out to seem downright amateurish compared to what she experienced at Prep.

And so Amelia Wheeler learned how to be mean. She tried to be cold and indifferent to criticism, accepting her lot in life as a misfit and being resigned to it. Maybe it was even good that she was a weirdo; she'd gone through a phase where people would tell her, "You're weird," and she would respond sarcastically, "Thank you." At least part of her meant that, and she got a tiny bit of satisfaction from their confused reactions.

After a while, she became more aggressive. If the other kids were going to keep pointing out what was wrong with her, then she was damn well going to turn around and start doing the same thing to them. Graham had a stutter, which made him sound like an idiot whenever he was called on in class. Lisa wore the same pair of jeans three days in a row without washing them, so they probably stank. Kristin started wearing make-up, but it looked stupid and made her big-ass nose look like an arrow pointing downward toward her lips, which were a jarring shade of bright red that didn't suit her.

Even physical aggression became a thing: If people were going to keep branding her as some big, fat, lumbering giant, then so be it. She'd bump into people in the hallways, sometimes unintentionally but not always, and she wouldn't even apologize, not anymore. Her desire to be a petite, dainty thing had long passed.

Her bitterness wasn't confined to what went on at school. Her family life sucked every bit as much. The whole reason that she — and Megan, now that she was old enough — were at this stuck-up school full of jerks was because of Peter, the asshole that her mother had married.

Amelia wasn't clear on where this guy had come from, how he'd made his way into her mother's life. It was something that her grandmother had been involved in, some kind of set-up. Learning that made her hate the old bat from that point on. Sure, it meant that Mom could stop complaining about money on a daily basis; the man was obviously very wealthy, the owner of some construction company in town.

There was, Amelia felt, an all too short dating phase that quickly led to an engagement, the beginning of which was punctuated by yet another one of those infuriating approval-seeking conversations with her mom.

"I've started seeing this man, and he's very nice, and... well... I need you to be okay with this."

Amelia looked at her, arms folded. Her father had been dead for just under a year.

"Okay?" her mother asked, her bug eyes glaring.

Amelia frowned, staring back. *No, it's not okay,* she wanted to say.

"Okay?" Her mother was adamant, demanding a response that Amelia didn't want to give.

But she did anyway. "Fine."

To be fair, Peter — or Pete, as he insisted the girls call him in the early days — probably wasn't that bad of a guy. Amelia would only admit this to herself much later on. He was rich, well off, and exactly what their mother needed in order to get back into the status of being a comfortable, married woman. That's what she had been before when Amelia's father had still been alive.

She never told anyone why, but she preferred calling him Peter because she'd learned that this was also a slang term for a man's penis. As far as she was concerned, this guy was a dick, and she would never accept him as a replacement for her real father. So naturally, it pissed her off when Megan did, even going so far as to start calling him "Dad" a few months into the new marriage.

It disgusted her the way the little brat sucked up to him. Amelia's feelings for her sister had always been back and forth, but now she definitely hated her. When she'd been younger, she was jealous of the way Megan had inherited their father's features, particularly his pale skin and red hair. That had looked good on him; he was tall and handsome. But Megan was an ugly little troll, the freckles on her face and arms making it look like someone had splashed her with tomato juice. How dare she betray the memory of their real father in exchange for toys and trinkets from this new imposter?

Amelia benefitted from this newfound wealth as well, but she wasn't happy about it. The expensive, brand-name clothes she found herself wearing did nothing to allay the criticisms of her appearance from the other kids. Savannah Prep, while it was certainly a nicer school than the one she'd been at for fourth grade, turned out to be full of jerks. Even the camera she was given for her eleventh birthday didn't do much to change her mind about how much she despised her stepfather.

She'd wanted to pursue photography in order to follow in her own father's footsteps, but this had been impossible before Mom married Peter. "That's an expensive hobby," she'd said dismissively when Amelia had asked for a camera for Christmas. And then, once she had it, she barely used it. There just wasn't a lot she felt like taking pictures of. It would prove to be an asset later, but for a completely different reason.

"Oh, don't listen to them," Tamara said. "All right, so you're not the skinniest girl in the world. But you still have a pretty face!"

It was a backhanded compliment, but she'd take it. "Thanks," Amelia said, trying not to roll her eyes. By about halfway through sixth grade, she'd managed to make at least a couple of friends, but she still wasn't sure how much she really liked them. Tamara was a misfit like her, one of only a handful of black people in the entire school.

Amelia didn't really understand the dynamics of race, prejudice, and things like that, nor was it clear to her why private schools had so very few black students in them compared to the public schools she'd known. Tamara's family was, like her own, well off, so maybe that had something to do with it. But there was something about the girl that bothered her, making her seem kind of incongruous, and not because of her skin color. Well, not exactly.

She'd known black people at her previous public schools, and they'd seemed a lot different. They weren't quite as sharp-witted and vibrant as the ones she'd seen in sitcoms like *Diff'rent Strokes, Good Times,* and the like, though they did sometimes try to be that funny. But for the most part, they were just regular people. To be fair, it wasn't like her own family or the other white people she knew were hilarious like the ones on *Mork & Mindy* or *Mr. Belvedere.* Anyone could seem a lot funnier with a laugh track accompanying them, but that wasn't real life. Hell, real life wasn't funny at all most of the time.

Even so, she could remember certain kids, like LaTonya at Kellerman or Wallace at the school before that, and they'd seemed a lot more, well, *fun,* at least in retrospect. They were the ones who would crack jokes in class and often get in trouble with the teachers, and while she'd found that annoying and disruptive at the time, Amelia kind of missed it now. She'd always been one of the smart kids, so she'd also been more reserved and well behaved. But what she wouldn't give for one of those witty, smart-mouthed kids by her side these days…

Instead, she'd wound up with Tamara and Meredith. They were okay, but not great. She'd fallen in with them because all three were outcasts, the girls that no one else wanted much to do with. The teachers adored them, but by this age, that was no longer an asset. Being polite (for the most part) and studious got you good grades, but it just made the less intelligent kids — that was the majority of them, Meredith pointed out as nicely as she could — jealous and even more mean. By this point, Amelia was mostly numb to that. She might have even felt sorry for them if she could have been bothered to.

Both Tamara and Meredith did their best to keep Amelia's vitriol at bay. It kind of worked. At least being able to hang out with them and vent seemed to help a little, but she still kept things from them. There was Meredith, the pale-skinned, dark-haired, lanky girl who for God knows what reason insisted that she wanted to grow up to become a nun — maybe she'd seen *The Sound of Music* too many times. And there was Tamara, a black girl who was so soft spoken and gentle that she seemed just as white, at least compared to Amelia's memory of cooler girls like LaTonya.

Perhaps it was unfair of her to think of them in such negative ways. But after all these years, she couldn't help but be critical; it was just in her nature. Even though she'd actually managed to lose some weight by seventh grade, everyone still thought of her as the fat girl, and sure, maybe she was still kind of dumpy and awkward. It probably wouldn't matter how much weight she lost.

"You do!" Tamara continued. "I wish I had a wide, expressive smile like yours."

"You're saying I have a big mouth?" She said it like it was a joke, but deep down, she was beginning to feel more self-conscious.

"No!" Tamara laughed.

Amelia sighed. "Well, pretty smile or not, that's going to get ruined soon, thanks to Peter." She spat out the name in her usual manner. "I'm really dreading the idea of getting braces. The guy actually thinks he's doing me a favor by insisting on that!"

Meredith, who already had braces herself, blushed. Whenever she did that — which was often because she was so easily embarrassed — it was like her entire body turned beet red. "That's not..." She paused, clearing her throat. "I mean, they're not *that* bad. Well, sometimes. Yes, okay, so they hurt when the orthodontist tightens them."

"Yeah, I'm really looking forward to being in pain all the time," Amelia said sarcastically. "And I'm sure that Simone and the Anorexic Whores will find a way to incorporate some insult like 'Metal Mouth' into their stupid little songs."

This was in reference to the mean girls in the grade above them. For reasons Amelia couldn't fathom, Simone had fixated on her as early as fifth grade, picking on her at recess for being fat and making up the stupid "Meals on Wheels" nickname and its accompanying song. She tried to ignore them, but it didn't work. Things escalated as the years went on, Simone and her group of bitchy little friends sometimes expanding on their musical taunts with extra verses. It was idiotic, but it still hurt. Naturally, this abuse was picked up by some of the kids in Amelia's own grade as well, leading to school being an overall miserable experience.

The teachers weren't any help, either. They would just say useless things about ignoring the "teasing," which sounded like such a trite word compared to how angry it made Amelia feel. And there wasn't any point in getting into physical fights with Simone or any of the others to try to make them stop; she'd learned that early on. Prep was particularly strict about fighting among the students, and multiple incidents could get you kicked out of school.

Back at Kellerman near the end of fourth grade, Amelia had come to blows with one particularly mean boy named Justin. It had been shortly after her mother had gotten married to Peter.

"Bullcrap," Justin sneered at her. "There's no way your grandfather got run over by an eighteen-wheeler and didn't get killed."

"Yes he did! You don't know what you're talking about!" Amelia knew that she was exaggerating: The truth was that the man had gotten into a car accident and come out okay, and yes, there was a truck involved, but no, it wasn't actually a semi. But this was something she experimented with from time to time, people's credulity. They'd already refused to believe that her father had been killed by vampires, but even as unlikely as that sounded, it was the truth. So every now and then, she liked to see just what people were willing to believe. This didn't do a lot for her reputation.

"It's just something else you're saying so people will think you're cool," Justin went on. "Like when you said your little sister was double-jointed and could twist her arm around over and over without breaking her elbow."

"Shut up," she said. Megan was in fact double-jointed, but this talent was much more limited than Amelia's tall tale: She could bend her thumb at an odd angle over the back of her hand and flare out one of her pinky toes.

"In fact, I'll bet that your dad isn't even dead! He probably just ran out on you and your mom because she's a lying witch like you, and you don't want to admit they got divorced."

"I said shut up!" Amelia shrieked, seeing red. Before she knew what she was doing, she'd punched the short little shit right in his face, noticing just before her fist made impact how the freckles on his screwed up nose reminded her of Megan. The blow sent Justin toppling backwards onto the playground, and he went running off to one of the teachers, unsuccessfully hiding his tears as he cried out in pain.

She'd gotten in trouble, but upon hearing the whole story, Ms. Tremaine had sided with Amelia, saying that Justin had been unreasonably cruel to her and had provoked the attack. There was some lecturing to both of them about fighting not solving anything, but Justin never bothered her again, not for the rest of the school year.

Unfortunately, this kind of justice wasn't available at Savannah Prep. When Amelia's repeated taunting by Simone and her friends eventually led to a similarly physical confrontation — Amelia delighted in the way that the older but smaller girl started shrieking, *"Stop it! Stop!"* as she pinned her down and got in what few blows she could — there was no sympathy for her from the teachers this time. Instead, Amelia was painted as the aggressor, stupidly advised that her only defense should be to repeat the useless mantra: "Sticks and stones may break my bones, but words will never hurt me." That was complete bullshit.

"Just take a lot of aspirin," Meredith advised during their discussion about Amelia's dread over her impending braces. "That's what I do. It helps."

"But not too much," Tamara said. "I heard that every aspirin you take makes the inside of your stomach bleed an entire teaspoon full of blood."

Amelia's eyes went wide. "Are you serious?"

"Totally!"

Meredith had gone paler than usual, if that were even possible. "That's not true," she said, shrinking back. Then she shuddered. "Gross."

A wicked smile began to form on Amelia's face, and she leaned forward in her desk, peering down toward Meredith's belly. "And how many aspirins have you had today?"

"Stop it!" she insisted, putting a hand to her torso.

"You know," Tamara said to Amelia, also getting an evil look in her eyes, "if the braces get to be too much for you, you could always do what I heard this one boy did."

"What's that?"

"He decided he just couldn't take them anymore, so he got a pair of pliers and just *ripped* them out…" She mimed doing this with her hand.

Meredith's entire body quaked as she clamped a hand over her mouth, her eyes full of horror.

"Really?" Amelia asked theatrically. "If you like, Mere, I could get some pliers from my stepdad's toolbox and bring them to school tomorrow…"

"Please stop," the girl pleaded, parting her fingers slightly to let the words through while screwing her eyes shut and turning her head.

The other two girls laughed. Then Tamara reached out her hand and squeezed Meredith's forearm gently. "Aw, calm down. We're just fooling around."

The three of them picked on each other like this from time to time, but true arguments between them were infrequent. Tamara might even make a crack about Amelia's height or weight, and she could retort with a black joke and get away with it. And then there was Meredith's squeamishness and tendency to get embarrassed, particularly if dirty words were used. Even if there were actual hurt feelings, none of them stayed apart from each other for long. After all, no one else would have them.

Deep down, Amelia always felt a disconnect from these friends, like they didn't know the real her. That was because she wasn't entirely honest with them. She liked them okay, but there was something at the core of her friendship with Meredith that she kept a secret: The girl was occasionally a useful source of information. It was all a part of a plan that had been brewing in Amelia's mind for quite some time now, something that started when a seed was planted in her mind during that physical confrontation with Justin all those years ago.

"Your dad isn't even dead." Amelia knew the vampire legend as well as anyone else her age. She just hadn't started to put the pieces together until that point. But the more she thought about it, and the more miserable her life became, a question began to develop within her that she couldn't shake: What if her father was still alive?

Yes, he'd died. That's what happened to people who got attacked by vampires. But they also came back to life as vampires themselves, right? She knew that it must not be something that happened immediately; she'd seen her father's body at the funeral, after all. The sight of that had traumatized her: He looked completely wrong, all still and silent in that casket, his face a weird shade of beige. As disconcerting as it was, the thought of him being alive again — even if it did mean that he drank blood like Dracula in one of those horror movies — made that memory less painful.

The idea wasn't without its problems, though. Why had she never seen him again? Did she even want to? Yes, yes, she definitely did. She missed him so much, and her life had turned to complete and utter crap after he'd left. Even if he was a monster, he'd still be her dad, and she knew he'd still love her and never hurt her. The story built up more and more as the years went on, complete with imaginary conversations and scenarios that depicted their eventual reunion.

She reasoned that he hadn't contacted her after his resurrection because he didn't want to scare her. Maybe he had some notion in his head that it was better that she thought he was just gone, not one of the undead. But she wasn't afraid of him. She needed him, needed to believe that he was still out there somewhere and that she'd see him again. It was this fantasy that kept her going, but she refused to believe that it was only that. It had to be true, even if she didn't have all the facts.

This made her hate her mother all the more for moving them to Savannah. If they'd stayed in Augusta, Amelia knew, she'd have been able to find her father again. She wasn't sure just how to go about doing that, but she'd find a way. But in order to do that, she needed to somehow get back to the city she'd grown up in. That hadn't even been part of the plan early on; early versions of the fantasy involved her father finding her in Savannah somehow. But once she found out that Meredith had family in Augusta and apparently knew something about vampires, that was when she'd decided to strike up a friendship with her.

Amelia had known the basics of what happened in 1983. Vampires had gone on a rampage for about a week, and lots of people had died, including her father. There was no real explanation for why the attacks suddenly stopped — or why they'd even started, for that matter — but they did, and life returned to normal for most people, if not for her. But according to Meredith's cousins, whom she'd visited shortly before school started in sixth grade, there had been more vampire activity in 1985.

Initially, Meredith and her friend Tamara had been wary of Amelia. She'd been pretty bitter and mean throughout most of fifth grade, though in her eyes, that was justified given how she'd been treated. She'd even picked on and been rude to Tamara and Meredith, but only a couple of times. She tried to limit her meanness to the people who were actively rude to her.

Once she turned up the niceness in order to get closer to Meredith and find out what she knew, things got better. None of the three girls would ever win a popularity contest, and they were always the ones to get picked last for teams during P.E. class. But at least they had each other to be nice to, even if that was sometimes uneven as well.

So Amelia learned what she could from Meredith about what had happened in Augusta the previous summer. She didn't know everything, just hearsay, and it was hard to get her to talk about it given the girl's inherent squeamishness. Also, Amelia didn't want to let on just how interested she was in the whole phenomenon for fear of appearing too morbid or weird, so she had to be careful. She was curious as hell, though.

That meant that she could only ask Meredith about the vampires in Augusta occasionally, getting her knowledge in bits and pieces. But it helped. With each new fragment that she learned, her fantasies became more intricate, as did her growing plan to find a way to run away from home. This was the main thing that helped get her through the bad times: Even though she hated most of her peers and her family, one day, she would leave this shitty life behind and go back to Augusta to find her father. And if that meant being turned into a vampire as well, she was fine with that, too.

It was the prospect of being forced to get braces that was the tipping point for her. Aside from the fact that she hated how they would make her even uglier and further ridiculed, she wondered if they might somehow interfere with her growing desire to become a vampire. After all, who ever heard of a vampire with braces? What if they messed up her fangs somehow, or maybe something happened the other way around, like the fangs twisting all the wires and metal up in a weird way?

She'd been planning to get out of town for years, or at least, she'd thought about it a lot. The actual planning, she found, was more difficult. She went through several options in her mind to try to figure out just how to get from Savannah to Augusta, wondering if she might be able to hitchhike, but she'd heard too many horror stories about that. There was a book she'd read when she was younger about a brother and sister who wound up living in a museum after sneaking away from home by stowing away on a bus, so she wondered if that was a possibility. Or maybe she could do the same thing on a plane instead?

What she ended up doing was riding her bike downtown, abandoning it on the sidewalk, then selling her camera at a pawn shop. In an earlier version of her plan, this would have been to pay for a bus ticket to Augusta, but by March of 1987, she already had enough money saved up from her allowance to do that. She mostly did it out of spite: She didn't need Peter's crappy gift anymore, just as she didn't need him or the rest of her family.

As she walked from the pawn shop to the Greyhound station, she briefly wondered if she was making the right decision. Would she eventually miss her family? Her thoughts drifted back to her younger days, back before things had gone so wrong. She could see herself crouched beneath the foot of her bed, putting on a puppet show for Megan, who sat against the headboard laughing and applauding as Amelia made Fred the Frog and Rhiney the Rhinoceros sing along to songs she'd taped off the radio. She smiled at the memory, then shook her head.

Things weren't like that anymore. They'd been that way back in Augusta, back when she'd been happy. She hated Megan for how she'd grown and changed, just as she hated her mother and grandmother for bringing Peter into their lives. Amelia was going to be her own person now, going back to where things had been better. There wouldn't be any puppet shows, she knew, but there would be new adventures to find. Most importantly, she'd find her father again, also transformed into a new person, and the two of them would be undead happily ever after.

CHAPTER TWENTY

SHATTERED

Joe was a good man. He'd fought in the war and defended his country. Not that anyone ever thanked him for it. Stupid damn hippies with their fucking pointless protests.

Joe liked to listen to the radio. Not any of that hippie shit from the '60s, but rock and roll was good. There was heart and soul in that music. He had his radio. It was his. He made sure it had batteries. It needed them. He needed it.

Joe was homeless. That's what they called people like him nowadays. There was a name for it. It was a term. A condition. Like the other things the doctors called him.

Joe had once had a family. And friends. He didn't miss them, not that much. When he'd come back from the war, they'd all looked at him funny. "What was it like?" "Did you kill anyone?" "Why are you acting so mad?" "You're home now." He wasn't home. Home was where things made sense. Why did it make more sense where he'd been before, surrounded by all that chaos?

Joe had pushed people away. He was too angry, too scared, too something. Whatever it was, he didn't fit. They tried giving him pills, but they made him feel funny. Not himself. He stopped taking them. Everyone insisted that this was wrong.

Joe knew who he was. He knew his name. He knew how he felt. He was disconnected from everyone. Nobody could understand him. He was better off on his own.

Joe heard people talking to him. He knew that they were in his head, but that didn't mean that they weren't real. Maybe they were demons, or maybe they were angels. Sometimes they were kind, and sometimes they weren't. He could learn true things from them, but if they got too loud, he had to tell them to shut up. If they wouldn't listen, he'd have to shout at them, even curse at them. But he didn't want them to go away. Then he'd be alone.

Joe had a place. It was under the bridge. The sound of the cars rushing over it had a music all its own. A rhythm, a song, like planes flying overhead.

Joe believed in God. He'd read the Bible cover to cover when he was a boy. He liked the Old Testament. The New Testament made him nervous, all that talk of judgment at the end, eternal fire. He didn't want to go through that again, flames right and left, east and west. He'd been through the fire already, like those guys in the Book of Daniel, come out alive.

Sometimes people gave him things. Sometimes he got food. Sometimes people would give him money. Sometimes people would avert their eyes and pretend they hadn't seen him. Sometimes other people who lived like he did were kind to him. Sometimes other people who lived like he did took things from him. Joe was used to looking out for himself. The only one who ever took care of him was Joe.

The world around him was an illusion. No one actually saw reality for what it was. It was all a fake. He felt sorry for everyone else, all of them living their deluded, pointless lives that they thought meant something. He knew better. He'd learned more. Life and reality was fragile, like an eggshell waiting to crack. A skull waiting to be smashed. A life needing to be snuffed out.

Joe heard the whispers. He had his ear to the ground, talk of the town. Roger, all signals coming in clear. Just keeping it going, waiting for the end. Judgment Day coming soon. Bats in the belfry. Must be

Reagan and the government doing another Agent Orange thing. They knew. They always knew.

Read the newspapers. There were things in there. Collect them. They were good for keeping warm at night, too. Stuffing. Little paper blankets. Could be lit on fire, too, if he needed the warmth, but it wasn't like that now. Summer was here. Fun in the sun, made in the shade. Though really, sleeping through the day seemed to work best.

Maybe that's why they came for him. Joe liked the night life. The bats came, then became. They were people now. Vampires, like they said on the radio. Joe had wondered why no one had talked about them for a couple of years. He also wondered why they looked so young, like kids. He wouldn't live long enough to find out.

CHAPTER TWENTY-ONE

STRAYS

Well, that sucked, Diane thought to herself as she walked towards her apartment. As she fumbled through her keys to find the one for the door, she suddenly stopped mid-stride as she approached the doormat. In the dim light, she peered down at it, making sure that there were no surprises waiting for her. She'd learned to be careful given what had happened recently.

Diane liked cats. She liked dogs, too, and she rejected the notion that some people had when they would ask her, "Are you a cat person or a dog person?" She would reply that she was simply an "animal person," caring for both equally. Unfortunately, neither were allowed in her apartment complex. She wasn't sure why the landlady was so insistent on that, but given the old woman's generally unpleasant temperament (which was a nicer way of saying that she was a bitch), it wasn't all that surprising.

Still, that didn't stop Diane from leaving out food for the stray cats that showed up around the place. Her goal with each one was to get them tame enough to where they would let her pet them and eventually feel comfortable coming inside, even though that was against the rules. Once this was achieved, she would try to find them homes elsewhere, adopting them out to co-workers, to friends, or to friends of friends.

She tried not to get attached to any of them, but she always felt a little sad whenever it was time for one of them to move on. But it was better that it happened that way rather than them getting snatched up by Animal Control, whom Miss Crabby Bitch Landlady had been threatening to call because of "all these damn cats that keep coming around." Diane had held her tongue during that conversation.

During her first year living at Water's Edge — she had no idea why it was called that, given that there wasn't so much as a stream anywhere near the property — she had been very careful, feeling a sense of urgency to get the cats tamed and re-homed in time to get them out of her place before the next visit by the apartment complex's maintenance guy, Skip. He came around each month to spray for bugs, but she suspected that he might also be being sent out by Mrs. Crosby (Miss Crabby Bitch Landlady's real name, and the one she called her to her face) to check to make sure that nobody was harboring any illegal, oh-so-horrible pets.

One time, Diane had been careless and forgot to put away the litter box that she'd had for a recently adopted cat, and Skip saw it in her kitchen. She froze when he paused to look at it, her mouth open as she tried to think of something to say.

"I'm going to pretend I didn't see that," he said firmly, but then his face broke out in a grin, punctuated by a wink. "It's okay. I won't tell anybody if you don't."

After that, Diane relaxed, knowing that she at least had Skip on her side. He was a nice old man, and he lived in the apartment building next to her, which made him easily accessible whenever she had any problems. He'd even tried to talk Mrs. Crosby into cutting Diane a break on her rent the month that the air conditioning had crapped out, causing it to run constantly without actually cooling the place and running up her electric bill. Not surprisingly, Miss Crabby Bitch Landlady would have none of that.

"I tried, I really did," Skip said, relaying the conversation to Diane afterwards. "But she's all, 'If she can't tell that it needs fixin' and dutn't report it in time, that's not my fault!'" He did a pretty accurate impression of the woman, and she could tell that he wasn't particularly fond of her. "She's always been like that." Diane wondered how long the two had known each other.

At any rate, while she still had to walk on eggshells around her landlady, she felt more confident in her mission to rescue as many strays as possible, knowing that Skip wouldn't tell on her. Most of the time, she was successful, but other times, a cat would show up once or twice but then disappear. Some of them were just too feral to tame.

And then there was the time very recently that a cat had been so grateful for her kind treatment of her one night that she showed her appreciation by leaving a dead mouse — with head and tail detached, no less — on her front doorstep the following morning. It was something she'd read about during her research on cats, a gesture they sometimes did to show affection. The display had horrified her, particularly given that she'd barely missed stepping on the mouse parts on her way out of the door that morning. But then she couldn't help but laugh. It was kind of sweet, sick and twisted though it was.

Fortunately, there were no additional dead mouse bits waiting for her upon her return to her apartment tonight. She did hope that the cat, whom she'd already named Isobel during their previous encounter, would show up again. For one thing, she'd appreciate the company. It had been a crappy night so far.

She'd been out with some friends at the Red Lion Pub, a local bar that had live music. It wasn't like Augusta had that vibrant of a music scene, but she still liked to go out, have fun, and support the local artists. That kind of thing had been more prevalent in nearby Athens, where she'd lived before moving here a year ago.

The night was cut short when the police showed up and made everyone leave. Diane and her friends were confused, wondering if maybe the band had been playing too loud, but it didn't seem like they were. The fact that they were playing at all was a bit of a shame given how terrible they were, and her friend Christina joked that their being cut off was a mercy killing. The headlining group, Thousand Eyes

Land, hadn't even gotten a chance to play, which they were pretty pissed about.

Things became more serious once everyone was outside and saw not only police cars but ambulances. Two guys from a local radio station that had been there to promote the show were talking to police, one of them visibly shaken, the other looking angry and saying something in a loud voice.

Word of mouth eventually revealed that some people had been killed, something to do with an upstairs room and a broken window. Diane felt bad for whoever the people might have been, then noted with disgust the way that one of the guys from the headlining band kept ranting to the police about how he needed to get his guitar, which was apparently in the same upstairs room where the bodies had been found. It struck her as remarkably self-centered and callous.

The police had been urging everyone to go home as soon as they'd arrived, and while there were some "boo"s and similar protests at first, things quieted down once the talk of the dead bodies started circulating. Diane was surprised by how cooperative most of the people then became, and there was one word that kept standing out among the various conversations: "vampires."

Of course, she'd heard the rumors even before she'd moved here that Augusta was known for occasional vampire attacks. But that was silly, probably just something drummed up to scare people, particularly tourists or new residents like herself. It was like how certain old hotels around the world would have a reputation for being haunted, so people would flock to the places hoping to see something spooky. It was good for business. It wasn't like a place would earn extra cash with a slogan like *"100% Ghost-Free!"* You had to invent the danger first, then lure people in with the possibility of being threatened by it.

That was her impression of Augusta and its vampire situation. The town was pretty boring, the only supposedly exciting thing going for it being the Masters golf tournament every year. But that didn't interest Diane, and the friends she'd made since moving here had a similar disdain both for it and for the people it drew to the city every April.

"Don't even think about going anywhere near Washington Road during Masters Week," Christina had cautioned her. "The entire area is just clogged with out-of-towners who don't know where they are or what the hell they're doing, and you're likely to get into a wreck. No one knows how to drive. And then after the tournament's over, all the tourists go home, and Augusta's back to being nothing again."

So Diane believed that vampire stories were periodically circulated in order to get more people intrigued and interested in the city. Tourists equaled money. But tonight, given the solemn faces and hushed whispers of the people surrounding her as they filed away from the Red Lion, she began to wonder if she were the callous one, not the opportunistic business owners. Christina seemed similarly subdued, urging Diane to go home with an uncharacteristically serious tone.

As she drove, Diane wondered what was really going on. She was a skeptic, but she wasn't a cynic. What little she'd learned in her time here about Augusta's vampire phenomenon suggested that the killings that had occurred — and she suspected that the number of them had been exaggerated over the years — were probably being caused by some kind of animals. That was a lot more likely than anything supernatural.

Once home, she checked outside the back door of her apartment to see if the dry cat food she'd left out had been eaten. Some of it had, though how much of that might have been eaten by Isobel, other strays, or the trail of ants walking to and from the bowl was anybody's guess. Being careful not to get bitten, she took the bowl back inside, dumped its contents into the garbage disposal, then turned it on as she rinsed the mix of kibbles and frantic ants down the drain. She felt bad for them, but she knew better than to let them live on to infest her apartment again.

She felt less guilty when she used the same bowl to splash some water onto the pavement outside where the remaining ants were still scampering around. That wouldn't kill them, just disperse them. She'd always had mixed feelings about ants. They were interesting creatures; one of her earliest memories as a little girl involved finding an article on them in the encyclopedia and reading the entire thing, fascinated by how they lived.

But there had been another time several years later when she'd successfully enticed a stray kitten from across the street to her front yard with some canned tuna fish, only to find that this had also invited the attention of some fire ants from a nearby anthill. What ended up happening was that the kitten, trying to enjoy his meal, was suddenly flinching and shaking his paw as the ants began to bite it. Diane intervened, getting bitten by the tiny orange ants in the process and scaring the kitten back across the road. He just barely missed getting hit by a car that happened to speed by at the same time.

Tonight, she decided to wait a half hour or so before putting another bowl of food out, giving the ants time to lose interest. If she heard Isobel's little meow outside sooner than that, though, she'd go ahead and go out there. Hopefully the cat had learned that this was a place to come for food.

Killing time, she watched TV for a while, procrastinating on studying. This was her first time taking summer classes at the local medical school, the reason she'd moved to Augusta after finishing up her undergrad at UGA last year. While some people took the summer off from school, Diane wanted to get through her degree as quickly as possible, but she was beginning to regret that choice. Unlike the fall, winter, and spring quarters, the summer ones were more compact, a lot of material having to be gotten through in a shorter amount of time. To say that it was stressful was a gross understatement.

Still, the sooner she got her degree, the sooner she could get out of here. She had no desire to stay in Augusta any longer than she had to, though she didn't exactly hate the place. It was just dull. She didn't really know where she wanted to go after graduation, but she was pretty sure she didn't want to go back home to her family in Whitesburg, Kentucky. If anything, that place was even more boring. But that was part of the reason why she wanted to become a physical therapist: to go wherever the work would take her.

She hadn't realized quite how late it was until the 11:00 news came on, which reminded her that it was already past the point when she'd meant to put out more food for the cat. She started to get up from the futon, but then what was on her TV made her sit back down. It was a report about the tragedy at the Red Lion.

The story revealed only a little more than she'd gathered by having been there herself, specifically that the people who had been killed were employees of either the bar or the radio station — it was unclear just which — who were on the roof of the building trying to make their way in through the window of an upstairs room from which they'd been locked out. Supposedly — and this was equally vague — they had then been attacked and killed by what may or may not have been vampires.

The wording of the news report bothered Diane, partly because it didn't fit with her earlier belief that these vampire stories were sensationalized in order to garner interest in the area. Instead, it was like the reporters were reluctant to even say the word "vampire," peppering the story with words like "supposed" and "allegedly."

But what disturbed her even more was the revelation that not only had there been similar deaths very close to the bar that same night — Monday — there had also been others Sunday evening in the same area. If she'd known that, she never would have gone down there the following night. Still, at least the attacks seemed to be concentrated somewhere far away from her apartment. She started to imagine what it must be like for the people who lived around there, how horrible that must be. Then she shuddered, trying to put the thought out of her head and be grateful that she was out of harm's way.

Her face brightened when she heard a faint and familiar *"rawwwr"* from outside. She needed the distraction.

"Don't hiss at me!" Diane said with a smile. It wasn't like the little orange tabby was anywhere near as threatening as she probably thought she was; she was just plain cute.

"Raaar. Raaar. Raaar." The cat seemed almost annoyed by Diane's presence, squinting at the fluorescent kitchen light whenever Diane's shadow moved to let it stream into the little beggar's eyes. But there she was just the same, her vocalizations seeming to say, *Feed me, feed me, I don't like you, but feed me.* When she'd tried to reach out and pet the visitor, it had drawn back and hissed at her, but it still didn't leave.

"Okay," Diane said playfully. "Calm down." She straightened up slowly, being careful not to appear threatening. The cat — maybe kitten, she wasn't sure — flinched, but she still sat there, repeating her pleas. *"Raaar. Raaar. Raaa-aar!"*

Leaving her back door open and keeping an eye on it, Diane moved over to the refrigerator, hoping that maybe the kitty would venture inside. It didn't, so she opened the fridge and quickly took out a slice of lunch meat, something she knew would go over well. If the cat returned tomorrow night, she'd be treated to some tuna fish, which Diane knew usually sealed the deal and made the cat content enough to be lured inside, slowly build up trust and let itself be petted, and eventually become tame enough to be a temporary roommate. Then would begin the process of finding it a new home, somewhere safe from Mrs. Crabby.

"There you go," she said as the feline panhandler dug into the slab of bologna that she'd lain down on the concrete. She giggled at how the cat had never stopped meowing at her perturbingly, but it was also eating at the same time, so the sounds had turned into something like *"raarrrmphble... raarrrmph... reeormpp..."*

She tried once more to pet the cat, eager to get to that step with this latest project. But as soon as her fingers touched the soft orange fur, the testy little thing jumped and bounced away from her, leaving the half-eaten meat behind.

"Sorry!" Diane pleaded, drawing back. "Sorry, sorry." She continued to stay squatting at ground level, shuffling backward across the linoleum floor. "It's okay," she whispered, then caught herself, remembering that whispering at a cat was probably something they interpreted as hissing. "Come on back," she said in a quiet, almost singing tone. "It's okayyy…"

Still looking annoyed, the cat she'd named Isobel cautiously approached the meat again, resuming its meowing. Something in her face seemed to say, *I dare you to try that crap again.* Imagining this made Diane giggle once more.

"Okay, I'll leave you alone," she said placatingly. With that, she gently closed the door, then listened closely, hearing the faint sounds of smacking coming from the other side.

A bit later on in the night, Diane was feeling proud of herself not just for helping out another stray but also because she'd finally managed to crack open a textbook and start reading at least a few pages of assigned material before bed. Her thoughts were interrupted by the sound of a barking dog from somewhere not too far away.

Like cats, dogs weren't allowed in the apartment complex either, the one benefit she could see being that it made for a quiet place to live, which helped in terms of studying. Still, she occasionally heard the ones from nearby neighborhoods, and she'd told herself that if a stray dog ever showed up at her place and needed food, she'd treat it with the same kindness and courtesy as any cat.

She had in fact helped a lost dog find its way home not long after moving here, and she'd done it before back home in Kentucky. Dogs were much easier than cats, more approachable and eager to be friendly, even if they were lost and scared. A gentle eye-level approach, a reaching out of one's hand to let the dog sniff it, and then some eager petting and encouraging words were usually enough to earn their trust. A quick inspection of the dog's tag led to finding its owner's phone number, and then it was just a matter of keeping the little guy safe and out of the street until someone came to retrieve it, grateful for what she'd done. Sometimes, money was offered as a reward, which she usually refused, except for one time when she'd been having a particularly bad month in terms of getting her bills paid. Lots of things had sprung up on her at once, including her faulty air conditioning unit.

Sometimes, when she was feeling particularly introspective, Diane wondered why it was that she was so eager to help these stray animals. There was certainly a good feeling it brought her, but why was that? Reuniting a lost dog with its owner was its own reward, and keeping cute little cats from being scooped up by the pound was another. But was there more to it than that?

Maybe it was because she felt a bit like a stray herself. Here she was in a town she didn't particularly like, far away from where she'd grown up or where she'd recently lived. Moreover, she didn't plan to stay here and would hopefully find herself in yet another brand new, unfamiliar place. She liked the friends she made wherever she went, but they always felt temporary. Dating didn't even seem like it was worth the trouble, not that she'd ever had great success in that department anyway. Most guys weren't interested in taller, plain-looking girls like herself. And she was fine with that for now: At this point in her life, she needed to focus more on school anyway.

The barking that she'd heard stopped rather abruptly, presumably because whoever owned the dog had reined it in. That was good; sometimes dogs would go on for ages, barking at nothing and ignored by their masters. As much as she cared for animals, that still got on her nerves, particularly when she was trying to read.

After a few minutes, Diane heard a more disturbing sound, this one more close by. It was a cat, but instead of Isobel's gentle but insistent plea for more food, this was a snarl, the kind cats made when either fighting or mating (and sometimes those two overlapped, she knew). Concerned, she got up from her bed, setting her textbook down but leaving it open. Grabbing her slippers and a flashlight, she ventured out the front door and in the direction of the noise.

Diane suddenly felt a bit foolish as she crept along the walkway to the street, wondering what she might say to anyone who might show up and ask her why she was out in the middle of the night in a robe and slippers, her long, dark hair tied up in a disheveled knot. But she barely cared; she just wanted to make sure that Isobel was all right.

Then she felt foolish again. Cats fought. It was just something they did. More than that, they were very good at taking care of themselves. A couple of months ago, Midnight, the black cat that she'd been taking in — though he still came and went as he pleased by that point in their relationship — had worried her when a really huge thunderstorm rolled through one night. Having seen it approaching on the weather forecast, she'd been planning to keep Midnight inside, but he hadn't shown up.

As the wind and rain pounded away at her windows, and the thunder and lightning continued for several hours, Diane got this terrible image in her head of Midnight being swept away in a torrent of water and down into a storm drain. But the following day, he turned up safe and sound.

So Isobel was probably fine, too, she told herself, but she couldn't get the sound of that feline shriek out of her head. She hoped that the fact that it had only happened once so far was probably a good sign: If there were any real trouble, the screams would have been ongoing.

Some movement up the road caught her eye, and she spotted what she thought was Isobel padding along the street. Cautiously, she ventured toward the figure, soon realizing that it wasn't the small orange tabby she'd been expecting. It was still a cat, but larger and all white, as she was able to tell once she'd directed her flashlight onto it to be sure. The cat stopped and turned its head, apparently noticing the beam, and Diane continued to approach it, tiptoeing along.

It always struck her as creepy the way that animals' eyes seemed to glow in the dark when bright lights were shone at them. It was something to do with the way their eyes were constructed differently than humans', she knew, but it still made her uncomfortable. She'd seen it happen with cats, with dogs, and even with the raccoons that used to frequent her family's yard back in Whitesburg. But what was strange here was that even after she'd turned off the flashlight, thinking that it might scare the cat she was approaching, it looked like its eyes were still lit up, glowing eerily. Diane paused, glancing around to see what other source of light might be causing this, maybe an approaching car. But there was nothing.

When she turned back, the cat's eyes were dark and normal, and it had sat down. It was still looking at her, unmoving, and Diane wondered what she should do next. Had this been the source of the screech she'd heard earlier? Maybe this cat had attacked Isobel, or maybe it was just another innocent stray in need of some food. Or had it been the one that had cried out? Slowly, she began stepping towards the white cat, speaking softly.

"Hey there," she said. "Are you okay?" She half expected the cat to bolt and run; they did that sometimes, particularly when they didn't yet know her.

The cat still didn't move, though it did blink a couple of times. Diane blinked back deliberately; she'd heard somewhere that cats did this as a means of communication, and returning the gesture engendered trust. When she was within a few feet of this new arrival, she squatted down and held out her hand, hoping that the cat would recognize her as friendly and step forward, hopefully giving her a sniff. Tame cats usually did that, followed by a friendly rubbing of their chins against her wrist.

"Come on," she said gently, her hand still held out. The cat got up and slowly walked towards her. "That's right. Do you want something to eat? I've got some food if you need it." She smiled, hoping she'd made another new friend.

As the white cat reached her, its eyes lit up again, a yellowish glow that looked very much like a firefly's luminescence. There was no reason for it, and Diane turned her head again to see if there might be a car's headlights approaching from behind her, despite the fact that there was no sound to indicate this. Her confusion was interrupted by the sound of swift movement and a sharp pain on left side of her neck.

Before she knew what had happened, she was falling back onto the pavement, her hands batting helplessly against the furry form of the cat attached to her neck. It had bitten down into her flesh, and she could hear a quick, faint swallowing sound as the cat's rough tongue rapidly lapped against her skin. As her limbs went numb and she found herself unable to fight back or even cry out, she realized what was happening, not just to her but to the entire town.

Too late, she'd solved the mystery. She'd been wrong about the vampire phenomenon, that it had been some publicity stunt to get people worked up about the boring town of Augusta. But everyone else had been wrong, too, thinking that the vampires were the traditional kind, undead people preying on the living. No one had ever known the truth. Who the hell would have ever expected anything like vampire cats? The idea was so ridiculous that it made her angry.

As the blood drained out of her, Diane bitterly thought that even if she could have survived, no one would ever have believed her.

CHAPTER TWENTY-TWO

PRECONCEPTIONS

Brenda heard the screams and raced in their direction, her weapon drawn. She wasn't even sure what she could do, but it was her duty to protect people. She'd always known that. As she got closer and the scene unfolded, memories flashed across her mind.

There was McCarthy, the chauvinistic pig, being condescending to her a couple of nights before on what turned out to be an uneventful outing. "If anything happens, you stay behind me." Jerk. She could hold her own, just like any other member of the Augusta Police Department.

There was her supervisor, saying some crap about how he didn't agree with putting women in harm's way. This was her job, she assured him, just as it had been her father's. Sergeant Bainbridge relented, reluctantly, for once not pointing out how she was "so young," something he often did to diminish her.

"Daddy's little girl," her father had said to her with a pained look the day she'd joined the police force. "It goes without saying that I'm proud of you. I mean it."

Brenda wondered if he could tell that she knew he was lying. He'd always wanted her to become a nurse instead. She'd always meant to tell him that, to call him on it before he'd died.

Another memory of McCarthy, this time of him calling in sick for tonight's shift. She'd been glad. She was tired of being partnered with that worthless piece of shit. She'd be fine on her own.

Snapping back to the present, Brenda began to wonder if she'd been right. But then, even if McCarthy had been here, what could they have done? She had no way to be sure if her gun would even be effective against these beasts. If both legend and the times she'd seen the confrontations in movies held true, it wouldn't be. She'd been pushing the idea at work of getting officers armed with wooden stakes, but everyone had just dismissed this as childish and stupid.

"This ain't no monster movie," Bainbridge had said to her, prompting laughs from everyone else. Asshole.

She surveyed the scene. People were fleeing in panic. Three others were down, being preyed upon by what were obviously vampires, their heads lowered to the necks of the three victims. Two of them were female, but she couldn't see the third one clearly because of the angle. Wouldn't that be interesting, she thought, if all of the vampires that had been terrorizing the city were in fact women?

She was just about to step in to intervene when she spotted someone else. It was a little kid, a boy, hiding in the bushes nearby and watching what was happening to the people in the middle of the street. She struggled with her options for a moment: confront the vampires or get this child to safety?

Opting for the latter, she ran up to the boy as quickly and quietly as possible, putting her gun away. She couldn't let the vampires become aware of her, nor did she want to scare this poor kid any more than he already must be.

"Quick!" she whispered harshly, startling the boy. His head whipped around to face her, and he was clearly tense. "Sorry," she said reassuringly. "I didn't mean to scare you. It's okay." The boy almost looked like he was more angry than scared.

A couple more screams erupted from not too far away. The situation was escalating. Reaching out her hand to lead the boy away, Brenda said, "It's not safe here!"

"I know," the dark-haired boy said, his face suddenly changing to a sinister grin punctuated by two sharp fangs. Impossible.

Too late, Brenda realized that this boy was also a vampire. He hadn't been hiding from the attack; he was watching it. She'd made a fatal mistake. She tried to jump back and run, but as the boy's eyes lit up like two small, amber flashlights, she found herself unable to move.

The boy began to creep closer, the menacing smile on his face never fading. She struggled against the supernatural grip on her mind, trying to will herself to move. It was like a nightmare, one in which you want to run but can't. Her life was about to end, and she felt completely helpless.

"But... but... you're just a *child!*" she cried. They were the last words she ever spoke.

CHAPTER TWENTY-THREE

WHITE PICKET FENCE

"I'm so glad it's finally done," Virginia said, squeezing her husband's hand as they surveyed the newly constructed addition to their house. It had taken months to complete, and they were both glad that all of the noise and construction was over with. It had been a lot to get through, but it had been worth it.

"We should take some pictures," she said. "You know, 'before' and 'after.'"

"Why don't we wait till tomorrow?" Arthur suggested. "When the sun's up. You can take some from outside that way, show everything that's been done. Didn't you take some outside ones before?"

"You're right," she said, nodding and smiling. "Always seeing the big picture, aren't you?"

The two of them embraced, then kissed gently. Drawing back from each other, they each breathed in deeply, enjoying the moment. It felt good to have gotten to this point.

"So when do we invite some people over?" Virginia asked eagerly. "We should christen the place with a party. Like a housewarming."

"We already had one of those," Arthur said simply, still grinning.

"I know. But... well... I don't know. It's a new wing on the house." Her eyes brightened, and she tapped her husband lightly on the chest. "A wingwarming!"

"Not sure I would call it a 'wing,'" he protested playfully. "Just two rooms."

"That counts!" She pushed away from his chest, dancing over to one corner of the new room. Then she began walking the entire perimeter of it, meaningfully stepping along the newly finished hardwood floor. "I like it. I really, really like it. Can't wait to start having parties and jam sessions in here. Well, not here, but the downstairs one."

Arthur nodded, picturing their friends coming to visit, musical instruments in hand. "We still need to get the furniture moved in up here for it to be a proper guest room. And we need to get some chairs for down there, too. You want to go to the market tomorrow to look for some?"

"Yes, definitely," Virginia said with a wide smile. "Something nice looking, not cheap, plastic stuff."

"I know," Arthur said in a pained tone. She'd never forgiven him for the time he'd come home with those generic, lifeless patio chairs, an old argument that she often brought up when she wanted to make a dig at him. They were supposed to be classier than that. "You want to take a look at the downstairs half?"

"Sure!" she said, but then she frowned a little, looking at the windows. "Too bad the sun's not out. I'd like to be able to see the mountains."

"Tomorrow," he said, holding out his hand to her.

Downstairs, Virginia repeated her move, lightly skipping by the baseboards that lined the room. Arthur watched her with admiration and amusement, her short, curly brown hair flapping about her ears as she moved. He knew how lucky he was to have been married to her for twenty years, and she acted just as young and free as the day they'd met at the dance, decades ago and two states away.

"Should I go get my fiddle?" he asked. "Since you seem so keen on dancing."

His wife stopped by the new French door to the backyard, giving him another wicked grin. Then she sighed. "No, I'm too tired for that. It's been a long day." She turned and put her face to the glass, shielding her eyes from the indoor light in order to see out. "We really should get those up, though. They're bugging me."

"The what? Oh." He remembered the leftover pickets from the fence at the far end of the yard. When the workers had rebuilt it after getting the last of their construction equipment off the property, they'd staggered the wooden planks slightly farther apart than they'd originally been, leaving a handful of them on the grass. The foreman had been apologetic about this, insisting that they break the fence down again and start over, but both Arthur and Virginia agreed that it looked better with the gaps. The man was overly nice and kept trying to say that if the workers had screwed up, they should fix it, practically having to be shoved out the door and convinced that no, they really did like the fence better this way.

The two of them later realized that by rushing the men off, they'd missed the opportunity to get them to clear away the rest of the refuse, which would have been helpful but wasn't essential. They could do it themselves in the morning. There wasn't that much of it, just pieces of scrap wood here and there, bits of concrete, and a random plastic bucket that had been overlooked and left behind. That last item would actually help with the cleanup.

But for some reason, Virginia had become obsessed with those leftover pickets. Arthur had suggested reusing at least one of them in the vegetable garden, inverting it into the soil and letting vines grow up it. "Only if I can paint it first," she said.

"It's already painted."

"I know! But I can decorate it! I'm thinking ladybugs, or maybe dragonflies. Or both."

"Whatever you like, dear," he said, acting exasperated but not really feeling it. He knew better than to get in her way when she was feeling crafty.

Still, he didn't see much point in her going out to mess with them now, not after dark. He tried saying as much, but she ignored him, rushing out to play with her latest toys. The woman could make a project out of anything, sometimes at the most impractical times.

"Come on out here!" she called to her husband, a plank of wood in each hand. He was still inside, and she'd started to head back in herself, then realized that she didn't want to bring these dirty things into their new, pristine room. In fact, if she were going to repaint them, that would also have to be outside, and — like Arthur kept saying — not now, but during the day.

She placed the pieces of wood onto the lawn, then looked back up to where Arthur was standing in the doorway, the light from inside silhouetting his figure. But then something strange happened. It was as if a strong wind had suddenly whipped up around him, his clothes and hair flapping around for a few seconds as he staggered backwards a couple of steps. But there was no breeze out tonight; the winds were calm.

Confused and concerned, Virginia ran forward, calling out her husband's name. She slowed her approach when she saw him more clearly in the light from the room, not sure what she was seeing. "What's...?" She was too stunned to finish her sentence.

The first thing she noticed was that his clothes had changed, but that was impossible. Somehow, the T-shirt and sweat pants he'd been wearing had been replaced by a complete outfit: pants, a vest, button-up shirt, and a long, dark-colored coat. There was something very odd about the ensemble that she didn't notice at first, but it came to her soon enough: The clothes looked decidedly old-fashioned, the collar of the shirt frilly like something one would wear in a historical movie.

Equally as impossible, his hair had changed as well. It still looked to be about the same color, red mixed with some grey, but now it was long, brushed back from his forehead and curling back behind his ears, almost like some old lady's coif.

"Arthur?" Virginia practically whispered.

"Arthur?" he repeated back to her in a strange, gruff voice. As he continued to speak, she became even more unsettled. His speech was halting and weirdly accented, like that of a foreigner struggling to choose his words carefully. "Nay, I am not this… Arthur. I did know of an Arthur Holmwood once. But he is, alas, no more." He began looking around the room curiously, like he was trying to remember something.

Virginia couldn't place the accent. German? Dutch? She barely cared. She didn't recognize that last name, either. But she'd already had enough of this, whatever it was. As she did on the rare occasions when she actually got mad at her husband, she called him by his full name. "Arthur Horsley, whatever you think you're doing, stop it right now. This is too weird."

He looked back at her, his face still obscured by the overhead light behind him. Then he continued to speak in that bizarre voice. "I… do not wish to distress you, kind miss. You must forgive me, but I seem to have forgot myself for one moment. If you would be so good as to indulge me, then perhaps I may regain some recollect of what happen."

His words seemed kind enough, but everything was so surreal that Virginia didn't know what to make of the situation. However he'd pulled off the magic trick with the clothes, surely he would explain himself if she played along for a bit. He'd begun to step backwards away from the door, his hand gesturing that she approach and join him. Even that seemed completely unfamiliar. Arthur was a gentleman, sure, but he didn't move like that. The body language was all wrong.

As she crossed the threshold, Arthur had turned and was walking slowly across the room, his back to her. As her eyes adjusted to the light, she took in more details of his strange clothes, right down to the boots that had somehow magically appeared on his feet moments earlier.

Her mind had been doing her best to rationalize the situation. Was this some attempt at role-playing, something to spice up their sex life?

Some of their other married friends had suggested that to them. But it wasn't like Arthur to spring something like that on her. Any time that they had occasionally gotten experimental over the years, they'd always discussed it first to make sure both parties were okay with it. As she pondered this, he turned back around to face her, at which point she screamed and ran back out the door.

The face she'd seen in the full light was not her husband's. It belonged to a completely different man. Older. Wrinkled. The wide blue eyes, the beak-like nose... It wasn't Arthur.

Her frantic thoughts were interrupted by her foot catching the bottom step at the wrong angle, and pain seared up her right leg as she tumbled to the ground. Those steps were new; she wasn't used to them. She cursed her carelessness as she struggled to right herself on the ground, horrified to see the stranger in her husband's body slowly following after her.

"I see," he said, slowly and in that horrific voice. "Now I see what I did not, why you run from me. And I, sadly, remember my purpose here."

Virginia tried to stand up again, but her ankle gave way beneath her, causing her to scrape her arms and legs a second time as she fell. She felt the tears welling up inside, knowing that at any second, she was going to lose control entirely.

And then the next weird thing happened. A sharp breeze seemed to blow through her entire body, again incongruous with the stillness of the night. Miraculously, it seemed to wash away the pain in her body, and Virginia felt like herself again. Still on the ground, she turned to face the approaching man, who looked at her strangely. There was something determined in his eyes, but it was laced with sadness.

"Indeed," he said solemnly. "I see you now for what you truly are." He bent down to the ground, picking up one of the pieces of wood that the construction workers had left behind. It was about a foot long and had a sharp point. Apparently, the workers had also left behind a hammer, because Arthur held that in his other hand.

"Arthur, please," she pleaded, "whatever's done this to you…" She choked, panicking, forgetting what she needed to say. "Don't do this. It's me. Virginia, your love." There was now something strange in her own voice, she suddenly realized. It was almost musical, coming from a different place within her. It wasn't the strong, diaphragm-focused voice that she used when singing, like during the performances she and Arthur did with their musician friends. She tried to find her normal speaking voice. But what was coming out of her was more breathy, almost seductive.

"Virginia is for lovers," she practically cooed. "Remember that old joke? Because we live here, and it's my name?" She was backing away along the grass, pushing herself with her hands, slowly becoming aware of the way she was cocking her head from side to side, her tongue lapping out to punctuate her words. She also realized that even though it was well after dark, she could see Arthur's newly transformed features as clearly as if they'd both still been inside the house and fully lit. And why was she now wearing a long, white gown?

"You are one of the undead," the man said to her solemnly. "I do now what I must, unpleasant though it be. May God have mercy on your soul." With that, he jumped forward, his foot catching her in the shoulder and knocking her onto her back. In a swift motion, he maneuvered himself on top of her and positioned the sharp piece of wood over her chest. She felt an urge to fly away, suddenly remembering that she was capable of that. But it was too late.

Pain unlike any she had ever known seared through her chest as the wooden spike was hammered into it, and she cried out in a deafening shriek. Screwing her eyes shut in agony, she lost sight of the fierce, set look on the man's face as he continued to hammer the wood through her heart and all the way out through her back, the point of it piercing the soil beneath.

"Mein Gott," Abraham Van Helsing whispered to himself, standing up from the horrid sight beneath him. At least the young

woman looked at peace now, her placid, lovely face framed by the long dark curls of hair that surrounded it. "Poor, poor girl."

Becoming aware of his surroundings, Van Helsing realized that he was in a crowded neighborhood. The houses looked unfamiliar to him, but he realized that it was likely that someone may have heard the screaming of this poor dead girl, and they might come to investigate what had happened. He needed to leave, and quickly.

Memories flooded into his mind, though he was frustrated that he could not remember what had caused him to have lost them in the first place. For the moment, he decided, it didn't matter. He needed to escape this scene before he was discovered. He could fill in the gaps later.

CHAPTER TWENTY-FOUR

PORTRAIT OF THE ARTIST AS THE YOUNGS' CAT

Crowley sat on the floor and thought. And that was just it: He *thought.* He hadn't really been able to do that before, not like this. Something had changed over the past few days. Even the concept of days, of linear, progressive time, events leading one into the other and then being able to be recalled in context later on… It was all new to him. Or really, it was old, just something he had forgotten.

Things had been simpler before. He was a cat. Four legs, covered in white fur, incapable of communicating beyond the limited vocalizations his voice box and cat-brain allowed him. Life consisted of exploring his environment, chasing down smaller animals, eating, sleeping, and coexisting with the much larger animals in his life, the humans. The sounds they made were comprehensible to him only in the most basic sense: He knew when their voices got louder that they were angry, and he felt safer and more calm when they spoke in a gentle tone. He even knew that the word that sounded like *"Row-ree"* was somehow directly associated with him, something meant to get his attention. Sometimes he responded, sometimes not. It depended on how hungry he was at any given moment or whether or not he was in the mood to let them touch him with their huge, imposing paws.

He knew the routines of his life, the repetitions and the associations. The rustling sound meant that soon, there would be a tinkling sound in the bowl from which he could eat the crunchy bits of food. The feeling inside of something rumbling near his tail meant that he needed to find his way to the box of dirt and do what needed to be done to relieve the tension. A loud, whirring sound was often — but not always —a precursor to his being given much nicer, moist food, one of his favorite things. Strong smells from the tall surface high above meant that he might get small pieces of food, so he was sure to stick around while the humans ate.

Warmth was everything. The humans provided that. The heat from their immense and imposing bodies as he lay on them calmed him, as did the stroking motion from their paws. It made him happy, eliciting the almost involuntary vibrations from the base of his throat. It was a sound he liked, and the humans seemed charmed by it, too. It was a nice, symbiotic relationship.

But these were all things that he'd just simply done and lived without ever really thinking about them, at least until now. The fact that he was aware of this was troubling, but he didn't see any point in trying to convey this to his human caregivers. He knew he couldn't.

Crowley remembered bits and pieces. There had been something before, another life. Another time. He hadn't always been who he was now, or even the smaller, simpler cat he'd been before the change. Whatever had been done to him, it had opened up a door in his small, feline mind, letting in things that probably shouldn't have been. He understood the humans around him more now. He'd been one of them.

Walking upright. Being tall. The world on a completely different scale. Thoughts, feelings, ambitions. Human motivations. Seeing the cats in the world as smaller, lesser things to be cared for. That had been him once. There was a word for what had happened, a concept, a belief. Reincarnation.

This disconcerted him, and he shuddered. He licked his paw to clean it, then his leg. It soothed him, distracted him. But the thoughts were still there, nagging at him.

He thought back, but not too far back. He'd been more energetic once, almost beyond his control. As a kitten, he'd constantly felt the urge to run, to explore, to enjoy things. Everything was new, exciting, and scary. He remembered the fluid he used to drink then, the thick, white, deliciousness of it. That settled him down, too, making him want to sleep. For no reason he could understand, that had gone away, replaced by the thin, colorless fluid that parched his thirst but gave him little other fulfillment. Why couldn't he have milk anymore?

He suddenly realized that he knew that word: *milk*. It was a human word. He hadn't known it before. But now he did. How?

His thoughts were interrupted by one of the humans lumbering past him, shaking the floor. Did they not realize how frighteningly big they were? Trying not to give away that he'd been startled, Crowley stood up and walked into another part of his world... no... another room of the house. That's what they would have called it. He hoped to find his traces in there, the scents he'd rubbed onto the furniture to mark places that were safe to return to.

There were no humans in this place. This room. He could hear them and their noises elsewhere in the world... in the *house*. It was dark in here, more comforting.

Crowley thought about the milk again. There was something else happening now that confused him, but it wasn't entirely unwelcome. Just strange. But nice. Even familiar. In the past, the humans had come and gone. Sometimes they were there, and he had to cope with their presence. Other times, he was left on his own. But lately, since the change, they had been taking him along with them outside the house.

The outside world was fun, though sometimes overwhelming. So many sounds and smells. Life inside the house was one thing, occasionally providing stimulation. But outside... Oh, that was wonderful. So many things to chase after and kill. To Crowley's feline mind, there was nothing more exciting than seeing some fluttering, fast-moving thing and pursuing it. Even if he didn't catch it, he still enjoyed the chase. It was something just built into him... *Instinct.* Another human word, one he'd forgotten until now.

Crowley began cleaning himself again, licking and pawing his fur. Tongue to fur, tongue to fur, over and over. It needed to be done. Dirty. Clean it. Make it clean again.

Another thing that was different now was the size of the prey. Left on his own, Crowley loved chasing down small things. But now that the humans — were they humans? They were calling themselves something different now — were bringing him out with them, he'd been taking part in something new. New food, new fluid.

The two main humans who had been providing for him — he'd always known them as *Carroww-rwrrn* and *Raaaee* — had taken him to new places completely outside of his world. There were other humans — *people,* another human word — around as well, but they didn't matter as much to him. He tolerated them, though.

Regardless, the important thing was that new, exciting stuff was happening, most importantly a new way to feed. Crowley could now feed on humans, biting their delicious flesh with his sharp teeth and lapping up their warm, red milk. No, not milk. There had been milk, and then there had been *water,* and now there was *blood.* That was what the humans — no, not humans… *vampires* — called it.

There were so many new words. His small, cat-sized brain couldn't take them all in at once. And sometimes, they would slip away, and he'd forget them again. It wasn't fun, not like when a cockroach scurried by and could be chased down. It was unsettling, forgetting something and then not even being able to remember what it was that had gone missing.

Sometimes, the clarity was equally as off-putting. He knew, at least for a while, the proper names of his caregivers, Carolyn and Ray. He'd been spending quite a lot of time with Carolyn since the change, and he did his best to listen to her and understand the things she said to him. How difficult that was ebbed and flowed. He also felt very protective of her, another emotion he wasn't used to.

He spent plenty of time on his own, too. It surprised him how easily he took to flying; he'd never been keen on heights before. Both he and the humans-now-vampires could turn into fluttering little beasts themselves, and it was weird how he sometimes felt the urge to chase after them and bite them mid-air. But he managed to suppress that urge somehow, maybe another result of whatever had brought about the change. There was another word he kept hearing bandied about: *potion.* Maybe that was what had changed him. No, not just him. Them as well.

That might explain why he felt more of a kinship to the people in his life than before. The change had given them more in common. It had something to do with the blood, too, he was pretty sure. The blood, the blood, the blood. Sometimes it was all he could think about. That was why he'd gone off on his own when the others weren't looking. But in some way that he wasn't quite clear on, this was found out, and Carolyn insisted that he not do it again. He got the sense that she had a good reason for this, so he obeyed. Again, this was not typical behavior for him.

Crowley hadn't asked for this. He enjoyed the new abilities, the new power, the new tastes and smells. But sometimes, he resented how it seemed to have been forced upon him. He didn't like it when the distant memories popped up, the ones from long before, when he'd been a human in a former life. It made him feel sad, like he'd lost something. He could just vaguely remember people from back then, family, but not clearly enough. Who had he been? What had he done? Did it have anything to do with how he'd wound up becoming who and what he was now? The questions — and the ability to ask them in the first place — were unwelcome. He'd just as well have let the memories stay buried. Things were simpler before.

Maybe this strangeness wouldn't last. For all he knew, there might be a way for him to go back to the way he was before. That was what he really wanted. Perhaps he could become normal again and forget all of these eerie, disconcerting things. Sure, there were some upsides to the situation, but he wasn't sure if they were worth it.

Everyone had been more tense than usual the past day or two. That much he could tell. Something had upset them, but there was also an element of excitement to it. Crowley had begun to feel the same way, even if he didn't fully understand why. As the group flew into the night sky, he went along with them as usual, following their lead and looking forward to the next time he could drink that precious blood.

There was another word being tossed around frequently — a new one — that he picked up on. No, not just a word, but a name: *Shelling.* Clearly this had some bearing on what everyone was so worked up about, and Crowley wondered what the rest of the night would bring.

CHAPTER TWENTY-FIVE

LAURIE'S STORY

Laurie had been having a crappy day. The night before had been lots of fun, the tail end of her trip to Atlanta. She and her friends had gone to a few clubs, had lots of drinks, then wound down at Ben's apartment in Buckhead partying even later into the night.

Everyone had slept well past noon on Friday. Laurie was hungover, as were most of the others. But they all agreed that, unpleasant though that was, it meant that it had been a great night. Little by little, helped by drinking lots of water, she started to feel better. She began the long drive back to Charleston, hoping to get there before dark. Unfortunately, that wasn't how things worked out.

Her car wasn't the most reliable thing in the world, she had to admit. But she liked taking road trips. Being behind the wheel for long periods of time gave her a feeling of independence and freedom, a way to feel truly grown up and on her own. When she was on the road, whether it was solo or with friends, her car was her private little world with her rules and her music. She enjoyed packing for a trip the night before, planning each day as she laid out the clothes, carefully choosing which outfit was appropriate for the activities ahead. The same ritual applied to her big case of cassette tapes, which looked like a cute little leather briefcase.

"Why don't you just fly?" Ben had suggested the week before over the phone. "Charleston's got an airport; Atlanta's got an airport. It'd save you a lot of hassle."

"Because I don't want to," she said simply. "I like driving. Besides, it's too expensive."

"Laurie, your dad's a travel agent, for Christ's sake. I'm sure he can swing you some kind of deal."

But that was just it: She didn't want Daddy's help. He'd always paid for everything: her car, her apartment, her tuition, her textbooks. She wasn't ungrateful, but she also had this desire to be her own person. She was fully aware that people who knew enough about her lifestyle had this preconception of her being some kind of spoiled little princess.

If only they could see her now, she thought bitterly, her legs aching and her feet just as sore.

Laurie's car had been acting strange not long after she'd made her way out of Atlanta. The temperature gauge kept going up and down, the needle creeping up into the "H" zone that indicated that the engine was getting too hot. Whenever she turned the air conditioning off, the needle went down. But that made for a miserable drive; it was the middle of summer. Rolling the windows down helped some, and she eventually consigned herself to being satisfied with that.

But after a while, she realized that things were getting too far out of control. When she stopped off at a gas station in Augusta, she noticed some kind of smoke or steam coming out from the car's front grill. Clearly, something was wrong. She popped the hood, then looked around at the incomprehensible inner workings of the car's engine. She had no idea what any of it meant.

The gas station attendant, who was rather abrupt with her, suggested that she take her car to a repair shop not far from where they were, so she did. The tall, unshaven man who ran the place listened to what she told him about the car's symptoms, looked it over, and told her exactly what she didn't want to hear.

He explained to her in what she felt was an unnecessarily condescending manner that he could fix the car, but it wouldn't be ready until tomorrow because the alternator he needed for it couldn't be gotten from the parts store until morning. The cost of the part and the labor to install it would be close to $300. She could just barely afford that, and only then by putting it on her credit card, which was nearly maxed out.

Laurie didn't have any friends in Augusta; she barely knew anything about the town. It was just somewhere to drive through. What she did know was that she was out of money and couldn't even afford to get a hotel room. If she did that, there wouldn't be anything left to pay for the car repairs.

She tried to talk the mechanic down in terms of the price, flashing him her best smile. That didn't seem to work, so she tried for the pitiful approach. No luck there, either. She wasn't used to that. Laurie was a small, thin, attractive girl with expressive blue eyes and chin-length blonde hair. She knew full well that she got a lot of mileage out of her looks, and they usually worked to her advantage.

But this time, the guy didn't seem fazed by her charm. In fact, as she would soon find out, he was just the first in a string of unfriendly people she would encounter in this strange city.

Negotiations at the repair shop had left her with little more than a "good luck to you" from the jerk of a mechanic. Even worse, he'd indicated that there was a chance that the auto parts store might not even be open the next day because of the July 4th holiday. She'd asked him if there were any hotels within walking distance, and he'd quipped, "Depends on how far you feel like walking."

By that point, Laurie had reached her limit, and she rushed out before she lost her cool completely. She was normally a nice, friendly girl, but things had been getting steadily more frustrating, and she didn't want to blow up at the man, even if he did deserve it. It had been clear to her that he was impatient and eager to leave for the day; she couldn't help the fact that she'd shown up just before his shop was supposed to close.

As she stomped along the side of the road trying to figure out her next move, she realized that she should have asked him to call her a cab. If he'd been any kind of gentleman, he might have thought of that himself or, better still, offered to pay for it.

But even if she could have gotten a cab, where would she go? She couldn't get a hotel room, not with the impending cost of the repairs. Her first goal, she decided, was to find a pay phone. Maybe she could call Ben. How much would a long distance call from here cost, though?

Then she cursed her luck again, remembering that she'd given the last of her change away to some homeless guy outside the bar the night before. Her Atlanta-native friends had discouraged her from doing that, but she'd blown them off. If the guy needed help, she was happy to give him what little she could. Now she wished she'd taken their advice. Here she was, a stranger in this town, effectively homeless herself.

A thorough search of her purse, which she hoped might yield some hidden coins but didn't, gave her more bad news: She was almost out of cigarettes. She did manage to find a five dollar bill, so if she could make her way to another gas station, or possibly to a grocery store instead, at least that problem would be solved. There would probably be some change left over, but she was also getting pretty damn hungry. What little money she had left would have to go to whatever snacks she might be able to buy. It was scary, finding herself unexpectedly poor like this.

Laurie walked and walked, feeling more tired and frustrated as she did. She'd believed she was heading back in the direction of the main road, the one off the highway, but she must have taken a wrong turn. She was pretty good at finding her way around in a car, but on foot, she had a much worse sense of direction. Somehow, she'd ended up in a residential area.

It was getting dark, but the neighborhood didn't look all that bad. She knocked on a few doors, but no one answered, not even at the houses where there were lights on and the sounds of TVs or radios coming from inside. She assumed that at least someone would come to the door, maybe help her out. But the whole place turned out to be distinctly unfriendly and closed off.

Cars whipped by her as she walked along the ever darkening street, and she considered sticking her thumb out like the stereotypical hitchhiker, but that seemed foolish. Hoping that she hadn't gotten turned around yet again, she decided to head back in the direction she'd come from. Surely that would lead to a gas station, or something. If she could get some more cigarettes and maybe a little bit of junk food there, she might have the stamina to keep walking, hopefully finding her way to the main road. Maybe the gas station workers might prove to be more friendly.

No such luck. She managed to get what she needed for the time being: a pack of cigs, a Coke, and some cheese crackers. But when she asked the unexplainably timid guy behind the counter if he had a phone she could use, he refused. She probably shouldn't have framed her question with the phrase "it might have to be long distance." Maybe that had been the deal-breaker, or maybe he was just as much of an unhelpful asshole as everyone else in this town.

Frustrated, starving, and on the verge of tears, Laurie shoveled the salty crackers into her mouth as she sat on the sidewalk outside the store, washing them down with the soda. She did that a bit too fast, she realized, when she tried to approach one of the other store patrons on their way from the gas pump to the door of the building.

"Excuse me, I'm wondering if yoOOOUUAAAHHP…" She'd let out a huge belch right in the middle of her sentence, and she slammed her hand over her mouth involuntarily. It might have been funny under any other circumstances, but the horrified look the woman gave her and the way she hurried into the store made Laurie realize that she probably looked a lot worse than she'd previously thought. A quick glance into the reflective surface of the glass as the door closed between them confirmed this. Her hair was a mess, and her make-up had practically melted halfway down her face. No doubt she also stank from all the sweat, walking for hours in this summer heat.

Embarrassed, she hid around the corner of the store and waited until the woman had gotten back to her car and left. She then slipped inside and hurried to the restroom, only realizing once she was in there how bad she had to pee. She hated using public toilets, but by this point, she didn't have a choice. She used the paper towels by the sink to scrub off her make-up, feeling more vulnerable as she did so. She wasn't even sure if doing so made her look less scary or, well, homeless.

Laurie steadied herself, her hands firmly pressed on either side of the sink. She didn't want to start crying. If she did, she might not be able to stop, and that would probably make her look even more like a crazy woman. At least the bathroom was private, just the single-occupancy kind with a lock on the door.

She tried to figure out what to do. For a moment, she wondered if she might be able to hide out in here indefinitely. There was a sink to drink water from and a toilet to use, after all. Had the cashier seen her when she'd slipped in? Maybe if she got lucky, he'd close the place up and leave. As bad as things had gotten, she found that she wasn't opposed to the idea of camping out the night locked in a convenience store. At least she wouldn't starve.

She laughed, despite herself. It almost sounded like a fun idea. But it was just as likely that the guy would check the bathroom before leaving, then kick her out. She needed to use whatever time she had left to clean herself up some more.

After a while, Laurie had used the paper towels and the rather unpleasant smelling soap to wash off her arms, legs, and upper body. She could feel the stickiness of the dried sweat coming off of her as she did so, wishing that she could just be back in her car and on her way home. If only there were somebody who would actually help her.

A thought flashed across her mind, then another. A plan started to form, if an incomplete one. If she could just make it to a hotel, well, she might not be able to afford a room, but maybe she could sleep on a couch or even a chair in the lobby until morning. But she'd already seen how helpful people were around here. They'd probably run her out of there as well.

But her second thought was of a friend of hers from school, Sheena. She worked in a hospital, and Laurie had been there with her more than once. People slept in the waiting room there all the time, like when they had relatives who were in surgery. Plus there were vending machines and even a cafeteria. If she could just make her way to one here…

Someone banged loudly on the door, making her jump. "Ma'am? Ma'am?" a voice called out.

Laurie wasn't surprised when she opened the door and saw the ugly cashier eyeballing her suspiciously.

"I'm going, I'm going," she said impatiently, pushing past him. If he was going to treat her like some kind of criminal, she might as well act the part. She stomped out of the store, not even looking back as he shouted a few more "ma'am"s at her.

Outside, she lit up another cigarette. The smoke felt good going down her throat and into her lungs, and she realized how tense she'd been. Too late, she decided that she probably shouldn't have been so rude to the cashier. Maybe if she'd tried turning on the charm instead, he might have let her use the phone after all to call a cab. She only had a tiny bit of money left, but maybe she could have at least found out if there were a hospital nearby. Hell, at this point, she'd even call her dad if she'd been able to.

She hadn't wanted to involve him or to ask for his help, but she was feeling pretty desperate, she had to admit. A year ago, he'd berated her for letting her car break down because she'd gone way too long without giving it an oil change. It was just something that had slipped her mind, but he'd gone on and on about it like she was the dumbest person in the world, threatening to take her car away if she did that again. This was why, among other reasons, she hadn't contacted him as soon as she'd realized that there was a problem with it this time. She hated being talked down to. She could cope with this herself.

"Good job with that, Laurie," she whispered to herself aloud, exhaling more smoke.

Not everything had been her fault, but she could have handled the situation better. And now she probably wasn't even going to make it back home in time for tomorrow night's Independence Day bash, something she'd been looking forward to for weeks.

Imagining her friends enjoying the waterfront party without her made her sad. There would be fireworks, and she wouldn't be there to see them. If she wound up stranded in this crappy town for another night, would she be able to catch some fireworks here? That would be nice, at least. She'd loved them ever since she was a little girl, as far back as she could remember. When she was very young, she hadn't even been able to pronounce the word "fireworks," so she'd called them "pow things" instead. It was one of those cute little kid things that her family had encouraged, only to ridicule her for it once she got older.

Coming back to the present, Laurie realized that there was no point in hanging around the gas station any longer. The creep inside was closing the place up, as evidenced by the sound of the door locking and the external lights being turned off. She'd better get out of here, or else he might call the cops on her for being the horrible vagrant that she apparently was.

She rolled her eyes at the thought, thoroughly pissed off. This town sucked. Determined to find her way back to the main road, she set off again, the soreness in her legs making her wish she'd taken a little bit of time to sit down.

"Sure, come on," the pretty brunette said with a smile, and Laurie's heart leapt. Finally, she'd met someone in this godforsaken city who wasn't some paranoid piece of shit.

After leaving the previous gas station, Laurie had slowly and painfully made her way along the street until it had led to where she'd hoped: the big, four-lane road that she'd been on when she'd gotten off the highway hours ago. The way the neon signs of the multiple businesses here lit up the area encouraged her; this felt more like civilization. There were even a couple of hotels, but as before, she figured that there probably wasn't any point in asking the people there for help.

The good news was that the gas stations here were still open for business, though their doors were locked. What few customers the places had this late at night had to go to a little window to pay for their gas, talking to the cashier through it.

Shortly after burning her way through another cigarette, she spotted a car, a greyish hatchback, that pulled up and parked at one of the pumps. The girl who got out and went to the window to prepay for her gas appeared to be about the same age as her, which she hoped was a good sign. Almost everyone else she'd encountered since she'd gotten to Augusta had been older.

Trying to play it cool, Laurie waited until the girl had completed her transaction, then approached her. At first, the girl seemed just as cold as everyone else she'd tried to talk to, seeming to mostly ignore her as she focused on the task of refueling her car. But then, thank God, her expression slowly softened as Laurie began to relay her desperate tale.

The girl, whose name turned out to be Susanna, pressed the lever to lean the driver's seat forward, then stepped aside to let Laurie maneuver her way into the back seat.

"Thank you so much," Laurie said for the third or fourth time. "You have no idea how grateful I am for this."

"Who's this?" a boy with a high-pitched, prepubescent voice asked from the passenger side. He was immediately recognizable as the girl's younger brother; the two of them had matching hair color and similar facial features.

"Ray, this is Laurie," Susanna said formally after she'd sat down. "Someone who needs our help."

"Help doing what?" the boy asked. Laurie recognized his type immediately: just on the verge of puberty, the age when boys start being overtly sarcastic as part of their attempts at being older and tougher, thinking that they're more clever than they actually are. Her own younger brother had been the same way at this age, and he hadn't fully grown out of it, either. Susanna scolded Ray for being rude, then gave him a quick rundown of Laurie's story.

"Right," Laurie added, trying to be friendly despite her exhaustion. It wasn't essential that she won the boy over, but it would make the overall experience more comfortable if she could. "I'm really sorry if this puts you guys out."

"It's no problem," the older sister said, starting up the engine. "Happy to help." She said this with a sideways glance at her little brother, which Laurie interpreted as meaning something like *mind your manners.*

"Yeah, okay," the boy said. He turned around in his seat to look at Laurie directly. To her surprise, his apologetic smile seemed genuine. "So where's this hospital?" he asked her.

Laurie of course had no idea; she was reliant on her rescuers to take her there. Susanna seemed confident on which way to go, so she put her trust in her. As the three of them rode along, they made small talk, Laurie sharing more details of her crappy day and how she was eager to make it back home tomorrow if her car could be repaired in time. Had it just been her and the girl her age, she might have peppered her story with more profanity to express her frustration, but she curbed her occasional desire to do so.

Another surprise came up during conversation, the fact that Susanna also lived in Charleston and went to the same college, studying English while Laurie majored in marine biology. That was probably why they'd never run into each other on campus, their classes being unrelated, but still, it was a neat coincidence, and it made Laurie smile. Here they were, two girls from the same school, running into each other in this unfriendly city.

Laurie wondered if there was something about their parallel lifestyles that led to Susanna being laid back and friendly enough to help her out, as opposed to all of the assholes she'd encountered in Augusta so far. But she wasn't sure how to say this; it became clear that both Susanna and Ray were from here, so she didn't want to insult them along with their hometown. She eventually managed to fumble out some semblance of these thoughts, which thankfully weren't as off-putting as she'd feared.

"No, it's okay," Susanna said with a laugh, one which her brother echoed. "Things have been, well, happening here lately. Bad things. So people are on edge."

"Yeah, lots of weirdos in this town…" Ray began, but something distracted him. He pointed across his sister's field of vision and said quietly, "There's the hotel."

"I see it," Susanna responded hastily and just as quietly.

This confused Laurie. "No, I said I needed to get a ride to a hospital," she insisted, "for the free place to stay. I can't afford a hotel."

"We know," Susanna said, uncharacteristically stern. Then she seemed to recover herself. "Sorry. That's where we were headed before we stopped off to get gas and a…" She paused, clearing her throat. "Before we picked you up. We'll be at the hospital soon."

"Good," Laurie said, then realized that it sounded bitchy. She forced a smile as she spoke again. "Thanks so much for doing this. I really appreciate it." She wondered if she might be able to ask them for some extra cash to get some snacks from a vending machine once they arrived, but that might be pushing it. It was good enough that they were giving her this free ride.

A lull in the conversation led Laurie to look around the backseat, and she saw something strange that had escaped her notice before. It was a yellow coil of nylon rope, not unlike the kind she'd seen used on her dad's boat. She considered asking Susanna and Ray if they had been doing any waterskiing, but she changed her mind. The question sounded silly in her head.

Something else occurred to her as she caught sight of the green, digital clock on the car's dashboard. It was almost midnight, later than she'd realized. As grateful as she was that these two young people had been around to pick her up from the gas station, she began to wonder just why they were out so late, particularly the boy. She thought of asking them about this as well, then again decided to keep quiet.

"This looks about right," Susanna said, her voice low as she turned the car to the right and onto another street.

Laurie noticed yet another strange thing at this point, the fact that they had turned off of the main road and were heading into what looked like another darker, more residential area. Surely the hospital they were heading for would be in a place more populated than this. Or maybe they were taking some kind of a shortcut.

"You sure we're headed the right way?" she offered, not wanting to be a backseat driver but doing it anyway. Susanna didn't answer, but Laurie was uncertain whether or not she might have nodded in the dim, intermittent glow of the passing streetlights.

Nervousness began to creep up inside of her. Sure, she'd always been told that hitchhiking was dangerous. But she'd been desperate, and these two young people, strangers though they were, had been kind enough to help her out. It's not like they were some creepy old guy who was going to take her somewhere secluded, then rape and kill her. And she didn't have any money, so she wasn't in any danger of being robbed. Even so, that rope made her uneasy.

"So," Susanna said, glancing over to her little brother, "should you tell her, or should I?"

Ray laughed in a decidedly sinister way, and Laurie suddenly felt a lot more nervous. "I will," he said, then once again turned around in his seat to face her, a wicked glint in his eyes.

Then something impossible happened. There was a weird puff of smoke that seemed to fill the entire front passenger side of the car, but only for an instant. Laurie leapt backwards in surprise, but there was nowhere to go, and her back slammed against the padding of the seat. The smoke dissipated almost immediately, and the boy seemed to have disappeared like some kind of magic trick. But there was something else where his head had been: a large, black bat hovering and flapping its wings.

She didn't have time to process what was happening; she just acted out of fear and instinct. The dark shape zoomed towards her, and she skittered around using her arms and legs to propel her body into the other half of the back seat, trying to avoid the tiny attacker. She just managed to catch a glimpse of the other girl, still driving along with a sick smile as another passing streetlight illuminated her face.

The boy seemed to materialize from nowhere again as his form rushed towards her, her skull nearly cracking as their foreheads met. She saw blackness and fireworks before her eyes as she cried out in pain, trying desperately to fight off the attack. Whether he had intentionally head-butted her or had done this by accident, she couldn't be sure, and there wasn't time to contemplate this.

A sharp pain shot into the side of her neck, and she cried out again, but the scream died in her throat. Her entire body went limp, and she felt the weight of the boy on her as he drank the blood from her veins. The car rolled along, its engine's hum and the vibrations from the road beneath singing her to sleep.

CHAPTER TWENTY-SIX

UNHAPPY ENDINGS

Mandy's head was full of conflicting emotions, but she was used to that. On the one hand, she loved her father. Usually. But she was so pissed off at him right now that she didn't know what to think. She was glad that he was still alive, but there was another part of her that wished him dead.

A week ago, he'd been attacked by one of these vampire things that were flying around town. He'd survived, someone in the hallway at the hotel finding him before he'd had a chance to bleed to death. He was whisked away to the hospital, given blood transfusions, and then he was fine.

Things were awkward in the hospital, no one wanting to talk about the big question that was on her, her mother's, and maybe even the doctors' minds: What was her father doing at that hotel? It was halfway across town from their house in South Augusta, and there was no reason for him to be there. But everyone knew the answer, or at least some version of it.

Her own father, whom she'd looked up to and admired as a righteous, upstanding man, had been cheating on her mother. Whether this was a one-time thing or something ongoing, Mandy wasn't sure. She tried to tell herself that she didn't care.

She felt like a fool. She'd always believed that her parents were good, churchgoing people with strong morals. Sure, there was some rebellion against that on her part, but deep down, she'd respected it just the same. But now she was beginning to wonder if the fact that she'd never seen her parents act affectionate towards each other in front of her — which she'd always assumed was some kind of prudish behavior — was in fact a sign of marital trouble. For all she knew, her twelve-year-old brother was the product of the last time the two of them had ever had sex.

Maybe Mom had driven him to this, who knows. The woman could be quite a bitch sometimes, that was for sure. But that still didn't excuse her father's infidelity. If he'd had any balls, he could have just divorced his wife and moved on, not stayed with her out of some old-fashioned sense of having to remain in a dead-end marriage.

Who had he been there with at the hotel that night? Was it some slut from his job that he'd been having a long-term affair with, or had he just gone downtown and picked up some hooker to fuck? Mandy wasn't even sure if downtown Augusta had hookers or if that was just a rumor. She did know that there were strip clubs, way down near the seedy part of town along East Boundary. Or was that where the drug dealers were? She never went to that part of town.

But she was going out tonight, no matter how much her parents protested. She was a high school graduate now, and she prided herself on the fact that things in her life had progressed to how she no longer asked permission to go somewhere with her friends; she just announced where she was going. Since her father's return from the hospital, things had been unusual, though, her mother encouraging her to stay home so they wouldn't have to worry about her, whatever the fuck that meant.

She just couldn't take it anymore. The silence around the house was deafening; no one wanted to talk about the real issue. Dinner was painful to sit through, all averted eyes and the clink of silverware on plates. Mandy was tired of staying home night after night for no reason, especially when she couldn't even stand to look at her father.

She wasn't entirely sure how the night would go, but she liked to think she had a pretty good idea. She would lie, telling her parents that she was going to the mall with Claire. The two of them would then drive to Claire's boyfriend Noah's house, and Andrew would be there. They'd all go up to the Hill, as it was called, a secluded place with a spectacular view of city lights of South Augusta. It was an ideal place to make out. And if Andrew played his cards right and didn't say or do anything too stupid this time, she was fully prepared to do a lot more than that.

She was tired of this virginity crap, "saving it for marriage" and all that bullshit. She'd had enough of uptight hypocrites and their supposed morals. If her father could fuck around, then so could she. As she got ready for the night, spraying and blow-drying her hair within an inch of its life, she imagined herself saying these things to her friends, to Andrew.

But she wasn't sure. Did she really want to tell them how much of a piece of shit her cheating father was? She'd probably just tell Claire, maybe. The girl did have a big mouth sometimes, so maybe that wasn't such a good idea. But then, she'd already been asking questions about Mandy's father, ones she'd been dodging. Everyone knew that he'd gotten hurt, but no one knew the details, like where he was when it happened. Thinking of this made Mandy mad once again, and in that moment, her brush snagged a knot in her hair. She yanked at it angrily, tearing out a few strands in the process.

She slammed the hairbrush onto the bathroom counter, then forced herself to calm down. She needed to stop being so pissed off. If she could just finish getting ready and get out of this damn house, she and her friends could have a really good night.

George Calvert stood in his kitchen, watching his little girl head for the back door. But she wasn't a little girl anymore. He wanted to tell her not to leave, but he felt like he didn't have a right to. He knew that she knew what he'd done, and if she hated him for it, he deserved that. He wanted to apologize to her, too; he'd already done so to Florence a million times, and that hadn't done much good, either. His every "I'm sorry" had been met either with silence or a quiet "I know."

"Be careful," he said to his daughter. He usually said that to her when she went out.

Mandy's back had been to him, but then she paused and spun around, her large purse clanging against her side as she did so. The look she gave him was so icy that it made him want to recoil. He wondered if he could ever make things right with her again, or for that matter, with the rest of his family.

"Don't worry," she said flatly, her voice sounding eerily like her mother's.

"I do love you, you know," he offered, then flinched at how weak and stupid it sounded.

"If that was true, you wouldn't have cheated on Mom." Then she spun on her heel and walked out the back door, slamming it behind her.

It was the last time George saw his daughter alive.

CHAPTER TWENTY-SEVEN

IN THE BASEMENT

"Man, this is pretty crazy, huh?" Damon said to Nick.

"You're not kidding."

The two of them sat on one of the many mattresses that covered the floor of the basement, each of which had a pillow and some sheets on them. Nick wondered which one of the people upstairs it belonged to, then decided that it didn't really matter.

Damon placed a Tupperware container between them and pried off the lid. Inside was a brown, rectangular shape, and he touched it with his finger cautiously. It felt spongy to the touch, not unlike a brownie. He let out a nervous laugh.

"You know," he said, "last time I ate a brownie like this, I was tripping out for hours."

Nick laughed. "You mean a pot brownie? I've never had one of those. Heard of them, yeah, but never done it."

"Well, I hope not!" Damon said. "How old are you again?"

"Thirteen," Nick said, suddenly perturbed. "Doesn't mean I haven't seen some stuff. Don't be a dick."

Damon frowned, then tried to bring things back to a friendly tone. "I'm not; chill out. Let's just do this and get it over with." He picked up the brownie and wobbled it in his hand for a moment, examining it. It seemed solid enough, but it would probably break in half easily. That was what needed to be done, but he didn't want to admit how scared he was to go through with this. He glanced over at Nick, seeing that he too was eyeing the squishy brown substance apprehensively. The boy caught his glance, then hardened himself.

Nick didn't want to appear weak. "Here," he said, grabbing the other end of the brownie, which wasn't a brownie at all. It was the vampire potion, the drug or whatever it was that was going to turn him and Damon into blood-drinking creatures. He pulled, tearing it so that it broke apart, but it didn't tear as cleanly as he'd hoped. What he ended up with was only a fourth of it, maybe less. "Shit," he half-whispered.

"Hang on," Damon said, recovering from the awkward clumsiness and using his other hand to tear off a bit more to divide things up correctly. "There you go." He handed Nick the remaining portion.

They paused, looking each other in the eye. It was like a dare. So they took it, gobbling down the substance simultaneously. It tasted funny, kind of like burnt toast but worse, almost what charcoal might be like to eat. But they got it down, swallowing hard.

They sat there, looking at each other and breathing for a few moments. "So," Nick said simply. "Now what?"

"Guess we're in it for good now," Damon said, smiling. "If what Carolyn and Ray said was true, we're going to start feeling weird pretty soon."

That was an understatement. They'd been warned about how the potion, which would eventually turn them into vampires after four hours, would cause them to have massive mood swings and changes in behavior. The first one was aggression, this sudden desire to beat the crap out of each other. In anticipation of this, Damon and Nick had positioned themselves on opposite sides of the basement, thinking that doing so would be the safest way to go. But it didn't work.

"Come on, you pussy," Damon said in a gruff voice that he didn't know he had, stumbling across the mattresses toward his intended prey. "Let's see what you've got."

Nick felt himself similarly roused and angry, his entire body filled with fire. He screamed as he lunged at his foe, fists flying as he did everything he could to destroy his older opponent. They wrestled and fought, so violently that at one point, Damon lifted Nick into the air and slammed him down onto an old wooden table, barely aware of what he was doing.

The table collapsed under the impact, and Nick scrambled up, seemingly unhurt. The fighting continued, and Nick felt stronger than ever. He lunged at Damon's taller form with all his might, causing him to stumble backwards into some shelves on the wall. Various items from them clattered to the floor.

Damon was angry as hell, determined to best his attacker, who had stepped back for a moment, trying to figure out his next move. The pause gave him time to rush around to the side of the shelving unit, which he then grabbed the top of, shoving it forward and trying to pin Nick under it. It crashed to the floor, unfortunately missing him; he'd jumped backwards just in time to avoid it.

"Whoa," Nick said, pointing at something behind Damon. "What the fuck is that?"

Out of breath, Damon turned around to see what his enemy was indicating. In the wall behind the piece of furniture he'd just toppled over, there was a big, empty opening. It looked like a rectangular doorway, but there was something strange about it. Rather than leading into another room, which would have been unusual in and of itself since this was a basement, there was nothing but darkness.

"What the…?" Damon said quietly.

Behind him, Nick started to get up from the floor and brush himself off, but then he seemed to slip. "Whoa," he repeated, putting a hand to his forehead.

Damon turned back around to look, his feelings of aggression suddenly melting away. Instead, he felt both compassion for his foe and regret over having attacked him. But before he could move forward to help, he felt all of his strength disappear, and he collapsed to the floor, dizzy. "Oh yeah," he said, struggling to hold himself up with his hands. "They said this would happen, too."

The effects of the potion continued, rotating between long periods of normality, strong emotional outbursts, then several minutes of exhaustion that became longer each time. It was a little scary, but at least they'd been warned what to expect, and they helped each other through it.

Damon and Nick did what they could to straighten up the place after their initial outburst, hoping that the Youngs wouldn't get too mad about the broken table. "Guess we should probably help them put that back together when there's time," Damon said.

"Or maybe we can fix it now?" Nick offered. "There's some tools and stuff down here, you know." He gestured around at the walls, one of which included a large board with various tools hanging on it.

"Not really my kind of thing, to be honest," Damon admitted. "I'm more of an artistic kinda guy, you know, with my music and all."

This was one of the many things the two talked about during their long imprisonment. Once the potion had finished doing its work, it would be safe for them to be let out and among the rest of the vampires. But for now, they had a few hours to kill.

Nick had wondered if it would be difficult making small talk with someone seven years older than him. He had trouble relating to older people, and he didn't have any siblings. But he liked punk music and that culture in general, and while Damon wasn't entirely into it himself, he could appreciate it and hold up a decent conversation, particularly when it came to music. He was, after all, in a band himself.

Having such a wide gap in their ages became less of a problem as time went on, plus Damon was a people person; he could get along with just about anyone given enough time. This came in handy in terms of the various girls he'd dated over the years, though winning them over was just part of the process. He'd also learned that it was important to ingratiate himself to the girls' parents and family members as well.

Nick was more of a loner and wasn't keen on joining groups, clubs, or anything like that. In fact, he questioned his decision to join Ray's group of vampires, but he'd kind of been roped into it. Whatever his motives, Ray had invited him in, and if he'd refused, he might not even still be alive to be contemplating this. He kept his doubts to himself, though, trying to focus on how cool it would be. He and Ray had done various bad things in secret before — mostly minor vandalism and a little bit of pyromania — but he had no idea that his friend was into anything this dark. Sure, it was a bit frightening to be going down this rabbit hole, but it was exciting at the same time.

Damon had similar feelings about Carolyn, having been simultaneously shocked and intrigued to find out that his girlfriend of several months had been involved in something so sinister. He'd always thought she was rather sweet and innocent, though he had of course seen her more sensual side, something she didn't reveal to just anyone. But the fact that this vampire situation, which had been going on for a few years now, was something she'd actually been perpetuating herself was more than a little unnerving. He and Nick talked about this some, but not explicitly. Neither one seemed to want to tip their hand and admit just how nervous it made them both.

"It's weird, huh?" Damon said, trying to keep things light. "Like, my girlfriend has actually killed people."

"Yeah, and my friends from school, too," Nick said, trying to hide his discomfort. "But hey, that's like, I don't know, the ultimate anarchy, right? Kill 'em all; let God sort them out."

"I think it was a military guy who said that, actually," Damon said with a frown, looking down at his canvas shoes and fiddling with one of the shoelaces. "Like my dad. I know he keeps hoping I'll join the Army like he did." He let out a small laugh. "Probably why I went for the rock and roll lifestyle instead. I know it pisses him off."

Nick laughed at this as well, even though it wasn't particularly funny. "Do you know anybody who's been killed? I mean, like, since Ray and the others have been doing this?"

"No," Damon said solemnly. He pondered for a moment how bad this was, what he and Nick were getting into. More than that, it was surely a horrible thing not only for the people who died, but for their families as well. But then he laughed again, not even sure why he did it. "You?"

"Nope. Guess it's just as well." He sat silently for a bit. "Pretty soon, we're going to be doing that, too. Killing people, I mean." He felt a grin spreading across his face.

"Yeah, we are," Damon said, smiling evilly. His expression didn't match his emotions, at least not at first. "We should probably feel really bad about that."

"Yeah?" Nick asked, nodding, and then he burst out laughing for no apparent reason. "We... we're..." He struggled to catch his breath, then remembered what had happened earlier, back when he and Damon had first locked themselves in the basement beneath the house. He pictured that big black open doorway, the one they had discovered behind the knocked over shelving unit.

"Okay, here it comes," Damon said, fighting down even more laughter. "The final stage. Last one on the list." He couldn't keep it in; the laugh burst out of him as uncontrollably as a sneeze.

"What have we gotten ourselves into, dude?" Nick practically shouted, feeling his entire body quake, almost like he was being tickled by an invisible force. "I mean, this family, these people..." He keeled over, barely in control of himself.

"Right?" Damon asked, cackling. "It was weird enough that they had this basement that could be locked from the inside, and I'm thinking... okay, maybe like a bomb shelter or something, I mean..."

"We're all gonna get nuked! Hide!" Nick blurted out, laughing his head off. He knew that there was no reason to find the thought funny.

"Maybe that's what that weird dark tunnel was for," Damon said. He burst out laughing again. "Good thing we covered it back up! Or maybe not! We need to ask them... what it's..." Out of breath, he passed out on the mattress.

Nick watched this with amusement, waiting for his turn. He felt happier than he ever had in his entire life, and he could barely breathe given how hysterically he was laughing. Some part of his mind knew that this wasn't right, and he really should have been a lot more disturbed by all the things he'd learned. Maybe it was the potion doing it do him, but he found that he was actually looking forward to becoming a killer. He could feel his consciousness starting to fade away… and maybe his conscience, too?

As his vision began to give way to nothingness, Nick wondered about the things around him, both physical and otherwise. The vampire attacks, the killings, the basement full of mattresses, and the hidden tunnel to who knows where… Just how many other secrets did these people have?

CHAPTER TWENTY-EIGHT

DANCE OF DEATH

The vampire stayed hidden in the shadows, waiting for the moment to strike. He found that he enjoyed being on his own; normally, he and the others attacked as a group. But because their group had recently gotten larger, it had become necessary for them to split up into smaller teams. It wasn't easy finding enough victims in one place to feed everyone.

Out here in the suburbs, it had proven even harder than they'd expected, so they'd split up again, which was how he'd ended up at this park. There was a young woman sitting alone on a bench, seemingly not doing anything. It was a dangerous thing to do in this city, and the vampire wondered why she would be so foolhardy.

The woman listened. She had a feeling that she was being watched, but she didn't know if that was just her imagination. She had been coming to this park for three nights now, weighing the possibilities ever since she'd gotten the news Thursday afternoon. She enjoyed the peace and quiet, the freedom from the ringing phone. The isolation helped her think.

The vampire took a step forward, but then he hesitated when something occurred to him. Here was what looked like an easy prey, but maybe that was the point. It seemed too easy.

Over the past few days, he and the other vampires had encountered more resistance than usual, both from the police and from a growing number of individuals who had taken it upon themselves to try to combat the threat that creatures such as him posed. It was understandable: Things had escalated quite a bit over the last couple of weeks. The town had been threatened by vampires before, but never for this long and to such a great extent.

Even so, he and his friends had no intention of backing off, though it was completely within their power to do so. He knew that, logistically, the time would come when they would have to take the antidote to the potion and change themselves back to regular human beings, but every time he thought about that, something within him rebelled. He didn't want it to end, this feeling of power and control.

Pretty sure that was a footstep, the woman thought. She felt an urge to turn around and look, but she resisted it. If she did that, it might scare the predator off. Surely it wanted to take her by stealth, if it were even there at all.

Realizing that she'd been holding her breath, she forced herself to relax. Maybe tonight would be the night. After so many days and nights of mulling over everything, she hoped that she was right.

His thirst for the woman's blood grew stronger. He hadn't fed tonight, and he needed to. But again, he felt hesitant. Something about the situation seemed wrong. All alone, vulnerable on this park bench, sat this free meal. But what if she were bait?

The vampire tried to figure out what to do. He was used to being sneaky, and not just when it came to preying on humans. Nearly always, he'd gotten away with his schemes, but recent events had made him feel less confident. He'd begun to question whether or not he might be getting in over his head.

There was only one thing for it: He'd have to use his psychic powers. It wasn't something he was comfortable doing, and for more than one reason. He'd always kept them hidden, even from his closest friends. Sometimes, especially recently, he questioned why he still did that.

It had come to light that other vampires in the group had been keeping the exact same secret from the rest of them, and the revelation had made him uneasy. It wasn't something that the vampire potion had given them; the powers had existed before. But the potion had certainly made the powers stronger, that was for sure.

Before, he'd kept quiet about his abilities in order to avoid ridicule. People would think you were a nut if you claimed to be psychic. It wasn't something he could help; he didn't even want it. But it was there. When it was revealed that the other vampires had their secret powers and had been keeping that from the group, that made him retreat within himself even more. Again, he wasn't entirely sure why. Maybe it was just something he wanted to have for himself, his own little skeleton in the closet.

Disappointed but slightly relieved, the woman decided that she must have been wrong about what she thought she'd heard. It was probably going to be another uneventful night. So that just left her alone again, having to think about what her future might hold, what there was of it.

The events of the past few days played out in her mind again: the things she'd been told, the things she'd known for years, and what she imagined her fate might ultimately be. It wasn't something she liked to think about, but by now, she'd gotten used to it.

The hunger was almost unbearable now. He had to find out if it was safe to go after this prey. He almost wanted to just fly away and try to find someone else, but something in him flared up and said no. This was who he was meant to attack tonight. He'd spotted her, and she was his.

Reluctantly, the vampire prepared to drop the shield he'd been keeping around his mind. He'd do this as briefly as possible, scanning around the area to find out if there might be policemen or wannabe vampire hunters hiding nearby. It would probably be a good idea to probe the woman's mind as well, just to make sure that she wasn't packing anything like garlic or a wooden stake in order to take him on herself.

He opened up his mind, letting the power flow through him. The familiar tingling sensation in his scalp was accompanied by a mental image of a radar screen, the kind he was used to seeing on TV or in the movies. His consciousness swept around his body in a loop, trying to pick up any blips of life, but there weren't any apart from the unsuspecting woman on the bench.

The woman felt a chill in the air, something unusual for a July night. There was that feeling again of being watched, but as before, she wondered if both that and the coldness were something she imagined. Maybe it was even wishful thinking. She began to feel foolish.

Maybe she should just go home. But she knew that if she did that, there would be the phone again. She could choose to ignore it, even turn the ringer off, but that wouldn't stop the answering machine from clicking into life whenever someone left a message.

And then she would have to hear them, whoever it was this time, offering their condolences, their advice, or whatever other useless crap they had to say. She knew that they meant well, but she was sick of it nonetheless. She regretted skimping on the answering machine she'd bought: She should have gotten the one that allowed her to turn the speaker's volume down or off.

The vampire was certain now that no one else was around. The woman would be his. He still needed to peer inside her mind to make sure she wasn't armed, and he wanted to get that over with as soon as possible. The unpleasant side effect of using his power was already beginning to get to him. It was the other main reason he usually kept it hidden.

Shielding it from the others and not exercising it was easy enough; that wasn't much of a problem. But he'd found that when he did use it, something else happened: His conscience returned. He hated how that made him feel.

He'd figured out a long time ago that one of the things the potion did to him and the rest of the vampires was to suppress their normal sense of morality. It made it easier to kill when there was nothing holding you back, no guilt that made you think about what you were doing. This was probably related to another thing he'd realized about the potion, how it clouded their memories once they changed back to being human. He wondered if that would happen this time around, though, what with the formula being different than it had been in the past.

But even though it didn't seem to be happening to the other psychics in the group, whenever he used his psychic abilities, it somehow countered the suppression of his conscience. It was like the human in him reasserted itself, making him feel guilty, even if only temporarily. He didn't know why it happened, but it made him very uncomfortable.

The sooner he got this over with, the better. He could only hope that once he stopped using his power and tucked it away again, his shame would go along with it. Focusing his mind, he reached out to the woman on the bench, picturing some kind of scanning beam zooming into her head.

He got more than he'd bargained for.

The woman felt something weird in her brain. Was that even possible? She'd heard or read somewhere that the human brain didn't actually have any nerves in it, so it wasn't possible to actually feel anything within that part of the body. Only the surrounding tissue could feel pain, something she knew all too well.

The vampire had only meant to find out what the woman was thinking, to see if she might have any weapons. Instead, a flood of memories surged through his mind, accompanied by a searing pain in the front of his skull.

The doctors' appointments. The phone call. The mysterious illness that no one could figure out.

He gasped involuntarily, trying not to double over as he put a hand to his forehead.

The woman was certain this time. She'd heard something. Against her better judgment, she turned around to see where the noise had come from.

The vampire tried to pull back from the woman's mind, but it was like his own was caught inside hers, snagged like a fishhook.

The migraines would continue to get worse. The medication was too expensive. Her health insurance wouldn't cover it.

There was a pain in his forehead that wouldn't go away. It was like someone was jamming a screwdriver into his skull. Through the tears welling up in his eyes, he could blearily see the woman, who had stood up from the bench and was now facing him.

The woman tried to make out the figure in the distance. It was there, but it looked so far away. No, not far, just smaller than she'd first thought. Then it began to run toward her.

She flinched, but she didn't make a move to run away.

The vampire barreled forward, fangs bared and ready to kill. He was simultaneously surprised and suspicious at the way that the woman just stood there, remembering that he was supposed to have scanned her for weapons. But he couldn't think straight; her thoughts were blaring over his own.

Finally. But why is he so... Is this just a kid?

He felt a flush of embarrassment over this dismissive attitude. He leapt over the back of the park bench, intending to grab her and tackle her to the ground.

The woman stepped to one side, and the vampire boy missed her by just a few inches. She felt a rush of air as his form zoomed past, one foot connecting with the seat of the bench just before he almost gracefully tumbled to the ground in a roll.

The vampire recovered and stood up, having felt the woman's emotions in addition to his own: fear, relief, bafflement, realization.

He steeled himself. It was time for the kill. Despite his earlier clumsiness, he tried his best to feel confident. Usually in this situation, he did. It had never bothered him before that many of the people he'd preyed on in the past were taller than him, but all of a sudden, he found himself feeling decidedly small.

"I thought you'd never get here," the woman said flatly.

"What?" the vampire said, confused by her nonchalance but also disoriented. Fortunately, the unpleasant sensation of her thoughts flowing into his mind had ceased the moment she'd spoken. But now, his own voice sounded loud and conspicuous to him, like being in a crowded classroom where everyone except him seemed to stop talking at the same time.

The boy's prepubescent voice clenched it. "You really are just…" she began, then rolled her eyes. The movement made her head hurt worse for a moment. Then she sighed angrily. "Unbelievable." She stepped towards the vampire.

He resisted the urge to step backwards, still confused by what was happening. The woman didn't seem to be afraid of him, but she wasn't making a move to attack him, either.

"Well, come on then!" she said, putting her arms out by her sides.

"What?" he repeated.

She took another few steps forward until she was standing right in front of him. With eyes full of contempt and bitterness, she looked down at her would-be assailant. "Look, I'll make this real easy for you." Using two fingers to brush her long, curly brown hair behind her left ear, she leaned forward.

Her neck was exposed, and he knew what he was supposed to do. But this entire situation felt wrong. Victims weren't supposed to volunteer themselves. It wasn't just that it took the usual fun out of the kill; there was something else, something that just felt *off*.

"Oh my God, just come here!" the woman practically shouted, grabbing the boy by the back of his head and yanking him towards the side of her neck.

Despite how bizarre everything was, the vampire couldn't resist his instincts any longer. Whatever this woman's deal was, he had to do what he'd come here for. He let out an involuntary hiss as his fangs extended once more, then sunk them into the waiting flesh, his lips closing onto it. He felt a familiar quiver from the woman's body as she flinched and let out a sharp cry from the pain, and the warm, salty blood rushed into his mouth just as it had done from countless victims before.

It happened again. Too late, the vampire realized that he'd forgotten to put his mental shield back up, and her thoughts were flooding into his mind all at once. He couldn't shut them out.

The Peace Corps. Their time in Africa. The bitter irony of how they'd gone to help those people and how it had left her totally screwed.

Normally, the initial rush of the delicious red fluid triggered an urge to bite down harder and start swallowing. It was an amazing feeling, this uncontrollable desire to commit to the act of killing after taking that first big leap. Wave after wave of salty hot goodness would rush down the vampire's throat, and he'd ride the sensation to its inevitable conclusion: a drained corpse beneath him, a finished meal. Smugness and satisfaction topped the whole thing off.

But this was completely different. During the scant, few seconds that he'd started preying on this woman, her grip on his head and her fingers entwined in his hair had both confused and appalled him. Everything about this felt terrible. Worse still, there was something wrong with her blood. It tasted dirty, like trying to drink from a polluted river. The thoughts that slammed into his head told him why.

The mysterious bacterial infection she'd picked up in Africa that the doctors back home couldn't explain. The fact that eating certain foods gave her so much pain that she couldn't stand it, and the migraines that followed. The endless tests and medications that sometimes helped and sometimes didn't. The unfairness of how she'd probably die before she turned 30. The hopelessness, the anger, the despair, the solution.

The vampire gagged, his throat refusing to allow the diseased blood into his body. The convulsion forced him to reach up quickly and slam the woman's forearm away from his head as he jumped back and coughed, blood spilling from his mouth as both he and the woman toppled onto the ground. He spat the remaining fluid from his mouth, wiping at it with his hand.

"NO-HOH-HOHHHH!" the woman shrieked with tears in her eyes, clambering over in the grass towards the vampire hysterically. Her eyes were wild, and the wound on her neck was streaming red as she reached him, trying to grab for his head once more. "You don't get to do that!" she shouted desperately. "Finish what you fucking started!"

"I can't!" the boy yelled, stumbling back from her as he stood. "I don't... I don't want to anymore!"

"Who do you think you are? What the hell is this all to you? Just some stupid game? Deciding who lives and who dies? What right do you have to decide that?" The blood was still pouring from her neck, and she held a hand to it instinctively, despite her wish to die.

"Shut up," he said through clenched teeth. "It isn't like that." It was.

"Bullshit! You're not the one who's dying already! I am!"

"I know," he said sadly, then regretted it. He was feeling it again, that conscience of his nagging at him. It shouldn't be there, nor should the pity he felt for this sick woman. But he couldn't shut it off. Her thoughts and memories were still pouring into his head, more revelations that he didn't want.

Despite the ongoing blood loss, the woman found the strength to stand, then staggered over to the vampire. "Kill me," she hissed. "At least have the balls to do that." She collapsed against his smaller frame, surprised by how sturdy it was.

He just stood there while she panted, trying to shut out the telepathic onslaught, but it wouldn't let up. He was seeing visions of the woman's life, now stretching back to before the illness, back when she'd been happy. With the wound in her neck continuing to hemorrhage, he wondered if it would be possible to just wait her out.

"That's really what it is to you, isn't it?" she practically whispered, but the sound was deafening in his ear. "A game. A stupid game. And it's not just you, is it? I can see them in your head… the others… How many of you are there?"

"Too many," he found himself saying, but he was distracted by this latest development. The mental bridge was apparently two-way. It had to stop. With a slow but deliberate motion, he maneuvered his arms up, grasping the woman's head with both hands. Then he snapped her neck, and her body crumpled, lifeless in his grip.

Finally, the unwelcome flow into his brain stopped, and he felt a sense of relief as the corpse slid down the side of his body and onto the ground. He stepped back a couple of paces, unable to take his eyes away from the heap at his feet. Feelings of guilt and shame filled him, and he felt like crying.

It took him a few moments to remember what else he needed to do: He had to put the shield up around his mind again to turn off his psychic powers. It had been down for way too long. A quick visualization of a sort of cylindrical prison cell — something he'd seen in an old science fiction show — slid up around his head, and the task was done.

He felt himself harden inside once more, and that should have been the end of it. But it wasn't. *Too many,* he'd said, and the words echoed inside his mind. What had he really meant by that?

The vampire felt sad, but he also felt determined. The dying woman had been right: It was a stupid game, one that had gone on for too long. Things needed to change.

CHAPTER TWENTY-NINE

THROUGH THE LOOKING GLASS

The apartment felt empty. That was just fine with Alicein, or at least, that's what she had told herself a week ago, and the solitude of the place was something she'd tried to find comfort in since getting back into town.

But now she wasn't so sure. She'd needed time to process everything, hoping that doing so would help her understand it, but she still didn't feel okay. She missed her friends, and she wanted to make things right with them. She wasn't sure how much she would tell them about all that had happened to her, nor was she entirely clear on the details of that. It had all been so confusing and strange, but maybe talking to someone would help. That hadn't been the case a few days ago, though, when she'd just wanted to be left alone.

"I'm Russ, by the way," the man on the bus said, holding up his hand.

She shook it politely as a reflex, something expected of her. "I'm Alicein. A-L-..." She'd started to spell out her name, another knee-jerk reaction, but then she realized that there was no reason to in this situation. She was exhausted and not thinking straight. "I'm sorry," she said with a weak smile. "I don't mean to be rude, but if you don't mind, I'd really rather not talk anymore. I just need to be alone with my thoughts right now."

"Fair enough," Russ said. "I understand." And he did, Alicein knew; he'd been through the same weirdness that she and everyone else on the bus back from Warrenton had experienced, whatever that was. It was all vague and rather frightening, particularly the way that no one could remember just what had happened to them.

Alicein turned in her seat, curling up in an attempt at a sleeping position as she leaned against the interior of the bus's window, staring out of it as the greenery rolled by. It was pretty this far out in the country, and while she normally found comfort in that sort of thing, she wasn't in the mood to contemplate the wonders of nature, not now. There was a big gap in her memory, and she didn't know just what that meant.

Russ had related to her his story, one not too dissimilar from hers or the ones she'd picked up on from other people now sitting in the seats surrounding them. He was a friendly, middle-aged guy, probably about twenty or so years older than her, dressed in jeans and a Polo shirt and sporting a day-old beard. She'd liked him just fine, and at first, she thought that talking to him might help her fill in the blanks in her memory.

"It was the weirdest damn thing, I tell you," he'd said. "The bats flew right out of the sky, eyes all lit up and red, like something out of a horror movie. We tried to get away, but then… There was this one… I swear it smiled at me. And then its eyes lit up real bright, and the red glow just seemed to spread all over me. Everything went black after that."

Alicein had shuddered at this description; it was pretty much the same thing that had happened to her. And like Russ — like everyone else — she'd woken up on her feet in the middle of a crowded auditorium full of people, disoriented and confused. Everyone seemed to be more or less okay, but then some woman in a hood got up on stage and started ranting about vampires, either warning them or threatening them; she wasn't sure. Then more bats flew in and started attacking people, and they all ran out of the building, most of them making it out alive.

The next few hours had been a blur. No one knew where they were, what was going on, or anything. But despite the earlier danger, things seemed to have calmed down, and Alicein was content to step back and let other people take charge. She had some idea of what might have happened, but it was conflicting with some of her spiritual beliefs, which she was beginning to question.

Alicein was a practicing witch, though not the stereotypical, pointy-hatted kind most people thought of when hearing that word. She wasn't some evil, cackling hag who cursed people or rode around on a broomstick. That was all fiction, stupid stories that other people made up to discredit her kind throughout history. She did believe in magic — or as it was spelled by those who knew better: *magick* — and she occasionally cast spells. But this belief system of hers wasn't about controlling others or causing harm. In fact, that was one of the core tenets of her religion: *An' it harm none, do what ye will.*

She sometimes felt silly when she remembered what brought her to this lifestyle, knowing what she knew now. True witchcraft had nothing to do with devil worship or anything bad at all really, but she hadn't known that when she'd first decided to delve into it. It was an act of defiance, a way to rebel against her uptight, super-religious foster parents, whom she'd fallen out with a few years back. The final straw with them had been when she'd decided to move in with her boyfriend at the time, and they couldn't handle her doing something so horrible as "living in sin" like that. But her rebellion against them had started long before, and her new religion was part of that.

Initially, she'd surmised that Wicca was something very dark and mysterious, a direct counterpoint to her fundamentalist Christian parents' beliefs. But once she truly got into it and did the proper research, she found that it was much more about nature and the interconnectedness of all things, something that resonated with her a lot more than she'd expected. It made sense, and there was none of the bullshit she'd grown tired of: no controlling, arbitrary rules, no shaming of people for having natural, sexual desires, no fat guy in a polyester suit standing in front of a bunch of other well dressed people every Sunday telling them what to think, when to stand up, sit down, pray, or sing.

She wondered what her real parents would have thought of her choice, and she liked to think that they would have approved. She could still remember them, but only barely; they'd died in a car accident involving a drunk driver when she was only seven years old. With no other relatives to look after her, she'd been plopped down into the foster system, which was how she'd wound up with the crappy parents she'd been given instead. They weren't terrible to her, not all the time anyway, but the older she got, the more she resented them and couldn't help but compare them to the much cooler mother and father she wished she'd grown up with. For one thing, they were hippies, which was how she'd wound up with her name.

"It's spelled differently because you're special," her father said, leaning forward in his easy chair and looking down at her. He was a huge, nice man with a wide smile partly obscured by his thick, bushy moustache. His straight brown hair covered his ears, completing the look that made him appear in her memories like a carbon copy of the singer Sonny Bono. Because of this, Alicein often pictured her mother looking like Cher, even though she actually had reddish, spirally hair, much like Alicein did herself.

"But I don't like it, Daddy," her five-year-old self whined. "Everyone says it's spelled wrong!"

"Well, then *they're* wrong," her father said, his smile never fading. "Your mom and I named you after Alice in Wonderland. 'Alice, in.' But pronounced like 'Allison.' Isn't that neat?"

It took Alicein a while to accept this; in fact, she only grudgingly did so long after her parents' death. Sure, it was a neat idea, but the name caused her problems growing up, her constantly having to explain it to people.

The older she got, she'd grown to dread the first day of school each year. Teachers would go down the roll and call out the students' names, then stumble when they got to hers near the end. "Ah-*lee*-see-in?" "Uh… I'm not sure how to pronounce this, but…" *"Ail-ih-sign?* I think…" "You may have to help me out with this…" The phrasing varied, but the message was always the same: *I don't get it, and I'm going to make a big deal out of this and embarrass you in front of the entire class.*

By the time she was in high school, she'd learned to save both her and them the trouble and just blurt out the correct pronunciation once she could tell that they'd gotten to her name on the roll. The more astute teachers understood right away and just let it go, but there were also ones who wanted a more detailed explanation. This also changed over the years, starting off as the whole story about the reference to *Alice's Adventures in Wonderland* but eventually being shortened to the quip: "My parents were hippies." That usually got a laugh.

This was also why she'd developed the habit of spelling her name immediately after telling it to someone new, especially when she had to deal with someone official. "Alicein White, A-L-I-C-E-I-N." The phrase rolled off her tongue almost involuntarily. One thing she kept to herself, though, was her father's nickname for her when she was little: Rabbit. That was another reference both to her name and the story that inspired it, plus it tied into the Jefferson Airplane song "White Rabbit," which Alicein guessed was probably influential in her parents' choice in naming her as well. Again, they were hippies after all, and the song came out around the same time she was born.

But that was just speculation. The sad thing about people being dead, she decided, was that once they were gone, you couldn't ask them things anymore. They could pass along stories and explanations and whatever else while they were still here, but once their lives were over, that was it.

If they'd lived long enough, she might have gotten the chance to tell them how much she actually despised the whole "Alice in

Wonderland" thing, how it felt like it had been forced upon her. She didn't like the Disney movie; everything about it and their other movies always seemed so hokey to her, all of the singing and high-pitched voices, plus it seemed like everyone smiled way too much the entire time in a creepy, unnatural way. Even the bad guys smiled. Real life wasn't like that, and she didn't have much to smile about. As for the book the movie was based on, Alicein tried to read it once but found it mostly boring.

So while her friends occasionally suggested that she change her name to the more common spelling "Allison" to avoid all of the confusion, she was defiant. The name was her cross to bear, a tribute to the mother and father she'd lost and would never get to know. In a sense, it was all that she had left of them. People would mangle the pronunciation and the spelling of it for the rest of her life, but at the end of the day, that was their problem, not hers.

And so Alicein was a misfit from day one, and she was perfectly fine with that. She wasn't terribly unpopular growing up, though. Sure, she was a little weird and kind of "off" as far as people were concerned, but she didn't have much trouble getting along. She did well in school and was able to sort of float around among the various cliques, her gentle manner of speaking and good sense of humor serving her well. Sometimes even she was surprised by how well adjusted she was given everything that she'd been through as a child. But basically she knew how to roll with the punches and get through things. Whatever life hurled at her, she handled it.

But even her tolerance and levelheadedness had been pushed to the limit with this latest experience. She wasn't used to being so weirded out, and this left her feeling isolated and disoriented. She'd been aware of the increasing vampire activity in her hometown and how out of hand it seemed to be getting this time around, but even then, she'd had faith in her belief that she'd be okay. Somehow, she'd gotten swept up in the madness, but instead of getting killed like she knew so many other people had been, she'd come out okay, and that didn't really make sense either.

As the bus — one of several that the authorities had arranged for — drove along back to Augusta, she tried to understand everything, but she just couldn't. For some inexplicable reason, she and hundreds of other people had been whisked away to some tiny town in the middle of nowhere some fifty miles out west, all of them suffering from anemia and with their memories of the past few days blank. What the hell had happened to them?

They weren't dead; they hadn't been drained of blood completely. This wasn't like what had happened back home in Augusta before. As far back as four years ago, handfuls of people had gotten killed each night in various parts of the city, their bodies found drained and lifeless. She had friends whose relatives had died this way, but she considered herself lucky that she'd never lost anyone that she knew firsthand. Two years later, in 1985, there was more alleged vampire activity, and it was coupled with lots of people disappearing altogether, never to be seen again. And now in 1987, some of the same stuff seemed to be happening once more, but with a different twist. Maybe she and the others disappearing to Warrenton was part of the overall story, but it was just too strange to fathom. Worse still, it made her question something else she believed in.

"Okay, time to go," Alicein said to herself as she approached the door leading out of her apartment. She could feel her breathing getting shallow again, so she paused, closed her eyes, and forced herself to inhale and exhale more slowly. *It's Tuesday,* she said in her mind. *You told yourself that you weren't going to stay inside anymore once it was Tuesday.*

Taking a few more steps forward, she touched the cold metal of the doorknob, which made her hesitate once more. The place was so quiet now, and she winced as she began to remember happier times, back when Travis and Amelia still lived here.

"Sorry," Amelia said. "I didn't know. I just thought maybe I…"

"It's fine," Travis insisted, an amused smile on his face as he scraped the mass of overcooked noodles into a bowl. "I think they're still edible. They'll just be kinda sticky."

"What did you *do?*" Alicein asked, walking into what passed for their kitchen. She waved her hand in front of her face dramatically, fanning the steam away.

Travis laughed. "She thought she'd cook some ramen noodles herself, but she did them for like fifteen minutes instead of three."

"God, I feel so stupid," Amelia said, looking ashamed.

"It's *fine,*" Travis repeated. "Just… Well, maybe leave the cooking to me and Alicein from now on." He said this as he handed the bowl to Amelia, blowing on it to further disperse the cloud of steam that was rising from the soup. "Careful," he added, flicking his index fingers along the rim of the bowl to indicate that she should handle it similarly.

She did, then sipped at the edge. The hot soup burned her tongue, and she complained the rest of the night about how she couldn't taste anything anymore. "Can't even cook ramen noodles right," she grumbled.

"Don't beat yourself up about it," Alicein said to her. She knew how sensitive the girl could be.

She really needed to patch things up with Amelia; they'd had a bad falling out and hadn't spoken since. As for Travis, she wasn't so sure. Maybe she'd overreacted, maybe not. But she'd been on her own for too long, the gap within her memory notwithstanding. She was beginning to think that living alone wasn't the best thing for her after all.

"All right, enough," she said aloud, then forced herself to open the door. *It's daytime. Nothing to worry about. They're not going to get you during the day.* The anxiety remained, but she did her best to overcome it one step at a time. She made her way down the stairwell, then out onto the sidewalk. People were walking around, and cars were driving up and down Broad Street. It was a perfectly normal day. That just made her feel even more out of place.

For a moment, she started to change her mind, to turn right back around and go upstairs to the apartment. But that wouldn't solve anything. She needed to stop hiding out from everyone. She was alive, she was okay, and she had people to talk to. Hopefully they wouldn't be too mad at her for having disappeared on them for so long.

Passing by Basement Records, she considered stopping in to see if Travis was working that day. But she decided against it; she couldn't deal with talking to him just yet. Maybe they could work things out and get back together, but that would be a long and difficult conversation, one that she wasn't prepared to have. Instead, she continued along the sidewalk toward Nina and Roderick's apartment.

Like her own and many of the other apartments downtown, Nina and Roderick's was a loft situated above a store along Broad Street. The two of them weren't a couple, though; Roderick was gay. She had no problem with that whatsoever; it was well established among their circle of friends that Roderick was a perfectly nice guy and a great friend to have. The main reason that he and Nina lived together was to save money. Sure, some jerks hassled him from time to time about his feminine manner and quirky way of dressing, but for the most part, people left him alone, particularly when he was surrounded by his female friends. They were used to sticking up for him.

Alicein made her way up the stairs to their apartment, worried that she might hesitate before ringing the doorbell. But being out and around people had actually started to help her normalize and feel better, so she found that it wasn't difficult to push the button and wait for the door to open.

After a few moments, she heard the chain from the other side being unlatched, and the door swung open. The sight that greeted her wasn't what she'd expected. It was Nicola, Nina and Roderick's younger friend who sometimes stayed with them, but she didn't look like her usual self. Instead of the aloof, sarcastic punk girl that Alicein was used to seeing, the girl was a mess, and she'd clearly been crying.

"Nicola?" Alicein asked, immediately concerned. "Nicola? Sweetheart, what's wrong?"

She burst into tears and collapsed into Alicein's arms.

Alicein had always liked Nicola. Like Nina and Roderick, she was a punk rock type of girl, very much into wearing funky looking black clothes and gothic looking make-up. Even though Alicein had always felt that the pale foundation, dyed black hair, and heavy eyeliner look was a bit over the top and silly, she still respected the effort that it took. It wasn't her thing; Roderick and the others affectionately described Alicein as "vanilla" in comparison, more plain and ordinary.

"Not that that's a bad thing," Roderick would say in his usual sing-song kind of tone. "You just be who you are and we'll love you just the same." The boy was what he jokingly called a "devout atheist," and he sometimes debated Alicein on her beliefs and insisted that Wicca was just as stupid of a religion as all the others. But they never got into any truly bitter arguments. She tolerated his occasional bitchiness — even found it kind of cute — and she knew full well that he copied a lot of his personality from the more interesting singers and artists he liked from the late night MTV show *120 Minutes,* which showed videos from lesser known, weirder groups.

Nina had similar tastes, and she also styled herself in exotic, dark clothes and such. Her fashion sense was adopted not only by Nicola but Amelia as well, once she'd gotten into town and hooked up with them. Alicein felt downright plain and boring in comparison, but not in a bad way. They were all different; everyone was a misfit in the way that worked for them.

Nicola had problems at home, her mother being this difficult, overly dramatic woman who always blew things way out of proportion for no good reason. She and Amelia were close to the same age, in their early teens, and Amelia's mother had apparently been similarly impossible. She'd once described her as being "basically not good for anything other than being a rich housewife." That was why she'd run away from home, leaving Savannah and coming to Augusta, eventually finding her way to Alicein and Travis, who took her in and let her live with them. Alicein had been wary of harboring a runaway in the beginning, but she knew that if Amelia got caught by the police, she'd either get sent back to Savannah or thrown into the foster system in Augusta, something she wouldn't wish on anyone. Travis also had a soft spot for the poor girl given some things that had happened in his past.

The gothic punk look suited Roderick and Nina, all spooky and threatening. That was the point; the multiple piercings in their ears were meant to make them appear tough. *I look scary, so don't mess with me.* For Nicola, it was kind of the same thing, though she always wore her hair in a ponytail; it was her trademark. And for Amelia, it also served as something of a disguise: If the cops from Savannah ever did come looking for her, they wouldn't have even recognized the girl. Her long, light brown hair was transformed into a short black bob, and the thick black eyeliner that she wore framed her brown eyes in a way that made her look even more creepy than usual. She had this thing she would do with her eyes when she was feeling surprised, widening them and rolling them around in a weird way that was disconcerting. She probably wasn't even aware that she did it. But when the heavy eye make-up was added, the effect was downright scary.

And so they had their strange group of friends, all of them weirdos and oddballs, getting along as they did. Alicein and Travis were a part of that, as were the other punks and bizarre people that had begun to congregate downtown. Augusta was a strange place, and lots of bad things happened all around and throughout it, so everyone did their best to survive and help each other. At least, that was how Alicein chose to see things.

She struggled to keep her arms around Nicola as they collapsed together onto the hardwood floor of the apartment. The girl was crying uncontrollably, her body heaving as she quivered. "Shh… shh…" Alicein assured her. A selfish thought crossed her mind: She'd been planning to come here to spill her guts to Nina and Roderick, plus she'd hoped to find Amelia here since she knew that she'd gone to stay with them.

"Where are Nina and Roderick?" she asked. "Did they go somewhere?" She hoped that the question would get a rational answer.

Instead, Nicola began wailing, prompting Alicein to hold her more tightly. It was a maternal instinct, she reasoned; she sometimes felt like an older sister to the fifteen-year-old girl. That was really Nina's role more than hers, though. But then she began to realize what might be happening.

She pulled back, still holding onto the girl with her arms straight. She tried to look her in the eye, but Nicola kept facing the floor, sobbing quietly. "Nicola," she said firmly, "I need you to tell me what's going on." The girl sniffled, but she didn't say anything. "Nicola!" she repeated sternly, giving her a shake. The anxiety was beginning to well up inside her again, and she needed to know. Maybe joking would catch her hysterical friend off guard. "Don't make me call you 'Nih-*cola.*'"

It worked; Nicola let out a quick laugh, one tainted by the roughness of her voice and the tears she was choking on. Their eyes met, and Alicein noticed that for once, the girl hadn't been wearing her make-up. It was just as well; it would have just streaked down her face in smudged rivers by this point. The joke she had cracked was a long-running one between them: Nicola's name was, like Alicein's, often mangled by people who didn't know her. "It's just like the guy name 'Nicholas,' but without the 's,'" she'd tell them. "Not 'Nih-*cola.*'" The only thing she hated worse than that was people mistaking it for "Nicole," and she had a somewhat irrational contempt for any girl she met who happened to have that name.

Struggling to get herself under control, Nicola sat back from Alicein, folding her arms. She wiped at her tears with one hand, still avoiding eye contact. "They're dead," she said simply. "And Amelia, too."

It was Alicein's turn to break down and cry.

It took a while, but eventually, the two girls managed to calm down enough to have an actual conversation, making their way from the floor onto the futon. It was heartbreaking enough for Alicein to have to hear about what had happened to her friends, but she also knew that this was even more difficult for Nicola, who had lost her older sister during another vampire attack years ago. She'd gotten away that horrible night, and miraculously, she'd managed to survive last night's attack as well. She knew how lucky she was, but that just made her feel guilty.

"I knew what was happening before anyone else did, I think," she explained. "Once the first screams broke out, it was like the YMCA all over again. I just knew. So I ran, not even looking back to see if Amelia and the others were following me. God, I feel like such a..." She sighed, looking up at the ceiling. "I guess it doesn't make any difference."

"What do you mean?" Alicein asked.

She shook her head. "I don't know. It's all... I mean, I guess maybe if I'd told them to follow me, they'd have gotten away sooner?" She gave a weak smile, not understanding why she did it. "I've run it over and over in my head, thinking that maybe I could have done something different, saved them somehow. That's probably stupid of me."

"No, it's not."

"But it is! I know full well that if I'd waited, if I'd been just a few seconds later than I was, I wouldn't have time to hide, and I probably would have wound up just as dead as the rest of them..." She shuddered, and Alicein put a comforting hand on her knee.

"So, you hid?"

"Yeah. In a dumpster. Not my most glamorous moment, you know, but it worked. I didn't even care how gross it was. And when I saw the rest of them heading down the alley towards me, I was just about to poke my head out and, you know, signal to them or something, but then I saw the bats fly in behind them, then turn into people. It was the weirdest damn thing."

"Wait… How could you see if you were in a dumpster?"

"It had this little metal door on the side. That's how I got in. Then I just…" She mimed sliding the door closed. "Left it cracked so I could see. I kind of wish I hadn't."

Alicein didn't understand at first, but then it clicked. "You saw them get killed." Nicola nodded.

"And this is the really fucked up thing. You know how Roderick…?" She paused. "No, I'll bet you probably didn't know that."

"What?"

She sighed once more, trying to choose her words carefully. "I kind of feel like it's not my secret to tell. But I guess it doesn't matter now." Alicein gave her a quizzical look, prompting her to continue. "Roderick wanted to die. He wanted them to kill him."

"What?" Alicein repeated.

Nicola nodded quickly. "He always had this… I don't know if you'd call it suicidal exactly, but maybe, I don't know…" She tried to find the right word. "Fatalistic, maybe? It was the whole thing about him being gay, how people didn't like him, and he'd spent his whole life with everyone telling him that he was *wrong* and *sick* and *perverted…*" She said these terms with contempt in her voice, not for Roderick but for the people who saw him that way.

"I never called him any of those things," Alicein said softly.

"No, you didn't. Neither did I. But people thought it, and he knew that. He told me — just a few nights before it happened, in fact — that he'd be perfectly okay with the vampires finding him and killing him.

He was just kind of fed up with life. And I told him to shut the hell up with that kind of talk. Because of, well…"

"Because of what happened to your sister," Alicein said, totally getting it. She'd had similar conversations with Amelia, but for a slightly different reason.

When Amelia had shown up at Basement Records a few months ago, she was homeless and destitute. She'd tried to play it cool as if nothing was wrong, but Alicein and Travis had seen through her bravado immediately. The girl was starving, clearly in need of help, and the two of them took her in and gave her a place to stay.

"That could have been me," Travis told Alicein privately, "if things had turned out different."

Alicein knew the story, which was kind of sweet in a way but also very sad. When he was younger, he'd had a girlfriend in New York that he'd tried to run away to be with, but he'd been caught by the police and sent back home instead. Plenty of things could have turned out badly if he had made it there, he realized once he'd matured and been able to look at everything in retrospect. His parents had berated him about this more than once over the years, too.

But that hadn't been the worst of it. His little sister had been killed by vampires while their parents had been out looking for him, and he'd never forgiven himself for that. He'd had a hard time living a normal life and had gotten into trouble with the police on more than one occasion, mostly for petty things like vandalism and minor shoplifting. This of course made his relationship with his parents deteriorate even further.

"You remember how you'd always turn the milk cartons around at breakfast so you didn't have to see the missing kids on them?" his father had barked at him one day, bringing up the running away thing again. "How'd you think your mother and I would feel if you were on there?" Travis didn't say anything. Aside from feeling guilty, he was also biting his tongue, resisting the urge to yell back at his father and tell him how stupid he was. The reason that he'd rotate those cartons hadn't been because seeing the missing children upset him; it was simply because he'd thought that they were ugly and didn't want their pictures staring at him while he tried to eat.

He'd left home as soon as he was old enough to, and he and Alicein had gotten together while working at the record store downtown. Despite the snide, aloof exterior he showed everyone else, Alicein could tell once they'd become close that there really was a sensitive, wounded guy underneath who felt — even to this day — guilty over the death of his sister. He'd been a fuck-up basically because he didn't think he deserved anything better.

Travis seemed to have gotten his life in order the past couple of years, but once the vampire activity started up again this summer, he'd started acting weird, as had Amelia. Alicein hoped that she would continue to follow her advice and keep her mouth shut about the real reason she'd come back to Augusta, uncertain of how Travis might react but knowing that it probably wouldn't turn out well.

Amelia apparently had this idea that her father, who had also been killed by vampires four years ago, had come back to life as a vampire himself and was a part of all that was happening. She wasn't repulsed by this, though: She actually hoped that she could find him again somehow.

"You need to keep that to yourself," Alicein warned her; the conversation had taken place not long after she'd started staying with them back in November. She went on to explain to her what had happened to poor little Sarah and how it had messed Travis up so much. "Besides, the people who get killed by vampires in this town don't come back to life. They stay dead."

"Are you absolutely sure?" Amelia asked in an odd, leading tone.

"*Don't* let Travis hear you talking that way," she said firmly, feeling protective of her boyfriend. "I can't even imagine what it would do to him to think that Sarah could have..." She squinched her eyes shut and shook her head quickly. "No. Just no. I mean it. Let's just keep this a secret between you and me."

They did, including the fact that Amelia was originally from Augusta. While they both wondered if she might happen to run into someone who recognized her, that never came to pass, probably because she was hanging out with people much older than her. The punk makeover she got from Nina and Nicola no doubt helped as well.

As these memories flashed through her head, Alicein felt a sudden burst of anxiety. "Oh my God," she said suddenly, grabbing Nicola's wrist. "Travis… Is he okay?"

"He's fine," Nicola said, looking confused and a little bit annoyed. "I thought you two broke up, and that's why you'd been hiding out from everyone lately."

"We did, we did," Alicein said, relieved and also slightly embarrassed. "I just…" She wasn't sure what else to say. "Doesn't mean I wanted him to get killed, though."

She thought back to why she'd broken up with him, wondering if she'd been unfair. It was because he'd started buying pot from some other guy in the downtown group, something he was supposed to have given up. It wasn't so much that she was a prude, just that she didn't like him bringing it into the apartment. If he got caught with it and the police got involved, then all three of them — Travis, Amelia, and herself — could wind up shit creek. Harboring a minor was bad enough, but bringing drugs into the picture was out of the question.

And so she'd kicked him out, telling him to get his ass straightened out if he wanted to come back. Amelia had blown up at her over this, accusing her of being a total bitch. She really liked Travis and looked up to him, and she felt that Alicein was being unreasonable, even when she tried to explain her actions.

"Well, if you're so damn concerned about the police, then I guess I shouldn't be here, either!" Amelia shouted, stomping off to her corner of the apartment. She then tossed her duffle bag onto the fold-out couch and began piling things into it.

"Where do you think you're going?" Alicein asked, immediately regretting sounding like her foster mother.

"Like you care," Amelia spat, avoiding eye contact.

There was some more back and forth, but Alicein knew that they'd been through this before. It wasn't the first time they'd gotten into a fight.

On her way out the door, Alicein stopped Amelia and handed her a cassette tape by The Smiths. "Give this back to Roderick when you see him. You can tell him I'm done with it."

Amelia snatched it from her, rolling her eyes and not saying another word. Then she left, slamming the door behind her dramatically. *She'll be back,* Alicein thought, locking the door but knowing full well that she'd taken her key with her.

But that was never going to happen now. Sitting here with Nicola, Alicein was feeling the memories flood through her and the tears welling up, full of regret. She broke down, collapsing into Nicola's arms and sobbing. Eventually, they rearranged themselves so that Alicein was lying on her back, her head in Nicola's lap. By then, her crying had died down.

"There was something Roderick said to me a little while ago," she said, sniffling and absently playing with the ends of her hair, pulling out stray tangles. "It wasn't an original thought of his or anything, just something he heard, I guess." She paused.

"What was it?" Nicola asked gently.

She adopted Roderick's tone, doing a vague impression of him. "'When you say goodbye to someone, you should tell them you love them. Because for all you know, that could be the last time you see them. You never know.'" Sure, it was a little hokey, even to a "fluffy-bunny New Age person," a term Roderick had used to describe her.

But it felt like a truth, underscoring all of the pain and regret she was feeling right now.

"Aw, that's sweet. He did always do that, didn't he? 'Love ya!'" She said this last bit in her own Roderick-like tone. "I never really knew why. Just thought he was being, you know, Roderick."

Alicein sighed. "I can't even remember the last thing I said to him. Or Nina."

"I can," Nicola said gloomily, but she didn't elaborate.

Alicein started to tell her about her and Amelia's last conversation, then decided not to. That would just upset her more, maybe even both of them. She sat back up, turning to face her friend, the one who had survived. Nicola looked like she was about to say something, but then she stopped. "What?"

Nicola let out a small laugh, but her expression was still sad. "I'm not sure if I should tell you this."

"Tell me about what?"

"Roderick. Before he died. Like I said, I saw it. I really wish I hadn't. But, I don't know… It's almost like a funny story, but not really."

Alicein wasn't sure what to say. She was curious, but she didn't know if she wanted her friend to continue.

"Okay, fine, I guess I'll go ahead and say it. Roderick, you know? He was all gloom and doom sometimes."

"Not always," Alicein insisted.

"I know! But sometimes he was. And like I said, he had this sort of fatalistic streak, or maybe a death wish, you know? But when the… When the vampires got him, or just before it, he started talking to them. Like he was giving a speech."

Alicein was confused. "A speech?"

"Kinda. I could only make out a little bit of it. Something about 'this life has always been darkness…' He even had his arms spread out, like he was… Well, yeah, I guess that's why I was thinking it was like a speech. Like he'd prepared it. He might have."

"What did they… I mean, did the vampires react in any way?"

"No, they just cut him down. The blonde one did, I mean, the girl." She let out another half-hearted laugh. "Just, 'this life has always been…' and then, *shoop,* she's on him, not another word."

"That's horrible," Alicein whispered, but another thought was beginning to creep into her mind, one that she didn't like.

Their conversation didn't go on much longer after that. Alicein was beginning to feel more uncomfortable, anxiety creeping up on her once again. Nicola's notion of making Roderick's death into some kind of joke rubbed her the wrong way, though she knew that this was a sign that the girl was feeling better, returning to her normal, sarcastic self. It was a part of the healing process, sure, but Alicein wasn't ready to go there herself just yet.

She made an excuse to leave, saying that she needed to find Travis, who according to Nicola was in fact working at Basement this afternoon. This seemed to bother Nicola, who still wanted her to stay and talk, but she just couldn't anymore. Things didn't end on as friendly of a note as she would have liked, and she found herself spouting out some advice that she wasn't even sure was correct.

"You shouldn't stay here in this apartment tonight by yourself," she said. "Go home. Talk to your mom about what happened. Be somewhere safe." She knew that the words didn't entirely make sense, nor was what she was describing something she felt like doing herself. She hated her parents and felt no desire to go back to their house and confide in them. But she needed to get out of there.

As she walked down the sidewalk in the direction of the record store, she contemplated whether or not she should approach Travis. That too filled her with anxiety, and she felt dizzy and shaky the more she thought about it. She wasn't sure if she could handle it. She'd wanted to talk to Nina and Roderick about what had happened to her, the unexplainable encounter she'd had with the vampires that had mysteriously relocated her to Warrenton, plus the frightening gap in her memory. Instead, she'd found out that they were dead.

What had set her off was Nicola's description of the way Roderick had tried to talk to the vampires before they'd killed him, how he'd apparently longed for death. And she knew, even though it hadn't been part of Nicola's story, that Amelia had probably done the exact same thing. For all she knew, Amelia had probably begged the vampire that killed her to do it, stupidly hoping that she'd come back to life as one of them and find her supposedly undead father as well. But that wasn't how it worked. Vampires just killed people, leaving bodies for the police to find and the news to report on.

Are you absolutely sure? Alicein felt a chill as Amelia's words ran through her mind. No, she wasn't. She wasn't sure of anything anymore. She remembered everything that had happened the past few years, the bodies piling up every time this happened, but then… Not every time. 1985 had been different. No bodies were found; there were rumors of vampires and killings, but the victims just disappeared. Was that somehow related to what had happened to her and the others, the ones who had turned up miles away in Warrenton? Maybe, maybe not.

There were other concerns, too. What about her job? About a month before her falling out with Travis, she'd taken a waitressing job at one of the chain restaurants downtown. It paid better than working at Basement Records, plus she'd realized over the months that working with Travis, dating him, and living with him was a bit too much. The two of them were always together, up in each others' faces, to the point where she felt like she never had any time to herself. Maybe that was why she'd been so eager to kick him out when things had gone badly. She wasn't sure.

That's why you've been hiding out from everyone lately, Nicola had said. The words stung. They weren't true. Maybe she'd meant to do that, to have the apartment to herself and take time to figure things out, and she'd even briefly toyed with the idea of moving back into her foster parents' house if they'd have her back. She hoped it wouldn't come to that. The real reason she'd been out of touch with her friends wasn't because she was being some kind of snob; it was because she'd been abducted by some supernatural force against her will. That wasn't her fault.

But how could she tell the people at Red Lobster about that? She'd disappeared on them and couldn't give them a satisfactory explanation upon her return, so they'd fired her, understandably. Should she beg to get her job back? Did she even want to? It wasn't like she actually enjoyed working there. Serving food to rude people who rarely tipped her seemed like such an insignificant thing now, something not worth trying to get back to.

She hated herself for how she'd let the depression get the better of her. After she'd gotten her blood transfusion at the hospital, they'd sent her home Friday morning. Maybe if she hadn't spent the next four days sitting at home freaking out and feeling sorry for herself, Amelia and the others might still be alive.

Alicein sat on the floor of her empty apartment, crying over the enormity of it all. She didn't know how to deal with everything that had been thrown at her. The fact that she couldn't even afford this crappy place and would probably be kicked out of it in a few weeks felt like the least of her worries.

Half of her friends were dead. Her ex-boyfriend probably hated her, and maybe Nicola did now, too. She'd been through something inexplicable, the vampires that were overrunning this town having somehow fucked with her but also leaving her alive after the fact, and she didn't have anyone she could talk to about it. It didn't make sense. Nothing did.

According to the news, things had gone almost back to normal for the city, or what passed for normal these days. There were still attacks occurring, but it wasn't like the huge spike of activity that had resulted in her abduction. That word kept running through her head, and it disturbed her.

Everything was making her re-examine her beliefs, her life, and herself. Her neopagan religion taught that she should respect nature, that there really was magick in the world, and that the supernatural was just around the corner, something to be in awe of but not afraid of. Now she wasn't so certain.

The old Celtic legends about faeries — not the cutesy, diminutive kind like in Disney movies, but the scary, malevolent ones that kidnapped people and made them lose their memories — had been popping up in her mind ever since she'd boarded the bus back to Augusta. Was that what had happened to everyone? She tried to remember if any of the old stories she'd read included faeries who also stole people's blood, then tried putting the thought out of her head. It didn't work.

She also remembered something she'd seen when she was at the hospital when they'd sent her home Friday morning. There was a flyer on a bulletin board, and it had caught her eye because of the word *vampire* on it. Apparently, there was a local group called Life Force that was for survivors of vampire assaults and for family members who had lost people for the same reason. She hadn't read it very carefully; the thought of anything to do with vampires scared her, particularly after everything she'd just been through.

But maybe it was something worth looking into after all. If she could ever summon up the courage to venture back out of her apartment and talk to Travis, he might be interested in it, too. She wondered what he might say.

CHAPTER THIRTY

ON THE ROAD

Audio cassette recordings made by Special Agent Leonard Tilden

Okay, is it going? Yeah. Okay so here I am doing another one of these, what I call "the babbling sessions" where I pick up the little handheld tape recorder and talk about what's going on in my life. Hope the batteries are okay... Damn, I should have checked that. Otherwise the wheels are gonna start going slow and when Iplayitbackit'sgonna speedupandstartsoundinglikethis! [clears throat]

But hopefully not. I'm hoping that this'll be interesting to listen to later on, you know, like the tape that I did on that Florida trip last year. I know it... [laugh] Well, I doubt anything will be as funny as the tape we did in the hotel room on the way back from New York in '84, me and Charlie and Jarrod... [laugh] "Naw, we're sleeping, dude. DEWD!" Damn, that was hilarious. Best trip ever. [clears throat]

But anyway, that's not what I'm supposed to be talking about right now. Oh, I forgot to say the date, just so I'll know it later on. It's Monday, July 13th, 1986. And I'm... Did I just say 1986? [laugh] It's 1987, damn it. I don't know why I keep doing that. It's this weird thing that's been happening ever since it became July; my brain keeps wanting to think it's last year for some reason. So, yeah. '87. And, well, this session's a little different since I'm not just going on a trip for fun; this is for work.

I... am... Hang on, gotta change lanes here; this slow asshole in front of me apparently doesn't know where his gas pedal is. [engine revving]

Yeah, thanks, jerk-off! It's the one on the right! [sigh] So anyway, what was I saying? Oh. I'm currently heading out of Atlanta to go to Augusta, and I'm really not too thrilled about it. I mean, normally the police there handle their own shit; Augusta's a big enough city not to have to ask for our help. And the GBI's supposed to be for helping out the smaller towns around the state. But they've had this supposed vampire crap going on there for a while, which I think is complete bullshit, by the way, but I guess... I don't know. I mean, yeah, people are dying, and that's a bad thing. But I really do think that buying into all this supernatural shit is a waste of time. And I know that Perkins feels the same way, which is why he's sending me there to deal with this instead of going himself. It... I don't know. It's like, who did I piss off in order to get this gig? Actually, I have a theory about that, which I'll mention in a second.

But what I wanted to say... I just thought of this... I should see if Conrad is still working at the regional office in Thomson. That's where they do the crime lab and forensics stuff for Augusta, and Conrad's a good guy, really down to earth. He'll probably know if they've found out anything about the bodies that could, you know...

WHOA! Yeah, really good driving, asshole! Jesus... That... Was that the same guy from before? Oh yeah, now *you wanna speed up and weave around through the lanes and cut people off. Prick.*

Anyway... Whooo, that could have been bad. Stupid piece of shit in a Toyota thinks he owns the road. But I'm okay. You know, I've sometimes thought that if I were to... Well, maybe talking on tape and driving at the same time isn't the safest thing in the world. If I ended up getting into a wreck while driving and doing one of these, well, what if I wound up dying and somehow this tape survived, it could be like the black box in an airplane, you know? Like someone could actually hear me getting killed. Bet that would be creepy.

Okay, well, that's enough morbidness. Is that a word? Maybe. Or I just made it up. Who knows.

[road noise]

So now I've completely lost my train of thought and forgot what I was saying. I guess it was... Hmm. About why I'm going to Augusta? Yeah, something like that.

So, yeah. The cops in Augusta wanted someone from the GBI to come in and try to help them try to figure out their supposed vampire crap. Apparently, it's been going on for a few years on and off, but it's gotten particularly bad lately. And there's all kinds of theories as to what it is, like maybe it's a serial killer, or maybe some kinda Manson thing going on, or gangs, or... Who knows.

[engine revving]

Okay, you know what? This traffic is just getting too complicated. We're up to four lanes now... The people are just... Just let me put the tape recorder down, and I'll tape some more later when I can.

[click]

[blank space for two seconds] [click]

Well, that sure was a hell of waste of time, I've gotta tell ya! Holy shit. This is a couple of days after what you just heard, and, well, initially I thought I was going to do more of these recordings while I was in town, but that wound up not happening. Instead, I'm on my way out, and thank God! I think I said something on the last bit about Augusta being big enough to handle its own shit, well, no, I take that back. They don't know what the hell they're doing there. I mean, maybe I'm being unfair, but... Actually, no, I'll give you an example.

You know how I said that I don't think it's anything really to do with vampires? Like, real, bona fide, "bluh bluh I want to drink your blood" kinda crap? Well, part of what I was supposed to do was find evidence of that, something conclusive. And you know what? I didn't. Because there isn't anything to find! It's just a town full of dumb-ass scared people running around making up stories about why people are getting killed because... 'Cause I don't know why! Maybe 'cause it makes them feel important or special.

Oh, right. The example. Well, like I said, evidence. Like had anyone ever gotten a picture of these supposed vampires. Guess what, they haven't! Except for one time, there was this photographer who supposedly did. Wound up getting killed, in fact. This was back in '83, apparently during the very first attack, a bunch of people getting killed in a big crowd at some racetrack. Since the photographer guy got killed, the police kept the camera and the film as evidence, even developed the pictures.

And then lost them! [groan] I mean, yeah, great job, guys. Turns out, though, Conrad had... Oh, I should mention this...! The woman in charge of their archives, files, microfilm, all that... already can't remember her name... but I swear to God, this woman wore so much damn perfume that you'd swear she was wearing gasoline. I mean, I was choking being around her, trying to breathe through my mouth instead of my nose... Damn it was horrible. But what was I saying about...? Oh yeah. Those pictures they'd lost, Conrad had seen the prints. That was back when he still lived in town, before he got married and moved to Thomson. Which, by the way, I think I'm coming up on the exit for pretty soon... Let's see... Mile marker... Oh, no, never mind. Still a ways to go.

But yeah, I called and talked to him, trying to track down the pictures. Like maybe he knew where they were. He didn't, and he wasn't that surprised when I told him that they'd lost them there. But anyway, he said that the pictures wouldn't have told me anything. It was all... What did he say... "Just a buncha people running around, well, except for the ones who'd already gotten killed. And in black and white, because, I dunno... Art." [laugh] That was funny. I could just see the look on his face when he said that, sneering and all... "Art." Because black and white pictures are sooo much more profound than color ones, right? Well, the guy did work for a newspaper, so maybe that's why. I only just now thought of that, though.

Oh, right, and the other thing he said. I asked him if any of the "vampires" were in them, and he said, "No, not exactly. You could kinda make out some black blurs of something in a few of them, but that was it." So, yeah, there were some animals flying around, like birds… or bats, even, but come on, people. All this talk about actual people vampires is just… It's hysteria!

Oh! And speaking of people trying to feel important: A recent development in town were these people… I think I just said the word "people" about four or five times there. Sorry. I do that when I get tired, and these past couple of days have been exhausting. It's also what makes me ramble. I mean, that's kinda the point of these babbling sessions, me just rambling on about my thoughts on what's happening. But not if it's going to be annoying to listen to later on, y'know? Hang on, let me stop the tape.

[click]

Okay, back now. I did that because I saw a sign for Thomson, and I'm kind of going back and forth on whether I want to go see Conrad. I was planning on it, just for being friendly and all, y'know, but now I'm just thinking I wanna get back home. I mean I… [sigh] Maybe I should. Well, I've got about five miles to decide.

So what was I saying? Oh, about the Life Force people. That's the name of… [laugh] I mean, it just sounds so pretentious, doesn't it? "Life Force." Like they're all important and are going to save the city from these vampires that don't really exist. But yeah, these dumbass vigilantes decide they want to arm themselves with all kinds of stupid shit like wooden stakes and crossbows and all, playing vampire hunters and going after people that they thought were responsible for the killings.

And of course, what ended up really happening was that innocent people got hurt, and all because nobody in that town apparently has any common sense and wants to believe in the boogeyman. It's just really, really stupid. I finally had to basically say, "Look, guys, I can't do anything for you here. You're on your own." Well, I didn't actually say it like that. I had to be more professional, of course. But seriously, I think that place is a lost cause. It's like they don't want a rational explanation.

Well, okay, so they weren't all like that there, to be fair. There was this one guy on the force... I've already forgotten his name... Milwick? Milford? Something like that. He was a straight-up guy, at least, and he didn't buy into all the vampire nonsense. What's more, his daughter was one of the ones who got hurt by those stupid-ass Life Force people in one of their assaults. She's okay and all, but still... Was she a vampire? Had she killed anybody? No, of course she didn't. Just a bunch of stupid people making shit up and trying to believe in it, then using it as an excuse to hurt people. I really thought Augusta was more progressive than that, I mean, it's the second largest city in Georgia, next to Atlanta. But I guess it's more small-town-minded than I thought.

So, yeah. Glad to get out of there. To be honest, I kept having that feeling the whole time I was there, like some little voice in my head saying, "you really don't belong here." Maybe that clouded my judgment, maybe not. Am I being a snob? Like, "I'm this big city guy from the Georgia Bureau of Investigation and you little bumpkins don't know what you're doing!" [sigh]

Maybe. I tried to be open-minded, but if I'm being honest with myself, I didn't want to go there in the first place. Maybe I should have been more professional than that. But damn it all if that wasn't a fucked up place. If Perkins wants to give me any shit about it when I get back to Atlanta, he can go there his own damn self and try to sort out those lunatics. And hey, if the D.C. job ends up coming through like I'm still hoping it will, I won't have to worry about it. I'm still waiting to hear back from them on that, which I guess I should talk about, too.

[sound of car driving for several seconds]

Okay, I'm coming up on the exit for Thomson. I'm still debating whether or not to go see Conrad...

Yeah, I guess I should. I may tape some more after I leave, or maybe that's enough for now. We'll have to see.

[click]

Leonard Tilden left the GBI not long after this tape was recorded, taking a higher paying job at the FBI headquarters in Washington, D.C. Fifteen years later, he disappeared while investigating an internet site that sold downloads of video clips depicting people being murdered in bizarre ways, allegedly supernatural in nature.

CHAPTER THIRTY-ONE

IN MEMORIAM

Obituary from *The Augusta Gazette,* July 17, 1987

Cassandra Allison Culpepper, 21, of Dresden Way, passed away Wednesday night due to acute blood loss. A graduate of Copeland High School, Cassie attended Augusta College, where she was a Communications major. She is survived by her parents, Joseph and Beverly Culpepper, and her sister, Valerie Elise Culpepper.

Funeral services will be held at Westmore Memorial Cemetery on Sunday, July 19th at 2:30 p.m.

Excerpts from Richmond County Coroner's report, July 16, 1987

Decedent: Cassandra Allison Culpepper
Race: W
Sex: F
Age: 21

Marks and Wounds: dual punctures over jugular veins on opposite sides of neck, bruising on wrists and ankles

Probable Cause of Death: acute blood loss

Narrative Summary of Circumstances Surrounding Death: Subject found in woods next to Forrest Hills Golf Course. Blood loss consistent with similar deaths seen recently. Multiple neck wounds of slightly different sizes suggests two assailants, not as common. Bruising on extremities indicates that body was carried from initial location after death, also unusual compared with recent victims.

CHAPTER THIRTY-TWO

UNLUCKY

Ruth just couldn't catch a break. "I have the worst luck," she'd tell people, and that was pretty much the truth. Her life wasn't particularly miserable, but it always seemed like bad things were happening to her, often in bizarrely coincidental ways. It was like the universe — or God, or fate, or whatever it was — had it in for her, constantly tripping her up, mostly figuratively but sometimes literally.

Her mother had always been overprotective, not wanting to let her out of the house because she was terrified that something bad might happen. Even going over to friends' houses was a huge ordeal: Ruth found that the only way she could ever get to go was to put her mother on the phone with a classmate's parent and get them talking, the parent reassuring her mom that everything would be okay and that Ruth would be returned home safely.

And what happened the first time that she went over to her friend Julia's house in third grade? She injured herself on a trampoline, bouncing off of it at a weird angle and getting the wind knocked out of her, the pain so intense that she was sure she was going to die. Fortunately, she recovered soon enough, and only Julia saw it happen. Ruth made her swear not to tell her parents, lest her own mother find out and never let her go anywhere ever again.

Her mother would take her clothes shopping before the beginning of each school year. That included getting new tennis shoes, the soles of her old ones being worn down almost to non-existence given how much she liked to play outside. There were, naturally, occasional injuries due to her inherent klutziness, various bumps and bruises accumulated along the way.

But one of the most embarrassing ones she acquired was due to the fact that because the treads on her new shoes were so much better, she found herself walking faster. It wasn't something she did on purpose, just a sort of unconscious thing that happened given that she wasn't as prone to slipping on the worn out soles she'd gotten used to. Nearly all of the floors in her house were hardwood, including in her bedroom, and she hadn't even noticed how much faster she'd been moving until one morning the day before school started.

She opened the door to her room as she began to head out of it, but because her forward momentum didn't match the speed at which she was pulling the door, she smacked her face right into the side of it, giving herself a black eye. It hurt, and she cried a little, but she got over it quickly, laughing at herself over how stupid the whole thing was. It really was just a dumb accident.

What was disconcerting was how some of the people at school didn't believe her when she told them what happened to her. Apparently, walking into a door and getting a black eye was some kind of cliché, an excuse that abused children would give when asked about their injuries so as not to implicate their parents. But Ruth wasn't an abused child; her parents loved her very much, maybe even too much, she sometimes thought.

She knew that her mother's overprotectiveness came from a place of love, but it got on her nerves just the same. At least her father was more laid back, his attitude being that their children needed to get slightly hurt every now and then to toughen up and learn how to deal with life. That balanced things out, Ruth decided once she was old enough to understand things better.

In time, the black eye at the beginning of fourth grade faded, as did the embarrassment. It wasn't a terribly traumatic thing, despite other people trying to make a big deal out of it.

But because the universe apparently liked to do stupid things to her and then point and laugh, Ruth got new shoes for school exactly one year later, started to walk out of her bedroom, and smacked herself in the eye with her door again and wound up with yet another black eye. This time, she started laughing immediately despite the pain.

"Oh, you can tell me what really happened," her concerned fifth grade teacher gently said, touching her arm.

"I *did*," Ruth said impatiently, and she couldn't help but roll her eyes and laugh at the same time. "Really. I just have really bad luck. You'll get it once you get to know me."

The following week, she destroyed a tape recorder that was propped up on a table next to a filmstrip projector, tripping over the power cord and knocking the player to the floor.

By the time she miraculously made it to the end of high school, it didn't surprise her in the least when she sprained her foot the day before the graduation ceremony. She was carrying a box of old clothes downstairs to give to the Salvation Army, but she couldn't see her feet. When she got to the bottom of the staircase, she thought she'd reached the landing, but there was still one more step to go. Her right foot bore all of the weight for a brief, agonizing second, and she dropped the box, falling to the floor. She hadn't laughed at that one.

The school would have given her diploma to her even if she hadn't gone to graduation, but she was determined to. And so she hobbled across the stage on crutches, her friends cheering her on as she did. Somehow, she managed to do so without falling over.

Her rotten luck wasn't limited to physical injuries. Her relationship with her boyfriend, Albert, had been winding down for a while, especially because they would both be going off to different colleges. Once her foot had been sprained, that had led to them being less intimate, and eventually, they called it quits. It was what people called "mutual," she and Albert agreeing to end things without getting into a huge fight. It was sad, but Ruth knew that the timing had always been bad: They'd gotten together a little over a month before graduation.

Still, there was some hope. There was another boy, Torrey, who lived down the street from her. They were friends, and she'd always wanted to get closer to him, plus she was pretty sure that he had feelings for her as well. But they were never single at the same time; things never timed out right. When she was single, he'd be dating someone, and whenever he was available, she wasn't.

Finally, it seemed like it might work out. She and Albert had broken up, and the last time she'd talked to Torrey, he hadn't had a girlfriend for a while. So of course, when she called him up in mid-July, he'd just met this amazing girl, and they'd started dating. In fact, she found out a couple of years later that they wound up getting married.

It was just as well, Ruth decided, Torrey hooking up with someone else. After all, she'd be going off to college in North Carolina in a couple of months, so it wasn't like they could have had anything long-term, not unless they were willing to try the long-distance thing. But she wouldn't have minded at least having had a fling with him, but by this point, there was no sense in thinking about either possibility.

So instead, she embraced the idea of moving away from home and starting over. It was time for a change. She'd been toying with the notion for a while of dyeing her hair blonde; she'd been a brunette her entire life. *Why not?* she figured, thinking that it would be fun to do something so drastic, something symbolic to commemorate this new era of her life.

She was barely surprised when it didn't work out: Her hair wound up being this ugly, uneven shade of greenish-grey. She had half a mind to just leave it that way, an act of defiance against the universe that kept throwing so much shit at her. But only a day's worth of teasing and snide comments from the few people she had contact with — including her family — was enough to make her change her mind.

Hiding as much of the disaster under a baseball cap as she could, Ruth drove to a stylist. Once she'd sat down in the chair, she tore off the cap, prompting a gasp from the effeminate man who had been so cheerful and friendly to her just seconds before.

"Oh, *honey,*" he said. "What did you do?"

"Fix it," Ruth said through clenched teeth.

Armed with a short, black bob haircut, Ruth was determined to have a good time that night. It had been a crappy few days, what with missing out on Torrey yet again and the subsequent hair mishap. In fact, it had been a crappy month, but her foot had mostly healed; at least she could walk without too much pain.

She was supposed to meet her girlfriends Rose and Jean for a movie at Columbia Square, some comedy about a guy in a spaceship who gets shrunk down to microscopic size and winds up inside some other guy's brain. She wasn't particularly thrilled with the choice her friends had made, but if the movie gave her a laugh, well, that was what she needed. She'd barely been out of the house in ages.

Her mother hadn't wanted her to go out, but then, she always found a reason to complain about that. "You know there's all those vampires out there!" she insisted.

Ruth sighed. "Mom, that's not even happening this far out. We don't live in downtown."

"There've been attacks in other places besides downtown!"

"And how do you know there's going to be any all the way out in Columbia County tonight?"

"Because I don't know that they're *not.*"

Ruth groaned, rolling her eyes. She bit her tongue, fighting back the urge to say *That's the stupidest thing you've ever said.* It was almost like her mother wanted something bad to happen to her; she was always predicting and warning her about things that never happened or even could happen. She seemed to have this freakish obsession with the idea of some terrible doom befalling her, like maybe if she could foresee it, that would somehow prevent it. Or maybe she was just waiting for the chance to say *I told you so.*

It was occasions like this that really made her resent her mother's overprotective streak. As Ruth had grown up, the woman had constantly railed against the fact that Ruth was getting older and wasn't a little kid anymore. It seemed like her mother probably wished that she had never progressed beyond the age of five, that she'd always stayed "my little girl." But that wasn't what raising a child was supposed to be about. You were supposed to bring them up into adulthood, to teach them how to be fully functional individuals, not coddled to the point of smothering.

And so, defiant, Ruth had gone out that night, arriving at the movie theater in Columbia Square with Rose and Jean, who had picked her up. She was going to meet them there, but driving was still somewhat painful; of course it had been her right foot that had been injured, not her left.

They responded favorably to her new look, telling her that it was cute. She hoped that they meant it; girls always complimented each other on new haircuts even when they didn't really mean it. In fact, Rose was just catty enough to do so when the real reason that she approved of someone's fashion choices was because it made the girl look less attractive in comparison to herself.

It didn't help Ruth's paranoia when Jean and Rose started talking about something in hushed tones while in front of her in line, but she knew that it might not be about her. On the phone earlier, Rose had said that Jean also needed a fun night out, but she wouldn't say exactly why. "You'll find out later," she'd said cryptically. And she knew she would: Even if there were some big secret between the two of them, Rose would eventually tell Ruth. She was too much of a gossip to do otherwise, which was why she'd learned not to trust her with any of her most private thoughts.

In fact, the two murmuring girls were so engrossed in their secret conversation that they didn't even notice when Ruth collapsed. It was loud outside the theater with all of the other people talking, and what she mistook for the sound of someone coming up behind her at the back of the line turned out to be a vampire bat flapping up and attaching itself to her neck. She didn't even have a chance to cry out; she'd been too surprised.

As she lay on the ground, helpless as the small creature fed on her, her mind went back not to her earlier conversation with her mother, but to thoughts she'd had before about how weird it was that she'd never encountered a vampire. Given her penchant for misfortune, it struck her as odd that living in a town repeatedly under siege from these monsters had never resulted in her being attacked. In fact, she'd never known anyone personally who had been killed, and she only had passing acquaintances who had lost people. She'd attributed this to living in the suburb of Martinez instead of Augusta proper; it seemed very unlikely that she'd wind up a victim living this far from the main action. But then again, if anyone were going to be so lucky, it would be her.

She began to feel dizzy, her mind wandering to something seemingly random, the way it did when she was falling asleep. She remembered the calendar on her bedroom wall at home, one featuring the cartoon character Ziggy. He was a short, fat guy with a big nose who was always having bad things happen to him, and Ruth had always found his exploits funny, but in an empathetic way.

Just before she lost consciousness, she heard a scream, possibly from Jean. There were other people shouting and saying things that she was already too far gone to comprehend, and she thought she felt — maybe heard — a flapping of angel's wings next to her head.

Ruth woke up in the hospital later, the left side of her neck sore and covered with a rectangular bandage. The glue on it irritated her skin, but the wound hurt if she tried to scratch it.

At first, she'd had no idea where she was; the stark whiteness of the room and the fluorescent lights overhead had briefly made her wonder if she were in Heaven, but then, Heaven probably didn't smell like antiseptic. *Or maybe it does; who knows,* she thought. This made her laugh slightly, and she tried to piece together what had happened.

Soon enough, the doctors and nurses explained everything to her, how she'd been attacked but not fatally, and they'd given her blood transfusions to restore her to health. She was going to be fine, and her parents were on their way to see her.

Oh, great, she cynically thought. *Bet Mom's going to have a field day with this one.* But once her mother and father arrived, they showered her with hugs and affection, grateful that their little girl was okay. There were no recriminations, no blaming her for what had happened. For the first time in ages, she allowed herself to feel loved by them without any resentment. She was grateful to be alive.

"I don't suppose this is going to do anything to change your mind about going off to UNC," Ruth's mother halfway joked.

It didn't. By the time she left the hospital the next day, she was feeling more like her regular self, but not exactly. Accepting and laughing at her misfortune was one thing, but the relief over surviving an attack that nearly killed her also made her feel angry. *So it was finally my turn,* she thought. *That was how I got attacked. Seriously, screw this town.*

All this time, she'd actually started to think that despite her bad luck in other areas, she'd somehow been immune to the vampire phenomenon, maybe the universe actually cutting her a break on that front. But no, it had happened to her just the same. She became more and more eager to move to Chapel Hill, to get away from everything she'd grown up with, to start over somewhere completely new.

She couldn't help but notice how the timing of things had played out in Augusta this time. While she'd almost managed to avoid the vampires throughout the years, she knew the pattern well enough;

everyone did. Every couple of summers, their activity would flare up, then stop with no explanation, just as there was no explanation of where they'd come from in the first place. Some people would die, some would survive, and others would disappear altogether.

So when did the vampire activity stop in 1987? A night or two after she was attacked, of course. Nothing more was heard from the mysterious monsters that year, though it was reasonable to assume that the town would probably face the same threat again, probably in another couple of years. As far as Ruth was concerned, she'd be long gone by then, hopefully never to return.

Sure enough, she later found out, the vampires did come back. She was well out of harm's way by that point, but she began to worry about her parents, wishing that they'd also move somewhere else. Now it was her turn to be the protective one, trying to convince her mother and father to be safe.

She was sad about losing contact with her Augusta friends, especially Rose and Jean, but she'd never quite gotten over her resentment at how they'd failed to notice that she was being preyed upon by a vampire just a few feet away while they were busy carrying on their private conversation. Their letters back and forth tapered off over time, and it got to where she didn't even bother trying to see them on the occasions when she went back home to visit her family.

Living at UNC-Chapel Hill was a good thing for her, though when a huge fire broke out in the campus library just days after she moved there, she wondered if she might have brought her bad luck with her, transferring it to a new place. Maybe that was a coincidence, maybe not, but it did still seem like misfortune and bad timing were things she couldn't shake.

Over time, things weren't that bad. She was there to study drama and found that she particularly enjoyed Stanislavski's technique, which emphasized physical movement in relation to the emotions an actor portrayed onstage. This made her more aware of her body and what she did with it, which in turn led to her becoming less clumsy and more aware of her surroundings.

A couple of years later, she transferred to the University of Southern California to further her acting studies. Given what she knew about both Los Angeles and her personal track record, she pretty much expected an earthquake to level the place as soon as she got there. In fact, she was so nervous about the possibility that her clumsiness began to manifest again, but she got it under control once she was comfortable with her classes and the new friends she'd begun to make. The ground not giving way beneath her feet and swallowing her whole was a plus, too.

One thing that did surprise her about L.A., though, were the news reports that slowly began to crop up about vampires in the city.

CHAPTER THIRTY-THREE

YOUNG LOVE

Excerpt from the journal of Raymond Adrian Young

Friday, September 18, 1987

Had a test in Bible (the class. I wonder why they call it "Bible" here at Bethlehem but it was called "Religion" back at St. Joseph's). I don't think I did too good on it, either. But something interesting happened before it. I'd lost my pen before class, so I had to try and borrow one from someone. But no one had one. I asked Annie first since she's in front of me: "You got a pen I can borrow?" But she didn't. So then I turned around and asked Jay. "Jay, you got a pen I can borrow?" And he didn't either.

So I had to get up and ask more people, and it got kinda funny, cause I had to keep repeating it over and over: "Ken, you gotta pen I can borrow? Jolene, you gotta pen I can borrow?" It became like a song. And nobody had one! Finally, Elizabeth had one, and she handed it to me with this look on her face. I can't really describe it. I've already talked in here about how FINE she is, and I've never been really sure whether I actually like her or not, at least not until now. But I do, I really do, I've decided. She's so hot!

Oh, about the pen: she told me not to lose it, and I said, "What if I do?" Like, joking around with her, trying to make her laugh. And she just said, "Then I guess you won't do very well on the test." I got embarrassed, but when I thought about it after, well, it was a pretty good comeback, you know? Mainly I was just feeling nervous talking to her, because, I don't know, something about the way she looked right then, I just knew. I've always thought she was pretty and all, but now it feels like so much more than that.

I probably bombed the test, but part of that was Elizabeth's fault. I just couldn't stop thinking about her and what she'd said, how good she looked and all. And when I tried to give her her pen back afterward, she just told me to keep it. I sure as hell will! But then when I tried talking to her some more, Melinda got all bitchy and pulled her away, saying "Come on, Elizabeth, quit wasting time talking to that loser." Like I didn't even matter. She said she was kidding, but it was so damn fake. I used to think she was pretty, too, but now I just hate her. And I'm worried that if she's that way, she's going to make Elizabeth not like me too, just like Andrea did with me and Valerie back in 7th grade. I thought things were going to be different at this school, that I could finally get a girl to go with me.

I really do <u>love</u> Elizabeth now. I just want her to love me back. I kept looking at her all day the rest of the day, liking how cool she was and all. I don't think anyone saw, but I couldn't keep my eyes off her, that gorgeous blonde hair, the way she looked all fine in her pink shirt and blue jean skirt, black pantyhose/tights (not sure what the difference is between those two). She has a really good body. I wonder what she looks like naked! I'll bet she looks even better than those girls in that dirty magazine Dennis brought to school in 7th grade. (Some of them actually looked pretty stupid, I remember.)

Anyway, it's getting late, so I need to wind this up. Hopefully I'll write in here some more soon; I know I've been bad about keeping up with this. But it's sometimes interesting to go back and read the stuff I wrote, especially when things change. Maybe next time when I write, it'll be about how me and Elizabeth are going together! God, I hope so. I hope I dream about her tonight. That would be so cool. And it would be a lot better than having another nightmare about "it," you know, being V_____'s. That's happened a few times since we last stopped everything, but I don't want to talk about that.

I love Elizabeth Morgan!!!!!

CHAPTER THIRTY-FOUR

LETTER

Tuesday, April 4, 1989

Dear Dr. Williams,

I am writing to you in regards to the behavioral problems exhibited by your son, Dennis. As you are no doubt aware, he has been assigned detention with increasing frequency throughout the school year for various infractions including truancy, vandalism of school property, and inappropriate behavior such as disobedience to faculty and physical altercations with his fellow students.

I have done my best to get through to Dennis and have tried to get to the root of his problems, but to no avail. I suspect that there may be drugs involved, but he is not very forthcoming when I try to bring up the topic. I understand that this is an unpleasant thing for you to hear, and believe me, I know from experience that raising a difficult child is a constant struggle. What concerns me most in this matter, though, is your son's future.

At your earliest convenience, I would like to schedule an appointment to talk with you and Dennis, first separately and then with your son present. We need to discuss whether or not he will be allowed to continue attending Copeland High School. I hope that we can come to a satisfactory resolution so that more drastic measures will not be necessary.

Please see the enclosed contact information so that you may call and schedule an appointment via the school secretary, Mrs. Branding.

Sincerely,

Simon Carter
Vice-Principal
Copeland Comprehensive High School
Augusta, GA

CHAPTER THIRTY-FIVE

VISITORS

"I'm telling you, it's starting again," Norman said firmly. "We're nearing the threshold."

"I'm not denying that," Russ said, then sighed. "The first part, anyway. I just don't think that you're right about everything."

Norman tried to keep his anger in check. When it came to this topic, he could get quite volatile if he wasn't careful, and that put people off, including tentative friends like Russ. Well, maybe Russ wasn't technically someone he could count as a friend, but he was a regular customer, and they often had conversations when he came in.

He leaned back on his stool, folding his arms. "It's hard to believe that you of all people could be in denial about this."

"I'm not," Russ said. "I'm just saying that I don't buy into your theories about what's happening. And you weren't there two years ago. You didn't see the things I saw."

"No, but I still know things," Norman said cryptically. "Things you wouldn't believe."

"That's certainly true." He said this with a slight smile, trying to lighten the mood.

Norman huffed. "You miss my point. The Greys…" He lowered his voice. "They get inside your head. Make you see things different from how they really are. That's what no one understands. They're making them think that there's all these vampires running around, but that's not it."

Russ sighed again, then glanced at his watch as an excuse. "Look, Norman, I've gotta go. I appreciate your concern, and hey, who knows. Maybe you're right."

"Actually, I know I'm right."

Russ reached for the brown paper bag on the counter, but Norman put his hand on it. "Hang on." He ducked behind the counter and came back up with a black and white newsprint magazine. "Here," he said, holding it up to display the cover. "It's called *Revelations of Awareness.* It's out of Washington. Not Washington, D.C., but Washington state. They know a lot about this kind of stuff."

"I don't think…"

"Just read it. It'll blow your mind. There's things in here the government doesn't want you to know about. Underground stuff." He shoved the flimsy booklet down into the side of the bag, fitting it alongside the stack of paperbacks Russ had purchased. "On the house."

"Thanks," Russ said weakly. "I'll… I'll look it over." With that, he took his bag and left, the bell over the door clanging as he left the bookstore.

"No you won't," Norman said under his breath. He wondered why he'd even bothered, knowing that he'd probably just thrown away four bucks. But it wasn't like anyone else was buying these newsletters since he'd introduced them to the store. He just hoped that maybe by giving one away for free, he might garner up some interest in at least one customer, encouraging him to want more. Hell, it might even save the guy's life, if he actually read it and started to understand what was really going on.

"No, I don't want to be told the truth," Norman said mockingly as he drove home that evening, pretending that he was talking in Russ's voice. *"I just want to keep being ignorant and take home my stack of crappy old books that don't mean anything. And here are some more stupid bodice-rippers for my fat-ass wife to read, too."*

He growled through his teeth in frustration. Sure, he was a businessman, and he knew what sold: the old paperbacks that people traded in, the glossy magazines full of meaningless shit, and the comic books for the younger kids and the adults who were really just overgrown kids themselves. It pissed him off that no one was interested in the more meaningful stuff he tried to get them to buy. But he knew why that was.

Norman knew things. He always had. He couldn't quite explain how, but he'd always felt connected to something bigger, things that regular, boring people couldn't understand. Some of this came from the things he read, but there was more to it than that.

Ever since he was little, he'd suspected that the world wasn't quite how everyone said it was. He didn't believe in fairy tales, but he knew that what was depicted in science fiction was at least possible. That was why they called it that: *science* fiction. Science was real. Space exploration was happening; it was on the news. No, there weren't green-skinned Martians with antennae coming down in flying saucers to kidnap our women; that was stupid. But those ridiculous ideas didn't mean that there weren't real aliens out there. There were. Norman knew it. He could sense them.

He couldn't remember his abductions, and he was glad about that, mostly. But they'd still happened to him, at least up until a point. Clearly, the experiences had been wiped from his mind by the aliens, or maybe the memories were just so terrible that he'd repressed them. He knew that he could probably get them back through hypnosis like other abductees had done, but he didn't want to. It was bad enough that this kept happening to him; he didn't need to add to his discomfort. On the one hand, he was terrified by the concept, but on the other, he felt defiant.

He'd first noticed the evidence in his late teens, not long after he'd started college. While taking a shower, Norman would find bruises on his body, but he had no recollection of how they'd gotten there.

Occasionally, there would be other marks as well, like little red dots on his skin that looked very much like hypodermic needle injections. Surely he would have remembered the reasons for these marks if they'd been due to natural causes. On some mornings, he would even wake up feeling unusually sore in various places as well, but nothing in his waking experiences could explain this.

And then there were the coincidences. It didn't take him long to notice that whenever he found these mysterious wounds on him, there would be helicopters flying overhead that day, more than usual, that is. Yes, helicopters and airplanes flew around the city for legitimate reasons all the time, but why was it that they suddenly increased in frequency every single time he woke up the night after a probable abduction?

It was because the government was in on the whole thing. As far back as the Roswell incident, they'd been in contact with the aliens, the Greys, those creepy little guys with the big bald heads and huge black eyes. Plenty of people had seen them and written about them. In exchange for superior technology, the government allowed the Greys to abduct people like himself for their experiments, whatever those were for. But even they didn't know the whole story, how they were being duped.

All of these things ran through Norman's head throughout the drive home. He had some ideas about why the aliens' tactics had changed, but they weren't fully formed, not yet. He'd figure things out tonight after dinner once he started drinking. It wasn't that he was an alcoholic or anything, but when he drank and the beers kept flowing, that was when things came to him. He made connections that he wouldn't have made while sober.

As he opened up his first light beer — he always stuck to that because it wasn't strong enough to get him trashed but just enough to lubricate his brain, so to speak — he pulled out his notebooks and folders, the ones he'd been compiling over the years. He spread them out on the floor and sat down among them, trying to decide where to start. Then he picked one, a spiral notebook he'd been writing in most recently.

Russ, he wrote. *One of the 1987 abductees. Still in denial of the Truth like everyone else. Thinks it's vampires. Mental rewriting by Greys?*

He stopped writing, setting down the blue ballpoint pen. He shifted slightly to the left, then opened up a Manila folder. In it were newspaper clippings, anything to do with the supposed vampires. This one was new and mostly empty, unlike the previous three he'd put together from earlier in the '80s.

"Hmm. I wonder," he said aloud, sifting through the scraps of paper. Nothing.

His eyes spotted another notebook. He thumbed through its pages, pausing occasionally to take a sip of beer. The words reminded him of something, and a wave of inspiration hit him.

"Wait a minute..." he said, a heavy sigh passing his lips. "That could be it."

He went back to the first notebook, hunching over it as he began scrawling more notes.

Recent activity— misdirection? Intentional throwing off of previous pattern to distract. Previous three waves of activity (Greys pretending to be vampires) every two years in the summer: 83, 85, 87, but not in 89 as expected. Proximity to Halloween this year instead: intentional? - - - Last ditch effort before photon belt?

The thought of this excited Norman. As he was well aware, Earth was due to enter the Photon Belt sometime before the end of this century, something that would herald a great change in humanity's existence. It was a wave of energy from the Pleiades that would change everything, transforming all life on the planet into atmosphereans, beings of light and energy. All of mankind's religions, however distorted they were from the real Truth, had predicted this, even inadvertently. Some saw it as the end of the world, but it wasn't that. It just the beginning of something amazing.

But that was why the aliens had come. The first influence of the Photon Belt had started in 1962, and they weren't happy about that. The Greys and the Blues wanted to wipe humanity out, to stop them before the great transformation occurred. Norman kept writing.

G's and B's don't want us to ascend, so they are attacking now to prevent it. "Vampire" tendency just them being more honest: killing/ abducting/culling..? Possibly related to the Restart.

Norman reached for another notebook, then began writing in it where he'd left off. *More on idea that they are trying to restart the experiment: humans the result of crossbreeding between Greys and apes thousands of years ago. Not happy with result: war, violence, etc. Abducting a select few for resettlement on other planet in the Third Quadrant. Possible to prevent this?*

He wrote in his notebooks for the rest of the night, staying awake as long as he could. Eventually, the beers would catch up with him, and he'd be too drunk to make sense. But sometimes, it was right at that point when he made an even bigger connection than usual, a major revelation. He knew that what he was realizing and writing was true. It wasn't a coincidence that his mysterious overnight wounds and injuries had stopped in June 1983, the very same time that the supposed vampires first started attacking Augusta. It was the aliens, the visitors to our planet, changing their techniques and trying to stop mankind's enlightenment.

All of this was part of Norman's efforts to create a coherent narrative, something that he could turn into his own article for *Revelations of Awareness*. Once he had it done, he'd submit it to the newsletter for publication, and it would blow the whole theory of UFOs and alien contact wide open. He had proof — his own experiences — and everything he'd realized over the years was part of that. No one had managed to put the pieces together like he had, not until now. He knew the Truth, and he was looking forward to sharing it with everyone.

As he stumbled off to bed that night, he thought about the article he would write, composing bits of it in his head as he began to drift off to sleep, something he often did. Perhaps, if he were lucky and clever enough, this new upturn in "vampire" activity in Augusta might even afford him the opportunity to encounter one of these aliens, to get real evidence. There had been people in the past who had formed a sort of vampire hunters club, so maybe if they started up again, he could get in touch with them. Then he could play along as if he believed in vampires as well, just enough to get close to one of the aliens, maybe even capture it. He'd probably win the Nobel Prize for that.

Norman eventually completed his article in 1991, calling it "The Truth About Aliens, Alleged Vampires, the Photon Belt, and the Restart." While driving to the Post Office to mail the typed manuscript to the editors of *Revelations of Awareness,* he was killed in an accident involving a bus driver who lost control of his vehicle when its brakes failed.

CHAPTER THIRTY-SIX

THE CUSTODIAN

Obituary from *The Augusta Gazette,* October 31, 1989

Jeremiah Elias Walker, 46, of Central Avenue, passed away Sunday night due to acute blood loss. With a long-standing career as Head Custodian at St. Joseph's Episcopal Elementary School, Walker is remembered by students and faculty alike as a warm and friendly presence, a man who always had a kind and cheerful word for everyone he met. He is survived by his wife, Hilda Louise Walker, and his children Camille, Rochelle, Tyrone, and Samuel.

Funeral services will be held at Wisteria Cemetery on Thursday, November 2nd at 10:00 a.m.

CHAPTER THIRTY-SEVEN

SHADOW

Nick didn't feel like himself. Worse than that, he could barely *feel* at all. But then, he wasn't himself, not really.

He vaguely remembered what things had been like before, the fact that he'd had various emotions and responses to situations, but it was all disconnected now. The memories were there, sort of, but there was an emptiness inside where the real feelings should have been. That might have made him sad, but only if he'd been capable of that.

The closest he had to anything approaching an emotion was resentment. At least there was that. And even though he was a vampire, a dangerous creature capable of taking life whenever he wanted, there was no pleasure in that, no evil glee in the power that it gave him.

In a way, he was a ghost, or maybe just a by-product. He was solid enough, not some wispy phantom, and he'd killed plenty of times since the emergence. But the real Nick Davies also existed, just another weak human being among many. They shared most of the same memories, but when he tried to think back to when he was still that stupid, emotional wreck of a boy, it disgusted him. Well, maybe that counted as an emotion, too.

But that was just it. What little he could feel was negative: resentment, disgust, anger. Back when he'd been human, there had been a lot more, he was sure. Happiness, joy, pleasure, even love: These were all just words to him now.

What had happened was this: About three weeks ago, Ray — that stupid, scheming control freak — had roped him into getting together with all of the former vampires to try to take the antidote to that damned vampire potion they'd taken a couple of years back. That was where it had all started for him, but apparently, he and his dumb sisters, plus some more losers from school, had been using it on and off for years, turning themselves into vampires and killing a bunch of people just for the hell of it. There was a part of him now that almost admired that, the gall of such a thing.

At the time, he'd felt similarly roped in — manipulated, in fact — but he'd gone along with it. He and Ray had been friends during seventh grade, though he could barely remember why now. It was something to do with how they'd both been smart-asses and rebellious, always talking back to the teachers and doing things that could get them in trouble. Sometimes they did, but Nick had usually managed to skate just this side of the line, almost always avoiding getting caught. But taking a potion that turned him into a vicious mythical creature was going a lot farther than sneaking a piece of chalk into the eraser in Mrs. Warren's English class.

He could see it in his head, the mean old bat trying to erase the blackboard and being surprised and angered at how instead, big white streaks appeared. The class had laughed, and he'd felt… what? Pride? Amusement? It was all lost to him now. He just remembered that it had happened, and that was it.

There was something else about Ray and his bringing him into the vampire group in 1987 that bothered him. Ray hadn't invited him to take part initially; it was more of an after-the-fact thing, like he hadn't deemed him worthy to begin with, then did for some reason. He'd never understood that. And it wasn't just him: There was also that older guy, Damon, one of his sister's boyfriends, whom he'd kind of liked. But again, he couldn't really remember why. Didn't they have something in common? Something they shared? The memory escaped him, which just angered him further.

Despite being latecomers, he and Damon had done their best to keep up, taking part in the delinquency and the killing. There had been some joy in that, hadn't there? All Nick could remember now was the resentment over having been left out for so long, Ray having kept this secret from him despite the fact that they'd been friends. In fact, he could recall how the two of them had been friends during seventh grade because they hated everyone else, all of the posers and fake people surrounding them. Now here he was with some of those same people, being in a big group with them and having fun that he was only allowed into as an afterthought. He hated groups; they were just one more type of conformity, and they always let you down. The way things played out just reinforced this opinion.

Everything fell apart when everyone turned on each other, and it was so bad that they were damn lucky to get out of it alive. The entire experience shook Nick up so much that he broke contact with Ray, refusing to talk to him anymore if he could help it. That should have been the end. But then things got worse.

His current memories of just what happened back then were confused, knowing that in a way, the version of him that he was now had been a separate entity, but still trapped inside the other Nick, the human one. Sometimes, he remembered what his human side went through, like the increase in violent thoughts and the nightmares. There had been other things, too, but again, they weren't things he could clearly remember feeling anymore, like guilt and remorse. He knew that the other Nick had felt them, but those emotions weren't within him.

He also remembered things in a different way, how he — the vampire —struggled to get out, to come to the surface and take over. He wasn't alone in this; the other former vampires were having similar problems.

And so, despite his better judgment, he agreed to meet with Ray and the others to take the antidote to the potion, which was supposed to get rid of the vampires within. But before that could happen, Nick felt himself being pulled inside out, and strangely, impossibly, the inner vampires materialized outside of their human counterparts, exact doubles of them in nearly every way.

Since then, they'd been free to roam the city and kill as they pleased, but this didn't mean that Nick suddenly felt a kinship with them. All of his anger and bitterness from the past two years remained, and he still didn't want anything to do with the others. He did occasionally wonder just how the emergence had happened, but for the most part, he didn't care.

At first, it had felt good to be free, but that dissipated almost immediately. So he went about his nights, killing people sometimes or just wounding them, trying to glean some joy out of it but failing. What was the point of being a vampire if there was no pleasure in drinking blood? He just existed; that was it.

He didn't like thinking this way, all gloomy and depressed. It reminded him of his mother, a pill-popping Valium junkie whom he'd always hated. That wasn't just his current view; he'd felt the same way when he'd been human. The woman was just pathetic — he now saw this more clearly than ever — wallowing in melancholy for no good reason. Their family was well off and had tons of money, not wanting for anything. He fully acknowledged that his affinity for punk rock culture was a rebellion against this; he didn't want to grow up to be some snooty, rich prep like his father.

And even though his current existence felt empty when he knew it should be exciting, he refused to give in to any suicidal thoughts that crossed his mind. One time, he'd considered just waiting for the sun to come up and letting it destroy him, but he'd dismissed the idea immediately, irritated that he could have come up with it in the first place. He still had a survival instinct, and even if life seemed pointless, he wasn't going to just give up like some loser.

One night while flying around as a bat, he happened to spot a black man walking out of a hardware store downtown. Nick recognized him immediately: It was Mr. Walker, the janitor from his old school, the one where he'd met Ray. This was the first time he'd encountered someone he'd known from his human life, and as he hovered in the air above, memories came back to him.

There was a ladder to the roof of the school building in a hidden location; not many people knew about it. Sometimes, Nick would use it to sneak away from his classmates during recess, hiding up there just to… Why? Had it been fun? He couldn't even remember now. Maybe there had been some enjoyment in getting away with something he wasn't supposed to do. That may have been it.

Regardless, he'd gotten caught by Mr. Walker one day and wound up getting in trouble with the principal, one of the few times he'd ever gotten caught doing anything bad. After that, he'd made it a point to make Mr. Walker's job of cleaning up the school even more difficult, including vandalizing the boys' bathroom on a regular basis and knocking over trash cans in the hallways when no one was looking.

Here was a chance to settle the score once and for all, so he zoomed in from the air and latched his fangs onto the man's neck, taking him down instantly. There was barely any struggle, and as he drank the blood down, he thought about all the anger he'd felt towards this asshole back when he'd been at St. Joseph's. The salty taste of the warm fluid was pleasant, but once the kill was over, the feeling passed. There was nothing, barely even a flicker of triumph. The stupid-ass guy was dead, and now it wasn't possible to hurt him any further.

The following night, Nick happened upon a young man who was clearly distraught. He'd just slammed the door to a building he was exiting, muttering to himself as he walked and — if Nick wasn't mistaken — wiped tears from his eyes.

"Hey, man," Nick said, catching up to him. "You okay?"

The tall, well dressed stranger looked to his side and down at Nick, surprised but clearly not in the mood to strike up a conversation. "No, I'm not," he said with a scowl, turning his head away and continuing along the sidewalk.

"Aw, what's the matter?" Nick said, keeping pace. It wasn't that he actually cared, and this man was going to be dead in a matter of moments. But it might be fun to play around with him first.

"Nothing you can do anything about, kid. Now get outta here."

"Not going to happen," Nick said blithely.

The man stopped, his shoes skidding on the pavement. He turned to face his pursuer. "You wanna rob me or something? You want my wallet? Here, take it." He angrily whipped out his billfold and shoved it into Nick's hands, surprising him. "In fact, take this, too." He tore off his watch, a rather expensive looking one, and practically threw it at Nick as well. It wasn't like he was pleading for his life, though; the man was clearly pissed off.

"Gee, thanks!" Nick started to joke, but he was cut off by what the man said next.

"Fuck you!" he screamed. "I've just been dumped out of nowhere for no fucking good reason by the woman I thought I was going to marry, my father's in the hospital probably dying from goddamn pneumonia, and I'm probably going to get laid off from my job by the end of this week. You think you can hurt me worse than that? Go right a-fucking-head, asshole."

Nick shrugged, dropping both the wallet and the watch to the ground uncaringly. "Okay." He then lunged at the man, shoving him and sending him toppling into a nearby alleyway. His fangs were bared, but he decided not to kill the man right away. He and the other vampires had done stuff like this back in the day, taunting their victims before drinking them, and he hoped that maybe he could regain some of that sense of fun tonight.

Recovering from having been knocked to the ground, the man stood back up, still looking more angry than afraid. A streetlight in the alleyway illuminated Nick's face, and the man's eyes lit up with recognition. "Oh, so that's it, you little shit? You're one of those goddamn vampires?" He'd said this with a defiant stance, like he was ready to start a fistfight, but then he relaxed, spreading his arms apart, then his palms. "Fine. Kill me. It's not like I've got anything to live for."

Nick thought for a moment. Then he took a step forward. "Man, you *are* pathetic, aren't you?"

He leapt at his victim, but rather than going for his neck, he just grabbed him and slammed his frame against the wall of the alley. One of the benefits of being a vampire was having superhuman strength, and he planned to take full advantage of that over the next minute or two. The man winced with pain, but the defiant look on his face remained.

Grabbing the front of the man's suit, Nick repeated his move, slamming his foe against the wall once again. This time, his head made contact with the brickwork, and he lost his resolve, going limp for a moment. He then tried to fight back, raising his arm, which Nick promptly bent backwards, a sickening crack coming from it as it broke.

The man cried out in pain, and Nick released him, allowing him to clutch his wounded arm with the other. He panted in quick gasps, then looked back up at Nick, defiant once again.

Nick expected him to say something clichéd like *"Is that all you've got?"* But rather than giving him the chance, he just belted the man across the face, sending him stumbling. He grabbed the man's left arm, noting with a sneer the horrified look on his face as Nick whipped it around fiercely, breaking it as well.

The man collapsed to the ground, his vocalizations mostly a series of grunts and gasps. Some words began to form, or really, just one word: *"Hnnh... hunnh... hahunnh... stop... hunnh... stop... hhh... hhh... hhh... STOP!"*

He flailed around pathetically on his knees, trying to reach for either of his arms, but they were both twisted at unnatural angles. His face was a mask of suffering, which he turned upwards to face his attacker.

"J… just… *STOP!*"

"Stand up," Nick said simply. The man just continued to writhe in agony, grimacing. "I said," he began, bending down and grabbing the lapels of the man's suit, forcing him upright. "Stand… up!"

He kicked hard with his right foot, forcing another wail from the man as his left kneecap was shattered. The body faltered, but Nick held it in place, repeating the same move to destroy his other leg. His pitiful moans echoed up and down the alley walls, and Nick let the limp form drop to the pavement.

"S…. sss… st…" he tried to say. There was blood streaming from his nose where he'd been hit earlier, and Nick wanted to taste it. *"Just… KILL ME!!!"* the man shrieked, his head turned to one side. The neck was right there, waiting for the bite.

"No," Nick said, suddenly coming to a decision.

As he walked up the alley and back towards the street, Nick could hear the plaintive sounds of the injured man fading behind him. Then he realized something: He was smiling. He stopped walking, then looked back at the quivering, crumpled form on the ground.

Returning to his victim, Nick bent down, noting with sick pleasure the tortured look on the helpless man's face as he tried to struggle. Nick rolled him over onto his stomach, straightened back up, and raised his right foot. He stomped down as hard as he could, shattering the man's spine.

The man's incoherent blubberings once again faded as Nick walked away, wondering how long it would take for someone to find what was left of this worthless piece of shit. Maybe the guy would wind up in one of those cool new wheelchairs that he could only steer by moving his head against a special control.

Nick pondered this latest development. Making someone suffer, *really* suffer, brought him pleasure. The sensation had been lost to him for so long that it was exhilarating to finally be able to experience it again. He just needed to get better at it.

There were other people he could settle old scores with, more important than random nobodies from his past like that janitor, and certainly more relevant than strangers like the guy he'd left crippled in the alley. He thought about the people who had wronged him in his life, envisioning his memories like the Rolodex on his father's desk, the note cards filled with contact information whipping by as he thumbed through them mentally. He'd revisit them one by one, getting his revenge. The idea made a wicked grin spread across his face.

Perhaps he was getting the hang of this vampire existence after all.

CHAPTER THIRTY-EIGHT

CHANGE

Excerpts from the diaries of Elizabeth Pamela Morgan

Sunday, June 10, 1984

We moved to Augusta (or Fort Gordon) this morning. I wish we hadn't had to leave Kansas, and I hate it here already, because it's so hot!!!

Mom was mad, too, because she wanted her and Dad to drink wine tonight (to celebrate, I guess), but the man at the store wouldn't sell it to her. I didn't really understand it all, but it was something about it being against the law here. "You've got to be kidding me!" she yelled. Dad said it wasn't a big deal and they could buy some tomorrow, but how? How can something be illegal one day and not the next? I don't get it.

Monday, September 21, 1987

Turned 14 on Saturday. Whoopty-doo. It doesn't feel all that different from 13. I did get a few nice things, but overall, I kind of didn't care. But I did my best to pretend. "Put on a happy face" and all that...

It's just hard not to feel sad, you know? Especially when things are supposed to be happy and celebrating and all that, and I don't feel like it. Sometimes everything feels so fake and forced, more on days like that that are supposed to be special occasions. It's like I feel guilty whenever I don't feel sad. I don't care how long it's been, it still hurts.

<div align="center">~~~</div>

Melinda was being kind of a bitch at school today, and Helen even told her that. She wouldn't say why, but I'm pretty sure I know what's up. I think she's still mad that I gave that new boy Ray (see August 20th and September 1st) a pen on Friday. I mean, come on. It's not that big of a deal. Yes, I can tell he likes me and all, but I'm not interested. Not interested in anyone, really; I've sworn boys off for a while, maybe forever, especially after what happened with Kirby. And I wouldn't be mad if Melinda admitted she has a thing for Ray. She keeps saying she doesn't like him, but if that's true then why does she keep talking about him over and over and over? Weirdo.

So far, Ray hasn't really talked to me all that much, but even if he did come out and say something like he wanted to go with me or whatever, I wouldn't. I mean, sure, he's kinda cute and all, if a little short, but I don't know anything about him. And since he barely talks (staring at me every time we walk past each other in halls is pretty annoying, actually), it's like there's not much to know. Or even if there is, it's not my problem.

And besides, if I did start going with him, Melinda would wind up hating me then, and I don't want that, even if she does get on my nerves sometimes. Me and her and Helen: we're Best Friends Forever (BFF), and that's more important.

Saturday, November 11, 1989

Just wanted to write a little (and kill some time) after dinner tonight before going to pick up Helen and Melinda. That's the "great" thing about being the only one of us who has a car: I get to haul their fat asses around town all the time! J/K I love them both and they're not fat. (Well, Helen is a little on the heavy side and could stand to lose a few pounds, but we'll just keep that between you and me. Whoever you are, imaginary third person reader. Who are you? How did you get your hands on this diary? I'm calling the police!

Hee-hee, I'm in a weird mood tonight. It's nice to be in a good mood, especially compared to some of those older entries I was reading over the past couple of nights. As usual, I got caught up in what was supposed to be just looking for something specific in my diaries, then wound up staying up late reading the stuff I used to write. God, I was pretentious sometimes! Don't even get me started on that horrible poetry. "...and then I start to cry." Come on, Elizabeth.

Well, maybe that's unfair to the girl I used to be. She had her reasons for being as sad as she was. But the older I've gotten, the more I've realized that you just have to suck it up and move on. Things hurt, but you can't wallow in it. I wish I could have told that to my younger self. Yeah right, like she would have listened.

~~~

Anyway. I just went back and reread all of that and realized I forgot to close a parentheses. Here it is:) Happy now? Maybe I can be a professional proofreader when I grow up. Is there such a thing? I should look into that. J/K

And it's getting closer to 6:30 and time to go pick the girlfriends up. That was mean what I said about Helen. She can't help it that she's, you know. And Melinda... well, one of the goals tonight (but she doesn't know it yet) when we're at the mall is to try to talk her into straightening her hair too. It will look good on her, no matter what she keeps claiming. She really should try it. Hopefully we can steer her into Great Clips. And I just remembered that I need to buy base at some point since I'm almost out. Eyeliner too, maybe? I should check.

Now that my diary has somehow turned into a shopping list that I'm not going to even take with me, I should stop. I'm not this superficial, I promise. Ha-ha, "Don't hate me because I'm beautiful!"
~~~

Elizabeth Morgan's body was found in the driveway outside of her house the morning of Sunday, November 12, 1989. The coroner declared the cause of death to be acute blood loss.

CHAPTER THIRTY-NINE

THE LISTENER

"It was in my pants."

That was where it had all begun, Owen Raforth reasoned, when he looked back on his life. Maybe if he'd explained himself immediately, things could have turned out better, but no one ever gave him a chance, not after that stupid mistake. The damage was done.

The incident had occurred during his first week of school in seventh grade, back in 1986. Being the new kid in town was always a difficult thing, but in the past, he'd always managed to make a few friends given enough time. That was the life of an Army brat, and he was used to the routine by then, whether it was in Monterey, Leavenworth, or even Heidelberg in Germany. Unfortunately, things didn't pan out for him as well as he'd hoped in Augusta.

Owen couldn't even remember what the question was that Mrs. Ward had asked the class, why she'd asked certain people to raise their hands. Were they volunteering for something? Or voting? It had been a few years now, so the memory had faded, and he only recalled a few fragments. Whatever it was, Owen hadn't been counted, so he spoke up to let the teacher know. There were different lists of students' names on the chalkboard; he at least remembered that.

When he pointed out that she should have written him down for whatever it was, Mrs. Ward said in a light, joking tone, "Oh, I'm sorry. I must have missed you. Where was your hand, Owen?"

"It was in my pants," he said sarcastically, hoping to get a laugh out of her and his new classmates. What he'd meant to say was "It was in my pocket," the implication being… What, exactly? Again, he couldn't recall his motivation at the time, why he'd tried to make that joke. Maybe the joke was that she'd been the stupid one to not see that his hand was up all along, so he tried to say something off the wall and ridiculous? In the past, he'd always been a bit of a class clown, and that was what had usually won him friends in the previous cities he'd lived in. But this time, he'd screwed up, and that other sentence had come out instead. He'd just used the wrong word.

Mrs. Ward's face fell, and she just said, "O… kay…" She slowly turned back to the dark green surface of the chalkboard and wrote Owen's name down among the others, whatever it was the whole thing had been about. The entire room had gone silent as well, and Owen felt himself blushing.

"Do you really think that's what it was?" Kei asked, laughing. "That one time?"

Owen laughed as well, trying to fight down his nervousness. "I don't know. Like I said, I didn't think *that* much of it at the time, but when I look back on it now, I feel like everyone thought I was a big old perv or something, trying to make some dirty joke. But I wasn't!"

"I know," Kei said with a smile, her hand brushing up against his as they walked.

Flinching inwardly, Owen glanced down at the girl's small hand. He was trying to play it cool, but at the same time, he couldn't believe his luck. Ever since his family had moved to Augusta — and certainly since that incident at school that unfortunate day — he'd been branded as a dork and a loser, and girls had avoided him like the plague. Even when he'd changed schools, the reputation had followed him.

And yet here was this cute little Asian girl he'd met at the coffee shop, and she'd seemed downright flirty with him from the start. That wasn't something he was used to.

He'd gone to Be Caffeinated a couple of times before, trying to hang out there and be cool like everyone else, sitting on one of the couches and pretending to read a book, looking intellectual. It was what the place was for, and he'd seen other people do what he'd been trying to do, hanging out and hooking up. It hadn't worked for him until tonight.

"Whatcha reading?" she'd asked him as she plopped down on the couch next to him, the leather squeaking under the added weight.

"What? This?" he asked, surprised. It was a worn paperback of *Lord of the Flies,* one he'd taken from a shelf in the shop. There were lots of old books there; he wasn't sure where they'd come from. Maybe they were there to give the place a sense of ambience. He'd been thumbing through it, remembering bits from when he'd read it back in sixth grade. He showed it to the girl, and their fingers touched as she forced the book closed to look at the cover.

"Oh, yeah, I remember that one," she said casually. Then she sat back against the couch, smiling. "I'm Kei, by the way."

"K?" Owen asked. "Like the letter K?"

She rolled her eyes, but her smile never faded. "Nooo... K-E-I. Pronounced 'kay.' You're *totally* the first person who's ever said that to me, though." She gave him a sarcastic sneer.

He let out a nervous laugh. "Sorry. I bet you get that all the time."

"Pretty much!" She giggled. "And you are?"

"Owen," he said, unsure whether he should shake her hand or something. He decided that it would be too weird, then tried to think of something to say. "So, um, you come here often?" He immediately regretted saying such a clichéd phrase, and something in his pained expression betrayed him.

Kei laughed. "No, not often. I was here with some..." She broke off, then rolled her eyes again. "Doesn't matter."

The girl was small and petite, with long black hair and narrow eyes, clearly of some kind of Chinese or Japanese descent. She didn't have a foreign accent, though.

"Are you Japanese?" he asked.

She rolled her eyes once more, her expression less friendly. "No, Korean. No one's ever made *that* mistake, either."

"Sorry! I didn't mean anything… I mean I just…"

"It's okay." Her smile returned.

Owen sighed. "I guess I'm not really good at this."

"Good at what?" Kei asked, positioning an elbow against the back of the couch and propping up her head with her hand. As she did so, some of her hair was bunched up in it, coming down in waves as she settled in. Owen tried not to stare at how beautiful the dark locks looked as they fell.

"All… this." He waved a hand around the room. "Hanging out. Meeting people. Small talk."

"Well you've met me! And we're talking. I'd say you're doing all right so far."

This put Owen at ease, but not entirely. He was still nervous talking to this girl, wondering what she wanted but not daring to believe that she might actually be interested in him.

But somehow, things had gone remarkably well. They continued to talk, and he was surprised to find out how old she was: eighteen, two years older than him. She laughed at this. "I know, I know. People always think I'm younger than I really am. It's because I'm so short."

"Well, and Oriental, too. I remember my dad pointing out that Orientals tend to look young."

"Asian," Kei corrected. "Not Oriental."

"What's the difference?"

"'Oriental' is something you say when you're talking about an object, like a rug or a piece of furniture. You say 'Asian' when you're talking about people." Owen wasn't sure if she was truly offended, but he apologized just to be safe. "It's fine. Just doing my part to educate the masses."

Not long after that, a rather obnoxious couple sat down on an adjacent couch, talking loudly. This made Owen uneasy, but at the same time, he liked the idea of people seeing him talking to this girl. It was a nice change from everyone passing by him while he sat alone, occasionally glancing in his direction but then looking away, uninterested. He especially hated it when girls did this, treating him like he was invisible.

"You wanna go for a walk?" Kei asked him.

So they did, and Owen wondered where the night was going to lead. He'd never been particularly attracted to Oriental girls (to *Asian* girls, he corrected himself mentally), but the fact that this one seemed inexplicably interested in him was changing his mind. Yes, the folds of skin over her eyelids that made them look like she was squinting weren't what he was used to, but that didn't mean that she wasn't attractive. The fact that she was so short — she only came up to his chest — wasn't necessarily a bad thing, either. She certainly seemed less threatening than the other girls he'd tried to get together with over the years.

There had been plenty of failures, and he wound up telling Kei about a couple of those later on. But before that, she'd started off their conversation as they left the loud interior of the coffee shop with an odd question: "So, what's the most embarrassing thing that's ever happened to you?"

"What? What are you doing, interviewing me?"

"I'm a journalism major," she said. "Well, I was."

"Was? Do you go to college here?" Owen still hadn't decided what he was going to major in, but at least he had a while to decide.

"I did, but I had to drop out. Some things came up. Anyway, *I'm* asking the questions."

Owen laughed. "Well, gee, let me think. I guess it was this thing that happened back in seventh grade." He told her the "it was in my pants" story, including how it had haunted him ever since, his reputation tarnished irrevocably. "In fact, I don't even know if you could say that that's the worst thing that's ever happened to me. There were plenty of other terrible things after that. The kids at that school would make fun of me, pull these stupid pranks, stuff like that. It wasn't a good time."

"Aw," Kei said. It almost sounded like she was making fun of him. Or maybe he was just used to people doing that.

"The kids there were pretty mean overall. Like there was this one girl, Louise, who apparently at one point back in, I don't know… maybe first grade or something, got head lice. And even as late as seventh grade, when I got there, she was still known as 'the girl who has bugs in her hair.' They used to called her Louise the Louse."

Kei laughed, and Owen didn't at first, but then he allowed himself a small chuckle. "Did they have a nickname for you?" she asked.

"No, well, not exactly. It was weird, but they always referred to me as Owen Raforth, my full name. Never just Owen. 'Owen Raforth,' like somehow that made me different, not one of them. An outsider."

"Hmm. I can relate to that."

"And then there was my birthday party, how I found out later that the only reason people showed up was because the teachers begged them to so I wouldn't…"

"Do you have a car?" Kei interrupted, stopping in her tracks.

Owen stopped as well, surprised. "What? Yeah. Sure I do. It's back at the coffee shop. Why?"

She frowned, looking distracted, maybe even sad. "It's getting late, and I should be getting home. Do you think you could give me a ride?"

"I… Yeah, sure, I guess." He looked at his watch. It wasn't really that late, only about 9:30. "Where do you live?"

"Not too far from here, near the canal. I'll give you directions on the way."

"Okay."

"Don't look so disappointed," she said, smiling once again. "I'm not saying I want you to just drop me off and that be the end of it." He wasn't sure what she meant, but she gave him a rather flirty smirk and a flick of her eyebrows, then turned on her heels and began walking in the opposite direction.

Holy crap, Owen thought to himself. *I really hope she meant by that what I think she meant.*

This wasn't the kind of thing that normally happened. Actually, it never did. Owen had never had a girlfriend, and the things this girl had been saying and doing all night almost felt like a dream come true. She was interested, forthright, and didn't treat him like he was a loser who wasn't even worth talking to. Just the opposite, in fact. He barely knew a thing about her, but that was exciting, too.

He realized after a minute or so of walking that neither of them had said anything, and he was beginning to feel uncomfortable, particularly because he couldn't think of anything else to say. He was far too distracted by the possibility that he might actually get somewhere with this girl.

"You've gone all quiet," was all he could think to say, but he did so with a laugh, hoping to get one out of her.

"Sorry," Kei said. "Just feeling kind of… preoccupied."

"Oh." More silence. Finally, his car was in view, so he pointed it out to her. They reached it a few seconds later, and he opened the driver's side, then used the automatic lock to open her door. They each got inside.

As he started up the car, he asked her, "So, which way?"

"Straight down here," she said, pointing, "then right on Greene Street. Then another right after that."

"Okay then," he said, again wishing he could have come up with something more clever. And then, it dawned on him that he could ask her what she was so preoccupied about.

She sighed. "Just thinking about my, um…"

Please don't say 'boyfriend,' Owen thought. The few times in his life he'd ever been able to work up the courage to talk to a pretty girl, that word had always come up eventually, turning the entire interaction into a dead end.

"…roommates, I guess." She paused for a moment. "Have you ever been in a situation where someone seemed really into you, and then all of a sudden, they changed their mind? Like, for no good reason?"

"No, not that I can think of." Almost no one ever seemed interested in him. Then he smacked his forehead, suddenly remembering. "Oh, right! Of course! I can't believe I forgot about that. But yeah, you're right, something like that did happen, just this summer, in fact."

The first disappointment had been once he'd realized that the only reason Gail had asked him about going to the concert was so he could give her and her boyfriend a ride to Atlanta. Owen liked Bon Jovi just fine, but he'd never been to one of their shows. Stupidly, he'd assumed when she first asked him if he was interested in going was that she wanted to go with *him,* not the boyfriend who suddenly materialized halfway through the conversation. Had he known about him from the beginning, he'd have just said he was busy or something.

But initially, he'd thought that he might get a chance to do something cool with his neighbor Gail, whom he'd had a secret crush on since moving to Augusta. That had never gone anywhere; he'd never had the nerve to tell her how he felt. And once he'd already talked things up about how much he liked Bon Jovi and that it would be cool to go to the show, it was too late to back out once she made it clear that it would be the three of them going, and to make up for the cost of gas, Gail and Danny would pay for his ticket. "Great!" she'd said. "I'll get the tickets for me, you, and Danny, and we can all sit together! It'll be such a good time!"

"And it wasn't?" Kei asked. "Oh, turn left here." She pointed as they reached another intersection.

"It… It was, in some parts. But I did get pretty sick of the two of them getting all lovey-dovey on each other and everything. I mean, I guess Danny was a nice enough guy; he was pretty funny, actually."

"But you were the third wheel."

Owen nodded firmly. "Exactly. But then, once we got there and the show started… Actually, no, it was just before. There was this other girl. Danny and Gail were on my left, and this girl was in the seat on my right. I had no idea who she was, but she was nice and all, and we got along really great. She talked to Danny and Gail, too, asking us where we were from, where we went to school, stuff like that, even telling us what kind of job she had in Atlanta. She was really excited, waiting for the show to start. 'Bon Jovi's the *shit!*' she said. That made me laugh."

"Sounds like you liked her," Kei said with a smile.

Owen began to feel nervous, afraid that this might put her off. "Uh… yeah. I did. But nothing ever happened. That was the other disappointing thing about the night."

He continued on with his tale, how the girl danced around and sang along throughout the show, being really cool and cute. This had prompted him to let loose and have fun as well, and he mostly forgot about his jealousy over the Gail/Danny situation.

"It was neat, the energy of everything. Like I said, it was my first live concert. And Bon Jovi was great, playing all their hits, 'You Give Love a Bad Name,' 'I'll Be There for You,' all that. They were great, the crowd was great, everything. I remember the girl getting really into another song called 'Blood on Blood,' sort of screaming the words along with the band, putting her hands up like this…" He mimed punching in the air with one hand, keeping the other one on the wheel as he drove.

"You keep saying 'the girl,'" Kei said thoughtfully. "What was her name?"

Owen sighed, putting his hand back down quickly. "That was the thing. I never found out."

"What? You never even asked her her name?"

"I didn't get the chance!" he said, emotion creeping into his voice. "After the show was done, she was all like, 'Okay, I have to go find my friend.' She'd come there with someone else, but they hadn't been able to get seats together because they'd waited till the last minute to get tickets. She'd told me that earlier, before the show started. That was why she was by herself. And then, all of a sudden, she was gone, just like that." He paused. "I never saw her again."

"And that was it?"

"That was it," Owen said firmly. "Gail and Danny were on me about it the whole night, asking me over and over: 'What was her name?' 'You didn't get her phone number?' 'Why didn't you ask her?' 'What's wrong with you?' 'She was really into you! I could tell!' And…" He let out a frustrated groan. "I was really torn up about it. I screwed up."

"Did you cry?"

"No!" he said angrily, then checked himself, glancing to one side to see the inquisitive look on Kei's face. There was something else there, a kind of knowing. "Fine. Yeah, I did. Once I was alone, anyway. We stopped off at a Waffle House before leaving town, still talking about everything, but it was weird because our ears were ringing from all the loud noise at the show. I went to the bathroom and let myself shed a few tears… Wait…"

Owen slowed the car down, realizing something. "I have no idea where we are. Are we near your house?"

"Pretty close," she said. "Pull in here." She pointed to a large, empty parking lot.

There didn't appear to be any houses or apartments nearby, only an enormous brick structure with what looked like a tall chimney, a place called Sibley Mill. Owen recognized it as one of Augusta's landmarks, but he never really knew what the place was for.

"This is where you live?" he asked, confused.

"Not exactly," Kei said. "I just wanted us to stop off here first so we can have some privacy. If we go straight to where I stay, well... My roommates will be swarming around and get all up in your face. I'd rather have you all to myself. Go ahead and park here." She pointed again, this time to a marked parking space among many in the vacant lot. There were no other cars around, only streetlights illuminating the area.

While confused, Owen decided not to argue. He wasn't comfortable with the idea of roommates in general, something that had weighed on his mind when he thought about going off to college in a couple of years. He preferred being on his own; he was used to it.

"No, leave it running," Kei said when Owen started to turn off the ignition. "So we can keep the heat on." After a pause, she added, "I'm cold."

"Okay," he said, then wasn't sure what to do next. He turned to look at her, noticing how pretty she looked in the dim light.

"So...?" she asked in a leading tone.

"So."

"You going to take off your seatbelt?" she asked.

"I... Hey, you weren't wearing yours the whole time, were you?"

"No. And don't get me started about that stupid new law."

Owen laughed. A lot of people had complained about the seatbelt law when it went into effect, but he'd always preferred wearing his. If he didn't, it felt like he was bouncing around in the car too much whenever he made a turn. But it made perfect sense for him to take it off now.

"I'm curious," Kei said, turning sideways in the passenger seat so that her entire body was facing him. Owen couldn't helped but eye her up and down, taking in every curve. "Did you ever go back and look for her?"

"Who? Oh, the girl at the concert. No, that would have been impossible. Atlanta's a big place." He paused, wondering whether to reveal this next bit of information. "I mean, yeah, okay, the thought did occur to me to get my hands on an Atlanta phone book and call every post production studio in town. But what was I gonna say? 'Hi, do you have a girl who works there who has short curly brown hair and the deepest blue eyes you've ever seen? And she went to the Bon Jovi concert last week?'"

Kei laughed, but not in a cruel way. "I'm sure that would have gone over well."

"Yeah. I mean, maybe, if I'd tried really hard, I could have done something. But the more I thought about it, it wasn't worth the effort."

"Not worth the effort," she said mostly to herself, looking away for a moment. "That's kind of something I've been wondering about lately."

"What?"

She shook her head, briefly closing her eyes. "Oh, nothing. Just… to do with my roommates. It's a weird situation. At first it was just me and this one guy, and I thought there was something really *there,* you know, but then he started bringing in all these other people. Made me question…" She stopped, seeing the confused look on Owen's face. "It doesn't matter. I'd rather not get into it." She shuffled closer to him, a wicked gleam in her eyes.

Owen felt nervous. Was this girl really going to make out with him? He'd never even kissed anyone. He suddenly felt very afraid that he might get it wrong. At least her eagerness had assuaged his fear that, like Gail, she might have been just using him for a ride. That voice of doubt had briefly sprung up in his head earlier, but he'd shouted it down.

"Put your seat back," Kei almost whispered.

He started to question why, but he just went with it. Reaching to his left, he pulled up the lever that made the driver's seat recline, and he pushed with his back. He almost fell backwards, surprised. He jerked forward again, and the seat came with him, so he had to force it down once more, remembering to release the lever to lock things in place. The entire thing felt stupid and embarrassing, and his face felt hot when Kei laughed. He wasn't handling himself well.

But still, she edged closer, her grin growing wider. "I said take this *off*," she insisted, pushing the button on the seat belt's buckle. The belt zipped across Owen's front, slamming with a *thunk* into the driver's side door. Part of him hoped that the metal hadn't scratched the interior, but the rest of him told himself to shut up about that and pay more attention to the sexy little Asian girl who was beginning to climb onto him.

It was too tight of a fit. "Hang on," Kei said. "Steering wheel up my ass. Let me…" She reached down behind her, and Owen realized what she was doing. He pushed with his legs, and the entire seat shifted backwards along the floor of the car, giving them more room. "That's better," she purred, and she was able to maneuver herself into place.

Kei leaned down, her face close to his. He thought they were about to kiss, and he swallowed hard, realizing suddenly how his breathing had increased. Hers had, too, and he could feel her cool breath on his skin. He was already starting to get hard down below, though he didn't know if she could tell. But she must have, because she let out a gentle giggle and then maneuvered one of her hands down to the fly on his jeans, undoing it.

He wasn't sure how any of this was happening, but that voice in his head spoke up once more, shouting: *Finally!* After years of being treated like shit by girls, here he was in his car, getting the treatment he'd always known he deserved. He was a nice guy, and nice guys finished last, as the saying went. Not anymore. This girl wasn't like the others. She listened to him, cared about what he had to say, and most importantly, her hand was going down the front of his pants.

Owen gasped at the coldness of it, the feel of her soft little hand on his private parts. But he wasn't going to complain. The writhing of her body on his, the pounding of his heart, the tingle he felt as her fingers enveloped his cock and balls, and the broad smile as she looked at him in the dim light… This was everything. This was perfect. Then it happened.

Pain shot through his entire body, starting at his crotch and spreading outwards like a million volts of electricity. Kei's grip had tightened immensely, her hand like a vise crushing his genitals. The rhythmic thrusting and grunting he'd been doing before was replaced by a piercing shriek, one that he didn't even realize was coming from him until he noticed the soreness in his throat. He tried to push back, to get her off of him, but her right hand was holding him down by the shoulder. It should have been impossible that a girl this small could have so much strength.

It went on and on, the agony increasing as he forced his eyes back open, seeing Kei's distorted face above his. It was like one of those comedy/tragedy masks, the kind he'd seen associated with historical theatre, and it took him a few seconds to realize that the girl was laughing — laughing at him — but he couldn't even hear it until he managed to gasp for breath. Her cackling was drowned out once more when he began screaming again, wanting to beg her to stop but unable to form the words.

Struggling helplessly against the impossibly strong girl, Owen noticed the fangs protruding from her hideous leer of a mouth, and suddenly, sadly, everything began to fall into place. He knew now what was happening, who this mysterious girl was, what she was.

The monster's face leaned forward and out of his field of vision, the sound of her laughter becoming audible over Owen's wails as that horrible mouth passed by his ear. The terrifying noise became muffled and then stopped as the two sharp teeth pierced the side of his neck, the pain from that barely registering as it paled in comparison to the continued torture happening between his legs.

He tried not to think about the sensations of crushing he could feel down there, the most sensitive part of his body being mutilated by this terrible, cruel creature. As the blood began to drain from his body and tears poured from his eyes, all he could think about was how unfair this was. Being killed by a vampire was bad enough, but why had she talked to him for so long beforehand, listening to his stories, pretending to like him? What was she doing these horrible things for? He would never find out.

His consciousness slipping away, Owen had one final thought, realizing where this girl's hand was.

It was in my pants.

CHAPTER FORTY

UNDER THE INFLUENCE

Officer Hatcher sat in his car outside of a house on Ingleside Drive, just past the intersection where it turned into Aumond Road. He'd been called there on a domestic disturbance, one of his least favorite situations to deal with. It was always uncomfortable for all parties involved, but at least this one hadn't been that bad, all things considered. By the time he'd arrived, the violence — shouting outdoors and then inside, followed by the sound of objects being thrown — had died down, and the husband and wife were already on their way to reconciliation. They'd been more embarrassed than anything else, ashamed that they'd caused such a ruckus that their nosy neighbor had thought it necessary to call the cops.

Even so, he had to do his job, but he dreaded having to act like an impromptu marriage counselor in these cases. The couple had — big surprise — been drinking, arguing over various things to the point where it escalated out of control. Also not surprisingly, this wasn't the first time it had happened, and bits and pieces of the family's troubled past came up while he talked to them. But then, Augusta was a troubled town.

Hatcher had been a bit apprehensive about taking a job with the Augusta Police Department and moving his wife and kids to the big city, but it was a good move career-wise. Back across the river in McCormick, South Carolina, he'd realized after a few years on the force there that he'd gotten as far as he could with those people. It was a small town, and there was only so high that they'd let a black man rise within the ranks. That was just how things were, whether it was fair or not. At least Augusta was progressive and more integrated, and people of color stood a chance of moving up.

And sure, he'd run into some of the same prejudices as in his home town, plus he occasionally got some grief from people about being from "out in the boonies" and all of the other stupid cracks people would make, black and white alike. Even in the few short months he'd lived here, he'd learned to tame his accent to avoid ridicule, no longer pronouncing the place he'd come from as "McCommick" like he had done his entire life. That was how everyone who lived there said the name, but nowadays, he made sure to emphasize the "r" in the second syllable so he wouldn't get made fun of.

Technically, it had been a lateral move, and he was still the same rank as what he'd been back in McCo*r*mick. But the pay was better, and even though the cost of living was higher here, his new salary was definitely an improvement. Also, he'd been assured by his colleagues that he would make Lieutenant within a year or two. *I'll believe that when I see it,* Sergeant Hatcher thought to himself on his more cynical days, but overall, these weren't bad people. At least here, it seemed more possible that his career could move forward, as long as he managed to survive, that is.

He wasn't sure how he felt about the notion of there being vampires in this city, whether he even believed it or not. Apparently, it was true, even according to other people on the police force. He'd yet to encounter any himself, and he hoped things would stay that way. Fortunately for him, nearly all cases of vampire sightings and bodies being found — at least this year — were confined to the downtown area and to the region known as South Augusta, far removed from where his job normally took him, the suburbs to the west.

"You'd better hope so," Lieutenant McCarthy said to him one day at the station, taking a drag off his cigarette. "If you never run across any of them, you'll be lucky." He exhaled sharply, blowing out a thick stream of smoke. "We've lost a lot of good people to those things."

"Hot dirty sex!" James screamed out the car window.

Lewis, who was driving, laughed. They were both fairly drunk, and the joke hadn't gotten old yet, even though it probably should have by now.

The night had started back at their apartment, the two young men drinking vodka in preparation for the party at Tiffany's place on the other side of town. They were all a part of what they called "The Sunday Night Crew," a group of friends from the local college who celebrated the fact that their schedules happened to line up so that none of them had any classes on Monday mornings. It was a weird coincidence, just something that Tiffany had pointed out when they were all comparing class times one afternoon at the student center, and she'd proposed the idea that they could have what she called "an extended weekend," partying on Sunday night while many of their fellow students could not.

Those who were part of their circle of friends who couldn't take part — the ones whose classes met early on Monday — envied them and delighted in their stories of what happened on those drunken nights. People puked, passed out, and did insane and hilarious things, just like most of the rest of them did on Friday and Saturday nights, but the Sunday Night Crew was something special.

"I really need to make sure I fix my schedule next semester," a girl named Jessica said to Lewis one day after class. "I want to get in on this. You guys have so much fun."

"Hell yeah, we do!" Lewis said proudly.

The first meeting of the Crew hadn't gone as well as they'd hoped, though. Everyone had gotten together at Tiffany's, but the drinks ran out quickly. They hadn't thought about the blue laws that made it so no one could buy alcohol on Sunday. From then on, everyone made it a point to stock up on plenty of beer and liquor the day before, bringing it with them each week.

It was also found over time, at least from the perspective of Lewis and James, that it was more fun to get a little buzzed before arriving at Tiffany's. James especially hated showing up sober to find that everyone else already had a head start on getting drunk, and he didn't like to feel outdone.

Lewis was the more rational one, the pair having been roommates for over a year. They were good friends and got along, but Lewis knew full well that the more James drank, the more obnoxious he became. The only way to tolerate James when he got like this was to get drunk as well; at least then he didn't seem like as much of a pain in the ass.

James also had this habit of getting stuck on a particular phrase on any given night, repeating it over and over. It started off as something funny in conversation, but after a while, the fact that he was saying the phrase became the joke. He did lots of different character voices: Sometimes he adopted a rednecky tone, this sort of low grunt that could make almost anything sound hilarious, or there was the loud, wailing one where he was intentionally sounding like a dumb-ass. That one had started last New Year's Eve when they'd been drunkenly wandering around the bars downtown, shouting "Happy New Years!" at irregular intervals, sometimes at total strangers to freak them out. By that point, everyone had forgotten how the joke had even started, why he wasn't saying "Happy New Year" instead. But it didn't have to make sense; it was just fun.

This Sunday night, Lewis and James had been downing shots as they prepared to go out, and James went off on a rant about this guy they knew at school whom neither of them really liked. They were grateful that he wasn't able to be part of the Sunday Night Crew, even though he'd expressed a desire to.

"Yeah, man!" James shouted, pretending he was the object of their ridicule and beginning to segue into his annoying wailing character. "I wanna drink with y'all and be part of the Crew! Then maybe I'll get laid and have lots of hot dirty sex!" Lewis laughed, which egged his friend on. "Hot dirty sex! I wanna have hot dirty sex! Hey Lewis, do ya think if I can come to the party next week and ditch class the next day and stay out with you guys that I can have *hot dirty sex!?*" By now, he was at full volume.

"All right, chill," Lewis said. "We should switch to beer to even things out so we can make it there in one piece."

"Okay, fine," James said, returning to his normal voice. "But do you think maybe this time, you could remember to bring the beer in from the car so it doesn't sit in there and get all hot... *DIRTY SEX!*"

Lewis groaned, but he couldn't help but laugh. The tone had been set for the night: James was going to work that phrase into every conversation he could.

On the way to Tiffany's, James had continued to repeat the joke, and it became a drinking game. Whenever he was able to fit it into something they were talking about, they each had to take a sip off their beers.

"Okay, seriously," Lewis said, not actually feeling all that serious, "you keep that shit up and I'm gonna end up driving off the road."

"Fine, fine," James said. "I'll stop. No more mentions of *hot dirty sex!*"

"Goddammit," Lewis sighed while his friend laughed, and they each took their sips. Lewis faked his this time, only pretending to drink.

James cleared his throat, then held up the nearly empty bottle, peering through its dark brown glass as the passing streetlights illuminated it. "Damn, mine's almost done. Maybe I should start another one."

"No, jackass. Give it a rest. It's bad enough that we're going to be showing up with only half a bottle of vodka and four beers. We should've bought more."

"Not my fault. I told you to go to the store yesterday."

Lewis fought down his anger, resisting the urge to say something like *You could have gone yourself.* If they got into an argument while drinking, things could get ugly; it had happened before. At least they weren't talking about politics this time. Fortunately, something came up to distract them.

"Hey man, look out," James said, pointing through the windshield.

"I see them." There were two people walking, a guy and a girl, right along the edge of the road. Lewis forced himself to concentrate, being careful to steer around the couple without losing control of the car. It was only then that he realized he'd been speeding: He was doing almost 50 in a residential area.

"This'll be good," James said, and he pushed the control to roll down the window. "Slow down a little."

Lewis didn't; he maintained his speed. James wasn't going to tell him how to drive. And while he hadn't wanted it to be funny, he couldn't help but laugh as his friend once again yelled his catchphrase of the night at the unsuspecting people on the road, followed by an enthusiastic *"Woo!"* for good measure. More than likely, those two would spend the rest of their night wondering why some stranger had shouted that at them.

James wasn't done. They were coming up on a sign by the road, one of those yellow diamond ones with a big black arrow on it to indicate an upcoming curve. Lewis had hoped that they might make it through the night without this happening, but it was another one of his friend's signature moves. The empty beer bottle was hurled at the sign as they passed by it, making a loud clanging sound that undoubtedly was heard by everyone within earshot. It wasn't the most original thing to do — plenty of other delinquents their age did this kind of stuff, including bashing mailboxes — but it was classic James.

In his patrol car, Officer Hatcher set down the notepad, having finished writing up his notes on the disturbance at the Emerson household. There hadn't been any reason to run either the husband or the wife in, though he did feel bad for them. It was sad that they were so miserable that they had to drown their sorrows in drink, occasionally to the point where they took out their frustrations on each other. But at least tonight, no actual crime had been committed, and he'd let them off with a warning to keep things down.

Hatcher's eye caught the pack of cigarettes in the console next to the gearshift, strategically placed as always so that the side with the Surgeon General's warning on the label was facing away from him. He knew that smoking was bad for him and that he needed to quit, and he'd tried plenty of times but failed. And every time he did, things had gotten scary.

No matter how many warnings there were, how many bad stories he'd heard, and right down to the fact that his own grandmother had died of cancer, he couldn't seem to shake the habit. Whenever he tried to — his record was one month — he wound up becoming such an emotional wreck that the only recourse was to start smoking again.

During his first attempt, things started off great: He'd found himself in a terrific mood, happy about everything and so glad that he'd made this choice to improve himself. But then tiny, inconsequential things made him angry as hell and made him want to put his fist through a wall, and he'd unfairly taken his anger out on those around him. He'd always heard that it was hard to quit smoking, but it wasn't until he'd attempted it that he realized what people meant when they said that.

It sucked being addicted. Maybe that was why he'd been so sympathetic to the Emersons, who were clearly alcoholics. He'd stopped short of suggesting to them that they start attending AA meetings, but looking back on it, he wondered if maybe he should have. But he also felt like that wasn't his place. He was glad that he hadn't yet encountered anyone in Augusta who was a crackhead or a heroin addict, but he figured that he probably would someday, given how big of a city this was.

Still debating whether or not to light up, Hatcher thought back to some of the more hairy situations he'd been through back in McCormick that involved substance abuse, plus there had been domestic abuse cases that had been much less civilized than the one he'd had to deal with tonight. Back then, he'd gotten pretty good at reading people and knew which patterns of behavior to look out for, but he was finding that he was having to relearn that skill at his new job. Augusta people were just different.

He let out a small laugh as remembered something that happened last year, the time that he pulled over two speeding cars that had torn through town on their way back to Augusta. That one hadn't gone like he'd expected at all.

After pulling them over, he'd stopped at the lead car and spoken to the driver, a white girl in her early 20s. She was clearly upset and angry, explaining to him how the guy in the car behind her was her boyfriend, and he'd followed her all the way out to McCormick and back. They'd been having some problems with their relationship, and she was scared and didn't want to talk to him.

Hatcher told her to wait and then went to speak to the driver of the other car. The question that greeted him after the boyfriend rolled down his window was a simultaneously panicked and angry: "Is she okay?"

The boy went on to tell his side of the story: He'd gone by his girlfriend's house to break up with her and give back her stuff, some things she'd left over at his house or whatever. But when she'd seen his car approaching, she'd jumped into hers and sped away, and he was worried that she was driving out to the lake (Clarks Hill Lake, which wasn't too far from there) to kill herself. Apparently, the girl was unstable enough for him to think that.

With this in mind, Hatcher went back to the girl's car and explained things, not sure which of the two parties was at fault. Maybe the guy was crazy and abusive, or maybe the girl was the one who was the kook. Regardless, they'd both been breaking the law by speeding, so he had to deal with that, and they'd definitely both be getting tickets. This wasn't anything he'd said to them aloud by this point, though.

After some deliberation, he decided to let the boyfriend — now ex-boyfriend, according to him — give the girl her things back, but he didn't want there to be a big confrontation or shouting match. If that kind of thing started up, he'd shut it down immediately.

"I'm gonna walk you up there to her car, and you can give her the stuff you were talking about. And then we're going to walk back here, and I don't want any trouble."

"All right," the guy said, still fuming. He was pretty sure that his anger was directed mostly at the ex-girlfriend, not him.

Surprisingly, it had all been just as straightforward as he'd instructed. The boy carried a small, open-lidded box of trinkets to the girl, who was standing by her car, arms folded and tight-lipped. Something in her expression changed as he handed the box to her, almost like she was surprised, and the boy simply said to her through gritted teeth, "You are *such* a child." With that, he turned on his heel and strode back to his vehicle, not another word said.

Officer Hatcher's reverie was interrupted by the sight of headlights approaching from behind, and in his rearview mirror, he could tell that they were moving quickly. Too quickly, in fact, and within seconds, the car had zoomed right past him. He caught a glimpse of a young man in the passenger side, and just for a split second, the two of them had made eye contact. In that short moment, he could see the boy's expression change from exhilaration to panic.

"Just as well I didn't light one up," he muttered to himself, and he cranked up his car, turned on the lights and the siren, and began his pursuit.

"Oh shit, oh shit, oh shit…" James kept saying.

"Shut the fuck up," Lewis hissed, fumbling around as he looked for the bottle cap. He found it, and with shaking hands, he twisted it onto the top of his unfinished beer. "Put this in with the others," he ordered, handing the bottle to James.

"Oh shit, oh shit..." he kept repeating, leaning over to the floorboard behind the driver's seat to put Lewis's beer away. As he did, he glanced back at the blue and white lights that danced and flashed on the roof of the car parked behind theirs, its headlights searing into his vision. He screwed his eyes shut, hoping he could somehow wish them away.

Lewis sighed angrily. "I can't believe you almost yelled 'hot dirty sex' at a cop car."

"You're the one who sped right past him!" James shouted, slamming back down into his seat. "I told you to slow down."

"Shut *up*. I didn't see it in time."

"Shit. We're going to go to jail. My dad's gonna kill me. Shit, shit, shit!"

Lewis looked in the driver's side mirror, wondering when the policeman was going to come talk to them. He'd been pulled over once before a few years back, but never when he'd been drinking. He was worried that James was right. They were so screwed.

Officer Hatcher had begun to take out the necessary forms, knowing full well that he was going to have to issue a citation. He'd already taken down the license plate number and called it in, and he wondered how complicated this particular stop was going to be. He was still craving that cigarette, and it annoyed him that he was having to wait even longer to have it. He had half a mind to go ahead, to make the dumb kids in the car ahead of him sweat it out and wait even longer. But he shouldn't do that, he knew; he had a job to do.

He thought again about the possibility of quitting. There had to be some way to make it happen without going out of his mind. And if he didn't, he knew what the consequences would be. He didn't want that; he wanted to see his children grow up, to be there for them when they needed him.

A tapping sound on the car window brought him back to reality, and he resisted the impulse to jump. There was a boy standing outside, motioning to him to roll down the window. He was tall and pale with dark hair, and he looked barely old enough to drive. What was odd, Hatcher realized, was that he hadn't seen anyone get out of the car he'd pulled over, but because he'd been looking down for the past few moments, he figured that the driver must have approached his position unnoticed.

He studied the boy as he set his paperwork onto the passenger seat, mentally noting the position of his gun in its holster. He hoped that there wouldn't be any reason to pull it out, but he was trained to consider every option and assume the worst, just for his own safety. But honestly, this kid didn't seem like he was a threat. The very fact that he'd come to talk to him reminded him of another incident from his past.

Shortly before he'd moved away from McCormick, he'd pulled over another young man of about the same age who had cut him off at an intersection, and rather than sitting and waiting like he was supposed to, the boy had stepped out of his car and tried to approach him, hands raised. It became clear almost immediately that the boy was lost, confused, and a bit scared, having never dealt with the police before.

Hatcher explained to him what he'd done wrong, how exiting the vehicle could have gotten him into more trouble. But this was an okay kid; his lack of experience in dealing with the law illustrated that. He was let off with a warning, tips on how to behave if he were ever pulled over again, and directions to get back to Augusta.

With this in mind, Hatcher figured that this boy was probably similar, and he rolled down his window. "Son," he said with authority, "I'm going to need you to go back to your vehicle."

To his surprise, the boy laughed, then mocked him. *"Mah vee-hicle?"* He turned to look at the car parked on the side of the road ahead of them. "Oh, that's not mine. I have no idea who those guys are."

"Then what…?" Officer Hatcher never got to finish his sentence.

There was a flash of movement as the boy reached through the window and grabbed him, lifting him up from his seat with superhuman strength. A second later, he felt a sharp pain in the side of his neck, and despite his screaming and struggling, there was nothing he could do.

His meal finished, the vampire leaned back out of the car window, licking his lips and wiping away the excess blood with his wrist. He let out a satisfied sigh, a huge grin on his face. "That was good," he said, turning to his companion.

"You didn't save any for me?" the other vampire pleaded, though he was also grinning and wasn't actually mad.

"Up there," the first one said, pointing at the other car. "Let's see what else is on the menu." The second vampire laughed, a wild and hungry look in his eyes. "Time for your first kill."

"I can't wait!" he said eagerly.

"Hang on." The vampire reached into the police car, then pulled something out. It was the dead policeman's cap, which he placed on his head. "What do you think?"

His friend laughed, then shook his head. "Afraid not, Carl. Doesn't suit you."

"Found it," Lewis said, coming up from where he'd been rummaging in the arm rest's compartment. He pulled out a pack of gum, then nervously unwrapped a piece and began chewing it. "Here," he said, pointing the pack at James.

"You know I hate that shit," he protested. "Too strong. It makes me gag."

"It'll cover up the smell of alcohol on your breath, dumb-ass. Just take it."

James grimaced, but he took the gum, unwrapped it, and forced it into his mouth. As he tried to chew, the sharp, putrid taste of concentrated sugar and cinnamon overwhelmed his taste buds, the scent shooting up the back of his throat and into his nose. As expected, he started choking and his eyes began to water, and he spat the disgusting substance out. It stuck to the dashboard.

"Goddammit, James!" Lewis shouted.

"Told you."

A shadow flickered across the mirror, and Lewis saw that the policeman was approaching. He could just barely make out his silhouette. "Just play it cool," he said to his friend, his breathing becoming more pronounced as he smacked his gum. "I'll do the talking. And I swear to God, if you blurt out anything about 'hot dirty sex,' I'll punch you in the face."

"I *won't...*" James began, then stopped, still trying to clear his throat and get the horrible taste out of his mouth. "Shit. There's two of them. Someone's coming up on my side of the car, too."

Lewis started to ask about this, but by then, a tall figure was standing outside the car. Nervous, he tried to press the button to roll his window down, but instead, he hit the one that unlocked all of the car's doors at once. He quickly shifted his finger over and managed to hit the right control, doing his best to look calm and apologetic.

As the glass hummed down, the man outside the car said firmly, "Please step out of the car, sir."

This wasn't what Lewis had been expecting. The last time he'd gotten pulled over for speeding, he'd just sat in his seat the entire time, the officer intimidating him and eventually giving him a ticket. But he did as he was told, hoping to somehow talk himself out of this and survive the night.

As he got up and stood to face the officer, he realized that something was wrong. This guy was wearing a policeman's hat, but why wasn't he in a uniform? He was just wearing regular clothes, and he looked pretty damn young, too. Was he some kind of policeman in training — a deputy or something — and the real officer the other one that James had mentioned seeing?

Lewis turned to look over to find out, but all of a sudden, he felt his entire body being slammed against the frame of his car. The pain from this was soon supplemented by the sensation of the man shoving his own body up against his backside, pinning him with unbelievable force. This wasn't fair; he hadn't done anything to deserve this kind of brutality. But then something else just as unbelievable happened, and too late, he understood. The sharp teeth sunk into his neck, and the vampire began drinking his blood.

Todd smiled as he watched Carl kill the driver of the car. Now it was his turn, finally. With extreme glee, he grabbed for the handle and snatched the car door open, delighting in the terrified and confused look the boy inside had on his face. He was a stocky, short-haired fellow, the same kind of beefy looking jerk who had always picked on him at school. But all of that was going to change. It already had.

With his new strength, he effortlessly lifted his prey out and pulled him up to his mouth, burying his fangs into the soft flesh of the boy's neck as he screamed and struggled helplessly. The hot, warm blood rushed down Todd's throat, and he loved every single second of it. It tasted better than anything he could have ever imagined, and the feeling of this strong, stupid jock going limp in his arms only added to his enjoyment. This was heaven.

He'd only been a vampire for a few hours; Carl had made him that way. Todd knew that this was just the beginning, and he was going to love his new life.

CHAPTER FORTY-ONE

THE CONVERSATION

"You cold?" Jordan asked.

"A little bit," Vanessa said. "Not really. It's been warmer than usual tonight."

"That's true," he said. "Doesn't mean we can't, you know…"

"Sure," she said, smiling as she edged closer to him. As she did, her thoughts drifted back to events that had led them to this moment, the night it all began.

Vanessa was sobbing. "Please," she begged, unable to struggle against the impossibly strong grip the vampire had on her. "Please just let me go."

"Oh, no," the man said, and she could hear the smile in his voice even though she couldn't see his face. He was holding her from behind, having forced her to watch as the other vampire, a young blonde woman, had killed her boyfriend Jordan. She couldn't believe that he was dead, but more than that, she was terrified of the prospect of joining him soon.

"Please!" she repeated, shouting this time. "I don't want to die!"

"Aw, sweetheart," the man said with mock sympathy. "No one wants to die. But how would you feel about living forever?"

Vanessa froze. "What?" she whispered.

"See if you can do it," he said, but Vanessa could tell from the way he was projecting his voice that he wasn't talking to her. Instead, his words were directed to the horrible monster that had just murdered the love of her life.

"Damon…" she began, standing up from where Jordan's lifeless body lay. There was something in her voice that suggested reluctance. "I don't know if I can."

"Sure you can," he said, and for the moment, Vanessa was relieved that his attention wasn't focused on her. If only he could stay distracted, then maybe she might be able squirm out of his arms and get away. But she knew that the chances of outrunning both of these creatures were slim, probably impossible.

"I don't know. I don't feel strong enough. It's like… I kinda know how, but not really."

"You see, Carolyn here doesn't think she has it in her, but I know she does," the vampire Damon said, this time more quietly and into Vanessa's ear.

Carolyn narrowed her eyes at him, sneering slightly. She seemed to be avoiding looking Vanessa in the eye, almost like she wasn't important. "You gonna eat that or what?" she asked, pointing. Vanessa let out an involuntary squeal of fear once she realized what the girl meant. She again tried to struggle, but Damon continued to hold her fiercely.

"I want you to do it," he said, a sick growl creeping into his voice. "I like to watch it when you do."

Carolyn's expression changed, a wicked grin spreading across her face as she began to slink forward. "You do, huh?"

"Yes," he said firmly. "And then you can try bringing this one back, too."

"All right, then," the vampire purred, sliding herself up onto the front of Vanessa's helpless form. She was sandwiched between the two bloodthirsty killers, tears streaming down her face. There was no point in begging for her life anymore.

She cried out in pain as the girl's fangs pierced her neck, then lost the will to fight back. It sickened her to hear the sound of her own blood being gulped down her attacker's throat, but then she also became aware of another sensation, one that disgusted her even more once she realized what it was. Damon's crotch had been positioned behind her back this whole time, but something had begun to poke into her, his erection. The guy was actually getting off on watching his girlfriend kill her. It was the last thing she was aware of before she died.

That had been just over a month ago, and Vanessa sometimes laughed when she thought back to the scared little girl she'd been that night. She was a vampire now, too, as was Jordan, and they enjoyed their new existence as citizens of the undead. There were other vampires around town, she knew, but for the most part, their small group kept to themselves, living by their own rules.

For a while, it had just been them, two vampire couples enjoying their time together, but then Damon had made Carolyn turn Maureen as well, bringing her into the fold. That had made the dynamic much more interesting. Vanessa and Jordan, while they did like killing and drinking blood, weren't as into the kinky stuff that the two older vampires were. S&M just wasn't up their alley, but Carolyn and Damon had explored that quite a bit. They were definitely darker and more cruel, both to each other and to their victims when they killed them.

"You know, sometimes I wonder if either of those two have a good bone in their body," Vanessa said to Jordan one night in late January. They were lying on their backs on the roof of the house, looking up at the stars. While a portion of the roof near the front of the building had a steep slope to it, the majority of its surface was flat, which was what made it a relaxing place to hang out. Half of the top floor was the apartment where they lived, the other three quarters of the place used for storage by the old man who owned it. The group had taken over the apartment after killing its former occupant, some girl that Carolyn had known before. What was funny was that the dumb old fart had no clue that the new residents were even vampires; he didn't care who they were as long as they paid the rent.

"Well, Carolyn probably has a certain bone in her right now," Jordan joked, which prompted a playful smack from Vanessa.

"Shut up," she said exasperatedly. "We came up here to get away from all of that."

Jordan laughed. "Yeah, no kidding. Only so much screaming one can take, right?"

Vanessa giggled. "I mean, yeah. Good for them and all. But, like, shut up already!"

"But I know what you mean. They can both be pretty damn dark. Like what you were saying earlier about the girl who used to live here. What was her name?"

Vanessa couldn't remember, either. They'd been talking about the night the four of them had come to the place, and the girl hadn't realized they were vampires until it was too late. She'd begged Carolyn not to kill her, trying to appeal to her good nature and bringing up tales of the fun things they used to do together, including how they'd joked around so much in Typing class back in high school. But Carolyn was completely cold to her; she'd forgotten all about that, and it didn't matter anymore. Soon after, she'd killed her former friend, and she showed no remorse about it whatsoever.

There was a flapping noise nearby, then the sound of footsteps as a human form approached them on the roof. "Hey guys," Maureen said playfully. "What are we talking about?" She sat down next to them, crossing her legs beneath her.

Initially, Vanessa had been bothered by Maureen's insertion into their circle of friends, but she'd warmed up to her once she'd gotten to know her. She was a pretty girl with thick, platinum blonde hair, and she'd been a stripper — or as she preferred to call it, a dancer — at one of the clubs on Broad Street before being turned into a vampire by Carolyn at Damon's insistence. Having that background didn't mean that she was some horrible, trashy slut, though. Still, she was certainly more into playing around with Carolyn and Damon when they got into their sex stuff, much more than Jordan and Vanessa had ever been.

From the beginning, sex had been this weird, interchangeable thing within the group, at least from Vanessa's perspective. A newly resurrected vampire, she hadn't protested much when it became clear that Damon was just as okay with screwing her as casually as he did Carolyn, and it wasn't like she didn't enjoy it. The guy was good, no doubt about that. It bugged her a little the first time that Carolyn also had her way with Jordan, but soon enough, she got used to the whole thing. After all, none of them were human anymore, so why should they live by their morals?

It was very freeing, the way that no one was exclusively bound to a particular partner like in traditional relationships. There were still rules to follow, but it was all based around trust and respect; it wasn't like any of them could just go off and fuck whoever they felt like without telling the others. It was kind of liked licensed cheating, everyone being open and honest about the situation, and no one was allowed to have sex outside of the circle. This also applied to creating new vampires; that would have to be agreed upon by everyone. That was how Maureen had been brought in.

"Oh, not much," Jordan said to Maureen. "I thought you were taking part in Fuckfest 1990."

She laughed, as did Vanessa. "Is that what we're calling it tonight? No, I couldn't keep up. You know how they are. I got my jollies and then decided to let them keep going at it." She pulled out her cigarettes, lit one, and took a drag.

"So it's the ceremonial cigarette right after sex?" Vanessa asked, though she wasn't being particularly serious.

"I suppose. Just habit, really, or routine. I don't even know if I'm even addicted anymore. Now that I'm a vampire, I mean. It doesn't affect me the same way." She exhaled another plume of smoke into the brisk night air.

"Well, at least you don't have to worry about dying from cancer or anything," Jordan joked.

"Right," Maureen said thoughtfully. "And maybe that's why it feels different. The danger isn't there anymore, so it's less of a thrill. Before, it always felt like I was getting away with something."

This reminded Vanessa of something she'd noticed, how things had changed for her and Jordan since their death and resurrection. They'd been seniors in high school before, both still living at home and having to sneak around in order to have sex. Every now and then when they were out at night looking for victims, she'd spot a secluded place and think for a moment, *Hey, there's a good place to park.* But she and Jordan didn't need to do that anymore, to hide out from their parents. It took some getting used to.

The three continued to hang out and talk, pondering their new existence. Everyone agreed that they'd been surprised at how quickly they'd taken to killing, how it didn't bother them nearly as much as it probably should have. Vanessa brought up what she'd been thinking earlier, how freed she felt from her former life, no longer subject to the rules that had governed them as humans.

"What about Carolyn and Damon?" Jordan asked.

"What about them?" Maureen asked, stubbing out the remnants of her cigarette. She picked up her pack, seeming to consider having another one. "Anybody want one?" she offered.

"No thanks," Vanessa said politely.

"Me neither," Jordan said.

"Come on, man," Maureen said tauntingly, holding the pack out towards them and adopting a strange voice. "It won't hurt you. Everybody's doing it."

The other two laughed, realizing what she was doing, acting like one of the pushers in those cheesy anti-drug films they used to have to watch in school. "Nah," Jordan said. "I'm thinking about taking up crack instead." This prompted more laughter.

"You'd better not," Vanessa joked. "I'm not sleeping with a crackhead."

After the joke died down, Maureen asked Jordan, "What were you saying about our two lovebirds?"

"Hmm? Oh. Well, I'd hardly call them that. 'Fuckbirds,' maybe. You ever notice how they never actually kiss?"

Maureen paused, and then her face lit up. "You know, you're right! I'd never even thought about that. But yeah, that's true. They'll paw at each other and not give a shit about who sees, but it's… I don't know…"

"Brutal," Vanessa said meaningfully.

"Exactly. You think they were like that before? Like, when they were human?"

The couple exchanged a glance. They'd known them longer than Maureen had, so they knew things that she didn't. Vanessa decided to let her boyfriend speak first.

"There's a lot of history there," he said. "We don't know all of it. You know how they can be kind of vague about their past."

"Yeah, I've noticed that."

"There was a break-up at some point," Vanessa said. "But it's not really clear on how they got back together. Maybe it was when they became vampires, but they've never really explained how that happened, either. What's strange is that sometimes, they'll talk like they're still broken up, or even… I don't know, like there are these alternate versions of them that still hate each other. It's weird. I've never understood that part."

Maureen seemed to consider this. "Maybe that's why they're so into all of the violent sex stuff. Brutal, like you said. They like inflicting pain as a way to punish each other for whatever it was they did wrong."

"You mean what broke them up before?" Jordan asked. "Could be." He thought for a moment. "That doesn't fully explain the duct tape thing, though. We all enjoyed that." Sensual giggles erupted from the two girls, and then Jordan let out something similar.

"Yeah, okay," Vanessa admitted. "That was pretty awesome."

A few nights ago, there had been some experimentation with bondage, another kinky sex act. It eventually resulted in Vanessa and Maureen being "mummified," their bodies covered head to toe in duct tape (minus some gaps over their noses so they could breathe), which was oddly but undeniably arousing. There was something about the helplessness of it, the vulnerability to their male counterparts, having to both trust them and surrender to them while Carolyn watched from afar. The sensory deprivation was interesting, too, being almost entirely cut off from all external stimuli, and Vanessa found the entire experience erotic and soothing at the same time.

"And when the tape came off," she continued, then let out a heavy sigh. "I mean, even though it hurt… It was still amazing. The *release*. It felt like being born." She stretched out her arms as if she were yawning, then pulled them back down, pausing briefly to tuck her chin-length brown hair behind her ears.

Maureen sighed as well, smiling broadly. "Yeah, it did." She settled down next to Vanessa, snuggling up to her in more or less the same way that Jordan was doing on her other side. The move wasn't met with any resistance. Then she perked her head up again, peering over at Jordan. "You should try it."

"Me?" He paused. "Yeah, maybe."

"You and Damon," Vanessa offered. "We can swap roles this time."

"Yessss," Maureen hissed. "That would be fun. And then we can zap *you* two with the vibrators so you can see how it feels."

Jordan seemed to flinch, which made his girlfriend laugh. "I'm really liking this idea."

"I don't know," he said, doubt creeping into his voice.

"Aw, come on. Don't be a baby. You'll like it. I promise."

"You think the other two will go for it?" he asked. "I don't know if I can see Damon, well, you know…"

"Giving up that much control?" Maureen offered. "Oh, I think he might. You'd be surprised what some men are willing to try." She paused. "If they're not afraid. And I bet Carolyn would get more into it this time, you know, instead of just sitting back and watching."

Jordan let out an exasperated groan, but he would probably come around with a little more persuading, Vanessa thought. "Maybe, maybe. We should go in and ask them what they think about the idea."

"Do you think they're done yet?" Vanessa reached out mentally, trying to sense what their two friends were doing, her mind stretching out to the bedroom in the apartment below. It was one of the new abilities she'd gained since becoming a vampire, and she could also sense that the other two were doing the same. "Nope." She then let her preternatural sight return to normal.

"Wow," Maureen said, apparently still looking in. "I should have stuck around."

"Don't spy!" Vanessa chided, nudging her sharply. "It's rude."

"What do you think she tastes like?"

"You mean, in her pussy?" Jordan asked.

"No!" Maureen almost shrieked. "Vanessa, smack him for me. I can't reach."

"Already did."

"I meant her blood."

"Oh," Jordan said. "Think she'd let you find out?"

"I don't know. Do you think we can feed on each other? Like, without any real damage? It's not like we're going to kill each other or anything, since we can't die."

"Hmm," Vanessa said. "Maybe. We should try sometime."

"She'd probably taste different now than she did before, you know, when she was still human," Jordan suggested.

"Ooh, I wish I could go back in time and try that," Maureen purred. She wasn't shy about her bisexuality, Vanessa knew, but the way things had been going and considering how much the lines kept blurring, it seemed like the other four of them had been heading in that direction. Their freedom from traditional morals had allowed them that. There hadn't been any indication that Damon and Jordan might cross that line, nor was she entirely sure if she'd be okay with that if it came to pass. But then again, why not? That was one of the things she loved about this new lifestyle, how it opened her mind to things she'd never even considered before.

"She does have a sister, you know," Vanessa said teasingly. "Still human. I bet she'd taste the same."

"Really?"

"Yeah," Jordan said. "They don't talk about their families much, but there was one night when that came up, just a mention of her. Carolyn seemed kinda pissed about it."

"Why?"

"Not sure. I think maybe Damon did something with her…"

"Back when they were human," Vanessa interjected. "I think maybe it was just that he tried to. Like, making a pass at her."

"Or maybe he just wanted to," Jordan added. "Who knows."

The trio lay there in silence for a moment. "Is she younger?" Maureen asked. "Older?"

Vanessa giggled, finding herself also wondering what their friend's sister's blood might taste like. "Don't know."

Jordan piped up, "For all we know, she might be a twin."

Maureen shuddered, clearly aroused. "Ohh, that would be…" She didn't finish her sentence.

"Yeah, it would," Jordan said, apparently thinking the same thing.

"Settle down, you two." But Vanessa couldn't shake the thoughts that were creeping into her head as well.

The night went on, and the three friends continued to keep each other company. Many topics were discussed, including their plans for the following night.

"What's tomorrow?" Maureen asked. "Friday? I tend to lose track these days."

"No, it'll be Thursday," Jordan said. "Well, you know, technically, it's already Thursday."

"Don't start," Vanessa said, gritting her teeth. This was an old argument of theirs, and they as a group had already agreed on referring to each night of the week based on when they got up at sunset, disregarding the official change of the calendar day after midnight.

"Bummer," Maureen said. "I was hoping it'd be Friday night. That's when the strip clubs have more customers."

"Don't you mean 'dance clubs?'" Jordan joked.

"Not the same thing," she said, slightly irritated.

Her wish that there would be more victims to choose from was based on their tentative plan — providing that Damon and Carolyn would go along with it — for everyone to split up the following night and have a sort of contest. The idea was that each of them would find a victim and kill them in the most creative, tortuous way possible, then compare notes once they got back together and see who won.

"What do we win?" Jordan had asked.

"I don't know," Maureen said. "Bragging rights?"

"That works," Vanessa said with an evil grin.

Maureen's plan was to revisit one of her old haunts, a place downtown called The Wild Card. "Most of the men who come to these places are sleaze," she explained, "just like you'd expect. They just want to see tits and ass. But every now and then, you get some guy, usually the kind who doesn't normally come to a place like that, especially when he's been dragged there by his other friends. And so you do this thing where you quote-unquote 'get to know them.'"

"And those are the ones you can get more money out of?" Jordan asked.

Maureen grinned. "Well, yes. But more than that, these 'nice guys' get it in their heads that they're somehow going to rescue you from this horrible life of being a destitute stripper. Like you have no control over your life; you're some sad, desperate girl who needs saving. 'You can come live with me… You don't have to do this anymore…'" She said this in a deeper register, mocking the hypothetical guy she was describing. "And they don't get that *I'm* not the victim here."

"Interesting," Vanessa said. "I like it. So… you're thinking of finding one of these nice guys, making him think he has a chance with you, and then…?" She made a chomping sound.

"Exactly."

The plan got altered once they went back inside and were talking to Carolyn and Damon. "Let's up the stakes," Damon insisted. "We'll put a time limit on it. Let's say half an hour."

"Half an hour?" Maureen protested. "That's hardly time enough for me to… well…" She hadn't told them her idea about seducing the guy at the strip club; they'd realized up on the roof that it would be better for them not to reveal their techniques ahead of time. That should be saved for the end of the game, everyone regrouping and telling their stories.

"I agree," Carolyn said flatly. "That will take some real skill, to do something creative and cruel in such a short time."

"Hmm," Jordan said. "I might have to rethink my idea, too. Not sure if that would give me enough time."

"How about an hour instead?" Vanessa suggested. "That'd be a little more time."

"We need to keep it short," Damon insisted. "If we're doing it at the beginning of the night, we're all going to be hungry. People could get sloppy."

"That could add to the challenge, though," Carolyn said. "Keep your shit together but still do something cool. To be honest, I could see myself failing on that front. I might get too eager. But that can be part of the contest!"

"I guess," Maureen said. She looked sad, plus Vanessa noticed that her eyeliner had gotten smudged over the course of the night, which added to the effect. "I'll have to come up with something simpler."

"Forty-five minutes, then," she offered.

"Fine," Damon said.

Not long after, everyone was winding down and getting ready for bed. Carolyn and Damon had retired to the apartment's only real bedroom; the other three slept on mattresses that were arranged on the floor of the kitchen. Black garbage bags covered the windows to keep out the sunlight during the day, held in place by tape. Jordan had already settled down, and Vanessa and Maureen were conducting their nightly ritual of helping each other take off their make-up with a roll of toilet paper.

"Have you figured out what you're going to do?" Vanessa asked, rubbing at her friend's eye to clear away the heavy black color.

"I think so," she said. "Kind of a stripped down version of my original plan."

"Ha ha, I get it," Jordan called from his pillow. "'Strip.'"

The two girls ignored him. "I'll just pretend I'm some little…"

"No, don't tell!" Vanessa urged. "Remember, not until after it's over."

"Right," she said, wincing slightly as Vanessa poked her other eye a little too harshly with the toilet paper. She whispered a quick apology.

The girls in the group were dependent on each other for this kind of maintenance, both at the beginning and end of each night, and sometimes at points in between as needed. Being vampires was great, they all agreed, but there was one big drawback: not being able to see themselves in the mirror. Everyone had to do each other's make-up and hair, and there was an agreement that they would be honest about their appearances and help them look their best.

"Promise to do me up really nice tomorrow night?" Maureen asked. "A little more racy."

"Of course. As long as you'll do the same. But not too much for me."

"Always. Your usual." She smiled, but it was distorted as Vanessa continued to rub the beige foundation off her cheeks. It was nice the way that they looked out for each other, this weird little incestuous family that they had.

The lights were out. Vanessa was snuggled up close to Jordan, their breathing and the rhythm of their entwined bodies beginning to lull each other to sleep.

"Hey," she whispered into his ear playfully.

"What," he hissed, mimicking her tone.

"What's your plan for the scavenger hunt tomorrow night?"

"I'm not telling you," he whispered with a smile, "or else you'll just come up with something better."

"Does it involve duct tape?"

"Not telling. Maybe. Probably. Shut up."

Vanessa let out a quiet, monosyllabic giggle, hugging her boyfriend briefly. She knew him too well.

"How about you?"

"Sorry," she joked, "shutting up now." That was the end of the conversation.

As she started to drift off, she thought through her plan once more, considering variations on it. She was going to find a park bench, probably somewhere near the river. She'd sit there, acting despondent, possibly pretending to be a homeless person. Maybe she'd even whip up some tears for good measure. Hopefully, some well meaning stranger would stop to talk to her or give her some spare change, maybe even offering to help her or listen to a sad story she had to tell. She hadn't worked out all the details yet.

And then, when her intended victim least suspected it, she'd start laughing cruelly and announce: *You're going to die!* They would be confused, caught off guard, and dead soon after.

She might not win the contest, but it was going to be a fun night.

CHAPTER FORTY-TWO

THE OUTSIDER

The girl stood outside the window, being careful not to get too close. It was nighttime, and the lights were on inside, so she knew that the occupants of the house would only see their own reflections if they happened to glance in her direction. But if she got too close, they might see that she was there. That would be a very bad thing indeed.

She wasn't even sure what she was doing here, why she'd come all this way to find them, which hadn't been easy. She'd missed them, but now that she was here, she was beginning to question her decision. They were her parents, or at least, they had been before she'd died.

What had she been hoping for? To check in on them, to make sure they were okay? To maybe reveal herself to them, letting them know that she was okay, too? She'd been a vampire for a while now, and she had more or less gotten used to the change, but it still bothered her to have been separated from her family like this. But it wasn't like she could just knock on the door and say, *Hi, it's me! I'm back!* That would just frighten them and probably horrify them, seeing that their daughter had come back from the grave as a blood-drinking monster.

And so, with her heightened, supernatural senses, she not only watched but listened to them through the glass, but she didn't like what was being said.

"I was just saying, maybe it would be good to get away," the father said. "I'd have enough leave time by next month, and it might be nice to see Florida again."

"Tom, how can you even..." the mother began, then shook her head in frustration, looking away. "No. Just no. Not if it means driving through... through..."

"Where? Through Georgia?"

The mother whipped back around, pointing. *"Don't* say that word. That name. You know how much I hate that godforsaken place, that shitty hellhole of a state. I don't ever want to set foot in it again, not for the rest of my life. Not after everything that happened."

This seemed to shock Tom. "Never? I mean, not even to see...? We could at least visit their graves. I thought you might..."

"Might what?" the mother spat. "See where our two little girls are buried again? They're dead, Tom. *Dead.* I don't need to see where their bones are. They're gone. Our girls are just... gone." She'd begun to choke up.

"Joann," Tom began, but then she slammed her hand down on the kitchen counter.

"Don't you *'Joann'* me. I don't want to go to Sanibel again. Or Ft. Myers, or wherever. That's where we used to go, back when we had a family. A real family."

The vampire outside winced, seeing the pain her mother was in. Her father was surely feeling it, too, but he'd always been the strong one. In a way, she felt responsible for their pain. It wasn't her fault that she'd died, she knew, but clearly her death was the cause of their grief. She wished that there was a way she could fix things.

"I think you've had enough of those," Tom said as Joann poured another drink for herself.

"Is that what you think," she said sarcastically, ignoring him.

"Look. I know how much it hurts. It hurts me, too. But you can't just keep..."

"Keep what? Drowning my sorrows? You fucking bet I can. At least for tonight." She tipped her head back with her lips to the glass, just after glaring at her husband and daring him to say anything else. After her sip, she added, "And I'll do it again the next time you suggest doing anything like that."

"Damn it, Joann, if you'd just listen…" He trailed off, at a loss for words.

"No, you listen. I know what you're going to say. You made all these sacrifices so you could put in for a PCS to your CO, and… CGSC, XYZ, blah blah blah, whatever else Army alphabet soup you're going to spout out… So we could move back here even though you didn't want to. Because I've got family here. You had a good thing going on at Fort Gordon, but your poor little fragile wife had her precious mental breakdown after both *her fucking daughters got KILLED*… Yeah, thanks for acknowledging that, Uncle Sam! Sorry that my own fucking *children* getting murdered in a shit-hole town in the South was such a fucking inconvenience for you!"

"Joann, stop it," Tom said, his temper rising.

"You stop it!" she shrieked. "If you hadn't let them transfer you there in the first place, our girls would still be *aliiiiive!*" She swatted at the empty glass on the counter, sending it flying across the room.

The vampire stood watching, faintly hearing the sound of the heavy tumbler as it clattered to the floor and broke. She remembered how distraught her mother had been back when her sister had died, but she'd never been quite this bad. They'd all been upset at the time and had dealt with it in their own way, but seeing her mother like this was heartbreaking.

She remembered what it was like before, the times her mother would break down crying, and she'd hug her and do what she could to comfort her. Or it would be the other way around, and she'd be the one needing to be held. And of course, her father had been a source of strength for both of them.

Back then, it had sometimes been difficult being the child who had survived. *"I'm* still here," she would sometimes say in attempt to comfort her mother, but then she would feel guilty. She was beginning to have some of those same emotions, this time over having been given a second chance to live on as a vampire.

"It hurts me, too," the father said. "You know it does. Don't act like you're the only one. What you're feeling… hell, what we're *both* feeling… It's survivor's guilt."

"Here we go. More psychoanalyzing."

"I'm just trying to make you…" He paused, exasperated. "I understand. I do. And you know I had to deal with that kind of thing after the war. Not just because of the buddies I lost, but the… the things I had to do. The people I had to… you know. And you know I'm not proud of that."

Joann stared at her husband, her lower lip quivering in anger. "Were any of them teenage girls?" she practically hissed.

The girl felt a chill, unnerved by the look on her father's face. It wasn't one she'd ever seen before. "No," he'd said firmly, but there was something very steely in his eyes. For a moment, it looked like he might lash out at her mother and physically attack her, but he seemed to be holding himself back. His fingers were gripping the counter tightly, his forearm beginning to shake.

Equally defiant, her mother stared him down. "I'm going to bed now," she said finally. "Don't follow me." Then she left the room.

Her father just stood there, unmoving, his breathing heavy but controlled. That strange look in his eyes became wilder, and then he screwed his eyes shut, turning towards the counter and supporting himself with both hands. Silently, his whole body began to shake, but he got himself under control in just a few seconds. With quick movements, he began to wipe tears from his eyes, and he continued to breathe rapidly, but still quietly. He didn't want to be overheard.

Seeing him like this was unbearable, the girl thought. She didn't even know that her father was capable of crying; she'd never seen him do it, not even when her sister had died. He'd always been the epitome of strength. She'd done her best to emulate that, especially after their family's first tragedy. At only eleven years old, she had suddenly been forced to grow up quickly, to learn to be strong for her mother's sake as well as her own.

Unable to take any more and fighting back her own tears, the vampire turned away from the window and began walking toward the street. Coming here had been a mistake. She was still uncertain why she'd done it at all, what she was hoping to find. If it had been relief, a chance to see her parents one last time and find that they had gotten on with their lives and were doing fine, well, that had been a complete failure.

She stopped walking when she reached the edge of the front yard, then stomped the ground in frustration. It wasn't fair, feeling like this. She was a vampire, a killer who drank the blood of the living to survive. She wasn't human anymore, so why was she feeling so emotional, caring about the tribulations of this unhappy married couple whom she no longer had any real connection to? She tried to steel herself, to embrace that way of thinking. But it just wasn't true. Maybe she should try to make it true.

She did care about them. But given everything she'd just seen, she wasn't sure if that feeling was turning into pity or hatred. She was a survivor, always had been. They *all* had been, at least back in the day. On the other hand, she couldn't blame them for being so distraught: Losing one daughter had been bad enough, and then, once she'd died, that must have been even worse. She'd always imagined this, their grief over having lost her just a few years later. Why had she gone through so much trouble, flying across so many states, just to see that grief firsthand?

Fuming, the vampire considered her options. She could just leave, counting her losses and moving on from here. She could also do what had seemed absurd to her before, knocking on the door and revealing herself to her parents, attempting to console them with the knowledge that at least one of their girls had survived death, albeit as an undead creature of the night. But there was no way in hell that would go well. And then, there was a third, more sinister option.

They were hurting. They had been for years, and it was obvious from what she'd seen through the window that things weren't getting any better. Maybe the kindest thing she could do was to end their suffering. It was certainly within her power to do so. She'd ended plenty of people's lives already.

She shuddered at the thought, knowing that living with that on her conscience would be quite a burden. Could she really take the lives of her own parents? It might be for the greater good, but still, she wasn't sure if she could go through with it. A decision needed to be made.

Later, the vampire found herself walking away from the house, sniffling as she wiped away the last of her tears. It was time to go back to Augusta; at least some semblance of a life was waiting for her there.

Before flying away, she turned and looked back at the house one last time, frowning. "Okay, don't ever put yourself through anything like *that* again," she said under her breath.

CHAPTER FORTY-THREE

DUTY

"Jeez…" the young man exclaimed, taken aback by the rapid-fire series of questions from the girl standing next to him at the bar. "Allgood. Leavenworth. Once."

"All… good?" the pretty blonde asked, tilting her head. "Is that, like, even a name?"

"Sorry," he said, shutting his eyes and shaking his head as if to clear it. "It's an Army thing, us calling each other by our last names. I'm here with my buddies over there." He turned his head and nodded to indicate the group of soldiers sitting at a nearby table. Then he looked back at the girl. "My name's Lawrence."

The girl giggled, tucking her hair back behind her ear with her right hand, then giving him a mock salute. She did it wrong, of course; civilians always did. "Well, Lawrence, nice to meet you."

"Likewise."

"So, we've established so far: Your name is Allgood… I mean… Lawrence, you're from somewhere called Leavenworth, and you've had a Buttery Nipple, but only once."

"That's pretty much it." Lawrence was impressed with the girl's forward manner, but he was still trying to decide just how attractive he actually found her. She wasn't really his type; she was a bit too heavy on the valley girl talk, for one thing. He thought that kind of way of speaking had gone out of style years ago. But she seemed pretty confident, and he was at the very least intrigued.

He'd walked up to the bar to get a beer; the guys at the table were still halfway through theirs, and he needed another one. A few seconds after he'd ordered, this girl had turned to him and loudly proclaimed: "Hi, I'm Stephanie! What's your name? Where are you from? Have you ever had a Buttery Nipple?" The final question was referring to a particular kind of mixed drink.

"Well then," Stephanie continued, "order us a couple more, and it can be your second time."

Lawrence started to protest. He hated doing shots; they sometimes made him gag or even throw up, and he was afraid of embarrassing himself. But then he decided to man up and give it a go. After all, given what had happened earlier today — and in fact why he and the others were at the bar in the first place — the sooner he got drunk, the better. The drinks were ordered when Lawrence's beer arrived.

"So, you're in the Army, huh?"

"That's right. Signal Corps."

"What's that?"

"Basically, we're in charge of maintaining communications among the different parts of the Army while in theater." Stephanie gave him a blank look, her smile slightly fading. He'd need to dumb this down for her. "Like, radios and telephones. Big satellite dishes. Things like that. So all the soldiers out there in the field can talk to each other. Have you heard about the stuff going on in Kuwait?"

"Ku-*where?*"

"Kuwait. In the Middle East. It's been in the news…"

"Oh, I don't watch the news." She giggled. "It's, like, too boring for me."

Lawrence fought the urge to roll his eyes. Fortunately, he was distracted by the bartender, who brought them their shots and set them down.

"That'll be eight-fifty," he said. "On your tab?"

"Sure."

"Thank you!" Stephanie said, faking surprise at his generosity, as if she hadn't been expecting him to pay for the shots all along. She picked up her small glass and gestured to him with it, and Lawrence reciprocated, clinking the glasses together in a miniature toast. They then kicked their heads back as they each downed their drinks in one gulp.

Recovering from the rush of alcohol, they quickly put their glasses back down onto the bar. Lawrence cleared his throat, secretly grateful that he hadn't had a worse reaction.

Stephanie fanned herself with both hands theatrically. "Woo! That was so good. Love those things."

"I don't really care for them myself," he said, suddenly feeling too honest.

"Well, you've got your beer," she said, pointing at it with a laugh.

"That I do." He picked it up and took a big swallow, feeling the bubbles fizz down his throat and beginning to wash away the weird, candy-like taste of the Buttery Nipple. He set the bottle down, for some reason acutely aware of the sheen of condensation on it. He pulled his fingers away, wiping them against each other.

Stephanie sat down on a barstool, not taking her eyes off of Lawrence as she did so. He did his best to maintain eye contact, resisting the urge to look at either her cleavage or the obnoxiously short length of her denim dress as she settled in and crossed her legs, one of her feet casually brushing his leg. Almost without thinking, he pulled another barstool into place behind him and sat.

They continued to talk, and for a little while, Lawrence found himself feeling attracted to Stephanie, but that was probably just the alcohol talking. Yes, she was pretty, but he could tell that she was just faking interest in — or even comprehension of — what he was saying. He had a lot on his mind and needed to process it, and talking about it to this stranger seemed like a good idea at the time. The fact that she had a nice rack was a bonus.

"So, tell me all about you," she'd said to him, putting a hand on his knee. And so he did.

He told her what had happened to him and the rest of the 67th Signal Battalion that day, how they'd been given orders to deploy to Kuwait to take part in Operation Desert Shield. Saddam Hussein, the ruler of Iraq, had invaded and taken over the small, nearby country of Kuwait last month. It was a big deal; if this bastard was left unchecked, he'd keep taking over whatever he wanted to and could wind up controlling all of the oil in the Middle East, which would mean bad news for the U.S. and the rest of the world. So the military was building up its forces to go in and drive the Iraqis out of Kuwait if necessary, that is, if diplomatic channels failed. And so far, it was looking like they might.

The reason the Signal Corps was brought in was because this war — if it turned out to be that — was going to have to be a different kind than ever before. The doctrine had changed; the Army was used to fighting in places like Europe where communications were already in place. "Basic stuff like telephones and radios, like I said before," Lawrence clarified. "They just don't have all that in the middle of the desert, where all this is happening. So they need us to set it up."

"Wow," Stephanie said for probably the tenth time. "That's really interesting." She took a drag on her cigarette, then exhaled, tilting her head back. It was still early in the night, but Lawrence knew that the longer it went on, the more smoky the place would get. He wasn't a smoker himself, and he didn't mind when other people did it, but eventually, he'd have to start stepping outside occasionally to give the stinging in his eyes a break.

"Yeah. They're finding out they need a lot more help with communications than they thought. They already brought in some troops from Arizona, but shit's just taking forever to get done. So they're sending us over there, and I hear there's some more being transferred from Germany."

"Wow. That's, like, a lot of soldiers."

Lawrence paused, growing tired of talking to this airhead. *Next, they're going to recall our forces on the moon and send them in, too,* he considered saying, just to see if it would pass. This made him laugh.

"What?" the girl asked with a playful smile.

"Nothing, nothing."

"Look," she said, gently placing a hand on his forearm. "It's getting kind of loud in here." She was right; the bar was becoming more crowded, just like any other Saturday night. Almost. "Do you wanna, like, go somewhere else?" She said this with a suggestive raising of her right eyebrow.

Lawrence thought about it. In fact, he thought about everything. The entire day had been like that, every little thing feeling very magnified and significant, like he'd taken them for granted until now. He'd be leaving the country soon, and his whole life was about to become completely different, so now he was noticing every single detail. He tried to ignore the tiny voice in the back of his head that wondered if he might be seeing all of these things for the last time.

Maybe it wouldn't be so bad to take this girl up on her offer. God only knew when he'd get to do something like that again. He took in her details: the long, flowing blonde hair with a few stray strands sticking up here and there, the gold earrings that looked kind of like door knockers, the scent of her perfume just barely managing to compete with the smells of cigarettes and alcohol permeating the increasingly loud room.

But then he remembered the bigger picture. "I'm sorry," he said. "I don't mean to be rude, but I really did come out here tonight to be with my buddies. I need to get back to them." Stephanie looked disappointed, but not as much as he hoped she might, he suddenly realized.

"Aww," she said, her tone shifting to what seemed like mock sadness. "It's okay. I understand. You go back and talk to your Army guys. Official stuff, I'm sure." She gave him a playful pat on his arm, then pulled her hand back and rested it on her lap. "But thanks for the drink! Maybe I can get another one from you later on?"

Lawrence stood up, looking down at her apologetically. "Sure, maybe. Nice talking to you." He didn't like lying.

As he made his way back to the table where his friends from D Company were sitting, it felt like he was walking from one world to another. Behind him was his old life, picking up on some bimbo at the bar. In front of him was his future, the men he'd be serving with overseas. He'd already felt some of that transition when he'd joined the Army a couple of years ago, but this was different.

Back then, it had just been committing to a new career, a new way of life, something that separated him from his civilian friends, but not entirely. He was still who he was, but the Army had sharpened him, improved him. He hadn't become some mindless robot who didn't know how to do anything but follow orders. That was the stereotype, something people got from the movies. The keyword was discipline, not obedience, and one of the main things the Army had taught him was how to solve problems, to get shit done. Orders were given, and authority was respected, but what was also expected was that you had to come up with solutions to problems and put them into action. And he was damn good at that, he liked to think. He hadn't always been that way.

Some of his friends outside the military understood this change in him better than others, and he'd had to accept that. It was all a part of growing up, moving on, and life after high school. Some people stayed in touch, hung out, and got along fine, and others fell by the wayside.

"Hey, Allgood," Westfall said with his usual wide-mouthed grin, "who's the hot piece of ass?"

"Shut it," Lawrence grumbled, settling down into his chair. "Just some girl. Nothing to write home about."

"What, you didn't give her the spill?" he asked, punching his arm. "Big Army man going overseas, gotta have one last fling, now get on your knees and smile like a doughnut?"

The table erupted in laughter, and Lawrence couldn't fight the urge to laugh as well. "Wasn't like that," he insisted. "Give it a fucking rest."

"So… so…" Afton said excitedly as he slapped the table with each "so," clearly already drunk. "So… Do ya think maybe I should give her a try?"

"Go ahead, shrimp," Westfall said, but then his expression changed into an exaggerated frown. "Ohhh!" He pointed towards the bar. "Looks like you've missed your chance, short stuff. She's found someone else."

The men turned and looked, and sure enough, Stephanie had started chatting up another guy, some tall jerk with long reddish hair. Lawrence fought back a pang of jealousy, then wondered why he'd even felt it.

"Guess she doesn't have a particular type, then," he said. "Whatever." He tossed back the last of what was left of his beer. He slammed the empty bottle down onto the table, clearing his throat once again. "Who's got the next round?"

The six men at the table continued to drink, talk, and smoke, sometimes about their impending deployment, other times just yammering on about trivial things. That was the whole point of this gathering, to have what might very well be their last night off post to get mind-blankingly drunk. The orders to go overseas had come down earlier that day, but it wasn't clear yet just when lockdown would happen and they'd no longer be allowed to leave Fort Gordon. The soldiers who had family in town would need time to get their affairs in order and leave their loved ones behind.

The higher-ups had been nice enough to be lenient about that. As Afton put it when the topic came up, "Augusta's got enough who've lost people unexpectedly. You know, because of all of the... you know."

"Yeah," Allgood said gravely.

"Yeah," Westfall repeated.

"To the lost," Merckle said, raising his glass, looking slightly intoxicated but serious. He was the most taciturn of the group, but often when he did speak, he had something profound to say.

The soldiers clinked their glasses together, but Afton spilled some of his beer onto his hand as he did so. "Goddammit," he said, recovering from the blunder and licking the excess beer from his thumb. They drank in respect to Merckle's toast, then set their glasses down.

"Oh, crap," Allgood said, spotting a man who had entered the bar and seemed to be looking around for someone. He knew it was him.

Despite what he'd said to Stephanie earlier, the plan for this night wasn't just for Allgood and the guys to get together and drink each other under the table. There would be some of that, and that was how they'd originally planned it, but then they realized that they wanted their civilian friends in town to join them as well. After all, the guys would be seeing more than enough of each other over the next few months, but they needed to say goodbye to the people they'd be leaving behind. There would no doubt be some emotional farewells, and it was fully expected that each of the guys would break off from the main group to talk with their non-military friends.

Upon their arrival at the bar, they'd each taken turns at the payphone by the restrooms to call whom they needed to, telling them the news about the deployment and inviting them out. In Lawrence's case, that person had been Julia, a girl in his circle of friends who was kind of the hub of that group. They'd get together at her apartment and watch TV shows and movie rentals, usually eating pizza or Chinese — and once or twice enduring Julia's attempts at cooking. Other times, they went out to eat or to the movies together, always having a great time.

Lawrence was still trying to decide whether or not he would take Julia aside once she showed up tonight. She had, understandably, sounded upset when he'd given her the news. He wondered if tonight would finally be when he told her what he'd always been afraid to, that perpetual fear looming overhead of messing up their friendship if he did. He hoped that if he were successful, she'd wait for him to come back from overseas.

What he hadn't hoped for was that Sebastian would be the first to show up, but it made sense given that he lived the closest to the bar. He didn't hate the guy, but he was his least favorite member of their group. He was tall, with blond hair, shockingly blue eyes, and a sort of hook-like nose. There was this obnoxious intensity about the man, and he came across as a bit creepy. Some of that was an affectation, though, Lawrence realized the more he'd gotten to know him. To put it more bluntly, the guy was often full of shit.

Lawrence didn't really want Sebastian to be mixing with his Army buddies, guessing that they would also see through his crap. So he excused himself from the table and walked over to meet him.

"Hey, man," Sebastian said. "Now do you see why I didn't want you to join the Army?"

"Shut up," Lawrence said wearily, trying to pretend that he wasn't as irritated as he was. He gestured towards the bar, indicating that they should head that way. He also glanced around, wondering if Stephanie might still be where he'd left her, but she wasn't. But then he spotted her farther down the bar, talking to yet another potential suitor. Where the previous one had gone, he had no idea.

Sebastian picked up his previous theme. "Bet you didn't think this was going to happen, huh? Cold War's over, no real conflicts going on around the world, and… *Oops!* Uh oh, crisis in the Middle East. Just thought you were getting money for college, huh?"

"You going to be this much of an asshole all night?" Lawrence asked, again pretending that he was joking.

"Sorry, man, sorry. You knew I was going to have to get in at least one jab." Lawrence nodded, faking a smile. "So, you freaking out yet?"

"What?"

"About having to pack up and go off to the middle of the desert. It gets pretty damn hot there, you know."

"No, really?" Lawrence feigned shock. "I'd never heard that before. It's hot in the desert. Who knew. You're fucking brilliant, guy." Sebastian laughed, but he looked uneasy, maybe finally getting a clue. "Hey, did you know? Those things are bad for you!"

Lawrence was pointing at the pack of cigarettes Sebastian had placed on the bar. He hesitated for a moment before taking one out, then continued as he shot back his own sarcastic reply: "No, I've never heard *that*, either. Fine. Point taken."

Lawrence knew that Sebastian didn't drink, so he didn't bother to ask if he wanted anything when the bartender stopped by. He sometimes wished that the guy did drink; maybe then he wouldn't be so tightly wound. He hardly ever slept and was very much a night owl.

"Anyway," Sebastian said, "Julia called me and told me what's up. The rest of them are on their way. Thought I'd beat the crowd."

"Well, I appreciate you coming out." He almost meant it.

"What's your dad have to say about all this?"

"Hmm? Oh, I haven't actually called him yet. Was going to do that tomorrow." He paused. "Not sure what he's going to say. Either he's going to be proud of me for following in his footsteps, or... I don't know. Freaked out?"

"He was in Nam, wasn't he?" The name sounded stupid coming out of his friend's mouth, as if he were some kind of veteran himself.

Lawrence nodded. He shoved back the thoughts that began to creep up in his mind, a fear that he might be going into a situation just as dangerous. It had been a topic of discussion among his fellow soldiers in the weeks leading up to this, but as of today, everyone had stopped bringing it up. Freeing Kuwait from the Iraqis might be difficult, or it could wind up being a simple matter. No one knew at this point. He didn't want to think about it, and something on his face must have betrayed him.

"Look," Sebastian said, lowering his voice and leaning in. "It's okay to be scared. I understand. Believe me, I do."

"I know."

There was something that their circle of friends didn't know about, a secret that the two kept between them. Everyone knew that Sebastian had been involved in the anti-vampire group called Life Force three years ago, but not to what extent. If the subject ever came up, he'd clam up about it, insisting that it was all behind him. But he'd do it in this annoying, cryptic way, almost like he wanted people to keep asking him, then refuse to give any details. He thought it made him seem mysterious.

The truth of the matter was that Sebastian hadn't just been involved with Life Force: He'd been the ringleader. The group had been well intentioned in the beginning, a way for the common people to fight back against the growing threat of vampires in Augusta, especially because the police didn't seem to be doing enough. But soon, these vigilantes got out of hand, and rather than curbing the vampire threat, they wound up making things worse, attacking innocent people whom they merely thought were vampires, often because they'd been misinformed.

Lawrence had never seen a real vampire. Like everyone else, he'd been aware of the results of their activities, and he knew plenty of people who had lost friends and relatives to the ongoing menace. But never once had he lain eyes on an actual blood-sucking person or bat firsthand. Back in 1987, in his naivety as a recent high school graduate, he'd been foolish enough to let Sebastian rope him into joining Life Force, albeit briefly.

The one night he'd gone out with them on a raid, not a whole lot happened. This had been shortly before everything went sideways, when Sebastian had gotten a tip from someone — Lawrence wasn't sure who it was, maybe some kind of informant who knew the vampires — that there would be some activity and killings downtown. But by the time they arrived, there were no vampires to be seen, only the victims they'd left behind. The sight of those bodies unnerved Lawrence, and he made excuses to avoid involvement with Life Force after that.

That had turned out to be a wise choice given that afterwards, Sebastian and his followers went on to commit acts of vandalism and violence that got the majority of them arrested. A handful of people had even died, both innocent bystanders who were suspected of being vampires and members of Life Force itself, though Lawrence had never been clear on the details of that. He was just glad that he'd gotten out when he did, and no one ever implicated him or mentioned his involvement. If they had, he might have wound up with a criminal record and would never have been able to join the Army.

Sebastian sometimes held this over Lawrence's head, again in that irritating, cryptic way that he liked to be. And really, the guy had been damn lucky to have gotten off as easily as he did; the judge had been sympathetic to his cause given that he'd also lost loved ones to the vampires. The Life Force members who had actually been responsible for the deaths of some anonymous homeless people had also managed to get minimum sentences.

The whole thing made Lawrence's stomach turn, and he didn't like to think about it. He'd distanced himself from Sebastian for a while after that, but by an unfortunate coincidence, the man had wound up in his life again a year later when the two of them happened to move into the same apartment complex. That was where he'd met Julia, and she'd "introduced" them to each other one afternoon, not realizing that they'd known each other before. Despite the city's size, Augusta was weird like that, people being interconnected in strange ways, everyone somehow knowing someone who knew someone else from your past. It was like a small town, but on a large scale.

Lawrence and Sebastian didn't talk about their past then; it was like they pretended it hadn't happened. In front of their growing group of friends at Oakleaf Apartments, they kept up this pretense. Sebastian was, frankly, a convicted criminal, but Lawrence wasn't going to pipe up and gossip about that; there was no point in doing so. The less the others knew, the better, and he certainly didn't want any of these new people in his life to know that he'd also been involved in something that nefarious as well, however briefly.

"So you're really going to do this, huh?" Sebastian asked.

"Don't have much of a choice," Lawrence said.

"You could, maybe…" Sebastian got that look on his face again, that obnoxious, overly enigmatic smile.

"What the fuck do you think you mean by that?" Lawrence caught himself; he'd shouted, and a few people at the bar glanced over at them.

Sebastian flinched, but he quickly regained his composure. "I mean…" he began, but then he looked around suspiciously. A couple of people were still staring.

Lawrence looked around, too, including back at the table where his D Company friends were sitting. None of them seemed to have noticed the outburst, and he was grateful for that.

"Maybe we should talk about this outside," Sebastian said calmly.

Lawrence nodded quickly. "You're right. We should. The smoke in here is getting to me anyway." He screwed his eyes shut and rubbed at them, then pointed at the cigarette held between Sebastian's fingers. "Put that shit out."

"No."

He sighed. "Fine. Do what you want."

The two men headed for the door. Sebastian said something once they got outside the bar about how the rest of their friends should be showing up soon, but Lawrence cut him short.

"Over here," he indicated, leading them to a spot by the concrete wall a few yards outside the entrance. Sebastian followed obediently, but he still kept his same arrogant air. Once they'd stopped walking, he fixed Lawrence with another one of his cocky looks.

"You're going to do it again, aren't you?" Lawrence asked him through gritted teeth. "Trying to get me to join your stupid little band of outlaws. Well, forget it."

If Sebastian were intimidated, he didn't show it. He took a drag on what was left of his cigarette, then dropped it to the ground and put it out with his foot. "We really could use someone like you."

"I couldn't even if I wanted to! You really think I can just say to my CO, 'Sorry, can't go to Kuwait tomorrow! I've gotta stay here and fight vampires with my friend with the criminal record, who was ordered by a judge not to pursue that kind of thing ever again, but he keeps doing it in secret because it makes him feel important.'"

"It's not just…" Sebastian paused, briefly appearing rattled once more. Then he looked at Lawrence more sternly. "There's another war here at home, you know."

"It's not a war!" He steadied himself, trying to keep from losing his temper. He turned away, closed his eyes, and forced himself to breathe in deeply. Then he exhaled sharply. "Look. We're not talking about this anymore. Go back inside and wait for the others to show up. I'll be in in a minute."

Sebastian looked like he was about to argue some more, but then he changed his mind. "Fine," he said simply, and he walked back to the entrance to the bar.

Lawrence stood there, fuming. He felt an urge to punch the wall, but once he took a good look at it, he realized that would be a bad idea. The wall was solid concrete, and he noticed the little pockmarks on its surface and the way they looked in the glow of the streetlights. If he moved slightly, little bits of something shiny in the material glinted and shimmered. He'd never noticed that before. Something about this detail calmed him, but not enough. He was still full of nervous energy, and he needed to walk it off. It wouldn't take long to go around the block and make his way back to the bar, and hopefully by then, he would have calmed down enough not to have to punch Sebastian in the throat.

As he walked along the sidewalk, he thought about their conversation. Sebastian could be fun sometimes, at least in small doses, but how could he be so stupid as to think that Lawrence could just abandon his responsibilities and go off with him? But as much of a dumb-ass as he was, he'd at least been right about one thing.

No, he didn't want to go to the Middle East. He actually was scared that something bad might happen to him. He might not survive, or he might come back as some kind of basket case if he went through a lot of shit. Maybe he'd even lose a limb or two. Not that he was supposed to be in combat, but who knows what might happen once they were over there.

But he shouldn't be thinking like that, he knew. Duty, honor, and country: These should be first and foremost in his mind. He thought about the work he'd be doing, like setting up and running the AN/TSC-85 as part of the TRI-TAC program. He was part of a large operation, the Signal Corps basically becoming the telephone company and keeping everyone in touch with each other. That was important and real, not like Sebastian and his band of underground freaks playing soldiers. Lawrence wasn't playing.

Thinking along these lines helped him feel better, and as he rounded the corner that led to the bar, he hoped that Julia and the others would have arrived by now. He'd talk to them, say his goodbyes, and possibly make nice with Sebastian, even if he was a pretentious asshole. He would miss hanging out with all of them, maybe even him. And if he didn't lose his nerve, he'd take Julia aside and tell her how he really felt. In some ways, the prospect of that was even scarier than the idea of deploying.

There was an alleyway to his left, and as he passed it, he heard some strange noises. He almost ignored them, but as had been the case this entire night, his heightened senses got the better of him. Maybe this was important.

He paused and looked, a single streetlight illuminating the otherwise dark passage. There was somebody there… No, not just someone, but two someones. He thought it might be a couple making out, but there was something wrong. In a situation like that, both figures would be standing up, and Lawrence would avert his eyes and leave them to it. Instead, these two figures were horizontal, one on top of the other, the upper one moving rhythmically up and down.

As he cautiously stepped forward, the picture became more clear. But why would two people be fucking on the ground in some dirty alley? Maybe this was a rape, and he should step in and do something about it. But if that were the case, how come the small woman underneath the bigger man wasn't crying out or struggling?

Something beneath Lawrence's shoe made a noise, and the man suddenly stopped, straightening up and turning to face him. His long, red hair whipped around his head as he did so, and Lawrence could see the blood smeared on his face. Despite that, he recognized him from his clothes, the grungy, outdated style that hippies and peaceniks wore, or at least people close to his age who liked to pretend they were from that era.

The vampire let out a noise that sounded something like *"Aha!,"* a sickening smile on his lips. He stood up quickly, his pants drooping around his legs and his penis exposed. His arms were held up in an attack position, hands poised like claws.

Lawrence's mind raced, his combat training coming back to him automatically. But he was distracted by the stillness of the woman on the ground, her blonde hair splayed about, and her dead eyes staring up at nothing. Even in the dim light, he recognized her earrings, the ones that looked like door knockers. Her short denim dress had been hiked up and crumpled against her waist, and for a moment, Lawrence found himself wondering which had come first, the murder or the rape.

The vampire suddenly disappeared, seeming to vanish in the dark of the alleyway. There was a faint flapping sound, and Lawrence realized what had happened. At first, he was relieved, but then he felt disappointed. He'd already been triggered into combat mode, his heart racing and senses even further focused. He thought he was finally going to use the skills he'd been taught, though if you'd asked him just five minutes ago, he would have said something about hoping to never have to do that. A mantra from Basic ran through his head: *To kill! To kill! To kill without mercy!* That's what he would have done to that monster if he'd been given the chance.

He looked down at Stephanie's poor, lifeless body, and he figured he should call the police once he got back inside. He also wondered if he should say something to Sebastian. But his thoughts were interrupted as the flapping sound suddenly returned, lasting only a couple of seconds and growing louder until the bat thudded into the side of his neck. Pain seared through him as it bit down, and he tried to grab the small creature and pull it away, but he collapsed too quickly.

The bat disengaged, and Lawrence wondered why. Then he saw the human form of the vampire appear above him. It knelt down and leaned forward, that same shit-eating grin on its pale, round face, which disappeared from his field of vision as the vampire zeroed in on his neck once again.

As his blood drained away, Specialist Lawrence Allgood felt both sad and angry. He thought of all the things he'd never get to do. He wouldn't get to serve his country in a foreign land, he'd never get promoted to an E-5, and he wouldn't get the chance to tell Julia how he felt. It was all ending here in this dark alley, some disgusting, worthless beast taking everything away from him.

In a way, Sebastian had been right, he hated to admit. There was a war here at home, and he'd just become its latest casualty. Just before he lost consciousness, he hoped that one day, Sebastian and his rogue group would find this vampire and destroy it.

CHAPTER FORTY-FOUR

LEFT BEHIND

"Evenin', ladies," the taller of the two police officers said with a nod as they passed the three girls on the covered sidewalk. He had that same macho swagger that all cops did.

Nicole let out a giggle. "Heyyy," she cooed.

Valerie rolled her eyes. "Quit flirting," she said, loud enough for the policemen to hear. She figured it would embarrass both her and them, but the cops didn't react and just kept walking.

"Shut up!" Nicole said, laughing as she playfully smacked her friend on the arm. "I am not!"

"She's just practicing for the next time she gets pulled over," their other friend Rebecca said with a grin. The three girls laughed.

"Hey, couldn't hurt!" Nicole said, flicking back a strand of her platinum blonde hair.

"I still can't believe you got out of a ticket by saying you got the brake pedal and the gas pedal confused," Rebecca said, shaking her head.

"Well, there was that, and a lot of batting my eyes at the guy. You know, if it works, why not?"

Valerie huffed. "Please."

"Don't be jealous, Val," she said, taking a drag off her cigarette.

"Don't call me 'Val,' *Nicky.*"

"Ohh, you bitch." Her eyes narrowed, but her smile never faded.

Nicole was definitely the pretty one of the group, and everyone knew it. They were all good friends, but Valerie often felt insecure about her own looks when the three of them were together. She wasn't ugly, just the least pretty of the three, with her wavy, dark brown hair that was almost black, and a nose that she always thought was too big. Rebecca, with her fiery red hair and delicate, narrow features, was somewhere on the middle of the scale.

"Settle down, *ladies,*" Rebecca said, mocking the policeman's accent from earlier. She leaned forward slightly and nodded as she said this, just as he had done.

They all laughed again, and Rebecca asked Nicole if she could bum a cigarette. She was only seventeen, as was Valerie; Nicole was the only one old enough to actually buy cigarettes. Valerie didn't smoke, and she wasn't thrilled with the fact that her two friends did, often telling them how bad it was for them and that they shouldn't do it.

This was the reason they were still outside, the fact that both girls wanted to smoke. Until recently, that was okay to do everywhere, but a lot of the stores in Daniel Village and other places around town had started making it so you couldn't do it inside. It was stupid, but those were the rules, so they complied. Once they were done, they'd go inside the record store and look for the music they'd been wanting to buy that night.

Rebecca flicked her lighter and inhaled on her "cancer stick," as Valerie called it, then exhaled the first puff of smoke. "So," she asked, "who does that make me, then? Becky?"

"Or Becca," Valerie offered. "Though, I don't know, Becky sounds more airheaded."

She laughed, then adopted a stupid, valley girl accent as she waved her head from side to side. *"Hi-eee, I'm Beckyyy! I'm, like, sooo stupiiid!"* She stopped her impression, then turned to Nicole. "Hey, at least you're not… Who was that girl? The weird one we met who got all pissed off when she found out your name."

She let out another laugh. "Oh, right. Nicola. 'Nih-co-*luh!*' Like, 'I hate meeting girls with your name because mine's different and I'm so damn special.'" She rolled her eyes. "Not my fault your parents named you something retarded."

"I think it's pretty," Valerie said.

"Yeah, you would," Nicole said, exhaling another plume of smoke.

That barely even made sense, so she chose not to respond. Instead, she changed the subject. "Anyway, nice job on your hair."

Nicole smiled, touching one end of it; it had been recently dyed. "Aw, thank you. I really appreciate that."

Valerie cringed inwardly. Her friend had this irritating habit of saying "thank you" and "I really appreciate that" in the most unconvincing way possible, and it was clear that she had no idea how fake it sounded. It was like she was trying too hard to sound sincere, but then, why was she doing that now? The compliment had been genuine.

The cops walked by them again, this time from the other direction, but they didn't say anything. It wasn't unusual for them to be here in this shopping center; after all, there was a police substation situated in the corner among the various stores. It was meant to make the place safer, and the general consensus was that it did. Augusta could be a dangerous place at night, but there hadn't been a vampire attack here for quite a while.

Even so, Valerie felt uncomfortable as the two men passed by, and Rebecca noticed the scowl on her face.

"Valerie, it's okay," she said once they were out of earshot. "They're not doing anything wrong."

"They're not doing anything at *all*," she said bitterly. "They never do."

Valerie didn't like the police; she hadn't for a long time. Like so many in this terrible town, she'd lost people, and she didn't think that the police were doing enough to stop the threat. For years, even before her sister had died, they'd denied that the vampires were even real, practically ignoring the bodies that kept piling up and not doing a damn thing.

When she was being fair, she could admit that once upon a time, she didn't believe in vampires either, buying into the story that the killings were just being done by some kind of wild animals, maybe rabid bats or something stupid like that. But the evidence grew stronger over the years as more and more witnesses reported seeing actual, human-looking creatures attacking people.

Then there had been Life Force, a bunch of ordinary people who rose up to take the vampires on since nobody else would. That was how her sister had died, but the exact details of her death were kind of murky. She'd been involved with them, Valerie knew, though she'd only been thirteen at the time, so it wasn't like Cassie had told her a lot about it.

Cassie's boyfriend, Phil, had been one of them as well, and even though he'd gotten out alive, he'd also been arrested by the police because of his involvement with the group, whom the police stupidly labeled as criminals because they were "taking the law into their own hands." That was rich, she thought, the idiot authorities arresting perfectly well meaning citizens, all the while not doing jack shit about the vampires themselves.

All of this led to her developing an extreme contempt for anyone in uniform, and not just the police. She didn't like the Army, either, and she occasionally saw men and women from Fort Gordon around town, resenting them almost as much. How come the military weren't doing anything? Surely they had the power to, if they'd just bothered to give a shit. But no, they instead wanted to go around the world and shoot at people and drive their tanks around in the desert.

Rebecca and Nicole were well aware of their friend's feelings, and they agreed with her up to a point. They certainly felt sorry for her because of all the pain she'd been through, but they weren't as vehement in their criticism of the people in charge. Even so, they'd also known people who had died; everybody did. It was just a fact of life in Augusta. Valerie was the only one of them who had lost a family member, though, so they cut her some slack when she got into one of her bitter moods.

"Don't worry about them," Nicole said, referring to the policemen. "Let's talk about something else."

Valerie breathed in deeply to calm herself, then regretted doing so as the smell of cigarette smoke filled her nostrils. She exhaled sharply, but then she noticed that she felt better. Maybe there was something to their whole "smoking relaxes me" thing after all, she wondered, but she still didn't want to take up the habit.

"I know, I know. You're right. It's just... I don't like them. And the idea of you flirting with them kinda pisses me off."

Nicole laughed. "It's not like I'm going to date one of them!"

"You'd better not."

"Plus they're, you know, old," Rebecca offered. "Gross."

Nicole laughed again, then fixed Valerie with a pointed look. "Oh, hey, speaking of that, how are things going with Brent?"

Valerie glared at her. "What do you mean, 'how are things going with Brent?' We're friends, that's all."

"Sure you are," she said, her wide brown eyes suddenly narrowing. "But you've been spending an awful lot of time with him."

"Because we're on the yearbook staff!" Valerie insisted. "That's all."

Brent was a friend of her boyfriend's, a guy named Frank. Things were fine between her and Frank, but it just so happened that Brent and Valerie had wound up with the task of selling ads for Copeland High School's yearbook. What was cool was that they got to skip class during the day and drive around town to go to various businesses, soliciting them for advertisements. The companies would pay a certain amount of money — the larger the ad's size on the page, the more it cost — giving them a way to help support the local school and pay for the cost of publishing the yearbook itself.

"But you do keep bringing him up," Nicole said, one eyebrow raised.

"That's very true," Rebecca added, smiling. "'Brent said this.' 'Me and Brent were talking, and he did this thing…' Brent Brent Brent. It's like you barely even talk about Frank anymore."

"Shut up! I do not! We're just friends. Frank's my boyfriend. End of story."

"What about the other day?" Rebecca asked. "How he held the car door open for you to get in?"

"So? So he's a gentleman. That's how he was raised. Nothing wrong with that."

"There it is again," Nicole said, shaking her head. "You always fall for that shit. I swear, a guy could hold a door open for you and then punch you in the face, and you'd still say, 'But he's a great guy!'"

"He *is* a great guy," Valerie fumed. "And I'm not 'falling' for anything. We're just friends, like I said. Me and Frank are okay."

"What about his car?" Rebecca offered. "You keep going on about that, too. Like, 'His car is so cool!'"

Valerie looked baffled. "So *what?* I like cool cars. He drives a restored '67 Mustang. It's a classic. Forgive me if I have an appreciation for that kind of thing."

"So long as that's all you 'appreciate,'" Nicole said, taking one last puff off her cigarette before dropping it to the ground and stamping it out with her shoe.

"I'd say she appreciates his stick shift," Rebecca quipped.

"Fuck off," Valerie said, flipping her the bird. "Besides, his car is an automatic, not a stick."

"Whatever," Nicole said airily.

"We're just friends," she repeated.

"Are you sure he doesn't want it to be more than that?" Rebecca asked, though her tone was more cautious than it was taunting.

"What? No! He and Frank have been best friends for... I don't even know how long! What kind of jerk goes after his best friend's girlfriend?"

"Yeah, Nicole, what kind of person does that?"

Nicole gave Rebecca an icy look. "That was ages ago. I thought we'd agreed we were over that." She pulled a second cigarette from her pack.

"Oh my God," Valerie exclaimed. "Seriously? Another one? Can't we just go in already?"

"Yeah, what's up with the chain-smoking?" Rebecca asked. Her own cigarette was almost out, and she turned the lit part of it toward her. Then she threw it down and put it out. "Come to think of it, can I have another one, too?"

The girls continued to talk and argue, but they had to be careful not to let things go too far. They often bickered like this, but they loved each other like sisters nevertheless. As was often the case, Rebecca found herself being the peacemaker of the group, doing her best to keep things light. She kept being distracted, though, by some guy nearby who was smoking as well, eyeballing them and probably listening in on what they were saying. He was tall and had short, dark hair, not all that bad looking, really. But something about him gave her the creeps.

They started gossiping about another girl they knew, Evelyn, who had apparently gotten pregnant by some jerk shortly after leaving her boyfriend, a nice guy named Chad whom she'd decided to ditch because she wanted to party and fool around some more. There had been some debate about whether or not the girl would keep the baby or have an abortion, but really, as Rebecca pointed out, it wasn't any of their business.

"I still think she should have it," Valerie insisted.

"It's not your life," Nicole said sharply.

"What about the unborn baby?"

"That's not your life, either."

Valerie stepped closer to her friend, then stopped, holding herself back. "You know what? Fuck you." With that, she abandoned the conversation, heading for the door of the record store that they'd been standing outside of for what seemed like forever. She then turned back and said, "I'll be inside. You two keep smoking it up out here until you're done. I hope you both get emphysema. Or cancer." She stomped her way through the door, wanting to slam it, but it had one of those mechanical arms on the top that made it close slowly.

"Bitch," Nicole said, exhaling another puff of smoke.

"Oh, come on," Rebecca said. "You know you love her."

"I know. She just gets so self-righteous sometimes."

"We'll make up with her in a few minutes. Give her a sec to cool off."

"Fine." Nicole took another puff, then frowned as she held out her cigarette to look at it. "You know, I don't even want all of this."

Rebecca laughed. "Same here." She watched Valerie through the window as she started to peruse the store. Then she giggled evilly. "So, how many times did she say 'we're just friends?' Four? Five?"

"I lost count. 'We're just friends. We're just friends. I'm not going to cheat on Frank. Me and Brent are just friends.' Please. He'll have her in bed within a month."

Rebecca sighed. "Oh, give her some credit. She might not."

"Want to bet on it?"

"Excuse me," a male voice said from behind them. They turned around and saw a somewhat odd looking boy close to their own age, maybe a little younger. "Sorry, I don't mean to bother you or anything, but… That girl you were talking to, the one who went inside. Was that by any chance Valerie? Valerie Culpepper?"

"Yeah…?" Nicole felt suspicious of this newcomer, but he looked harmless enough.

Rebecca was more friendly. The guy was kind of cute, but more in a sweet way than anything else, not the big kind of beefy guy Nicole would have gone for. There was something almost mouse-like about his squinty, blue eyes, and he had tight, dark brown curls. "Do you know her?" she asked him with a bright smile.

"I used to, yeah. We went to school together a few years ago."

"You want me to go get her?" Rebecca asked.

"Actually," Nicole said, taking a step forward, "she's not in a good mood. Right now might not be the best time to approach her."

"Aw, it'll be fine," her friend insisted.

"No, no, it's okay," the boy said, holding his hand out to them and waving it dismissively. "It's not a big deal. We weren't really great friends or anything. I just remembered her, and I thought it might be funny if…" He trailed off, looking to his right, then back at them. He had a strange, conspiratorial grin on his face. "You see that guy over there by the white car?"

The girls looked to where he was pointing, a spot halfway across the parking lot. They could just barely make out the two figures standing by the vehicle, a boy and a girl. "Who's he?" Rebecca asked.

"Someone Valerie and I used to know. I was thinking of going up to him with my arm around her," — he mimed doing this as he spoke   "and being all, 'Hey! How's it going?' Like she and I were a couple. He used to rag on me for being a loser, you know, not having a girlfriend. So I thought it'd be fun to fool him. Just for a laugh, really."

"Or to show him that you're not still a loser?" Nicole offered, sounding more snide than she meant to.

"Something like that," he said, apparently unfazed. That won him some points, at least with Rebecca.

"Well," she said, "maybe one of us could stand in for her. You know, pretend to be your girlfriend and all."

The boy continued to smile, looking back and forth between the two of them. "That's just what I was thinking! So, who's up for it?"

Rebecca volunteered, but then she was afraid that she might be seeming a little too eager. She was starting to like this guy, even though he did seem a little weird. There was something about his simultaneous state of being awkward and charming that appealed to her. "No, wait," she said, pointing to Nicole. "You do it."

"Me?" She seemed to think for a moment. "Well, I suppose I could… No. You do it."

"*You* do it! You're prettier. If we're supposed to be making the guy over there shocked or jealous or whatever, you'd be a lot better at that than I would."

"Hmm… Yeah, okay. Whatever. I'll do it." She shrugged and smiled, then stepped forward to take on the role of pretend girlfriend.

"Great," the guy said with the same conspiratorial smile. The two put their arms over each other's shoulders, turning their backs to Rebecca as they left. He glanced back at her one more time, a wicked twinkle in his eye.

"So, what are we going to say?" Nicole asked as they walked off towards the unsuspecting couple by the car. Rebecca couldn't quite hear the boy's response.

She was going to watch the encounter from afar, wondering how it might go. But then she jumped when someone behind her gently touched her elbow. She whipped around to find herself staring up at the creepy man who had been eyeballing her earlier.

"You shouldn't be leaving those there," the deep-voiced man said, pointing at the cigarette butts on the ground. "That's littering."

Rebecca wanted to say something sarcastic, but the man was right. There was even an ashtray right next to them, something that looked like a small trash can with a silver top filled with a substance not unlike kitty litter. Or maybe it really was kitty litter; she had no idea.

"You're right," she admitted. "Sorry." She bent down, picking up the butts she and Nicole had carelessly left on the ground. Then she straightened up, disposing of them properly. After that, she looked up at the imposing man, who was still standing there.

Inside the record store, Valerie was thumbing through the cassettes in their plastic cases, but she was barely paying attention to what she was doing. She was supposed to be looking for music by specific artists, but she was so mad from her earlier conversation with Rebecca and Nicole that she spent more time thinking about that than the reason she was actually there.

How dare they accuse her of wanting to cheat on Frank? Yes, Brent was a great guy. But that was no reason to screw things up with her current relationship. And who the hell was Nicole to get all judgmental? She was the type of girl who would float from boyfriend to boyfriend, changing her personality to fit who he was and what he wanted. When she was with Billy, she'd suddenly started liking country music, which she'd made fun of for being stupid before that. When she got together with Royce, she got all interested in politics and started championing all these dumb causes. Her next boyfriend would probably be some hippie kind of guy, and she'd start wearing tie-dyed shirts and claiming she liked the Grateful Dead. Or maybe she'd hook up with that cop she'd flirted with and get into whatever the hell his useless ass wanted her to.

Her thoughts then shifted to her resentment of the authorities. Not too long ago, it had occurred to her that maybe she should try calling the FBI. If the local police weren't doing anything about the vampires, and the Army weren't helping either, maybe they would. She quickly gave up on this idea when she realized that she didn't know just how to contact the FBI, or even if she could, what would she say? It was a dumb fantasy, just like plenty of others she'd had.

She'd also recently tried to get in touch with whatever remained of Life Force; there were rumors that the group was still around, at least unofficially. The only link she had to them was through Phil, but she didn't actually know him, not anymore. After Cassie's death, her parents had shunned him despite his genuinely feeling guilty over what had happened to her, and Valerie knew that he was sincere. But because he was so much older than her, there wasn't much reason for them to continue to have contact.

Fortunately, Frank's older brother knew him, and she'd managed to get him to arrange for them to get together on the phone one evening. It was weird hearing his voice again; he sounded exactly the same as she remembered, even though they hadn't spoken for years. As they talked, she could picture his mannerisms, like the way he'd wobble his head in that weird but cute way when he was feeling confused or frustrated.

He did admit to still being a part of Life Force's underground movement, but as she feared, he'd been reluctant to let her in on things, worrying that she might get into trouble, or worse. In time, though, he came around, and he said he'd talk to their leader, who would have final say on whether or not she'd even be allowed to meet with them, let alone join them.

"What's his name?" she'd asked.

"Can't tell you that, either. It's all really hush-hush, for ours and everybody else's safety. Can't risk getting in trouble with the police again."

"Fair enough. I understand. Just let me know something as soon as you can."

And he did, but it wasn't what she wanted to hear. She'd halfway been expecting this mysterious, unnamed leader to shut her out, but what Phil had to tell her was even stranger.

"I don't know what happened," he said. "He just… I can't explain it! It was like he suddenly lost interest."

"Lost interest? In what?"

"The whole thing. Vampires, hunting them down, everything. We were talking, and at first everything was normal, just like it always had been. Then he seemed to… I don't know… space out or something. Like he wasn't listening. And then he kinda came back, but he was like, 'What were we talking about?' So I told him, and he suddenly got all dismissive. 'I don't think we should worry about that anymore. There's nothing we can do about it. I think it's time we stopped.' Just... weird."

Valerie could picture him doing that head-wobbling thing again, and she almost did it herself, baffled by what she was hearing. It barely made sense. "Do you think he was, well, maybe lying or something? Like he didn't want you to get me involved for some reason?"

Phil let out a frustrated sigh. "I don't think so. He seemed really insistent, like something had suddenly changed his mind, and he wouldn't hear another word about it. He basically just walked off and told me to go home, and from what I heard, he did the same thing to the rest of the people who were there."

"That is weird," Valerie agreed. "Is he always that moody?"

"What? Well, yeah, kind of. But this was something different. I'll try to talk to him again in a day or two, see where his head's at. I just can't believe that he's seriously doing an about-face and abandoning this. Maybe he's up to something; I don't know. I'll let you know what I find out."

That was the last she heard from Phil.

It was frustrating, the way everybody kept letting her down. There were people out there who were supposed to be doing good, fighting against the bad things in this world. But they weren't doing enough. She wanted to help, to do her part, but she didn't know how.

She had lost people; everyone had. One would think that this would motivate others to take action and get something done. It wasn't just Cassie that she'd lost; every now and then, she'd hear about or read in the newspaper how someone she knew or used to know had died. She'd almost gotten used to it, but it still hurt every single time. She wondered who would be next.

Unfortunately, she would find out the answer to that question this very night, and one of her friends would be dead. She'd spend the rest of her life regretting the last thing she'd said to her.

CHAPTER FORTY-FIVE

PLAYBACK

"Please, guys, be careful," Janet said, her hands clasped nervously beneath her chin as she looked on.

"He'll be all right," Fred said, holding up one of his friend's legs to balance him as he slowly maneuvered his way through the missing pane in the window. Donald was holding the other one.

"You got it, Barry?" he asked.

"Almost," he said. "Little further." He was halfway through the window now, using his arms to support his upper half on the back of the couch near the wall. He was a small, skinny guy, which was why he'd been chosen for this task.

And then the vampires attacked. Janet went down, then Fred and Donald, who dropped Barry. His body was sliced open by the broken frame and glass beneath him, and if that didn't kill him, the vampires soon did.

That was how Hugh imagined it had gone down; he could never know for certain just what was said or in what order things had happened. But he knew the victims, their personalities and the kinds of things they would have said and done. He'd been the one who had found the bodies, and he'd run the events over and over in his head more times than he could count for the past six years. No one had blamed him, not directly, but he had never forgiven himself for letting it happen.

The radio station, WFNS, had changed formats in the intervening years. At the time of the incident on the roof of the Red Lion Pub, they were a rock station, playing both classic artists and recent stuff that had a hard-hitting feel to it. There was no pop or easy listening crap allowed; they weren't Top 40. Their music had an edge.

These days, things were different. Starting about a year ago, new management had changed everything to a format they called "alternative." It was part of a larger movement that began in the early '90s, with these weirder, more contemplative groups becoming more popular and mainstream. The playlist became a strange melee of recording artists who were modern and yet almost throwbacks to the '60s and '70s, mixed in with new wave and punk hits from the early to mid '80s. There was also the rise of a harsher sound called grunge, making things even more of a mixed bag.

Even so, Hugh went with it and managed to keep his job, adjusting his tastes to match the demands of the time. Even if he didn't actually like much of the new music they were being forced to play, he could fake it, and in time, he actually grew to like some of it. He'd been encouraged to do this by his supervisor, Jack, with whom he had a tense but functional working relationship.

Jack had always been something of an asshole, but he was good at what he did. He had the perfect voice for radio, this booming, authoritative sound to him that skated the line between harsh and friendly, entertaining the listeners and making them want to stay tuned. He also understood the business very well, knowing that while 99 percent of the population thought that radio existed just to play songs, the real reason it was there was to play the commercials between them. That was what paid for them to be on the air in the first place. The more successful the station, the more they could charge for ads from both local and national businesses.

Hugh knew all of this, and he'd come a long way since his days as a wide-eyed, unpaid intern back in the "97 FNS" era. Back then, he'd been all about the music, and he'd been delighted when his sister's boyfriend had gotten him a job at the station working under Captain Jack, the name the DJ used on the air at the time. It came from an old Billy Joel song, and Jack would start his evening shift every night by playing it. That was his trademark.

Meeting him had been a bit of a shock. Hugh had heard Captain Jack and other local on-air personalities all his life, putting together mental pictures of what they looked like. But as it turned out, once he started working in radio himself and began to meet some of them, nobody was anything like what he'd expected. Jack, for instance, had this cool swagger to his voice that caused Hugh to picture him resembling David Hasselhoff from the *Knight Rider* TV show, black leather jacket included. In reality, he was a plainly dressed, overweight man with an oddly round-shaped head and a dark, full beard. It took Hugh a while to reconcile the voice with the man's true appearance.

The night of the tragedy at the Red Lion back in '87, a group called Thousand Eyes Land was supposed to play. Jack had been Promotions Director of the station, which meant that he was in charge of events around town where the station van would show up and broadcast live, and station employees and interns would hand out things like T-shirts and bumper stickers to listeners. Often, these events were band performances at bars like the Red Lion, but it was just as common for them to be at other venues like car washes, newly opened restaurants, or charity events. The idea was to get the station name and brand out there for people to see, increasing exposure both for them and whoever paid them to show up and get the community interested.

Things usually went well, but not always. For instance, there was the time when the remote broadcasting equipment broke down, so Jack wasn't able to do his breaks on-air. They had to make do with coordinating with the board operator back at the station and using a payphone to get Jack's voice on the air, something Hugh had suggested. The sound quality wasn't great, but at least they got the job done. When one of the interns failed to bring the helium tank from the station for the balloons at another remote at the newly opened Nestor's Car Wash, it was Hugh who remembered that his dad had one in his garage, left over from his little sister's recent birthday party. He'd sped home and back to get it to the remote.

It was this penchant for last minute problem solving that put Hugh in good standing with Jack, which led to him being promoted from a meager intern to paid part-time staff, filling in overnights and on weekends, being a real DJ. He bristled at Jack's insistence that he didn't use his real name on the air, though; he liked the idea of people he'd known in high school suddenly hearing him on the radio.

"Sorry," Jack said, clearly not sorry at all, "but Hugh Levine just isn't a good radio name. Doesn't have the right kind of sound. And besides, if you do get really well known and all, you don't want to wind up with some crazy stalker fan who looks you up in the phone book and shows up at your house one day. That happened to one of my old PDs back in the day. Scary shit. Long story." He'd always say "long story" when he didn't feel like fully explaining something.

"So that's how you became 'Michael Clifton,'" Marvin said. Then he nodded. "Yeah, gotta agree with the Captain on that one, for once. Hugh just wouldn't have worked." He pinched his nose and continued: *"Hugh. 'Hi, this is Hugh on Finesse 97.'"*

"Don't be a dick," Hugh said, slightly miffed but still smiling. He liked Marvin, who was a cool guy, an intern who had started at the station back in late '92.

"It can get confusing, though, having two names," Hugh continued. "Pretty much everyone around here calls me Michael. But I'm still Hugh to my family whenever I talk to them, or if I get close to someone." He frowned for a second, then rolled his eyes. "And if we ever do manage to get you on the air, *don't* get involved with any of your listeners. I dated this one girl who kept showing up to my remotes at the Ace, and she had the hardest damn time calling me the right name, no matter how many times I tried to tell her."

Marvin laughed. "Can't imagine what she was calling out in bed. 'Michael! I mean Hugh! I mean… Who are you again?'"

Hugh let out a small laugh, not wanting to admit how true this was. "Well, yeah. Plus even when she did get it straight, she also had this freakish obsession with getting married. She was practically begging me to propose to her after something like two months of dating. I had to call things off with her after a while."

"Weird," Marvin said.

"Yeah. But that's what I'm saying. Radio's a cool job and all, but the more you… Well, there's a thing about people who are really into it. Non-radio people, I mean. The kind who'll call you up in the middle of the night and talk to you when you're off-air. You've seen it."

Marvin nodded. "Yeah, like that time Clark had that drunk girl on the phone, then told her to go get a carrot from the fridge, and… I told you about that, right?"

"Yes," he said firmly, shuddering. "And the less said about that, the better. That guy was a fucking creep, and I'm glad he's not around anymore. Worst Music Director we ever had." He paused, lost in thought. "But that's what I'm saying. People who'll sit at home and listen to you for hours on end and call you up and talk to you off-air, and they think they're your friends… Well, they're kind of losers, honestly. Not all of them, but yeah, a lot."

"I get it."

"Yeah, you do. And that's why I think you'd be a good fit for being on the air. You're not like the other interns, just dumb high school or college kids who want to hang around and get free CDs and shit."

"Nope. I want to actually *do* something here. Make a difference."

This was why Hugh liked Marvin: The guy's attitude and ambition reminded him a lot of who he'd been several years ago. He still needed some polishing and guidance, plus a little voice training and help learning how to run the control board more tightly. But overall, Hugh was pretty sure that Marvin belonged on the air. If only they could manage to convince Jack of that. Now that he was Program Director, the decision would be up to him.

Hugh also liked Marvin because, like him, he was a minority but refused to let that get in his way. Marvin was black, but for whatever reason, he wasn't into the typical things that other young black people his age were. Instead of rap or R&B, he was fully into the alternative music that Finesse 97 played. That was the new name that the station went by after the format change, and Hugh had always found it pretentious and lame, but he went along with it. You had to do that to survive in radio.

Marvin didn't strike Hugh as some kind of sell-out, though, as he sometimes feared that he might be himself. He was Jewish, and it wasn't like there were that many guys like him on the radio in a small, southern town like Augusta. That didn't really bother him, even if he did sometimes feel out of place. He was who he was, and if anyone wanted to make a stupid quip about the Menorah around Hanukkah or question him about "all those weird holidays you guys have" or whatever, he was more than used to it. He'd run into his share of bigotry over the years, but in most people's eyes, he was still considered white and was treated as such.

He wondered how much racism had affected Marvin's life, but the guy never really mentioned it. If the topic did come up, he'd dodge it, often with jokes. He once quipped that he wasn't "really black" because of all of the atypical things he was into, including science fiction and martial arts. He also didn't seem interested in getting in touch with his African roots, something that had become trendy among black people in recent years. "Just doesn't appeal to me," Marvin had said when asked about it. Hugh could relate; he wasn't all that interested in his Jewish heritage, either, much to the chagrin of his family.

"Have you come up with any more ideas for your mock air check?" Hugh asked Marvin.

"Not a lot. Well, okay, barely any, to be honest. I'm still not sure what I should do. Was kinda hoping you could give me some pointers on that."

Hugh nodded. "I wrote some stuff down before I came in tonight. It's in a notebook on my desk." He pointed in the direction of his office, then checked himself; it had recently been mentioned to him that he tended to point a lot. Now that he noticed it, it bugged the crap out of him. It was just a habit he had, thinking visually; he'd even point behind himself when talking about something that had happened in the past.

"You really do need to get a move on that," Hugh insisted. "I mentioned to Jack that you'd expressed an interest in getting on the air, and he said that Nick was thinking about doing the same thing. I'd *really* rather see you on the air than that little prick. And Jack seemed into the idea. Of Nick, I mean. Wait, hang on."

The song that had been playing was nearing its end, and Hugh quickly slipped on his headphones. He punched the mic button on the board, and the studio monitors went silent in order to prevent feedback. Marvin stood there quietly, used to the routine.

"Finesse 97! From the album *Ten Summoner's Tales,* that was of course Sting with his latest, 'If I Ever Lose My Faith in You.'" Hugh spoke in his practiced radio voice, smiling as he talked. It wasn't that he was actually feeling happy; this fixed grin was a technique he'd learned from Jack during his early radio days. If you smiled while talking, people could hear it in your voice. "It's been on the charts for quite a while now," he continued, "and it shows no signs of going away anytime soon. So… I guess if you like Sting, that's a good thing, and if not, well, hey, too bad!"

Hugh was being sarcastic, one of his usual gimmicks on the air. Some of the other DJs did this, occasionally poking fun at the artists and groups that they played, particularly ones they didn't like. But

Hugh liked Sting just fine; his stuff was a lot less "out there" than a lot of what the station played these days.

He continued on with his break, turning to read from one of the laminated, laser-printed sheets of paper propped up behind the board. "Hey, don't forget, if you're looking for something cool to do tomorrow night — and who isn't, right? — then be sure and check out tomorrow night's show at the… at the, uh… Red Lion Pub. Doors open at 8:30, and the action begins at 9:30 with Toothpaste Gag! And then at 10:30, it's Athens-based band Right Lane Must Turn Right. Tickets at the door are just three dollars, and I'm tellin' ya, you really need to check these guys out. They put on a great show.

"This is Michael Clifton, and you're tuned in to the best alternative for Augusta, Finesse 97. But you knew that, right? Well anyway, now it's time for us to pay some more bills." Hugh pressed the button to start the first commercial playing. He then turned off his mic, and the red *ON-AIR* light on the wall of the studio went dark.

"Man," he said, taking off his headphones and roughly placing them down on the counter. "That sucked."

"What?" Marvin asked. "I thought it sounded just fine."

"Didn't you hear how I faltered there? Sounded like an idiot."

"No you didn't. I didn't notice a thing. I'll bet no one listening did, either."

"Yeah, well. *I* noticed. And I'm sure Jack did if he happened to be listening. At least I got the segue right." It was an art, running the board like this, and while he was proud of himself when he did it right, he hated himself when he got it wrong.

Hugh was Production Director of the station, which meant that he was in charge of all of the prerecorded elements that went on the air. That was the job he'd gotten promoted to after all these years, but now he was afraid of losing it. The longer he'd been in radio, the more he'd come to realize how unstable of a career it was. Everything depended on ratings, and if you didn't perform well in those, your job was in jeopardy.

He liked to think that he was good at what he did, and he'd had years to hone his craft. It was his job to make sure that everyone, himself included, sounded good on the air, at least on the production side of things. If mistakes were made, either live on the air or when recording things for later broadcast, he was very critical because he was supposed to be. This very precision had landed him in bad favor with Carrie Crenshaw, the woman who had replaced that creepy guy Clark as the station's Music Director a few months earlier.

Hugh's production studio was more or less identical to the air studio, except that it was meant for recording, not broadcasting. Everyone knew how to use it, that is, everyone on the air staff, not the sales staff, the other side of the operation. Not-so-affectionately known as the "sales geeks," they were the ones who sold the ads and wrote commercial copy for the on-air talent to read. When Hugh was in the studio, he was in charge of creating the more complicated spots, but he couldn't be there all the time. So it was perfectly normal for the other DJs to record commercials and promos on their own.

"So, what was the problem?" Marvin asked. "Did she do one wrong?"

"She's always doing something wrong. Well, not always, but a lot. Getting a word wrong here and there, using a music bed we're already using for something else... Just, always something. And when I'd check a spot and point out to her that she needed to redo it, she'd get all huffy."

"Jeez, can't imagine that," Marvin said, rolling his eyes.

"Well, she wasn't like that in the beginning." Hugh knew that Marvin had already had a bad encounter with her a few weeks earlier. "At first, she was all fake smiles and 'Oh, sorryyy! I'll get it right! Tee hee!' Like she was trying to flirt with me or something. I mean, she's not bad looking, but, you know…" He shuddered. "No. Just no."

"No, I know what you mean. She's all right at first, but then you get to know her, and it's like she becomes less attractive. Sorry, Frog-face, you're not as hot as you think you are."

Hugh choked back a laugh. "Did you just say 'Frog-face?'" He stood there for a moment, his gaze slightly to one side as he pictured Carrie in his mind. Then he snickered again. "You know, you're totally right."

Marvin put his hands up to his face, forefingers and thumbs almost touching, and he moved them back and forth slowly. "I mean, her eyes… they're all big and just a little too far apart. And her mouth, it's too big, too." He bugged out his eyes and widened his mouth, making a gumming gesture with his lips as he made a sound like *"meh-meh-meh-meh."*

Hugh cackled, and he slammed a hand down on the control board. Then he stopped laughing immediately, looking down in fear. He was worried that he might have hit one of the buttons and messed something up, but fortunately, he hadn't. He let out a sigh of relief, then realized that it was time to kick off the next set of music; the commercials were almost done. He did his intro over the opening of the song, timing it just right so that the singer's vocals started right when he stopped talking. Nailing that one made him feel a little better.

"I just think it's funny that you've come up with your own name for our precious Music Director," Hugh said, picking up the conversation where it had left off. "Me, I've taken to calling her 'Old Yeller.'"

Marvin looked shocked. "What? Like the dog? Come on, man, she's not that ugly."

"No, not that. It's because she yells all the time. Old *yell*-er. You ever notice that? She gets on the mic, and she's all like, 'FINESSE 97! THIS IS CARRIE CRENSHAW! WE'VE GOT NEW MUSIC COMING UP FROM BLAH BLAH BLAH BLAH!!!'" Marvin laughed, as did Hugh. "I mean, come on lady, give it a rest! You're going to break the mic!"

"My ears are bleeding!" Marvin said, adding to the imagined conversation. Then he came back to the present. "Yeah, you're right. She does do that."

"It's like someone's crouched down under the board and pulling on her pinky toe or something." Marvin laughed again, but Hugh felt a twinge of regret. "Okay, to be fair, that's one I stole from someone else."

"Who?"

"Kirk, from the morning show. He calls her 'Yabba Dabba Doo.' Seems like everyone's got their own name for her."

"Wait, why? She definitely doesn't look like Fred Flintstone."

"No," Hugh said with another laugh. "But the way Kirk put it, she gets up there and is all…" He stood close to the microphone, making a quick check to make sure it was still turned off. If this conversation accidentally made its way onto the air, he'd definitely be fucked. He'd once known a guy who had lost his job that way.

Taking a deep breath, he did yet another unflattering impression of his co-worker. He used some of the same words as before, but they came out in a rapid, increasingly incoherent stream: "FINNEH NINNEH SEBBEN THITH ITH CAWWIE KENTHAW WE GOT NEW MOOGICK COMING UP FWUM AN I'M SO EXCITING BECAUSE I'M SO FUCKIN LOUD AND YABBA DABBA DOO YABBA DABBA DOO DIDDLUH BLAH BLAH LULLALUH…"

Hugh broke off, not quite out of breath but having made his point, and noticing that Marvin was almost on the floor laughing. Trying to bring things back to a sense of normality, he continued in his regular voice. "I get why she's doing it. It's her way of trying to sound excited, so that way, the listeners get excited and into it, too. But it's just really, *really* obnoxious."

"You're not wrong," Marvin said, recovering. He sighed, grinning widely and wiping his eyes. "Man, that was hilarious."

Hugh was fine when he could joke around like this, and it was a welcome distraction from what had bothered him just a few minutes earlier. The reason he had faltered during the break was the mention of the Red Lion Pub. He wished that any reminder of that place didn't still bother him after all these years, but it did. He'd never forgotten the horror of that night, finding the bodies of his murdered friends.

If he were lucky, the name would just make him twitch, usually only on the inside. But there were other times when he would go into full flashback mode, clearly seeing in his mind the mangled corpses and remembering the panic he'd felt that night. Sometimes, if a group of people started talking about the Red Lion, he'd have to make an excuse to remove himself from the conversation. On really bad days, he'd have to isolate himself in the restroom until he got his breathing under control.

That didn't happen as often these days, and he'd learned to cope with this post-traumatic stress disorder, which is what his therapist called it. She'd explained to him that it was the same thing that soldiers sometimes had when they came back from war, which at first struck him as ridiculous.

"But I haven't been in a war," he insisted during one of his early sessions. "I didn't get shot at by anyone. I wasn't all huddled up in a foxhole, getting dive-bombed by enemy fire."

"PTSD isn't a contest," she said calmly but firmly. "No one 'deserves' it more than anyone else. Lots of people can experience it, and for lots of different reasons. Women who are victims of rape, for example, they get it, too. I had a patient who, after her experience, couldn't stand for her husband to hug her from behind under any circumstances. That was because, at the time she was assaulted, the rapist snuck up from behind and grabbed her. So, even though her husband was trying to make an affectionate gesture, her mind immediately snapped back to that moment. Was it rational? No. But was it understandable? Absolutely, given how the human mind works."

Hugh was grateful to have such a reasonable, level-headed therapist as Emma was. She listened, she didn't interrupt, and when she did have something to say, it was sensible and to the point. Hugh was well aware that Augusta was teeming with tons of mental health professionals, some of them more qualified than others. With so many people like himself traumatized by the way things were in this city, there was a huge market for counseling.

The good thing about this was that the cost of being in therapy was much more reasonable than in other parts of the country. It was the law of supply and demand, plain and simple. Therapists needed to be competitive because there were just so many of them, and offering their services at a lower rate meant getting more clients. But that also meant that sometimes, cheaper rates meant lousy therapy. You really had to shop around to find someone who didn't suck.

Funeral homes were also plentiful in Augusta, though Hugh thought that the rates they charged were so high that they bordered on extortion. It was unfair, he felt, that they would bilk tons of money out of grieving people when they were at their most vulnerable. They'd lost a loved one, and now they had to pay thousands of dollars just to put them into the ground and give them a headstone.

Even so, just like it was with the therapists around town, some of the funerary businesses were savvy enough to be competitive. The station had even advertised with one that offered discounts for families whose loved ones had died from acute blood loss. One of the sales geeks had tried to get Hugh to voice that particular commercial, but he'd handed it off to Jack instead, who understood why.

Jack was a jerk in a lot of ways, but he'd always been understanding when it came to Hugh's occasional anxiety. He'd been there that night, and even though he'd acted like a dickhead at the time, he'd later apologized for that, something he rarely did.

Thousand Eyes Land was the headlining band playing at the Red Lion, but by some stupid accident, their instruments had gotten locked inside the green room. The bar was actually a large house that had been converted into what it was now, the downstairs being where the main stage was and where drinks were served. Upstairs was the green room, where the performing acts could hang out in private, plus a public area that had pool tables and a couple of video games, but hardly anyone ever played the latter.

There was a window on this upper level that led out onto the roof of the building. Not many of the bar's patrons ever noticed it or even knew about it, but back before his promotion to part-time, Hugh and the other interns had discovered it. When shows were well underway and their services (like handing out station paraphernalia or helping with the remote broadcast equipment) were no longer needed, they'd go out onto the roof to relax, get away from the noise, and have fun. They would either sit on the angled, coarse surface beside the window or meander about on the level area close by. That could be a bit precarious, particularly the more they drank. A little bit farther down was the window to the green room, which they would sometimes peek in on to see what was happening in there, if anything.

Hugh had been a part of this, along with Janet, Fred, Donald, and Barry. They all joked around and picked on each other, the way friends did. Janet even got drunk one night and started singing songs; Hugh was surprised at how good her voice was. He was so tipsy that he thought about making out with her once they were alone, but he decided against it. Donald, who was meaner, threatened to jump off the roof and kill himself if she didn't stop singing. That just made her sing more.

The night of the incident, none of the bartenders had a key to get into the green room; the only set had been accidentally left on a couch inside. It was Fred who suggested trying to get in via the window on the roof, and then they could unlock the door from inside and let the band get to their equipment. Hugh okayed the idea, another thing he would always regret. He'd never know whether it was Barry himself who had volunteered to squeeze through the open window pane, or maybe one of the others had brought it up. It probably wasn't Janet; she'd have likely protested such a dangerous maneuver but then been ignored.

If only Hugh had gone out there with them, he could have stopped them. He'd assumed that they were just going to try to reach through the open pane to unlock the window, and they'd probably tried to but then couldn't reach the lock. Hell, he wasn't that much bigger than Barry, so he should have been the one to take the risk of climbing through. As the new Promotions Assistant, he was in charge of the interns, responsible for them. And yet, no one had ever actually blamed him for what happened, even though he thought that they should have. But it didn't matter; he blamed himself.

He would often run the scenario through his head, or more often, alternate scenarios, the "what ifs." And he knew that, had he been up there on the roof with them, he'd have wound up just as dead. Sometimes, he wished he had. In his therapy sessions, Emma urged Hugh to eschew thoughts like that.

"That doesn't do you or anyone else a bit of good," she'd say. "You survived. You were lucky. And that *is* a good thing. So is owning responsibility for your part in what happened, but beating yourself up for it is not."

Everyone had been so understanding, more than he ever felt he deserved. Emma was the only one he told his dreams to, though, the nightmares. In the weeks following the accident, he'd see his friends' bodies in his mind's eye all the time, and he'd run the entire sequence through his head. He felt more than heard the crashing of the window, and even that he was unsure of because he could barely hear anything over the sound of the crappy opening band downstairs, Starfish Amputee. But there was this big *thump* that seemed to come from the room, and he wasn't sure what was happening. He waited for longer than he should have before heading out onto the roof to check on everybody, and when he finally did, that was when he saw them. What was left of them, anyway.

Early on, he'd fantasized that he had made it out there in time, and somehow, he'd fought off the vampires and saved the day. But that was stupid; how could he have done that? And it wouldn't have helped Barry, anyway, who had already crashed through the window and been sliced in half. Then he started imagining that he too had been caught and killed, and that just made things worse, culminating in the recurring panic attacks that eventually landed him in therapy.

The dreams he had weren't much better. At least he could wake up from those, but when they were particularly disturbing, the imagery stayed with him for days. Again, the intensity and frequency of those diminished over the years, but they'd never completely gone away.

They weren't replays of the actual events, though, not like it was on TV. Not once did he dream about what really happened, or even a twisted version like his daydreams in which the vampires got him as well. Instead, he would find himself in a situation with one or more of the now dead interns, just something ordinary and mundane. But then he would remember what had happened to them in real life, and things would get scary.

In one nightmare, he was at the station with Janet, and she was helping him pack some boxes of T-shirts for an upcoming remote. Everything was normal until he remembered that she was supposed to be dead. He didn't say anything, but somehow she'd known what he was thinking, and all of a sudden, she was this demonic, powerful vampire, rushing at him with a hideously distorted face full of fangs. She screamed, too, this horrible, hoarse sound like some kind of turbine engine, and as her body slammed him up against the wall of the small room, the fear shocked him awake. Hugh had lots of nightmares like this over the years, so often that he eventually learned how to force himself to wake up, what he called "the ejector seat."

Many other dreams were much more mild, never getting to the point where he realized during them that his old friends were supposed to be dead. They were just there, either individually or in any combination of Janet, Barry, Fred, and Donald. It wasn't like he was dreaming about the past, that it was still 1987 and he was still that young. Instead, it was the present day, and there were his friends beside him, doing ordinary things. Then he would wake up and be sad, remembering the truth.

Another variation was that the incident on the roof of the Red Lion had occurred, but somehow, everything had been a mistake, their dying, the funerals he'd gone to, all that. One or more of his friends was still alive, and they'd turned out to be okay somehow. As long as Hugh stayed deep enough in sleep not to think about things too logically, he was fine, but he'd still wake up with that same disappointment and regret.

Even though the more intense and horrific dreams lessened over time, Hugh still hated them whenever they occurred. He also grew to despise the less threatening ones, like when his former friends showed up and were living their lives normally as if nothing bad had happened. He felt like his subconscious mind was somehow disrespecting them, not letting them just be dead and gone, and he wasn't even allowed to miss his deceased friends. They lived in his mind, but falsely, which gave him a weird sense of guilt.

Emma was helpful about this as well; it was her job as a therapist to do so, after all. She suggested that Hugh try to take control of his dreams when he was able to, and instead of becoming a victim when his dead friends showed up, he should confront them, even when they weren't doing anything wrong.

"Tell them that they shouldn't be there," she told him. "Say 'You're gone, you died, you're not supposed to be here anymore. Move on, and let me live my life.'"

He tried it the first time he was able to. Dreams are weird, and sometimes control is possible, other times not. But the first time he felt like he could do it, he stopped Fred in his tracks and said, "You are *not* here. You are *not* real."

Fred began to leer at him, and Hugh's sleeping mind knew that he was going to do something tremendously scary any second now. Before he got a chance to, Hugh found himself holding a gun, and he blasted three shots into Fred's chest, subduing him.

Hugh started awake, clutching his pillow and feeling his legs jerk beneath the sheets. In a split second, he remembered where he was, who he was. "Well, that pretty much sucked, too," he mumbled to himself. Oddly enough, though, he didn't dream about Fred for a long time after that.

It was a long road to recovery. Maybe he'd never get there. Maybe there wasn't a finish line, and Hugh was just who he was, struggling to get through one day after another.

"Howard Johnson," Marvin said.

"But that's a hotel," Hugh said, looking baffled.

"I know, but that could kinda be the… I don't know… the 'hook,' maybe. If the station can be named after a brand of shampoo, I can have an air name that's the same as a hotel. 'Hey, you're listening to Howard Johnson on Finesse 97. That's right, all the ladies get to stay overnight with me.'"

Hugh let out a chuckle. "That's probably a bit over the top. I don't think 'the Captain' would go for that."

He said his boss's air name with a sneer; he'd never gotten used to his shortening it to that after the station changed formats. But he'd gone along with it, and he'd produced some new bumpers for him to use between songs. In one, Hugh's voice — run through so many heavy processing filters as to be almost unrecognizable — announced: "You're listening to the Captain." This was followed by a sound bite of Robin Williams from the movie *Dead Poets Society:* "O captain! My captain!" A quick sound effect was added to give an extra punch, and then Hugh's voice came in again: "On Finesse 97."

It was always fun producing those short little bits, using phrases out of context and making things sound cool, weird, and off the wall. Marvin had a good ear for these sound bites, too, and he often came in with tapes of useful little things for Hugh to incorporate into his production. He'd even taught Marvin how to make some bumpers and commercials himself.

Sitting in a chair in the studio, Marvin continued to look through the notes Hugh had made for him, suggestions for his mock air check. People who were already DJs and looking for new jobs made actual air checks, which were compilations of recordings of them on the radio, showcasing how good they sounded and the kinds of things they did. It was sort of like a recorded audition or résumé. But for guys like Marvin and Nick, they would have to create pretend ones, playing the role of an already employed DJ.

"It's not out of the question that you use your real first name, by the way," Hugh offered. "So you could be, for instance, Marvin Johnson. Or something more hard sounding, maybe a little rhythmic, like, let's see… Marvin McClellan." He wobbled his head a bit as he said this, adding a slight swagger to his voice.

Marvin considered this. "Hmm. Maybe. Seems like there are a lot of *kh* sounds in DJ names. Michael Clifton. Carrie Crenshaw. The Captain." With each of these names, he over-emphasized the hard *Cs.*

"True. It just sounds good over the air. Hard-hitting, rock. Ro*ck.*" He lightly punched the air with his fist as he spoke.

Marvin pointed at another phrase written in the notebook: *some kind of gimmick?* "Oh, and I've thought about this too, since you mentioned it the other day. I was thinking I could go, 'Hey, this is…' Well, let's say I still use Marvin… 'This is Marvin, the world's tallest DJ, here on Finesse 97.' And then, next time I get on, I change it to, 'This is Marvin, the world's shortest DJ.' 'Marvin, the world's best looking DJ.' 'The world's only battery powered DJ…' Like that. Changing it up each time to be funny."

"That might work. I'd say give it a shot. Jack's pretty big on gimmicks. That's why I suggested it. Kind of like how he does his airplane pilot bit where he says, 'This is your captain speaking…'"

Marvin smiled evilly. "Or I could just say, 'This is Marvin, the station's token black DJ.' How's that for a gimmick?"

Hugh laughed, despite feeling slightly uncomfortable. But he knew that Marvin was hoping for that reaction. "Nah, don't put that one on there." He hadn't said anything about it until now, but he did wonder if Marvin's race might be a factor. For all he knew, Jack might favor Nick over him simply because he was white. But Marvin was definitely more skilled and belonged on the air, at least in Hugh's opinion.

He voiced some of this concern to Marvin, then followed it up with: "I suppose this could be a way to find out whether or not he's a racist."

"Yeah, I guess," he said, shrugging. "But if Nick gets it, I won't be heartbroken or anything. A little pissed, yeah, but not that much. Just kinda bummed."

"Well, don't give up before you've even tried, dumb-ass," Hugh said with a grin.

"I know." He thought for a moment. "At least he's got the right name for the job. Ni*ckkhh!*" He paused again, looking thoughtful. "What do you think he'll use for a last name, though? Maybe he could be Nick Dick." They both laughed. "Or maybe… heh…"

"What?"

"Well, I was just thinking, if he does get the job instead of me, you should act all nice and supportive, and you can say to him, 'You know what would be a really good on-air name to use? Nick Head. That'd sound really cool.'"

Hugh laughed again, but something was beginning to bother him.

Marvin wasn't even on the radio yet, but he seemed to have already picked up on one of the core tenets of the industry: In order to succeed and build yourself up, you had to tear other people down. Everyone in the business was like this, nice to people to their faces, but stabbing them in the back any chance they got. It was just how things were, and that was due to the very unstable nature of having a career in radio.

Everybody who worked in it feared for their jobs on a daily basis. Whenever book came in — that was what they called it when Arbitron seasonally reported their ratings for each DJ's air shift — everyone's job was in question. If your ratings were up, you might get promoted to a better position, but if they were down, you might get demoted or even fired. Both Jack and Hugh had managed to navigate this treacherous career successfully so far, but this last time around, book coming in meant that Hugh had been moved from afternoon drive to nights, 7 to midnight. Any more slippage in the ratings, and he might well be out of a job.

And it wasn't like anyone ever talked about this openly. It was just understood. You didn't tell a DJ ahead of time that he or she was about to be taken off the air; that was too risky. If a Program Director said to someone, "Sorry, your ratings were just too low, so we're going to have to let you go at the end of this week," that same person could go on the air and say something to thousands of listeners like, "This station fucking sucks, my boss is a cocksucker, and everyone who works here is a piece of shit." And then the radio station would get in trouble with the FCC and get fined hundreds of dollars. So it was just the status quo that anyone who got fired from a radio job wasn't warned of it ahead of time; they were just shown the door.

This made for a very competitive, almost paranoid work environment. Hugh liked the excitement of the job, the pseudo-celebrity status, and getting to meet recording artists when they came to town to play shows. Not many big-name people came to Augusta, though; those kinds of acts usually went to Atlanta and Columbia, the two nearest capital cities. Still, he'd met a handful of performers he'd grown up listening to, and that was fun, except when some of them turned out to be assholes in real life. But that was hit or miss; some of them were perfectly nice and cool, and he had a lot of good memories of his time at the station.

But he'd also done some things he wasn't proud of, at least now that he was getting old enough to look back on them. He had occasionally stepped on people to get where he was. He'd been guilty of gossiping about his co-workers behind their backs. He was the one who reported Clark to Jack about how he'd been messing around with some underage girl and even bragging about it, which led to him getting arrested and losing his job.

He was also considering telling Jack about his suspicion that Carrie had a cocaine problem, sometimes coming to work high and with bloodshot eyes. But should he? Was it really his business, as long as she came in and did her job like everyone else? As he struggled with this, he tried to rationalize it by telling himself that her drug use was affecting her job performance, but what if it were something more petty than that? Was he just wanting to go and be a tattletale on someone simply because he didn't like her?

Carrie was an unlikable person, but then, most people in radio were. Hugh was finally getting to the point where he could admit that, and it wasn't just that he'd begun to grow tired of the people around him. It was that he didn't like the person he'd seen himself becoming, if he hadn't gotten there already. Maybe it was time for a change.

Throughout his almost seven years in radio, Hugh had seen plenty of people come and go, many of them falling victim to the unstable nature of the business. Most of the people working at WFNS had come from other parts of the country, hopping from place to place and trying to succeed. The ones who had left, voluntarily or otherwise, usually moved somewhere far away to start over at a new station. He wondered about the ones who had families, like the guy who had done their morning show before Kirk and Kristy had been brought in to replace him. He wasn't even sure where he, his wife, and two small children had ended up after that.

Hugh wanted a wife and kids someday. He was nearly 27, and while he enjoyed the single life in a lot of ways, there was another part of him that wanted to settle down. He'd been briefly tempted to with Penelope, the marriage-obsessed ex-girlfriend that he'd mentioned to Marvin earlier in the night. But she wasn't the one, he knew. He'd hooked up with her one night thinking it would just be a fling, but then he'd found himself in a full-on relationship. It was nice at the start, but he quickly grew tired of her. Sure, he wanted to get married one day, but not to her. But how could he support a wife and kids if he kept working in such a volatile career?

He wondered if the advice he was giving to Marvin was the right kind. Maybe the most humane thing he could do was to tell him to drop the idea of being in radio and go find something else to do with his life. Or it could be that he just needed to tell himself that, not shoot down somebody else's dreams.

"Nick did say something funny the last time we were working a remote together," Marvin said. It was almost midnight, and they were waiting for the overnight guy to show up, the one Marvin was hoping to replace. Of course, they couldn't let on about that to him. "It was at the Ace."

"Yeah?"

"Yeah. Turns out he doesn't like Jack either, not really. I guess he can kind of see through his bullshit, too, like us. But anyway, his name came up… I forget why. But I said something about Jack, and he said, 'Oh, you mean Mr. Off?' And I just looked at him, like, 'What?' And then he said, 'You know, Jack. Jack-off. So I just call him Mr. Off.'"

"That's…" Hugh began, but then he stopped, something occurring to him. "You know, that *is* funny. Back in the day, when we were still 97 FNS, and I didn't like him back then either, you know… I did the same thing. He was Captain Jack, so when I was mad at him, I referred to him as Captain Jack-off."

"But not to his face, I hope."

"Well, no."

Marvin thought for a second. "Is Jack even his real name? Or is that just another *kh*-sounding name for radio?"

"Nope, it's John. Not that anyone here ever calls him that."

"Figures."

The overnight guy showed up as scheduled, a part-timer who had been given the 12 to 6 shift after the shake-up from the last book. Hugh and Marvin were friendly to him as usual, and they said their goodbyes to him as they prepared to leave the station.

"You wanna grab something to eat?" Hugh asked, not ready to end their conversation yet. There were a few more things he wanted to advise him on in terms of how to do his air check, plus he had at least one more story to pass along to him about Carrie and how she'd messed up some commercials she'd done.

The main one he wanted to tell Marvin was one that he'd meant to include in their earlier conversation about her, but he'd gotten distracted by the other stuff that had come up. It was a screw-up on multiple levels, and what was worse, the commercial had made it onto the air before he'd pulled it.

Hugh was a smart guy, and even though he'd dropped out of college to pursue radio full-time, he still had a good grasp of proper English. So it got on his nerves more than a little when he heard a commercial for the Ace last summer, back when it had changed its name from the previous one. The spot opened with Carrie doing what she called her "sensual voice," announcing in a sexy purr: "Change is the only constance."

"Constance" wasn't even a word; it was a girl's name. The sentence should have read: *Change is the only constant.* That was bad enough, though not entirely Carrie's fault. The sales geek who wrote the copy got that part wrong. Maybe if Carrie hadn't been as grammatically ignorant as whoever that was (Hugh wasn't sure who had the Ace account), she would have caught the error. But it also irritated Hugh that Carrie had recorded the commercial and gone ahead and added it into rotation without first letting him review it. That was his job.

She'd gotten pissy about it when he reprimanded her for the error and made her redo the spot, but Jack had backed him up on it. Once he was in the room and was reminding her of the proper procedure and workflow, Carrie had gone from hellcat to sweetness instantly, acting like she wasn't mad at all and could laugh at her own mistake.

These days, Jack and Carrie weren't as tight, but back then, Hugh had been pretty sure that they'd been sleeping together. He suspected that was how she'd gotten her job in the first place. At least he didn't have to see her as much anymore, what with getting moved to nights; Carrie's shift was from 10 to 3.

Hugh planned to tell Marvin this story once they got to the nearby Waffle House, and then he remembered another one that he could tell him as a counterpoint. He'd made Kirk redo a different commercial for the Ace a few months later because of the way he'd pronounced a couple of words, but Kirk had been fine with it. In fact, he'd found it hilarious once Hugh pointed out to him that the way he'd said the phrase "Ladies, you're in free until midnight…" came out sounding instead like "Ladies' urine free until midnight…"

He chuckled at the memory, walking slowly to his car in the crisp night air. Marvin had walked out of the building with him a few moments ago, but then he'd realized that he'd left Hugh's notebook on the chair in the air studio and had to go back for it.

Hugh wondered again whether or not he should advise his young friend to just give up on radio and do something better with his life. But perhaps he shouldn't be so cynical, he thought. Maybe Marvin — if Jack would let him get on the air, that is — could actually shake things up and make a difference, just like he'd tried to do when he'd started out.

He also wondered if there were something deeper going on here, something related to why Marvin was pretty much the only intern at the station that he had anything to do with. It was a holdover from the incident at the Red Lion Pub, how his friends, the four interns under his charge, had died. He'd always felt responsible, like he'd let them down. Since then, he'd shied away from interns. Just the presence of them was another trigger for him, something to set off his anxiety. But if he could help this hopeful young upstart get to where he wanted to be, maybe that would be a step towards redemption.

His thoughts were interrupted by something that sounded like a bird flying nearby. But even before his suspicion was confirmed, he knew what the sound really was. A part of him had always wondered if this moment would come, if it would one day be his turn.

He'd heard enough stories of what vampire attacks were like. Granted, a lot of the people who had fallen victim to those didn't live to describe them, but there were plenty who did, either because they weren't drained to the point of death and managed to survive, or they'd escaped unharmed while people around them died.

As soon as he heard the flapping sound, his heart sank, and he felt angry with himself. He had no weapons on him, nothing to guard against an attack. He'd gotten lazy. Vampire killings had become much less frequent in recent years, but that didn't mean that they didn't still happen.

More than that, they were even less common here in North Augusta, where he lived and where the station was located. That had always seemed weird to him given that North Augusta was just across the river from Augusta proper, the downtown area that had once been so rife with vampire activity. Regardless, it was well known — even if no one could explain it — that attacks in North Augusta were extremely rare but not unheard of. He knew now that he would pay the price for his complacency.

What surprised him most was the figure of the woman who materialized in front of him, seeming to appear out of thin air. It was just an illusion, though, the vampire bat having chosen its place to land between Hugh and his car and then change its form to something human, yet not human. The parking lot was well lit, and there was his ex-girlfriend, leering at him wickedly.

"Hello, Hugh," the vampire version of Penelope said. At least she'd gotten his name right this time.

As she fed on him, drinking from his prone body on the cold black pavement, Hugh quickly grew too weak to resist. It was just like all the stories he'd heard, or worse, the scenes he remembered from the horror movies that he'd long since sworn off because they freaked him out too much. There was also something disturbingly intimate about it, being pinned down and consumed by a girl he had once loved. It surprised him how philosophical he felt, and he would have laughed about how stupid that was had he been able to.

She'd been surprisingly beautiful before she'd pounced on him, still the same pale-skinned girl with the slightly shorter than normal nose, and she still had that irresistible smirk that he'd always liked. The fangs were an unwelcome addition, but there was nothing he could do about that now. In the months since he'd last seen her, she'd grown her hair out, something he'd always been trying to talk her into doing, and it looked good on her. And somehow, under circumstances he'd never know, she'd wound up becoming a vampire as well.

He tried to wonder about how that had happened, but his mind was beginning to break apart, the same way it did when he went to sleep. Random thoughts were intruding on the moment, distracting him from the fact that he was dying. But then he'd remember that again, try to struggle, and be unable to move. It wasn't the worst way in the world to go, he thought. Had it been that way for Janet?

What was left of his mind was a jumble. His attacker, his former lover, was no longer on him. He just lay there, nearly lifeless. There were sounds, movement. Someone calling out. Marvin, maybe? *Please, don't let it happen to him, too.* He could hear running, but he couldn't see anything anymore.

As he began to fade into nothingness, he wondered whether or not Marvin would escape. Maybe he'd make it back into the building in time, maybe not. And even if he did, there was no guarantee that Penelope couldn't get in there after him. But if Marvin did survive, then he'd have to live with the memory of this night, the horror of seeing his friend killed, and the guilt of having survived. Or maybe he'd just be dead. Hugh wasn't sure which of the two outcomes he wished on him.

CHAPTER FORTY-SIX

TAPE

maxwell IEC TYPE I NORMAL POSITION EQ 90

A DATE ___ N.R. ☐ YES ☐ NO

Bloodletting (The Vampire Song) —Concrete Blonde
Moon Over Bourbon St. —Sting
Forget Me Not —Bad English
Self Control —Laura Branigan
Close My Eyes Forever —Lita Ford & Ozzy Osbourne
Black (Live) —Sarah Mc Lachlan
Man Eater—Hall & Oates
Friends —The Police
Murder By Numbers —The Police
Kiss Me Deadly —Lita Ford

B DATE ___ N.R. ☐ YES ☐ NO

Only The Good Die Young —Billy Joel
Forever Young —Rod Stewart
Forever Young —Bob Dylan
Abracadabra —Steve Miller Band
November Rain —Guns & Roses
Night & Day —Bette Midler
Forever Young —Alphaville
I'll Be There —The Escape Club

CHAPTER FORTY-SEVEN

THE WATCHER

He sat in his tall, ornate chair, alone in the vast, empty room. All was quiet, save for his slow, steady breathing. His growing smile was partly hidden by his forefingers, which poked up from the folded hands resting on his chin. His elbows were comfortably settled on each of the polished arms of the chair.

He knew everything that was happening, and he was pleased. Things were falling into place, just as he always knew they would. He could see that. Not literally, of course, but his mind's eye was sharp and focused.

The chess pieces were moving, going about their merry way, having no idea that they were being nudged, manipulated, and influenced. He was in control of the game, at least up to a point, but that was the fun part. Even he wasn't sure just how everything would play out, but he still had confidence in his plans, how the story would go.

The end game was near.

CHAPTER FORTY-EIGHT

WEB

From: <djuraszek@defender.net>
To: <s.hensley@cujaguar.edu>
Date: Friday, May 2, 2002 2:14 AM
Subject: site

Hey Steve… You really need to check out this website:
http://www.vampiredeaths.org/index.html

The video clips are right up there with that twisted shit you're into, like that Faces of Death stuff you showed me back in the day. Really sick. I don't know if it's real or not, but it sure as hell looks like it…. I can't say for sure. But damn man, take a look, tell me what you think…… Is this really people getting killed??

You have to pay to see the really deep shit, but they have these short previews, too. They still take a long time to download, though. What the fuck??

CHAPTER FORTY-NINE

THE EXPERIMENT

Dr. Yeoman's patients were literally beating down the door to get to him. That was a true statement; he hated it when people misused the word "literally" when they meant "figuratively." As the loud knocks pounded against the locked door to the lab with increasing ferocity, he looked around frantically, fighting down panic as he tried to figure out what to do.

It had all started off so well, so innocently, he tried to tell himself. But things had gone horribly wrong. He'd had the best of intentions, using chelation therapy to try to combat the effects of aging by flushing out the toxins that people put into their bodies. That was what made people grow old, he'd learned, and if his hypotheses were correct — not theories, by the way; he also hated it when people misused the word "theory" — he may have found a way to change the course of human history.

He should have kept a better eye on the side effects, but it didn't help that his patients kept lying to him. What began as a craving for raw meat was soon revealed for what it truly was: a need for blood. Once he knew this, he'd tried to treat the symptoms by giving the patients what they needed, disgusting though it was.

The small quantities of animal blood that he fed to them seemed to stave off their violent urges, but only at first. It was a downward spiral, and the more he tried to fix things, the worse they got. The patients' hunger became more intense, and their self control eventually abandoned them. Subtle manipulation on their part gave way to madness, and once he realized that the first few clients were no longer coming to him for treatment, it was too late. The rest followed suit shortly afterwards, and it wasn't long before reports of people being preyed upon by so-called "vampires" began to crop up around the city.

Over the next couple of years, Dr. Yeoman tried to find a way to correct his mistake. He wanted — and had tried unsuccessfully even before his patients went off on their own — to develop a counter-treatment, something that might restore them and stop their murderous behaviors. Administering it to them would be difficult given that he had no idea how to find them anymore, but he had to take things one step at a time.

With his test subjects gone, he'd considered recruiting others, but he knew how unethical that would be. At least he still had that much of a conscience. Trying his experiments on chimpanzees would be his best bet, but getting those proved to be too difficult. It wasn't easy to justify that kind of work when he had to keep lying to people about what he was really trying to do, and getting the necessary funding was next to impossible for the same reasons. Maybe he could try using lower mammals like rabbits or even mice, but the farther his intended subjects strayed from actual human DNA, the less certain he could be.

"Please, doctor, you have to help me," Maggie said, her voice hoarse and brittle.

Dr. Yeoman was shocked by the sight of the barely recognizable woman in the parking lot. He'd been working late that night, which was just as well. Otherwise, Maggie wouldn't have been able to approach him. Like traditional vampires, the ones he'd accidentally created also had an aversion to sunlight. As near as he could figure out, that had been somehow related to the early days of the treatments when he'd encouraged his patients to avoid it. The sun had aging effects on the skin, after all. But somehow, along with everything else about their condition, this antipathy had mutated into something more sinister.

"Maggie, my poor…" He choked back tears, horrified not only at what he saw but the fact that he was responsible for it. "I'm so, so sorry." He had half a mind to pull her to him and hug her, but then he remembered how dangerous that would be. In fact, he wondered why he hadn't run screaming from her in the first place.

"It's all…" she began, then broke off with a cough. "It's all gone so wrong. Everyone's like this. We don't know what to do." She sounded pitiful as she limped toward him, and Dr. Yeoman realized that this was why he hadn't run. Once a dark-haired, blue-eyed beauty in her late twenties, Maggie had been reduced to a wrinkled, grey hag. Even if she were a bloodthirsty killer, she didn't look like much of a threat to him now.

"What's happened to you?" he asked.

"I was hoping you could tell me," she said bitterly, and for a second, she almost sounded like her younger self. But then she softened, looking like a sad, old woman who had lost everything. "I know you didn't mean for this to happen. The others… They're not so forgiving. They hate you, and they want to see you dead. They don't know I'm here."

"If I can get you inside, run some tests on you…"

"I know," she barked, back to sounding like someone at least three times her real age. "Way ahead of you on that, doctor."

They worked late into the night, Maggie being as patient as she could while the doctor poked and prodded, took samples, and did his best to figure out what he could do for her. He noted the size of her teeth, which reminded him of something from his research from a while back.

In his desperation to find a cure, and having exhausted all avenues of traditional medical research, he'd turned to folklore, the vampire myth itself. He didn't believe that there was such a thing as real vampires, people who died and came back to life to drink the blood of the living. But maybe, just maybe, there might be an answer in the old wives' tales.

As it turned out, modern science had established that most if not all historical cases of vampirism were based around primitive misunderstandings of death and disease. Somebody in a village would die, and then others would, probably the result of a plague. But then the survivors would have bad dreams or hallucinations that led them to believe that the first victim — patient zero, in a sense — had come back from the dead and was the cause of everyone's suffering.

They would exhume the body and, to everyone's horror, the corpse would look as if it hadn't decayed at all and was still full of blood, maybe even with dark red flecks around its mouth. What's more, its teeth looked longer than they should be, but this was due to the gums receding as they dried up. This was natural decomposition, just as the body swelling and overflowing with fluid was. But common people back then didn't know this.

Even more damning was the fact that when the traditional method of hammering a stake through the heart was employed, methane gas that had built up in the lungs was forced out through what remained of the corpse's vocal chords, which produced something akin to a demonic scream. Blood spattering up through the mouth was an added bonus, all lending credence to the notion that this was indeed a vampire that the frightened villagers were "killing."

It was, at the end of the day, all bullshit, and it was easy for a matter-of-fact 20th century scientist to look down on these primitive people for their ignorance. But then, Dr. Yeoman thought, he'd been just as much of an idiot for thinking that he could cure aging, even with the tools of real science.

There wasn't an answer for him or his unfortunate patients — or victims, he sometimes admitted — in folklore. So he worked with what he had, and he put forth a proposal to Maggie this night.

"I want to try another injection of the serum," he said cautiously. "The same one as before."

Maggie seemed to recoil, starting to straighten up but then wincing as it clearly caused her pain. "You can't be serious."

"I mean it. Remember what this was supposed to be all about in the beginning. Fighting the aging process. The theory is still sound; we proved that before. I'm not saying this will outright cure you, but it should be a step in the right direction. If we can get you back down to a point where you were before, then we can figure out how to proceed from there."

Maggie still looked skeptical, and then her expression abruptly changed to plaintive. "Can't I just have a little more of your blood?" Her voice was almost a whisper, and despite her looking like a 90-year-old woman, she suddenly sounded like a frightened little girl.

Dr. Yeoman had already drawn some blood from himself and let her feed on it; doing so had calmed her down tremendously, making her a lot less anxious. But the blood wasn't enough, he was sure. It had to be administered along with the serum. If he was right, that's what had gone wrong with Maggie and the other vampires.

According to what she'd told him, they'd been drinking blood and staying young because of it for almost three years now just fine, but over the past few months, they had all started to age rapidly. If he didn't do something soon, the doctor knew, they might die. Or worse, they might just keep on going, deteriorating but still somehow living, maybe a very literal version of the term "undead."

He explained all of this to her, then added, "It's up to you."

After a few moments' thought, she nodded determinedly, her long grey hair bouncing on her shoulders as she did so. "All right."

The results were staggering. Another vial of his blood — which she downed like a shot of alcohol — was administered along with an injection of a variant on the penicillamine-based serum he'd first used on her three years ago. Initially, he thought he'd made a terrible mistake. Within seconds of the injection, Maggie had begun to shudder, the table she was sitting on quaking as she started screaming and clenching her arms to her sides. Tufts of grey hair fell off of her head, some onto the table and others all the way to the floor. Dr. Yeoman backed away, afraid that the woman might suddenly explode into a giant mess like in some kind of horror movie.

But after only a few seconds of this, a remarkable transformation occurred. The hair that had fallen out was replaced by a combination of grey and dark brown strands, sprouting out of her scalp like hundreds of tiny streams of meat through a grinder. Almost instantly, her face was framed with chin-length salt-and-pepper hair that mixed in with what remained of the shoulder-length hair that she'd had before. Once it stopped growing, what resulted was a strange but almost fashionable layered look, and the way it had grown so miraculously had distracted Dr. Yeoman from the change in her face.

The lines on it weren't gone, but they had become decidedly less pronounced. It was like she'd aged backwards. Instead of resembling some ancient hag, she now looked like a respectable middle-aged woman, maybe age 60 or slightly less than that. There were still frown lines around her mouth and crow's feet by her eyes, but there was no denying it: The treatment had made her grow younger.

"What?" Maggie asked, breathing with exhaustion.

The doctor realized that he'd been staring. "Sorry. I think it... It worked."

Maggie reached up to touch her face, but then she snatched her hand back, scowling at it. The skin on her hand still showed signs of aging, dried and with occasional liver spots. "No it didn't!" she shrieked.

"Maggie, Maggie, calm down," he said, reaching forward to steady her by the shoulders. "Here, let me show you..." He looked around, trying to find a mirror. He then remembered the handheld one he had in his desk drawer, which he occasionally used to check his bald spot.

Once back at the table, he held it up to Maggie's face, which she touched gently.

"I'm… But I'm still *old,* " she whined.

"But you're younger than you were! That's the point. It means that we're on the right track."

Maggie looked away from the mirror, obviously not satisfied. She rubbed her face again, moving her fingers up to her forehead. Then she fixed him with a look that was mostly stern, but there was a hint of a smile in her eyes. "Okay, do it again," she said.

Dr. Yeoman wasn't certain that another treatment so soon would be a good idea, but he was curious as hell. "You sure you're okay?"

The middle-aged woman nodded eagerly, a charming, wrinkled grin on her face. "Yes."

After another round of blood and serum, Maggie had nearly been restored to her former glory, almost as lovely as the day she'd first walked into the clinic. She wasn't all made up and well dressed like she had been back then, and maybe if she had been, that would have made all the difference. But for all intents and purposes, she was a young woman again.

During this transformation, Dr. Yeoman had paid more attention to her face than to her hair, which was now long, straight, and chestnut brown. The anti-aging was almost chilling the way it happened so rapidly; it resembled a computer-generated effect in a movie, but much more realistic. It was like the skin was sucked back onto the skull more tightly, but it looked no more unnatural than a person's abdomen deflating as they let out a breath.

Maggie's face lit up when she looked in the mirror to see the results of the change, and she immediately began touching her hair and combing back strands of it with her fingers, turning her head left and right to examine different angles. Then she set the mirror down beside her.

"Oh my God," she said, smiling at him gratefully, her voice now velvet smooth and feminine. "Thank you. Thank you so much."

"We're still not done," he said firmly. "How do you feel?"

"Perfect," she said.

"And the cravings?"

She looked at the floor, seeming to examine herself internally. "Still there, but a lot less." Then she looked him in the eye, a twinkle in hers. "I don't feel like a murderous evil bitch, if that's what you mean."

He laughed, despite his nervousness. Most of that was buried under his excitement over how things had gone so well. "Good, good. Now if we can just keep you this stable, we can work towards undoing the rest of the damage. You don't know how long I've wanted to have this chance, to right the wrongs I've done."

"You and me both," she said, sighing and looking up at the ceiling. She then shot her head down again, her brow furrowed. "Those fluorescent lights are still bothering me, though."

"That's understandable. We can't expect to turn you completely back to normal all at once."

"Maybe another injection?" she offered. "It could... I don't know... flush the rest of the stuff out of me?"

"We'd really better stop here. It's late, I'm exhausted, and I can't keep sticking myself and taking out blood. I'm already feeling a bit loopy. Though, like I said, that could just be the lack of sleep."

Maggie pouted slightly, but then she nodded her head once more. "You're right, of course. I'm just..." She stretched out her arms and splayed her fingers, looking back and forth at her restored body. "I'm just so happy to feel like *me* again." She scooted forward and stood up from the table, enjoying her renewed strength and mobility. Then she turned to the doctor, her expression still cheerful and bright. "So what happens next?"

"Let's see how well things hold. Can you come back tomorrow night?"

"Sure, I guess so, I..." Her expression darkened, becoming sad. "You know, I just realized. I don't really... I can't go back to the others, not like this. Pretty obvious that something's happened, you know."

Dr. Yeoman considered offering to let her come stay at his place for the night. But he wasn't sure if he should. It wouldn't be proper, for one thing, and he had already found himself feeling plenty of inappropriate feelings toward his patient. She really was gorgeous, and he'd started to entertain fantasies that her gratefulness could somehow translate into something more.

Maggie was an actress, or at least, she had been before he'd ruined her life. But then again, half of the people in this town were either actors or wannabe screenwriters. Originally from New York, she'd moved to Los Angeles in hopes of making it big, but the most high-profile thing she'd managed to land before he'd met her was a national commercial for a major car manufacturer. In it, she portrayed the date of the car's driver, a rugged, handsome man on his way to her home while she got ready and dressed herself up. Dr. Yeoman remembered seeing the commercial when she'd told him about it.

Many of his other clients, including the ones who had succumbed to the ill effects of his so-called treatment, had done similar small-time gigs, like guest starring on sitcoms or playing bit parts in movies. Others were aging trophy wives who were afraid of getting too old and being replaced once their looks faded. He knew full well that L.A. was a vain city, the perfect market for him to exploit, and not a day went by that he didn't hate himself for having done so. Even he wasn't immune to vanity; it was something the place just did to you, infecting one like a disease.

Both to avoid temptation and to keep himself safe in case Maggie's vicious tendencies resurfaced, Dr. Yeoman called her a cab and gave her a wad of cash to pay for that and a hotel room. When she thanked him and said goodbye, she also hugged him, obviously full of glee over the prospect of being cured soon. His heart leapt at such an intimate gesture, and for a second, he wondered if she might kiss his cheek the same way she'd done to the guy in that car commercial. But she didn't, which was probably just as well. Best to keep things professional.

On his way home, he thought about all of the things he'd done, good and bad alike. Often, he felt like both a failure and a fraud. His experiment with the chelation therapy had been a wrong turn that had gone from bad to worse, but what he normally did for a living was much more tame, though still not entirely honest. He didn't like to admit that, and a lot of the time, he talked himself out of doing so.

The purpose of his clinic was to offer alternative treatments to counter the effects of aging. These took on a variety of forms. Some of them were of the "new age" kind like meditation and yoga; a lot of the books he recommended were on that topic. But there were other things that took on a more medical bent, like encouraging clients to exercise and improve their diets. There were also the pills and herbal supplements, many of which Dr. Yeoman knew full well didn't actually do anything.

But the power of the placebo effect was undeniable. He'd seen it throughout his career, and it was clearly evident in most of the people who came to him. They reported results, claiming to feel better and really meaning it, many of them using phrases like "I feel so much younger!" That was encouraging, both to them and to him as a practitioner, fraudulent though he was. But no one had to know that, and as long as he kept under the radar of the FDA and the AMA, he was safe.

His doctorate wasn't even in medicine, but like everything else, he kept that quiet. It was actually in counseling, and he had quite enough psychology credits from school under his belt to fake his way into seeming like a real doctor to the people who didn't ask too many questions. Moving from San Francisco to L.A. helped with that; he was able to start anew after he'd gotten sick of listening to basket cases and lowlifes whine about their problems to him, never taking his advice.

It bothered him sometimes that he essentially sold snake oil to the gullible masses, and L.A. was a hotbed of people in need of a cure for the inevitable effects of aging. He didn't want to get old and die, either. He was already in his mid-thirties, and he could see his own body starting to sag, his hair growing marginally thinner, though this was apparently only noticeable to himself so far.

But he could give people hope. That made him happy, or at least fulfilled, and any lies he told were quashed by the comfort he got from that. People could create their own reality through belief.

His attempt at using chelation had been a mistake, and he kicked himself for trying to do something legitimately medical and scientific when he clearly wasn't qualified to do so. But he'd read such great things about it, how it could possibly be expanded beyond its intended use.

Originally, it was something used to treat heavy metal poisoning, like when people were exposed to mercury. Injections or orally ingested serums contained other metals, which bound themselves to the bad metals and flushed them out of the body. Research — or at the very least speculation — suggested that this same methodology could be applied to other ailments.

Several leaps of logic later, Dr. Yeoman had decided to try to use chelation to take on mankind's oldest enemy, the specter of death. If he could find a way to make this particular science eliminate aging altogether, he could save his neck from the inevitable noose, plus countless others. He would be a hero.

And then it all went to hell. The women he tried to help had turned into monsters. He hadn't meant for them to, but it had happened just the same. He really did want to bring them back from that, to use his skills to turn them back to normal. If he could do that, maybe he could sleep well again.

"Hello again, doctor," Maggie purred, and he felt ashamed over how much her appearance and manner aroused him. He'd been waiting for her in the clinic's parking lot at the appointed time after dark, and she'd finally arrived, looking astoundingly gorgeous. The sexual fantasies about her that he'd fallen asleep to the night before suddenly felt both embarrassing and inadequate.

There she was in her short, tight, black dress, all made up and looking every bit as sensual as she did in that commercial from all those years ago. Her perfect, smooth legs were clad in black pantyhose, and her shiny black high heels clicked along the pavement as she walked slowly and seductively towards him. Her face looked just as flawless, expertly painted, her lips an alluring shade of red. But she wasn't alone.

Behind her, a dozen or so much less glamorous figures followed. Even though they were almost unrecognizable, he immediately knew who they were. He felt for them, and he certainly had plans to turn them back to normal as well, but not yet. Aside from their advanced age, there was something else strange and unnerving about the vampires' appearance, but he couldn't quite put his finger on what. Maybe it was just because there were so many of them.

"Maggie," Dr. Yeoman began, "it's too soon. I told you we needed to wait, to make sure your treatment held."

"Looks like it's working to me," she beamed, holding her arms out from her sides and gesturing with her hands. Her walk took on more of a slink, and she never slowed her pace.

"Fine! But you shouldn't have brought them with you." He glanced at the other women, who kept time with Maggie's approach. "I'm not ready for them yet. I do have enough of the serum, but I only procured enough pig's blood for you. The treatment will only work if I can administer both."

"Oh, there's plenty of blood here," Maggie said, now close enough for him to see the hungry gleam in her eyes. She eyed him up and down, much as he'd done when he'd first spotted her moments before, but for an entirely different reason. Another glance at the aged vampires behind her revealed that they shared her intention. His chest tightened, his body went cold, and he felt his hair stand on end.

He raced for the door to the building, hearing increased movement behind him as the vampires began their pursuit. He managed to make it to the keypad combination lock and frantically typed in the entry code, making it inside and forcing the door closed behind him just in time.

They were a horrific sight, their faces distorted in nightmarish grimaces as they shrieked and clawed at the locked door, which was mostly glass surrounded by a metal frame. It wouldn't hold for long. The elderly looking vampires were a horrible sight to see, but even Maggie, for all of her youth, beauty, and fashion, was equally terrifying. He couldn't believe that this was the same woman who had been so civil and cooperative the night before.

As he turned to flee deeper into the building, it suddenly occurred to him what was different about the old vampires: They'd moved every bit as quickly as Maggie, not slowed down by their apparent age. He cursed himself as he took off running, realizing that he'd been a fool.

Maggie was an actress. He knew that, and he'd remembered that, but what he'd allowed himself to forget was that there was another word for what she did and what she was: *liar*. Not only had she not been weak and infirmed like she'd pretended to be, but she also wasn't some defector who had come to him unbeknown to her fellow vampires. If anything, she was the ringleader, and he'd fallen for her pitiful act, thinking he could save her.

As he reached the door to his lab, slammed it behind him, and locked it, he heard the distant sound of shattering glass as the vampires broke through. They would catch up to him any minute now. He was pretty sure he was going to die, but it wasn't just his blood that they were after. They could get that anywhere. What they were really here for was the serum, and he'd been the one who had stupidly revealed to Maggie that they needed both that and blood to stay young and pretty. Maybe they'd already figured that out, but he'd gone and proven it, probably signing his own death warrant in the process.

Desperate, Dr. Yeoman tore open the refrigerator and began flinging the vials and syringes about, shattering them on the floor, walls, and countertops. At least he could destroy what remained of the serum. But as the door began to give way, he remembered that the formula for it still existed, both on his computer and in various hard copies around the lab. There was no way he could get to those in time.

He looked around for something flammable. If he could start a fire, maybe that would do it. He might not survive, but he needed to do whatever he could to prevent these monstrous harpies from continuing their rampage, killing people around the city just to satisfy their bloodlust, to say nothing of their vanity.

Then he hesitated, wondering if there might be another way. Setting a fire, maybe burning the entire building down, even with him and the vampires in it, felt wrong. How far might it spread if it got out of control? Would other places go up in flames, too? The city had only recently recovered from the Rodney King riots, after all.

It was too late. Maggie and her demonic accomplices had kicked the rest of their way in, and she stood in the doorway, beautiful and murderous all at the same time. Her hair was in shambles given all of the physical effort she'd been through, some of it strewn across her face. She must have been aware of this, because she smoothed it back with her hands as she stepped forward and leered at him.

"There!" she announced proudly as the wrinkled and grey— but clearly not old and weak — vampires piled into the room around her. They settled into a sort of arc formation, pausing as they gazed at him, eyes wild with evil and delight.

"You're too late," Dr. Yeoman announced to all of them, panting from both exertion and fear. "I've destroyed the serum. You can't have any more."

"Aww," Maggie said dramatically, feigning disappointment as she strutted over to the computer on the desk nearby. "But it's still on here, right?" With a single tap on the keyboard from her finger — the nail perfectly painted red — the zig-zagging pattern on the monitor disappeared. There was the formula for the serum in all its pixelated glory, green characters on a black background. She turned her head back to face him with a sickening smile. "Like you kept showing me last night?"

The doctor's heart sank. There was no way he was getting out of this. "Please…" he began, the word passing his lips almost involuntarily. "You don't have to kill me. Can't we just…" He broke off.

He realized that he was about to misquote Rodney King, the same way that so many other people had done since his appearance on the news a month or so ago when the riots and protests were at their height, and he'd tried to tell people to calm down and stop committing violence in his name. He'd actually said, "Can we all get along?" But in the weeks since then, the quote had gotten distorted, everyone reciting it in a sort of sing-song way: "Can't we all just get along?" It sounded like some kind of hippie-dippie, peace-loving catchphrase, and it had already become something of a joke. He hated it when people did that; it diminished the intent of the original quote.

But being pedantic wouldn't save his life. He knew that, and he knew that he was done. He felt both sad and scared as Maggie pointed, directing her accomplices to descend upon him with a single word: "Ladies?" But it wasn't a question. She'd done what many actors dreamed of eventually doing: She'd become a director.

Her subjects obeyed, and they began to quickly move towards him, fingers raised like claws, their mouths opening to reveal long, menacing teeth. They didn't have fangs like traditional vampires, but that wouldn't stop them from tearing him apart.

It wasn't fair. All he'd ever wanted was to try to help young women — and men, for that matter — hold on to their youth and beauty. He'd wanted to do the impossible, something unique, and he'd almost succeeded, but everything had gone so terribly wrong. He had no idea how much longer this would go on for after his death, these vicious, bloodsucking women taking innocent lives to sustain themselves, his serum helping them along the way. Maybe it would never end, and they'd go on forever, immortal.

But he was certain of one thing: Nothing like this had ever happened before, not anywhere else in the entire world.

CHAPTER FIFTY

THE HITCHHIKER

Narrative from incident report filed by Officer Ernest Darrow,
Richmond County Sheriff's Department

On November 11, 1991, at approximately 8:15 p.m., I was dispatched to the Circle K gas station at the corner of Alexander Drive and Washington Road. An ambulance was already on the scene at the time of my arrival. I spoke with the caller, Shane Turner, who was distraught but managed to adequately convey the details of what transpired.

Turner stated that he and his girlfriend, Theresa Collins, were travelling along Milledge Road at approximately 7:30 p.m. Along the block between Battle Row and Gardner Street, they spotted a young woman waving her arms at them, appearing to be in distress. They pulled over onto Gardner and spoke to her, at which point she asked them for help, claiming that her car had broken down nearby and that she needed a ride to somewhere with a payphone so she could call her boyfriend. The two of them complied, but when Turner offered to instead take her back to her car and take a look at it for her, she was "kind of vague" and insisted that she be taken somewhere with a phone instead. Turner added that she said something about her boyfriend getting jealous if someone else helped her, adding that it "didn't make a lot of sense."

Upon arrival at the Circle K, Turner noticed that his car was running low on gas, so he parked at the pump and got out to refuel while the hitchhiking girl went to a payphone on site. The girl then returned to the pump and informed him that the phone was not working, so he, after conferring with his girlfriend (Collins, mentioned above), agreed to take her to her boyfriend's house, which she stated was not far from there, a location off Washington Road "not far from Westchester Suites." The girl thanked them for their help, then got into the backseat of the vehicle.

Turner went into the store and paid for the gas, and upon arriving back at his car, he found Theresa Collins dead in the front passenger seat, drained of blood and with two puncture wounds on her neck. The girl was nowhere to be found. "That's when I knew she was a vampire," he stated, then became upset again. Presumably, this was when he went back into the store and called 911.

The suspected assailant is described by Turner as approximately 5 and a half feet tall, slender build, with straight blonde hair past her shoulders, and wide blue eyes. The name she gave to him and his deceased girlfriend was "Elizabeth," though this may have been a false name.

CHAPTER FIFTY-ONE

FAMILY RESEMBLANCES

Heidi drank the blood from her victim's neck, savoring every swallow. The blood was warm and salty, and she loved the shiver that ran through her body once she got her first taste of someone. The man that she was drinking from tried to struggle against her, but she was too strong for him. She loved that, too.

As the man began to weaken, she loosened her grip, sliding her left hand up his chest while she continued to drink. When it got close to his chin, she began to playfully walk her fingers the rest of the way up his neck, then onto his face. They went over the bridge of his nose, up to his forehead, and stopped. She slid them back down slightly, three of them settling on his cheeks, the middle and index finger positioned over each of his closed eyes. Then she pushed those two fingers down, plunging them past the eyelids and straight into the sockets.

This was her signature move, something she did to all of her victims. She enjoyed the squishy feeling of the eyeballs as her fingers pushed through them, reaching all the way back as far as she could. Sometimes, she'd withdraw immediately, feeling the coolness on her fingers as the aqueous and vitreous humour, mixed with blood, met the dry air. Other times, she'd probe around in there for a little while, exploring the backs of the sockets as she obliterated the remains of the victim's eyes, feeling little bits and pieces of tissue.

Precisely when she did this during a kill varied. She had to time it just right, depending on her mood. When she'd first done it, it had been before she'd even bitten the person, a girl around her own age.

But the way the girl had screeched and carried on so much had been more irritating than entertaining, and she'd bitten her and drained her quickly, more to shut her up than anything. It was more fun to do it during the process of draining someone once they were in that stupor, seeing just how much of their consciousness and awareness was left to react. If she did it too soon, they'd freak out, which she sometimes liked. If she waited too long, though, they'd be too far gone and not give enough of a response. That was disappointing, but there was always the next time.

Heidi hadn't always been this cruel, but then, she hadn't always been a vampire. Both changes in her life and personality were due to her mentor, Carl, the boy who had made her this way.

Growing up, Heidi had always been an overly sensitive person, caring too much, even about things that didn't really matter. She first noticed this about herself around the age of twelve, when she was feeling upset about something: school, a boy, maybe both. It was too long ago to remember. She'd been using a plastic tape dispenser, and when the tape slipped off of her finger and stuck to the roll, she'd gotten angry, then slung the dispenser across the room in frustration.

It clattered along the floor and came to a stop, and then she suddenly felt very sad for it, as if the plastic thing actually had feelings of its own, and she'd been unfairly mean. This made her want to cry, and as she walked over to where it had fallen, she felt the need to tell it she was sorry. Then it occurred to her how strange this was.

"Well, sure," the boy named Carl said to her on the concrete bench at the rest area, back before she'd died. "I guess that's kinda weird, but it's not all that crazy. You were just upset about the other stuff."

"But it's not just that," she said, laughing at herself, though she was still shaken by what had happened recently, the reason she'd pulled off of the highway. "There's this other thing I'll do, like when

I see a balloon floating up high in the sky. Not a hot air balloon... I mean the kind with the helium, little string attached, you know."

Carl nodded. "Like a kid would be holding." He held up his fist as he said it.

"Right! But the fact that it's floating up way in the sky like that, well, that makes me think that there must be some little kid on the ground, however far away, crying because he accidentally let it go. And that just kills me." She let out another small laugh, mostly from embarrassment.

"It's okay," he said. "I understand. You're just a sensitive person. Otherwise you wouldn't have pulled off in here after what happened."

The incident he was referring to had occurred just a few miles up the highway, when Heidi had been driving along I-20 on her way home from college. Not long after she'd crossed the Georgia border, a possum had been trying to cross the road. Just before her car struck it, it had stopped, stood up on its hind legs, and covered its eyes with its front paws. It was almost cartoonish, like it was thinking, *Oh no! My life is over! I can't watch!* And then her car plowed over it with a dull *thunk* that she both heard and felt beneath her feet. It all happened so quickly, and there was nothing she could have done to prevent it, no time to brake or swerve out of the way.

"I know what it was really doing," she'd told Carl when she explained the whole thing to him shortly after they'd met. She'd gone into the bathroom at the rest area to pee and to clean up her face from all of the crying, trying to calm down. She was supposed to get back into her car after that, but upon approaching it, she noticed bits of possum remains on the lower part of her front bumper, just barely visible in the artificial light. That set her off again, and she collapsed onto a nearby bench, sobbing.

It was shortly afterwards that the boy had approached her, asking her if she wanted to talk about it. It was such a nice gesture from a stranger, and she was feeling vulnerable, so she'd taken him up on it.

"Possums are really sensitive to light," she continued. "My dad told me this... We get them sometimes around our house. So what it was doing was shielding its eyes because my headlights were blinding him. He wasn't *really* saying, 'I'm so scared!' But it still looked like it." She could feel herself starting to tear up again, and she hated herself for it. "God, why do I have to be such a wuss?"

There was more to it than that, other things she didn't like about herself. She wasn't all that unattractive, but she'd always been kind of a nerd, somewhat awkward and goofy. A term often used to describe her was "quirky," which was supposedly meant in an affectionate way, but it still felt like an insult. People would tell her that she was funny, and she tried to make the most of that.

The friends she'd had in high school had treated her like a doormat, and she'd begun to suspect that things weren't going to be any different in college, even though she was dealing with entirely new people. In an effort to reach out and make friends, she'd joined the campus choir. It seemed counterintuitive for someone as shy as she was to get up in front of people and sing, but that was why she'd done it: to push herself. The performances made her nervous, but at least she was surrounded by other people doing the exact same thing, which helped a little.

What she mostly got out of the experience was the social aspect of it; she barely cared about the singing. There were about thirty students in the choir, eight of which were part of a smaller, audition-only group that sometimes performed separately. They were the elite, the ones who truly sounded good, and this improved their social status. If this choir were a microcosm of high school, then the members of High Notes would have been the cheerleaders and the jocks. Therefore, they were a bit snobby.

So it surprised Heidi that she'd somehow fallen in with them, getting invited to hang out after rehearsals and being encouraged to audition next semester. Cynthia, one of the leaders of this clique, had inexplicably taken her under her wing, and the rest of the group seemed to accept her as well. But as time had gone on, something felt weird.

They all talked like they liked her, but she still felt picked on a lot of the time. She was the funny girl, the comic relief, and sometimes the butt of their jokes. "Oh, we love you, Heidi," Cynthia would say, often with her arm around her, but there was a thinly concealed condescension in her voice. "It's all in good fun. You know that." The girl wore too much mascara, maybe trying to go for some '60s-style look, but instead it got all clumpy, making her eyelashes look like spider legs. Heidi thought of pointing this out, but she was afraid that it might piss Cynthia off, which she knew was a bad idea. She could be brutal to the people she didn't like. Everyone in High Notes could.

The more she examined this precarious relationship with her new friends, the more it bothered her. It was nice to be in with the popular crowd, but was it real? And was it a good thing to be the court jester? What if they turned on her one day, kicking her even farther down the totem pole than where she'd been before?

All of this ceased to matter the night she'd met Carl. Her first semester of her sophomore year complete, she'd been on the way home to Augusta on the Saturday before Christmas. She hated how warm the weather had gotten: Despite the fact that it had been in the 40s all week, it had suddenly jumped up to the 70s, and the forecast for the next couple of days was the same. She really hoped that it would get cold again by Tuesday, or else things just wouldn't feel right. When she'd been little, there had never been the proverbial "White Christmas," but at least it had always been cold and actually felt like winter. That was part of the holiday experience. Chestnuts roasting, all that.

She had no idea why the weather had gotten so screwed up over the last several years, going back and forth between hot and cold like that, but it pissed her off. Still, the fact that it was as mild as it was meant that it was comfortable enough for her to hang around outside at the rest area, recovering from her ordeal with the possum and talking to what appeared to be this nice, young stranger willing to listen to her vent. She hadn't realized that it had all been an act on his part.

She should have known better. Augusta had its reputation for vampire attacks, something that always made her nervous when she'd go back home, but nothing bad had ever happened to her. The number of deaths had declined in recent months for God only knew what reason, but sitting around after dark talking to a total stranger was still a stupid thing to do. She hadn't been thinking straight, and Carl seemed like such a nice and unthreatening guy. He even reminded her of her younger brother, something she mentioned to him during their conversation.

"Really?" he asked, still putting on the fake charm that she'd fallen for.

"Yeah! You've got a lot of the same features as him… well, as me, too. Can you see it? The pale skin, brown hair and eyes, heart-shaped face. And we've kinda both got this thing going on with the bridge of our nose…" She reached up and ran her finger along hers as she said this.

Carl laughed. "Yeah, I guess so. We could be long lost cousins!"

Heidi laughed as well. "Given how big of a small town Augusta is, that wouldn't surprise me. Seems like everyone's connected in some weird way or another."

"True." He looked down at the ground, like he was thinking about something. They'd talked for a long time, and she'd told him way more than she'd meant to about herself, including some of the drama she'd gone through at school, the friends she was uncertain of. It was really nice to talk to someone who seemed genuine and neutral, though it had never even occurred to her to ask him why he was there in the first place.

"So," he asked, still looking down, "you feeling better?"

She sighed. "Yeah, I think so. Thanks. You've been a really good listener. I should get going."

Carl straightened up, just as she had done, and he turned his upper body towards her, arms extended. "You want a hug?" he asked with a silly grin.

Heidi laughed sweetly. "Sure, why not." She leaned into the embrace, and she was dead a few moments later.

At first, she was appalled by what had happened to her. Getting killed had been traumatic enough, but then to be brought back to life as a vampire, that was too much. She'd already hated Carl as he bit into her neck and drained her blood, but at the same time, she despised herself for falling for his sympathetic act so easily. She'd been a gullible idiot, plain and simple.

And now, he'd condemned her to eternity as a bloodsucking fiend. She found the very idea repugnant, and she spat countless curses at him as the reality of her situation sunk in. Phrases along the lines of "How dare you?" and "What gives you the right?" were peppered with other words like "fucking" and "bastard" and "filth."

Sometime between her death and resurrection, Carl had moved Heidi's body away from the well lit bench to the woods far off from the road. It was here that she'd awoken, and once he'd explained to her who he really was and what he'd done to her, she'd been furious.

But all of that fury had evaporated the moment she'd made her first kill. In the middle of all of her fuming, her ranting at the boy who had killed her, she'd caught a scent on the wind.

"That's it," he said encouragingly. "You smell it, don't you?"

"Fuck you," she hissed, still mad at him. But her eyes had gone wide, and maybe her nostrils had, too. It felt like they had; she could smell human blood nearby. "I... I don't want to do this..." But then she was walking up the grassy hill towards the eighteen wheeler parked nearby. When she'd come back down the sloping ground to meet Carl again, her mouth was a wide, fanged grin, blood smeared across her face. The salty taste still lingered on her tongue, and she wanted more.

Over the next few months, she'd learned how to be a completely new person, the vampire Heidi. Carl was a great teacher, even if he was cold and distant a lot of the time. There was nothing romantic between them, which was just as well given how closely he resembled the younger brother she'd left behind after her transformation. She missed him and the rest of the family sometimes, but not as much as she'd expected to.

What she'd lost was so insignificant compared to what she'd gained, and whenever she thought back to who she'd been before, she almost laughed. Pre-death Heidi had been a joke. Now she was strong, feared, and ruthless. She, Carl, and the rest of their small group of vampires had the power of life and death over anyone who crossed their path.

Putting out her victims' eyes had been something Carl had started her off on not long after she'd become a vampire, an offshoot of his own tendency to torture his prey before killing it. In a twisted way, it was her tribute to the possum, the one she'd blinded just before it died. At least, that was how it began, but now it was just something she did because she enjoyed it. It was evil and cruel, just like she'd become.

"That's one of the best things about being a vampire," Carl explained. "All restraints are gone, and you can finally be who you always wanted to be, who you never could be before."

Heidi snickered. "That's a lot of 'be's." Carl seemed less than amused. "No, I get it! And you're right. I love being like this." She hugged herself as the two of them walked down the darkened corridor.

Their hideout was beneath the campus of Augusta College, the location of which had once been an arsenal during the Civil War. What not many people knew was that there was a network of catacombs left over from the war days, now sealed off and unused, but still accessible if one knew where the entrance was. It was the perfect place for vampires to be, underground and safe from the outside world, day and night.

Upon first seeing the tunnels, Heidi again thought of her brother, who had a thing for exploring abandoned buildings and such. She didn't share his passion, but she could understand the thrill of it, especially having to avoid getting caught, which he always managed to do despite a couple of close calls with the police. He would tell her about his exploits whenever she'd come home to visit. If he'd known about this place, he would have loved it.

It occurred to her once that maybe she could go to her brother, then kill him and bring him back as a vampire as well. That would be neat, having him in the group along with the guy he so closely resembled. He was close to the same height as Carl, too, as was she. Most guys were either close to her height or shorter; it was another thing that had always made her feel awkward.

But she didn't know quite how it worked, what it was that made some victims come back to life and not others. There was some mechanism for it, but Carl hadn't explained it to her. It might have been as simple as merely wishing it, or decreeing it, or who knows what, as opposed to just letting the dead person stay dead. She didn't know, not yet.

She wasn't even sure if Carl fully understood it himself; he'd get evasive whenever she brought it up. That was partly her fault, though, because of another idea she'd once had for being particularly cruel to a potential prey. As mean as it was for her to blind hers like she usually did, she decided that something even more tortuous would be to put someone's eyes out, kill them, and then make them immortal. They'd have to endure being blind forever. Or she might grow tired of the game and kill the blind vampire, putting it out of its misery once she'd had enough fun at their expense.

She'd expected Carl to compliment her on her viciousness, given how he was all about the torture. Instead, he had vehemently forbidden her to do such a thing, but he was vague as to exactly why.

He was that way about a lot of things, and it was an aspect of him that she found frustrating. He rarely talked about his past, and for a while, Heidi wondered just how old he might be. Sure, he looked like a teenage boy, maybe four of five years younger than her, but for all she knew, he might be decades or even centuries old. When she asked him one time, he just changed the subject, and she got the hint.

Still, there were plenty of good qualities about him. He was definitely a good leader, certainly the most experienced vampire she'd ever met. She'd encountered other ones around the city, but she hadn't been that impressed by them, so she tended to stick by Carl's side, though they didn't always go out together to kill. Despite the fact that he could be aloof and sometimes bossy, what she liked about him the most was how fiercely loyal he was, very protective of her and the other vampires in their coven.

It was a small group: just her, Carl, and a pair of twin boys, Sam and Ty. They'd already been a part of things before Carl had brought Heidi in. She liked them just fine, but there was something unsettling about them. She'd known them for about two months by now, but they still made her feel uneasy sometimes.

"They're… I don't know." She was trying to explain her discomfort to Carl one night when it was just the two of them, waiting in the catacombs for the brothers to return from their hunt.

"You have a problem with them?" Carl asked, his tone disapproving.

"No! They just kinda…" She tried to choose her words carefully.

"Is it because they're black?"

"No! Not at all! I'm not prejudiced. You know that. I've tasted people of all colors."

"Then what?"

"It's the way they move, I think. In sync. Have you ever noticed that? When they walk, their arms swing the same way, and their legs, too…" She held up her lower arm and swung it by the elbow in a rhythmic motion, back and forth, back and forth. "It's like they're two soldiers walking in a really small formation. And because they look identical, it just adds to the effect."

"Well, that's the thing about identical twins. They're *identical.*"

"I know! But I've known other pairs of twins before. They weren't that, well, *i-den-ti-cal.* Like these girls I knew back in high school, they were twins, but one had short hair; the other had long. And I knew some others: One was the nice girl, the other one meaner. It was like they wanted to differentiate themselves. But Sam and Ty, it's like they don't want you to know which is which. They're nice guys and all, but they're just creepy!"

Carl's face remained impassive, but a hint of a smile passed across it. "Shouldn't that be fitting for a vampire? To be creepy?"

Heidi sighed. "I guess."

"It's the way we should be."

"You're right, you're right." She thought of something else that she'd noticed about them, recalling a racist joke she'd heard many years ago from someone at school. She couldn't remember the joke itself, but the punch line had something to do with seeing a black person walking around at night, and all that was visible was their teeth and eyes, the way people looked in cartoons. It wasn't true, of course; black people's eyes and teeth didn't glow in the dark, no more than white people's did.

However, there had been a few times when the four of them had been hanging out in their main room underground — sort of a makeshift living room with bean bags and numerous candles — and she'd looked over at Ty, his face barely visible in the flickering light. Then he would smile, and his teeth glinted, a huge, white grin against a dark, featureless face. It didn't happen all the time; the lighting and his position had to be just right. She'd never noticed it happen with Sam, maybe because he usually sat in a different part of the room, better illuminated.

There was something unsettling about this effect, but given what Carl had just said, Heidi wondered if Sam or Ty had ever used it to their advantage. Or maybe they weren't even aware that they could do it. But for all she knew, the very last thing that some of their victims ever saw was a set of gleaming, fanged teeth framed against a dark face as it descended upon them. She liked the idea, the thought of a prey feeling that much more threatened just before it died.

She considered sharing all of this with Carl, but given how the conversation had gone so far, she didn't want to wind up sounding like some kind of bigot. Fortunately, Carl brought something else up, and it surprised her.

"I have a twin, too, you know."

"What? Of course I didn't know! How come you never mentioned it before?"

Carl smiled, this time more genuinely. "I wasn't sure if I should. But now that I think about it, you need to know. So do the guys. Because if you ever happen to run into him, you need to steer clear."

"Why?"

"Well, for one thing, he's human. I haven't seen him for a long time."

Heidi's mind raced. "Is he…? I mean…" What she wanted to ask was how old this twin was. If Carl was as old as she suspected he might be, this twin brother of his might be middle-aged. But she'd gotten so used to him avoiding talking about anything personal, she wasn't sure if she should ask. "Identical?" she offered.

"Yes, more or less."

"Same age as you, or older?" Under most circumstances, that would be a stupid question to ask about twins.

Carl seemed to ponder this. "The same." He was looking away from her as he spoke, pensive. "More or less," he repeated. At least that answered one of her long-standing questions.

Then he looked up at Heidi. "We're linked, me and him," he said, lightly touching his chest as he spoke. "He's the one human being in this entire town that, if you encounter him, you can't kill him. And he may try to kill you if he knows you're a vampire."

She wasn't sure where this was headed. "So… I should just let him?"

"No! I mean you should get away. Just leave him alone. And tell me if you've seen him, so I can steer clear, too. I've done a good job of it so far, but…" He trailed off, looking away.

"Sounds like you're afraid of him."

"I'm not…!" he began to shout, but he caught himself. It was the most emotional Heidi had ever seen him become, even if it did only last a couple of seconds. Then he was back to his more quiet self. "Fine. Maybe a little. But not for the reason you might think. It's… complicated."

Heidi wasn't sure what to say. She settled on the safest option. "Okay. Whatever you say. Human Carl: bad news. Stay away. Got it." She punctuated this last brief statement with a comical thumbs up, and Carl seemed satisfied.

There was a noise from down the hall, the sound of a heavy door being closed, reverberating along the brick corridors. A muffled voice could be heard, soon differentiating into two identical voices, Sam and Ty talking as they neared Heidi and Carl's position. They were back from their night out.

The group talked well into the morning, but it wasn't like staying up late was an issue for them. The sun could rise, but it wouldn't touch them. After some initial discussion centering around Carl's revelation to the boys about his own twin, the topic had shifted as it often did to everyone trading stories about who it was they'd killed that night, how much fun it had been, and what creative things they'd done to torment their prey.

"We did the 'teleporting' thing again," Ty said.

"Again?" Heidi asked with mock exasperation. "That's getting old, you guys."

"But it's such a good bit!" Sam insisted, laughing. "I swear the girl almost shit her pants when I showed up right in front of her, and Ty was still a few blocks away. She screamed her damn head off."

"And I heard it," Ty added, "from that far. I almost fell over laughing and had trouble running to catch up."

"Did you reveal it to her at the end this time?" Heidi asked, her expression bright and eager.

"No, there wasn't time," Ty said. "She was dead by the time I got to them."

"Aww, darn. I'm telling you, that would be a great twist. A real mindfuck right at the end. 'Look, sweetie! It wasn't just me popping up out of nowhere! There's two of us!'"

"I know, I know," Sam said. "We're going to do it at some point. Just got to get the timing right."

"Yeah, that can be a thing," she said with a wicked grin. She wondered what the girl they had killed must have thought. "Aw, poor little meal. Did she have a name?"

"Sure she did," Sam said.

"No idea what it was, though," Ty finished.

They often talked like that, kind of like an old style comedy duo, riffing on each other's sentences. For the first time, Heidi found herself admiring that, thinking that it was neat. Before tonight, she'd seen it as kind of freaky or even annoying. But her earlier conversation with Carl had given her a new perspective, and she was glad to find herself in such interesting company, her adopted family.

"It's too bad you can't bring your own twin in on this," she said, turning to Carl, who had been silent for quite some time. He did that a lot, sitting back and listening while the rest of them talked. "Or could you?"

"No," he said firmly, and the room seemed to darken. Heidi immediately felt like she'd put her foot in her mouth. Apparently, that subject was off limits from now on. Sam and Ty seemed to pick up on this, exchanging a glance first between themselves and then with Heidi. Everything was unspoken, but understood.

It was time for everyone to settle down and sleep, and Carl had already retired to his private chamber. Heidi had her own as well, and she was saying her goodnights to Sam and Ty in theirs. As she did, she thought about Carl and his estrangement from his twin. They were all cut off from the families they'd once had, and while they seemed perfectly fine with that, she wondered about something.

"Do you ever think about them?" she asked quietly.

"Who?" Ty asked. "Our family?"

"Well… Sorta. I was thinking more of the bigger picture. Not just our families, but the ones of the people we feed on. The ones left behind. You ever feel bad for them?"

The two boys pondered this. "Not really," Sam said.

"Not anymore, anyway," Ty added. "The way I see it, we *were* those families once. But now we've been brought up, risen above that."

"We were the prey, and now we're the… well, preyers."

That sounded odd to Heidi. "Is that even a word?"

"Sure it is," one of the boys said, and she wasn't sure which one it was because she hadn't been facing them.

"'Say your preyers,'" the other joked.

"I think you mean 'predators,'" Heidi said, addressing them both. "But you're right."

"We lost our father to a vampire a little over… How long has it been?"

"About a year and a half," Ty said. "No idea who did it, if they're even still around. And sure, we suffered. But being like this, who we are now…"

"It's like payback. We got hurt, and now we get to *do* the hurting. Fair's fair."

"I suppose so," Heidi said. A memory flashed across her mind, and she nodded decisively. "I mean, everyone's lost people, everyone in this town, right? I had an Aunt Brenda who died. A policewoman, killed in the line of duty. Plenty of stories like that to go around, I'm sure."

"I say it's better for us to carry on than mope around," Ty said. "Make the most of what you've got."

"Fair enough," Heidi said. She wasn't sure if she meant it, but the conversation had run its course. "Good night."

About a week later, Heidi was alone in the catacombs, the first one to make it back after the night's hunting. The hallways were always eerily quiet, save for her footsteps, but she'd long since gotten used to that.

A faint sound came from the door that led into the hideout, and she wasn't sure what it was. The door was heavy and weathered with age, so sometimes, depending on the humidity outside, it could be unwieldy. But this sound was different. Rather than forcing it open with superhuman strength like she, Carl, or the twins sometimes had to do, it sounded like someone on the other side of it was being much more cautious: scraping, nudging, and maybe trying to sneak their way in.

Something like this had happened once before, about a month into her time as a vampire. As Carl had explained to her, the security guards at Augusta College knew about these tunnels, but they never patrolled them, at least, almost never. There was no need to.

One night, they had all heard the door open down the hall, and everyone leapt to their feet, listening to the approaching footsteps. Heidi was scared, still new to her powers and afraid that they were going to get caught, or worse. But they made short work of the security guard, later dumping his body in another part of the campus.

That time, the guard had just stumbled into the place, perhaps as part of some very infrequent but routine check of the catacombs.

This would-be intruder, though, was being much more careful and deliberate.

Heidi was angry with herself; the person had probably seen her outside and followed her. She'd gotten slack lately, not being as stealthy as she should have been. Then she felt mad at the person on the other side of the door. How dare they try to force their way into her home? She wasn't scared this time.

With confidence and determination, she stomped up to the door and grabbed the handle, pulling hard. The door resisted, though it had already been pushed partly open from without. In a practiced move, she pulled up on the knob, maneuvering the uncooperative door into position in the frame so she could then swing it open. She had hoped to be greeted by the sight of a shocked campus policeman, but her earlier fumbling had lost her the element of surprise. She could see a figure running away down the dark hallway.

"Oh, no you don't," she hissed, smiling.

As she pursued her quarry, she felt her jaw involuntarily twitch, her teeth clicking together. Her index fingers did the same, pulling in on themselves in a quick motion. *Come here, little possum,* she thought, *sneaking around in the dark where you don't belong.*

Up on the surface, she began close on her target, now fully visible in the purplish, electric light. From behind, she couldn't tell the person's age, but this certainly wasn't a man in uniform. It was a boy, several inches shorter than her, with brown hair and a faded denim jacket that didn't quite match the darker blue of his jeans. Who was he? Maybe she'd interrogate him after pinning him down, just before putting his eyes out.

The thought crossed her mind that this might be another vampire, hoping to do her in. She was aware of some infighting among some of the vampires, but she, Carl, and the others had done their best to stay out of that. This was another thing that Carl seemed to know more about than he was saying, so maybe this was someone who had designs on him, not her. But if that were true, why would he have run? Why not fight?

Frightened little possum... Time for you to play dead... She was faster than the boy; her legs were longer. Any second now, she would reach him, tackling him to the ground. She could hear his labored breathing, and it looked like he might be clutching at his chest with one of his hands. Had she chased him to the point of having a heart attack, or maybe an asthma attack? He was slowing down, too, his footsteps pounding heavily on the ground as he seemed to stagger.

With a triumphant cry, Heidi leapt forward as she reached her prey. But at the same time, the boy abruptly stopped and spun around, holding something in front of his chest. It was an expertly crafted move, and she was unable to stop her forward momentum as she slammed into the wooden stake, the colliding pair toppling to the ground together.

Her chest seared with pain as they rolled over, and she was vaguely aware of the boy moving away from her. But she could barely comprehend what was happening; all she could feel was the pain from the stake in her heart. She cried out, trying to grab for the piercing object to pull it out, but it was already too late. Her screams were cut off as she choked on the blood forcing its way up her throat, and she lay there on the grass, quickly losing strength.

Everything had happened so quickly, but the details she remembered — before her mind began to fracture — surprised her. The night she had run over that poor possum, it had been similar. The amount of time it took for her to see the white flash of fur on the road, recognize it for what it was as it stood up and covered its eyes, and then plow over it with her car as she screamed and cried out in horror: All of that had taken maybe two seconds. But as everything sank in, it played back in her head over and over, like a film in slow motion. She could see with alarming clarity the gleam of the possum's whiskers, the pink nose and pointy ears, the fineness of the fur on his face, and the reflection of her car's headlights in his opalescent eyes just before he covered them up with his hands — paws — with their tiny little clawed fingers.

The same thing happened here. There was her surprise over the boy suddenly turning around, the smug look on his face as she impaled herself on his stake, and — as trivial a detail as it was to notice — a faint scar on the boy's left cheek. It was barely a shadow, infinitesimal, like the moon-shaped imprint left by a fingernail pressed into the skin. But somehow, there it was, visible in the streetlight. Then, as the film sped back up to normal, they had collapsed together onto the ground, and he'd extricated himself from her as she lay dying.

She could no longer move her limbs, and she could even feel her fingers withering to the bone, the skin tightening and drying out along with the rest of her body. Her pitiful, burbling cries had stopped, and even though her ear canals were atrophying, she could just barely make out the sounds of shouting and struggling nearby.

She couldn't be certain, but it sounded like Carl was yelling, and someone else was saying something in response more calmly. Gloating, perhaps. She hoped that Carl would get the better of him, whoever he was. As her world went silent, she also hoped that he would miss her.

CHAPTER FIFTY-TWO

CHANGED

Excerpt from the journal of Raymond Adrian Young

Friday, February 9, 1990

I'm reluctant to write in here; it's been so long. It was nostalgia that drove me to find this old thing and look through some of it, which wasn't easy since I forgot where I'd hidden it at first. I'd forgotten that I changed its hiding place when I rearranged my room a couple of years ago.

But anyway, as always, I read some past entries, but I didn't get the same joy out of it I used to. Doing that used to make me happy. But now I read over these things and just think how stupid I used to be. All that talk of "it," "being V______'s," or even the worst thing we ever called it: "the game." It wasn't a game; it never was. I was just too young and stupid to know it. And the things I said about Elizabeth back when we first met, how dumb and naive I was... It's just embarrassing. Or maybe it's more than that.

So much has changed, and I'm not the same person I was before, in more ways than one. Everything's different now. There are things I have to do, but I don't know if I can. Sometimes, I don't even know which side I'm on.

You know what? Never mind. I thought I was going to go into detail, to explain everything, but forget it. It's all too complicated, and I'm in a crappy mood. The more I write, the more pissed off I'm getting, not just at the situation but at myself. I wish I could talk about it, but it's too private, even for this. I can't.

CIRCLE

It was late on the night of November 17th, 1989, in a cemetery off Wheeler Road. Elizabeth, the vampire, had the boy, Ray, pinned beneath her, struggling helplessly on the cold ground. He shouted his protests, trying to free himself from her grip, but it would do no good.

She delighted in his fear as she smiled down at him, fangs bared. As she leaned forward, she saw his expression change, his defiance withering as he became resigned to accepting his fate. Her triumph complete, she drew in closer, anticipating the warm, salty taste from his neck.

TO BE CONTINUED

ABOUT THE AUTHOR

T. Marshall Bunn grew up in Augusta, Georgia, and has lived several places up and down the east coast since. He currently lives in Rockville, Maryland and works as an audiovisual preservation librarian.